True Colours

True Colours

Karen King
and
Nann Dunne

YellowRoseBooks
a Division of
Renaissance Alliance Publishing, Inc.
Nederland, Texas

ISBN 1-930928-17-3

2nd Edition

First Printing 2001

9 8 7 6 5 4 3 2 1

Cover design by Linda A. Callaghan

Published by:

Renaissance Alliance Publishing, Inc.
PMB 238, 8691 9th Avenue
Port Arthur, Texas 77642

Find us on the World Wide Web at
http://www.rapbooks.com

Printed in the United States of America

This is for two Texans whose love for each other has made me believe that just maybe my soulmate is out there. And I'd like to thank Nann who has shown me that friendship can endure anything.

— Kas

For my parents and all the other people whose shining beacons have guided my path. For my dearest, lifelong friend, Sandy, whose passing darkened my world. For my daughter, Maggie, who understands me and loves me anyway. And especially for the woman who "got down on her knees" to lift me up from sad and lonely mourning; who restored my zest for life; who awoke and nurtured my passion for writing; and who has become my cherished friend, Kas.

— Nann

ACKNOWLEDGEMENTS

We wish to thank Sue Cole for generously sharing with us her knowledge of horses and her unique sense of humor; our Texans, Phyllis Belanger and Jennifer Allum, for their unfailing support and encouragement; and Bob Clements for applying his assiduous and meticulous attention to detail to our story.

But I see your true colors
Shining through
I see your true colors
And that's why I love you
So don't be afraid to let them show
Your true colors
True colors are beautiful,
Like a rainbow.

Chapter
1

"Mary Theresa Gillespie, get up off your duff and get moving!" The veterinarian, known as Mare to her friends, turned to look at the speaker. The wall mirror next to the desk reflected a young woman of average height with long, golden hair, noteworthy green eyes and a wry grin. "Okay, okay, I'm moving."

A week of 100-degree weather had been hard on a number of animals in the area and the doc had been scrambling to keep up with the mounting casualties. Most of them were suffering from heatstroke. The condition could be life threatening, so there wasn't the luxury of saying, "I'll be over later." When the call came, you hustled to get there.

And ailments didn't stop just because it was bedtime. Much of last night had been spent sitting up with a sick cow. Coming home and eating breakfast had probably been a mistake. *I should have grabbed something from the fridge and kept going. That would have been easier than slowing down and having to start back up.*

Pouring the last of her coffee down her throat, Mare pushed her chair back and stood up. She glanced at the appointment pad lying next to the phone on the small desk. No new calls had come in, but she had a couple of recuperating patients who needed to be checked.

As if on cue, the phone rang. Mare picked it up and leaned into the headpiece, catching it between her head and hunched-up shoulder. She picked up a pen and moved the appointment pad closer. "Dr. Gillespie," she said with a briskness she didn't feel.

There was a moment's pause. "This is Dr. Gillespie?"

"Yes, it is." Mare's booted toe started tapping the floor.

"Dr. Gillespie, we need you at the Meridian ranch, right away. One of our horses looks really sick. Can you come?"

"What seems to be wrong?" Mare scratched "Meridian ranch" on the appointment pad.

"She's breathing hard, her head is drooping and she's kind of listless."

Sounds like another one with heatstroke, Mare considered. *Wouldn't be surprised. Didn't cool down much last night.* "See if you can get her to take extra water. I'll be right out." Next to the ranch name, she wrote, "horse— heatstroke?"

"I'll meet you at the barn, Doctor. Do you know how to get here?"

"Sure do." Mare hung up the phone and stared at her reflection in the mirror.

Who could be out at the Meridian ranch? It's been closed for ten years. The voice had been female; maybe someone bought it. *Well, whoever it is, I gotta go see a sick horse.* Mare grabbed her ten-gallon hat, slapped it onto her head and picked up her "little" black bag. She strode out to her dusty four-wheel-drive, Dodge pickup parked next to her house. Dressed in her usual worn jeans, plaid shirt, and short-heeled work boots, she set her bag in the empty spot behind the driver's seat and climbed in.

The bag held a sampling of what Mare called her "quick-fix stuff" including such items as: gauze, tape, suturing needles, sutures, stethoscope, peroxide, ace bandages, painkillers, etc. The camper back of the pickup carried more of the same supplies. It housed a wide array of additional medications, stored in a refrigerated compartment, plus the bulk of the equipment needed to care for large animals.

Mare and her mother had pooled nearly all their resources to outfit Mare's practice. The second-hand truck was purchased three years ago, in her next-to-last year of studies, and the equipment was added gradually as their earnings enabled them. Last year, when Mare graduated and started her own practice, everything was ready to go.

Doctor Mary T. Gillespie, D.V.M., was the only vet within fifty miles of Meridianville, Texas. Actually, there wasn't much of anything within fifty miles of Meridianville. She sometimes wondered why she stayed. In the nine years she had been here, nothing had improved. *Mother loved it here. And she's buried here. Maybe that's why I stay.*

Today's heat was as oppressive as the rest of the week's had been. Mare laid her hat on the truck seat and turned the air conditioner's deflector toward her face. It was quiet in town this morning; only a few people were up and about as she drove down Main Street. Mare waved hello to Rochelle, who was opening the door to the Pot-O-Gold diner, and smiled at Jess Perkins when he whistled at her.

Jess had become the closest thing to a best friend that Mare ever had. His family, residing in Meridianville since it had been founded, ran the general store. Mare's frequent trips to pick up stationery supplies for her mother provided an opportunity for him and Mare to become fast friends. In Jess, she found a like-minded individual who tended to keep to himself and refused to get involved in the petty disputes that others their age squabbled over. Nearly six-foot tall with light brown hair, Jess was an especially talented athlete. Everyone expected him to go to college on a baseball scholarship but he surprised them by winning a coveted Information Technology scholarship to Stanford University.

Now, as well as helping out his folks at the store, he ran a successful web and graphics company from his home. Jess and Mare often got together for a beer and snack, talking about whatever was in the news or what was going on around town. Mare made a mental note to ask him if he knew anything about the folks out at the Meridian ranch.

The vet followed Main Street out of town past the last few paint-flecked houses. Immediately, wide vistas of fenced range opened up, dotted with stands of trees, and, to the left side of the road, ranch or farm houses with outbuildings and an occasional field of corn. The only movement outside of Mare's truck came from a flock of birds, silhouetted against a solitary cloud.

As Mare continued the eight miles to the ranch house, the results of Tom Meridian's callous abandonment of the town ran through her head.

Ever since Tom Meridian, great-grandson of the town's founder, had departed, the town had been slowly dying. Meridian sold off his huge herd of cattle, closed down the meatpacking plant he owned, took his family and left. Nobody seemed to know why he left, but everyone was bitter about it. The name Meridian was not heard without s-o-b in front of it.

Most of the people in Meridianville had worked at the meatpacking plant, just like their parents before them. With the town's biggest industry shut down, the residents were hard-pressed to provide for themselves. Many went back into farming, living off land rented from someone else and trying desperately to survive; hoping that someday things would get better.

Even children learned to make do: wearing worn-out hand-me-downs, eating only twice a day and finding simple ways to play. They rolled up discarded newspapers, tied them with string begged from the butcher shop and used them as balls; then sawed the handles off worn-out mops and brooms to use as bats. Other children fashioned little playmates from corncobs and husks garnered from the patches of land their parents worked. The surrounding ranches and large farms weren't as hard hit, but the town's depressed economy had some effect on all of them.

Mare's mother, Jane, had been a free-lance writer. A major newspaper chain engaged her to come to Meridianville to write an ongoing series about the town's difficulties in adjusting to the loss of its main source of income. She and Mare arrived about six months after the closing of the plant, and spent six more months gathering material for the articles. They both fell in love with the beauty of the area and the strength of the people. They decided to stay, and Jane bought a small home on the edge of town.

During the summer, and on weekends, Mare traveled throughout the area with her mother, assisting with interviews of those people most severely affected. From meeting so many desperate people and hearing their stories of hardship firsthand, Mare developed a deep-seated loathing for the Meridians. That dislike filled her mind as she neared the ranch.

All the land, as far as you could see on the right-hand side of the road that Mare drove along, had been part of the cattle baron's holdings. Mare turned into the lane that ran a half-mile up to the Meridian ranch house. As she reached the house, she could see that it and the other buildings were clean and fresh looking.

Gigantic in proportion even for Texas, the white stucco house sprawled from an attached, four-car garage to another building connected to it by a covered walkway. At a right angle beyond that building sat the barn, with a good-sized corral to the far side of it, containing two horses. A blacktop parking area formed a huge oval that started in front of the garage and sent a finger over in front of the house before completing its oval shape at the barn.

Looks like someone's done a lot of fixing up here, thought Mare. She pulled in front of the barn and stepped out of the pickup, her booted feet meeting the springy surface of macadam. A woman dressed in a short-sleeved,

tailored cotton shirt, jeans and high-heeled boots came
through the open door and hurried over.

"Dr. Gillespie? I'm Erin Scott." The woman was several inches taller than Mare. The blonde, curly head tilted
and cool brown eyes skimmed across Mare's face and form
as the two women shook hands. "Follow me. I'll take you
to the horse."

Well, hello, how are you, too? Mare snorted to herself.
Not too much southern hospitality being wasted here. She
nodded, got her bag from the truck and followed the
woman into the barn, noting her smooth, athletic walk.
Nice, even, rich-girl tan. Wonder if she's the owner?

Mare welcomed the cooler interior of the barn, even
knowing that it soon would seem just as hot as the outside.
As she looked for the ailing horse her peripheral vision
caught nameplates hanging at three of the six stalls and a
large tack room just to the left of the barn entrance.
Through the open tack room door, she could see part of a
worktable with cupboards above it and a deep sink standing next to it.

Erin stopped in front of a large palomino mare whose
nameplate said Faithful Flag.

A cursory look indicated that the horse was in obvious
distress. Her head hung low, she seemed listless and her
breathing was rapid, with her nostrils flaring. All were
classic symptoms of heatstroke. The vet set her bag down,
opened it and took out the stethoscope, which she hung
around her neck. Slowly walking into the stall, Mare
reached up to the high shoulder and patted it. "Good girl,
just let me take a look at you." There was no sweat on the
animal's body; though, in this heat, there should have
been.

Mare lifted the stethoscope's earpieces to their resting
place and listened to an elevated heart rate of 70 beats per
minute instead of the usual 40. For a final confirmation of
the diagnosis, Mare took the rectal thermometer from its
plastic case, dipped it into a nearby water bucket, shook it

down, then inserted it into the barely responsive animal's rectum.

"How long has she been this way?" Mare inquired.

"I noticed how she looked when I came into the barn this morning and I called you right away." Erin chewed at the inside of her lip.

"Has she been drinking a lot of water?"

"I gave her extra when you told me to and she drank most of it. Is Flag in danger?"

When Mare withdrew the thermometer and saw a reading of 103, the diagnosis was confirmed. "She's suffering from heatstroke. Heatstroke can kill but it looks as though you caught it quickly so there shouldn't be any problem treating it." The woman visibly relaxed at her statement and Mare realized the woman's brusque attitude was probably due to worry over the magnificent horse.

"Not used to dealing with horses?" Mare used Flag's tail to wipe the thermometer, put it back in its plastic case and set it back into the bag. She strode out to the truck to secure medication from the built-in refrigerator.

"More like not used to dealing with them in these conditions," replied Erin, following the vet. "Take me up north, give me several feet of snow and I'm okay. Present me with heat and humidity like this and I'm sort of out of my depth. And I can see that this is going to be a steep learning curve."

"You got that right. At least you were quick to notice that something was wrong." The doctor continued her explanation when they returned to the barn. "I'm going to give Flag a tranquilizer to bring her heart rate down and another injection to bring down her temperature. You want to come around here and hold her still for me? Better snap a lead rope onto her first."

Erin walked around the other side of Flag, snapped the lead rope onto the halter enclosing the palomino's head, and hung onto it.

Mare chose a 21-gauge disposable needle, attached it to a disposable syringe and pulled 3cc from the bottle of

Acepromezine. She injected it directly into Flag's jugular vein, then went through the same motions with 10cc of Dipyrone. She dropped the syringes into a plastic trash bottle she kept in her bag for their disposal.

The vet went out to the truck and brought back four bags of Ringer's solution and IV equipment. She went over and picked up a pitchfork she had spied on her way in, brought it back to the horse's side and leaned it against the wall of the stall. "That's good, hold her nice and steady. I'm going to put a catheter in the jugular vein."

When the catheter had been inserted, Mare connected a bag of Ringer's to the IV tubing, opened the drip regulator hooked to the tubing and let some Ringer's run through, pushing out the air. She then attached the tubing to the catheter. She reached for the pitchfork and hung the Ringer's on it, lifted it enough to keep the bag high, then adjusted the drip regulator. "I'll have to give her three or four of these to combat the dehydration."

As she ran the Ringer's in, one after the other, Mare explained some of the aftercare that would be needed: temperature taking, more injections, hosing down, adding electrolytes to the water. Erin looked a little skeptical. "Think I can handle that. Will you need to come out to check her again?"

"Yeah I'll be out tomorrow. In the meantime, Flag's going to need the care I've explained to you. I've had so many cases of heatstroke this past week that I've printed out the directions. I'll just fill in the figures and you can follow right along. You need to keep an eye on the other horses, too. Keep them out of the hot sun. Spray them down once in a while. Bring some fans in here and move them in here before midday. Until this heat breaks, all the animals are in danger."

Mare had finished with the Ringer's IV and she unhooked everything, walked out of the stall, and laid the apparatus on top of her bag. Reaching in her breast pocket, she extracted and unfolded a sheet of directions. She pulled a pen from a pocket in her jeans, clicked it open and filled in figures based on Flag's condition. She grinned to herself as she realized that Erin was still holding Flag's lead rope. "You can come out now."

Mare clicked the pen closed and replaced it in her pocket. As she handed the directions to the curly-headed blonde, she said, "Come here and I'll show you where you need to make the muscle injections." The extra-wide stalls made it easy for two people to walk side by side next to the horse. Mare pointed out the muscle area and looked to make sure Erin understood. The woman's earnest look reassured her somewhat.

"You're sure someone will do this? It's absolutely necessary."

Erin bit her lip again and nodded. "Don't worry, Doc. I might not be too keen on the idea, but we'll do whatever we have to do."

"Do you have a thermometer? If not, I can leave you one." Mare picked up the IV tubing and her bag and went to the tack room sink to rinse the tubing off.

Following her in, Erin opened the cupboards on the wall above the worktable. "I think we most likely have one; there's a lot of stuff in these cupboards that's probably still useful."

Curious, Mare strolled over and looked for herself. The cupboards were filled with a hundred items that could be used in the care of animals. *And they left it all here. That's odd.* Mare reached over and pointed, "Here's the thermometer you need. I'll leave you some disposable syringes, needles, the medications and some bags of electrolytes, and you have the water and hoses and fans. You're all set."

Erin grinned and raised her eyebrows. "I sure hope so. When will Flag be better?"

"Once she starts sweating and stops the rapid breathing, she'll be pretty well over it. That might take several days, especially in this heat."

"Okay, that's great." Erin looked at the vet and smiled, glad that the young woman had been able to help

Flag. The atmosphere was bad enough at the ranch without the death of TJ's beloved mare adding to their worries.

Erin frowned as she thought of her friend up in the house. Her mood this week had been mercurial, swinging from a joyous high to deep depression in a matter of hours; but neither she nor Paula had been able to figure out why. Still, Flag would be all right, according to the doctor, so that was one thing less she had to worry about.

She turned her attention back to the vet who was just finishing laying out the syringes, needles, and electrolytes on the worktable. Mare removed the proper medications from her bag, held them up and lifted an eyebrow. "Got somewhere cold I can put these? They usually don't need to be refrigerated, but in this heat I'd rather play it safe."

Erin took the bottles from the vet and opened one of the lower cabinets on the far wall to reveal a small refrigerator. Pushing some sodas out of the way, she set the bottles inside.

Mare watched Erin close the fridge and swing back around. "Flag should be okay, but you will need to keep an eye on her for a while. I'll come back tomorrow to give her some more Ringer's and to check on her progress."

Erin smiled and picked up the vet's bag, turning to walk slowly out of the barn. "Thanks. We appreciate your coming out so quickly. Believe me, it would have been disastrous if anything had happened to that horse."

Mare followed the woman out. She removed the drip tubing from under her arm where she had stashed it, and placed it back in the camper. "It wasn't a problem. So, how long have you been up here? Nobody in town even knew the place had been sold."

"Oh, we've been planning this for a while. Seemed such a waste not to use the land since it was just sitting here. And the land hasn't been sold. Well, not as far as I know."

Mare looked at the blonde who was a couple of paces in front of her. *Must be renting or leasing then.* "This must be costing you a fortune to rent." Mare's curiosity was piqued.

"Nope, we don't rent."

Mare laughed, her voice sarcastic. "Please don't tell me that the Meridian Corporation is letting you stay here for free."

Erin was truly puzzled by the vet's attitude. She knew that the town had suffered because TJ's father had closed the cattle ranch down, but she hadn't realized that the people around here held the family in such disdain. "Well, it's like this..."

Mare finally caught on and held up her hand. "Hold on a minute. Are you trying to tell me that you are the Meridian Corporation?"

"Well, not me, personally; but yes, I work for Meridian."

Mare's eyes hardened as she stared at the woman. "I can't believe they had the gall to set foot in this town again... but at least they had the sense to send a flunky." Mare realized how that sounded. It wasn't this woman's fault she'd been sent down here. She let her eyes soften. "Sorry. That wasn't meant as a personal attack. You have to understand that the Meridians are neither liked nor welcome in this town. They all but destroyed it when they pulled out."

Erin stopped her walk and looked at the vet again. "That's okay, no offense taken. I didn't realize they were so disliked down here."

"Well they are; and I'm sorry to say it, but even though work is hard to find around here, as soon as they know it's your corporation I doubt you will find many willing hands who will work for you."

Erin smiled. She liked this vet despite her attitude; she had spunk and wasn't afraid to speak her mind. "Thankfully, I don't have to worry about that side of the running of this place. That is my partner's domain."

"So you'll be seeing to the practical side of things."

"Yeah, Paula will do the hiring and I have to tell you, Doc, that she has a way of getting what she wants even from the most resistant of people." *Well, she got me down here and convinced TJ to carry on with her plans for this place, so I really can't see us failing to get the people we need.*

Erin handed Mare's bag to her. "How much do we owe you?" Mare named a figure and Erin pulled a checkbook and pen from a pocket and wrote her a check. When she handed it to Mare, the doctor noticed it had been pre-stamped with T. J. Meridian's signature.

"Will you have any problems looking after the live-stock? We are expecting to turn this back into a working ranch and we were hoping to sign you on a retainer. Or would you prefer we get someone from out of town?"

Mare considered this for the moment. Looking after the ranch livestock would be profitable and would enable her to do a few more things for those who weren't able to pay for their animals to be looked after properly. Still, wasn't agreeing to work for Meridian almost like selling out to them?

"Why don't you think about it and then let me know when you have made a decision?" Erin offered her hand to the vet. "Thanks again for your prompt help. As I said, it would have been hell on earth here if anything had happened to that horse."

Mare took the proffered hand and shook it. "Okay. I'll let you know my decision when I come back to do the follow-up on Flag." Mare noticed a delivery van, pulling up beside her truck. "Looks like you have something to take care of. I'll see you tomorrow."

Erin let go of the doc's hand and looked over her shoulder. "Yep, you're right. Thanks." Turning, she walked over to the delivery van.

Mare slung her bag into the truck, her mind still mull-ing over the opportunity that had been presented to her. She absently listened as the driver of the van shouted over to the blonde approaching him. "You have a Miss T. J. Meridian here? I have a personal package that needs to be signed for!"

"I can sign for it," replied Erin as she reached the man. "She's not available right now."

Mare felt a chill roll down her spine. *One of the Meridians is here? Well, well, well. Maybe I ought to drop in and say hello? Welcome them back after all this time?*

Erin was signing for the package as the vet breezed past her with an air of determination on her face. "Dr. Gillespie?" she yelled as the woman rapidly climbed the three steps to the porch and entered through the open doorway. *Ah hell, this is not going to be pretty.* She quickly unclipped the cell phone on her belt and punched in a number. "Paula, honey, we have trouble at the house."

Chapter
2

TJ sat behind the office desk, staring at the screen-saver on her computer, not really noticing the black panthers and other big cats that prowled their way across the screen. She knew that she ought to be working. She should be on the damned machine in front of her, looking at the proposals for upcoming business developments. But the inclination just wasn't there and hadn't been for a long time.

She pushed a strand of her long, dark hair back behind her ear. She didn't want to be in here. She would much rather have been in her room. But Erin and Paula had insisted she get out of bed today, and she wasn't capable of resisting when they forcibly got her up. All her screaming and cursing, all her threats did nothing to dissuade them from their task and make them leave her alone. She thought she might have hit Paula, and in some place she felt sorry for inflicting that on her friend. But, as with everything else these days, the feeling meant little to her.

She had only agreed to come down here to the ranch because they went on about it so much while she was in the hospital. The only way she knew how to shut them up was to agree and then, for seven blissful days, they left her alone.

She nearly succeeded in getting away from everybody then, but the night nurse had come in on her rounds and found her bleeding. A quick call to the doctor, and several stitches later, and she was tucked back in a clean bed— under observation this time. Erin and Paula were furious with her, and from that moment on had insured that some- one was with her at all times.

She hadn't realized that her failed attempt to kill her- self would result in more doctors and more tests. Still, she eventually escaped the clutches of the medics after they instilled in her enough skills to cope with her disability; but the proviso was that she still have counseling sessions and that she still go to physical therapy sessions twice a week. She hoped that, by returning to the ranch and giving Erin and Paula so much to do, they would forget about that. But her friends were hard taskmasters and always made sure that one of them was free to drive her to her appointments.

She picked up a pencil and started twirling it through her fingers. She had another session with her counselor scheduled for this afternoon and that was what had put her in this foul mood. Her last session hadn't gone so well. Peter wanted to talk about her father and TJ adamantly refused. He had nothing to do with her current situation; in fact, it was about the only thing in her life that she couldn't blame him for. She didn't see how talking about him could help her now. Peter said that she had demons to lay and that they might as well tackle them all, but TJ pulled her silent, I'm-not-in-the-room act on him.

He left the room then and had a long talk with Erin, who was in the waiting room. She knew she was being stubborn, but why couldn't anybody understand that the mere thought of her father was repulsive to her? He ruled her life while he was alive and she wanted nothing to do with him now that he was dead.

Erin lectured her all the way back to the ranch, wanting to know why she refused to cooperate with her treatment. Why bother going if she was going to be obstructive? TJ pointed out that she had no choice in the matter since she and Paula wouldn't allow her not to go. She hadn't wanted to see Peter in the first place and would rather all of them would get on with their own lives and stop fussing with hers.

The last hour of the drive was completed in silence. On their return, TJ asked to be taken out to see Flag but Erin told her coolly that she and Paula would be tied up for the rest of the afternoon and it wouldn't be possible. Which, of course, had sent her mood spiraling downward even further. She would be glad when the alterations on the house were completed and she could get about without assistance.

Then last night they had a big argument. Erin and Paula wanted to get someone in full time to help TJ. What they meant was that they wanted to get a nurse in. TJ was vehemently opposed to the idea. It had taken her long enough to allow Paula and Erin to help her; there was no way she would allow a total stranger to see her in this manner.

The pencil she was playing with snapped. She looked at it, stunned, not realizing she had been holding it that hard, then threw the pieces across the room in frustration. This afternoon she would make Erin take her out to see Flag, or she wasn't going to the counseling session.

The sound of voices in the hallway drew her attention. Erin was trying to stop someone from doing something, but the voice she didn't recognize wasn't having any of it and quite vocally stated that she was going to give "Miss Meridian" a piece of her mind. The door to her office was flung open, and in stormed the unknown voice. TJ watched as the intruder came quickly toward her, pulling up short several feet from the desk.

A small, longhaired blonde stood before her, her face flushed from her march through the house to find her target, her breath coming in uneven gasps. Erin rushed in through the door not a second later, a pleading look on her face. TJ sighed and felt her mood darken further. *Today was not turning out to be a good day.*

Mare had entered the big ranch house with ease. Finding the person she was after was a little harder; but she had scoured the ground floor, with Erin following her. From the look of her, the woman chasing her could have physically removed her from the house; could even have called the police on her. Though, Mare smugly thought, Chief Jackson would only have made a show of reprimanding her, especially when she told him who was in the house.

For some reason the blonde hadn't done either one, trying to get her to leave the premises through argument. Eventually, Mare had turned around to her and told her she wasn't leaving until she had given Miss Meridian a piece of her mind to her face. Then she had flung open a closed door, stormed through and found herself staring into crystal-blue eyes.

She took a deep breath, trying to calm her breathing. "You T. J. Meridian?" she inquired eventually. After all, she could have been Erin's partner, but the dark-haired woman sitting behind the desk gave a short nod. Mare put her hands on her hips and stared hard, trying to quiet her anger, so that what she was about to say would come out coherently.

"You and your family have some nerve coming back here. Don't you think that you've done enough damage to this town?" Mare strode forward till she was leaning her hands down on the desk. "Ten years ago, your father destroyed this town, destroyed the livelihood of everyone in it. They made your father and his company a fortune, then he upped and left. Hell, he wouldn't even sell the land to them so that they could work it themselves, and now you have the nerve to return. Just what do you hope to achieve here, Miss Meridian?"

At any other time Mare would have noticed the paleness of the woman before her, would have recognized the lifelessness behind the ice-blue eyes. But her anger was so high that these things were beyond her today. She waited silently, staring at the woman, refusing to let her hide from her emerald gaze.

TJ listened as the blonde vented her tirade against her and her family. How was she meant to respond? What she said was true. If the woman had known that the reason her father had pulled out from the ranch was to prevent TJ, herself, from becoming obsessed with it, no doubt she would have had more choice words to say. She knew that coming back here to put things right would be difficult. That was why she had planned to appoint a manager to oversee the project, but the injury changed all that. She had hoped to keep her presence here quiet but that would, for obvious reasons, not work.

The young woman's words hurt. She wasn't her father. But nobody seemed to be able to remember that; they always tarred her with the same brush. Even in death, he still ruled her life it seemed, and it looked like she would spend what was left of her life repaying his considerable debts.

She felt her anger build: anger at her situation, anger that Erin and Paula were being stubborn about her seeing Flag, anger at the world in general for not letting her lie down and die like she wanted to. "Have you finished?" she asked quietly.

Mare was startled when she heard the woman's voice; she thought it would be stronger. She nodded.

"Good. And you are?"

"Dr. Gillespie," she said tersely. TJ raised her eyebrow. "I'm the local vet."

Erin wanted to hide. They had kept Flag's illness from TJ, knowing that it would upset her. Now that the vet had decided to take things into her own hands, that was going to backfire terribly. She wished that Paula would hurry up and get here. She wasn't that far from the ranch when Erin radioed.

"Ah I see, Dr. Gillespie, and do you make a habit of bursting into people's houses?" TJ inquired condescendingly. "Doesn't seem like that would be a good way to attract business, if you asked me. As for your opinions on my family, they are neither wanted nor appreciated. I suggest you leave quietly, before I have you thrown out."

Mare observed the stirring embers of anger developing in the crystal-blue eyes. Her lip curled. "I come here to treat a sick horse and discover the return of a sick family." The fire in the blue eyes flamed and TJ opened her mouth to respond, but just then Paula came charging into the office.

Instead of speaking, TJ's glance went from Paula to Mare, then back to Paula, and she tossed her head to the side, signaling dismissal. Paula didn't know what was going on, but she recognized TJ's signal. Without question, her hand reached around Mare's arm and tightened as the vet scowled. Erin spoke up with an urgent tone in her voice, "Dr. Gillespie, Miss Meridian has asked you to leave and I think it might be wise for you to do so."

Mare's gaze had been locked on TJ's during this whole exchange. "I'll be back tomorrow to check on your sick horse." The vet's voice flattened, giving a false sense of spent anger. Her eyes switched to Paula's. "I would like to suggest that you take your hand off of me. I'm leaving."

Paula hesitated and looked at TJ. TJ's eyes were narrowed and her jaw set, but she nodded and Paula released Mare's arm.

"I'll show you out, Doctor." Erin started to exit, then looked back to make sure Mare was following her. The vet hadn't moved. She stood where she was until the blue eyes swept back to her. With one last challenging look, Mare turned away and followed Erin out.

* * * * * * * * *

Paula nervously watched TJ. She could see the anger building in the blue eyes and knew if she didn't say anything soon that it was going to be hell on earth around the ranch for the next few days. Maybe Erin should have told her Flag was ill. At least, then, that would only be one thing she was mad about. In fact, knowing TJ, that was probably the only thing she was still mad at; she was used to fending off insults aimed at her family. But her horse was another matter. These days the animal was the only thing that kept her going. She took a deep breath as she saw that TJ was about to start her tirade.

"Why did we require a vet for one of the horses?"

Paula frowned. This was much worse than she had thought. If TJ wasn't shouting, she was furious

"Erin went to the barn early this morning and thought one of them looked a little distressed. She thought it would be wise to err on the side of caution and have the vet check it out." It was unlikely that TJ would let her get away with not naming the horse involved but it was worth a try.

"Was it Flag?" TJ asked softly.

Ah hell, Erin, how do you always manage to weasel out of these situations and leave me to deal with them? "Yeah, it was."

"What was wrong? Is she going to be okay?" Paula noticed that TJ had picked up a pencil and was twirling it through her fingers, another bad sign.

"I don't know. I haven't spoken to Erin yet."

"Fine. We'll wait for her to come back then." The motion of the pencil quickened in her hand.

Oh yeah. Hell is about to materialize on a little-known ranch in Nowheresville, Texas.

* * * * * * * * * *

Mare stalked out of the ranch house, muttering and cursing under her breath. *I can't believe Miss High-and-Mighty just brushed me off like that. At least I told her what I thought, let her know that her kind weren't welcome here. No way on earth I'm working for them. I'll treat the*

horse but they can find someone else to use their retainer.
I don't care how much it would help to have that money.

Erin walked a pace or two behind the vet as she made
her exit from the house and stormed over to her vehicle.
She liked the vet and would still like to have her looking
after the animals for them, especially if the passion she
had just shown transferred to her work. What she didn't
like was her attitude toward TJ.

Erin had first met TJ at Harvard and over the years
developed a strong friendship with her. But in the beginning, it
had taken her months to break through TJ's icy reserve; she
was distant with everybody and rarely socialized. If provoked, she was openly hostile; even violent if pushed too
far. It took a long time to be able to see past that, but when
Erin was cornered one evening by one of the more aggres-
sive homophobic groups from the campus, TJ came to her
rescue.

Silence descended on the jeering group. They stopped
shoving her around when TJ's voice was heard. They just
stood there and looked up at the tall figure, assessing her,
trying to figure out whether she was actually a threat. The
first mistake the group's leader made was to smile, because
when he did, so did TJ. It was chilling to see and Erin
couldn't understand why none of the group could see the
danger they were in.

Their second mistake was not believing that the
woman standing before them would be able to use the
strength her tall, muscular body held. If there had been a
weapon among them it would have been a bloodbath. As it
was, a few broken bones later, it was all over.

Erin had immediately changed her opinion of TJ
Meridian and spent the next few months breaking down
barriers and generally pestering the woman until she
gained acceptance and friendship from her. In that time
she learned a lot about her: her contempt for her father and
his practices; her mother's constant badgering over what
was right, and what wasn't, for her daughter; her lack of

free time; the way she constantly studied, trying to appease the demands of her family.

The only thing that seemed to make the woman happy was when her younger brother visited. The look on her face when Lance told her he'd got into Harvard Medical School was priceless.

When the women's time together at Harvard came to an end, they kept in touch via the Internet, snail mail, and the occasional phone call. And Erin's admiration for the woman grew. After TJ's parents died, she took over the corporation and began to make changes. Market analysts said she was mad, that her changes were economic disasters. They were wrong. The shareholders loved her; their holdings rose and everyone was happy. Except TJ.

For some reason, everybody thought she was her father. The press said she was ruthless, more interested in profit than the repercussions her decisions had on those involved. The day TJ hired Erin and her partner, Paula Tanner, as consultants on the ranch project, there were protesters outside the building. Not protesting about the corporation, but about the person running it. The woman Erin saw that day was a shadow of the one she had been. The pressures were already taking their toll.

Yes, TJ had restructured the company and yes, people had lost their jobs, but it was nothing like what her father had done. Severance packages had been more than adequate, and where possible, people were moved to other positions within the corporation. In some cases, TJ had given financial incentives and help to other companies, to encourage them to relocate to areas where she had pulled hers out. But unlike others, who would have paraded their generosity for all to see, TJ refused to take credit for, or publicize, anything she was doing.

Erin's listening to the vet vent her anger on her friend hurt, and it had hurt TJ, too, though she would never admit it.

"You know, that was kind of nasty," Erin commented to the vet's back.

Mare swung around and stared angrily at Erin. "You have no idea what this town has suffered because of her. You have no idea what she's like." Mare turned back to the pickup only to feel a hand grab tightly to her arm and swing her back.

"No!" Erin said forcefully. "You have no idea what she's like. You haven't been through the hell we've been through with her the past year; you haven't been through the pain she has. What happened here happened ten years ago. At a guess, I'd say you were fifteen, sixteen years old? Well, she was eighteen. Do you think an eighteen-year-old girl had anything to do with making decisions about closing manufacturing plants and factories? TJ isn't her father, and it's about time people started realizing that."

"Look around you, Erin." Mare made a wide sweep with her arm. "Where did all this come from? Where did those prize horses come from? That one I treated today is worth more than my house is worth. The Meridian ranch is probably worth more than the whole town."

The vet's lip curled. "You're asking me to feel sorry for her because she's being blamed for the things her father did? Well, maybe she didn't make the decisions, but she sure as hell laid back and let the money drop into her lap, didn't she? Where would she be today without her father? Would she be a part of Meridian Corporation? Sure, tell me you believe in the Easter Bunny, too."

Mare took a ragged breath. She was exhausted and this argument was emotionally draining. "While she was living like a princess, people in Meridianville were wondering where their next meal was coming from, worried not for themselves but for their children. I don't think I was nasty. I just told her the truth."

"You dislike her because she's rich?"

"No, I dislike her because her father produced that money by climbing over the lives of people from places like Meridianville. You want me to believe she cares about them? Tell her I'll believe in the goodness of her motives when I see her turn that money over to them."

Erin's anger had died away to plain frustration. "Have you ever heard the expression, 'Give a man a fish and he'll eat for a day; teach him how to fish and he'll eat forever?' Well, that's what TJ is trying to do. She wants to rebuild the economy here and bring people's lives back to them."

"Right." The doctor was suddenly too tired to argue any more. She climbed into the pickup truck and started the motor. "I'll be back to see Flag. Make sure you follow those directions." Stifling a yawn, she put the truck in gear and left.

Erin walked slowly back to the house, her eyes cast down. *If I can't convince even one person that TJ's motives are good, how are we going to convince a whole town?*

Chapter
3

TJ's office was ominously quiet as Erin approached the room. She gently pushed open the door and stepped in. Paula stood over by the window, gazing out at the horses in the corral. TJ was still seated behind her desk, hands angrily twirling one of the many pencils that she kept in her desk caddy. Paula turned around, grimaced and indicated she should close the door. Erin already knew from the silence that they were in for one of TJ's infamous outbursts of anger. *Oh, this could be very painful indeed.*

"Has she left?" asked TJ in a precisely controlled voice.

"Yes." Erin didn't elaborate, knowing that it would only annoy TJ further and that when the woman wanted to know anything she'd ask.

TJ flung the pencil to the desk, leaned forward and stared pointedly at Erin. "Just when were you going to tell me that Flag was ill?"

Uh-oh, she's not yelling; this is definitely worse than I had imagined. "I only noticed this morning that she was distressed. I got the vet out right away and I would have told you once I found out the prognosis."

"And just what is the prognosis?"

"Flag has heatstroke. We'll have to watch the other horses as well, at least until the temperatures drop. With the proper treatment she'll be fine." Erin felt Paula come up behind her and rest hands on her shoulder, silently giving her support.

"Fine. You can leave now." TJ turned her head back to the computer screen.

Ouch! We're gonna get the silent treatment. She is more than just a little mad about this. "TJ, look, we weren't trying to..."

"Get out," ordered TJ, her voice growing colder. Erin winced as she heard the change in her tone.

"But, TJ..."

The plaintive plea in Erin's voice broke what little restraint TJ had over her anger. "Last time I looked I was just a cripple, not a child, though for some reason you insist on treating me like one. Now, get out and leave me alone."

Erin opened her mouth to try again, but Paula tugged her away toward the door. "Not now." She turned her gaze back to TJ, who was still staring at her computer screen. "TJ, I'll pick you up in two hours to take you to your session."

"I'm not going," she replied without looking up. Paula sighed and led Erin out of the room with her, then closed the door.

Erin pulled her arm out of Paula's grip and looked at her. "Are you going to let her get away with that?"

"She's upset. It won't do us any good to antagonize her. Let's go check on Flag and let her cool down. In an hour or so, I'll go get her and take her for a visit to Flag, then I'll kidnap her and take her for her session."

"She isn't going to be happy about that. She'll tell you again that you're treating her like a child."

"Yep, she will; and when she stops having temper tantrums like this, we'll stop treating her like one."

Erin turned and started to walk down the corridor. "Problem is, this time we gave her a reason. I should have told her about Flag."

"Yes, but I don't think that is really what she is upset about. It is just her excuse, since she'll never admit that what the good doctor said hurt her." They entered the kitchen and Paula walked over to the coffeemaker and poured two mugs of coffee. She added creamer and sugar to Erin's, then sat down at the breakfast bar.

"I tried talking to the doctor, tried to tell her that TJ wasn't her father, but she wasn't very receptive," said Erin, taking her mug.

"Maybe bringing TJ here wasn't such a good idea. The atmosphere isn't going to be great around here and that might not help toward her recovery."

"Maybe not, but we can't exactly go back to the city. You never know, maybe the attitude of folks around here will be the incentive she needs to pick herself up again."

"Yeah. Either that or it will kill her."

The two friends stared at each other as that thought whirled around in their minds. "We can't let that happen." Erin's face conveyed her determination even as a note of uncertainty sounded in her words.

Paula sat up straighter and a note of resolve filled her voice. "We won't let it happen. But at this point, we can only play it by ear, see how things go. Which reminds me, what's the story with Flag?"

"The vet is coming back here tomorrow for some more treatment. In the meantime, there are some things we need to do." Erin reached into her pocket for the directions Mare had given her and she cleared her throat. "Here's a list of the care Flag is going to need for the next several days." She put it into Paula's outstretched hand.

The dark-haired woman's deep brown eyes skimmed down the list. She looked up at Erin and her eyebrows came together in a frown. "You're going to do all this?

Erin's short laugh burst from her throat. "Nuh-uh, my friend. We are going to do all this. It will be a learning situation for both of us."

Paula whistled and her eyes took on a gleam. "When do we start?"

Erin shook her head. It never ceased to amaze her that Paula was always eager to try something new, no matter how much work was involved. "Right now would be good. We need to get some fans set out in the barn with one of them fixed on Flag and we need to give her a bath every few hours. You can see there are a couple other things on the list that we can do right now, and some to do later."

Paula handed the list back to Erin, put the coffee mugs in the dishwasher and grabbed a handful of cookies from the cookie jar. Chocolate chip cookies were her downfall and Erin always made sure to pick up some when she went food shopping. "Okay, let's get to it." She handed a couple of cookies to her partner as they left the kitchen in search of fans.

* * * * * * * * * *

The door closed behind her two friends and TJ let out a ragged breath. She slumped back into her chair, eyes staring sightlessly at the computer screen. *God! Those two are as bad as my mother used to be. She couldn't let me make a decision, either, that she didn't agree with. Anybody would think I was a two-year-old child instead of the CEO of a major corporation.*

She pushed herself further from the desk, maneuvered her chair from behind it, and wheeled herself to the window. The office was on the first floor, just like her bedroom and all the other amenities she needed. The sunken living room had caused a problem but it hadn't been too hard to rig a ramp to allow her access. The stair lift wasn't being installed till next week, and neither was the concrete ramp that would allow her to get off the front porch by herself.

At the moment she was totally dependent on her two friends, which she hated because it only made her feel more like a child. All she wanted was to be left alone, but they hadn't allowed her that since the hospital. Even now, although she had promised them she wouldn't do anything stupid, they still didn't trust her fully. Flag's illness was a classic example of that.

What did they think I was going to do, kill myself? Yes, they probably did, the more logical part of her mind reminded her. *They should have told me about Flag. Yep, they should have, but Erin was right: you would have worried yourself sick until the vet arrived. She did the right thing in not telling you till she knew what was going on. Let's be honest. If it hadn't been for the vet bursting in like that you wouldn't have known until Erin told you, and you wouldn't have had a problem, would you?* TJ grudgingly admitted it to herself. *So now you're going to have to apologize for being such an idiot and for losing your temper.*

TJ looked out the window as she heard laughter. Paula and Erin were walking over to the barn, arms loaded up with equipment. *Looks as though my outburst really upset them, didn't it? Great, now you're going to pout all day because they can see Flag and you can't. No wonder they treat you like a two-year-old child, when you act like this.*

* * * * * * * * * *

Paula hooked the last fan to the rafter, making sure it pointed toward Flag's stall. "Okay, that takes care of the fans. Each horse will have one. What's next on the list?" Paula put aside the stepladder, brushed her hands together and cocked an eyebrow at Erin who read from the doctor's instructions.

"Some of these things—shots, temperature taking— don't have to be done till about 4 o'clock. We're not to give her as much grain and we need to add some salt to her feed to make her drink more. And put a bag of electrolytes in her water. The doc left the stuff for the shots and a cou-

ple bags of electrolytes. They're over there on the worktable. The medications are in the fridge."

Paula was taking care of these as Erin read them off,
one by one. "Now," Erin continued, "we need to give Flag
a bath. Well, not actually a bath, we need to spray her
down, especially her head and up inside her legs, to keep
her cooled off."

She looked up at Paula who was waiting for the next
direction. "Put a lead rope on Flag and take her out of the
barn. I'll get the hose."

Paula clipped the lead rope on Flag and led her out,
noticing how listless she seemed. "She still doesn't look
all that great."

Outside, Erin turned on the faucet and unrolled the
hose from its carrier, pulling it toward the palomino. "The
doc said it might take a while. Best thing we can do for
her is to follow the instructions." Erin flipped the nozzle
to the spray setting and lifted the hose toward Flag's head,
showering her thoroughly. Erin stifled a grin as Paula, still
holding the lead rope, jumped out of the way.

"Yo! Watch it will ya? Flag's supposed to get the
bath, not me."

"Sorry," Erin sniggered.

She sprayed along Flag's back, then leaned down and
sprayed the undersides of the horse's hind legs. She made
sure to get plenty of water on the large veins as the vet's
instructions said. Spraying the underside of Flag's body,
she worked her way to the forelegs and sprayed the large
veins there, too.

She could see Paula's jeans showing between Flag's
forelegs and somehow the hose slipped and sprayed her,
too.

"Yeow, Erin! You know how cold that well water is?
Cut it out!"

Erin stood up and looked at Paula with raised eyebrows, the picture of innocence. "I'm so sorry. You don't
think I did that on purpose, do you?" She walked up past
Flag's shoulder until she was about four feet from Paula

and grinned wickedly. "Now, this is on purpose." She flipped the nozzle adjustment to the stream setting and doused her fuming friend. "You know, you really look like you need to be cooled down."

Paula led Flag quickly back into her stall and unhooked the lead rope on the move. Even before Flag was in place, the soaked woman was squishing after Erin. As she rounded Flag's hindquarters and shut the stall gate, Erin had followed her in and got her again with the stream of water. The blonde put her finger on the nozzle to narrow and strengthen the stream and caught Paula full in the face.

What Erin hadn't noticed was the extra bucket of water sitting next to the stall gate. She also hadn't noticed the kink in the hose. As she pulled the hose forward, the kink closed, cutting off the supply of water to the nozzle. Erin turned her laughing face back to see what had happened to the hose and when she turned forward, Paula let loose with the bucket of water, right toward her laugh.

"Yaaaaaaahhh!" Erin dropped the hose, threw crossed arms over her head and ducked, too late. While she hid her head, Paula grabbed the hose, flipped out the kink, and doused her with the stream of water until there was not a dry spot left on her body.

"I give up, I give up," Erin gurgled, trying to run away.

"You'll give up when I say so," Paula growled, chasing her but keeping herself between Erin and the doors. She finally took pity on her after a full minute of the water treatment and turned the faucet off.

The two of them, dripping wet, looked at each other and got a fit of laughing. Erin pointed at Paula and gasped. "You looked so funny, trying to hold onto Flag and get out of the way of the water at the same time."

Paula's laugh mingled with a snort. "You should have seen your face when the kink stopped the water and you turned back around to see a bucket of water coming at you! Thought you had the upper hand, huh?"

"I should have known better. You always seem to come out on top."

Paula waved her eyebrows and made a lecherous grin and the two went off again into gales of laughter.

They took a breath and had almost stopped laughing when Paula reached into her breast pocket and scooped out a couple of dissolved chocolate chip cookies. Her chagrined look re-ignited the hilarity.

The two finally got themselves under control. "I know one thing for sure." Paula waved a finger at Erin.

"What's that?" Erin's laughter still bubbled in sporadic bursts.

"Next time, you get to hold the horse and I get to hold the hose."

* * * * * * * * * *

TJ had continued sitting at the window. It was a pleasant distraction from having her head in a computer all day. In a short while, she saw Erin and Paula bring Flag out for her bath. It was apparent that the golden palomino wasn't up to par. Her head, usually lifted so proudly, hung down and her walk was sluggish.

TJ's eyes shifted to the distance as she remembered the first time she had seen Faithful Flag. Her father had squelched TJ's near-obsession with horses when he had closed the ranch. After his death, she determined to make up for lost time and promptly hunted for a jumper to start training for competitions. As soon as she saw the glorious part-thoroughbred, the two fell in love with each other. TJ hired the best teacher money could buy and had him train her and Flag together.

Picture after picture ran through her mind of times past when she and Faithful Flag moved as one: soaring gracefully over jumps, striding perfectly between them and winning over all comers. Twin, solid-oak display cabinets with mirrored backs sat in adjoining corners of the office filled with trophies and ribbons won by the tall, blue-eyed rider as she put her beloved horse to the test. And always, Flag came through.

With these reminiscences, TJ's eyes started to mist but squeals from near the barn drew her attention back to the present. As Paula ran Flag back into the barn, Erin was chasing her with a streaming hose. Several shouts were heard and presently, the two women exited the barn, dripping with water and laughing.

At that moment, the wealthy, beautiful, supposedly arrogant TJ Meridian felt very much alone.

Chapter
4

Paula ran lightly down the steps, all showered and changed after the water fight. *Feels good to get out of those boots once in a while.* She headed to the kitchen, hoping Erin had some sandwiches ready. Paula had waited while Erin jumped in the shower first, because TJ would be waiting for her lunch, and that was Erin's responsibility today.

"Good girl." The dark-haired woman smiled as she entered the kitchen and saw two places set, with sandwiches and iced tea waiting. She sat down and waited for her friend.

Erin entered from the hall that led to TJ's office. "TJ decided to eat at her desk." Erin sat down at her place and started eating and Paula joined her. "Guess you have to change your plan about "kidnapping" her, there's not enough time for her to see Flag before you need to leave for the therapy session."

Paula nodded. "I'll just go in there and tell her she's going, or else. See what happens. She can see Flag later."

The two women ate quickly then Paula rose. "Maybe TJ's right about us treating her like a child. Let's see how far I get treating her like an adult."

"Lots of luck." Erin smiled sympathetically.

She knocked on the office door, then opened it and walked in. "Time for your session, TJ." She couldn't tell whether TJ had actually been conducting some business or was just hiding behind the computer screen. Her empty lunch tray had been pushed aside.

Inscrutable blue eyes looked up from under coal-black brows. "I told you I'm not going."

"TJ, you say you want us to treat you like an adult, but when we try to, you act like a stubborn kid." Paula walked over and half perched on the edge of the vast desk, her voice stern "You know, you set the tone around here. If you want us to think you're a grownup, then you have to start acting like one. Because, so far, you haven't been."

TJ's eyes shifted downward, then she turned her head and lifted her gaze toward the window. Her fingers found an ever-present pencil, picked it up and started a quick tattoo on the desktop. Paula was on tenterhooks, not knowing what to expect, or whether she was even going to get an answer.

The even tattoo became ragged, slowed and gradually stopped. TJ sighed. "Go get the van."

Surprised at her easy victory, Paula jumped up and moved swiftly to accomplish just that. "I'll pick you up at the porch," she responded unnecessarily as she went out, leaving the door open for TJ's easier access.

TJ sat for a little longer, still gazing out the window. *Maybe if I go through the motions of cooperating, they will leave me in peace.* This morning sure hadn't been peaceful. As far as TJ was concerned, the vet had been an intruder—an annoying one. Why didn't she just take care of Flag and mind her own business?

For some reason, TJ couldn't get her out of her mind. Maybe it was her unaccustomed brashness. Most people quailed in front of the Meridian power, but it didn't even slow the doctor down. TJ shook her head to release the short reverie and wheeled herself out to meet Paula.

Paula worked the wheelchair down the steps and over to the open door on the passenger side of the van. TJ's long arm easily reached the bar that had been installed above the doorway and she hoisted herself in and fastened the seat belt. Paula folded the wheelchair, opened the sliding door and placed the chair on its side on the floor behind the front seat. Closing both doors, she jogged to the driver's side, got in, hooked her seat belt and started up.

They drove for a while in silence then it occurred to Paula that TJ would want to visit Flag. "I'll take you to see Flag when we come back, if you'd like. Erin and I have to give her some shots just about then and maybe you'd like to come watch us. We'll probably have to give her another bath, too."

"So it was Flag who got the bath today?" Paula's head jerked around for a quick glance at TJ, then came swiftly back to the road. But that glance had been enough to see the tiny quirk at one side of TJ's lips, a precious look that had been absent for too long.

"Why, TJ, I do believe you are teasing me." Paula automatically flicked the back of her hand at TJ's thigh then suddenly realized the woman couldn't feel that friendly gesture. Turning her head quickly to the left, Paula blinked rapidly and swallowed hard to arrest the unexpected tears that threatened to strike. "I guess that means you saw us come out of the barn, dripping wet, huh?"

"Yes."

Paula had started to grin, but the yearning so evident in that one word cut it short. She was glad they were pulling up in front of the counselor's office building. She jumped out, got TJ back in her wheelchair and took her in for her appointment. She left TJ in the small waiting area when Peter appeared and beckoned Paula into his office.

A few minutes later, Paula returned, wheeled TJ into the office and left. Peter came out from behind his desk and sat in a stuffed chair across from TJ. Mahogany shelving filled with leather-bound books rested in the corner near his neat workspace. Several large, signed, abstract prints hung randomly about the buff walls, interspersed with framed diplomas, testifying to Peter's expertise. A couch and matching chair made a cozy nook against the far wall with green carpeting and soft overhead lighting completing the décor.

"Well, TJ, Paula tells me you had some excitement this morning. With the vet?"

Peter was gratified to see that the usually cool blue eyes stirred a bit. "You could have asked me if anything had happened, you know. You don't need to have one of my own employees spying on me."

"Paula isn't spying on you. Actually, I just wanted to get her impressions of whether these sessions seem to be helping you any. She volunteered the information about this morning. You want to tell me about it?"

The counselor put his elbow on his chair arm and leaned his chin on the back of his hand. A man of medium height and build, Peter wore his light brown hair short and a darker mustache and beard graced his fair-complexioned face. Wire-rimmed glasses covered eyes that were, disconcertingly, of two different colors, one blue, one brown. It gave one the eerie feeling that two people lurked behind his personable face.

TJ shrugged. "Not much to tell. She came to take care of a sick horse and when she found out I was in the house, she came charging in and let loose a diatribe about my family ruining Meridianville. Old news."

"Did you get mad at her for running down your family?"

"No, what she said was right." *The more I think about it, the more I admire her guts. She was wrong to burst in on me like that, but most people wouldn't even try.*

"And did you feel responsible for it?"

"Me responsible for what my father did?" TJ shifted her shoulders in her chair. "Of course not."

"How do you feel about what your father did?"

TJ slammed her fist down on the arm of her wheelchair and exploded. "This is not about my father! Get that through your thick skull. I refuse to sit here and discuss him. We're supposed to be discussing my suicide attempt and what caused it, aren't we? That had nothing to do with my father. He's dead. D-e-a-d, dead. You got that?"

Peter tried to soothe TJ with a soft voice. "Don't you see, TJ, the reason you get so upset when I ask you about your father is because you have some unresolved issues about him. We need to get those out in the open to see what bearing they have on your attempt to end your life. You need to talk about him."

"Well, Peter, if that's the only way you think you can find what pushed me to try suicide, then we are both in trouble. I will not, I repeat, I will not discuss my father with you or with anybody else. Period. Go get Paula. This session is over." TJ leaned her head back against the chair and closed her eyes.

Peter could taste the bitterness of frustration. *Such a beautiful, intelligent woman but she seems filled with self-hatred. How can I reach her? How can anyone reach her?*

Peter knew from past experience that waiting for TJ to change her mind was a waste of time. "When you come next week, we won't talk about your father, TJ. We'll explore other avenues."

I won't be here next week, TJ wanted to scream, but knew she couldn't. The only thing standing between her and being committed to a mental hospital was the promise to attend these sessions. *And I will not be put in a mental hospital. I will die first.* TJ's eyes flew open, but Peter had gone to call Paula. *I didn't mean that, I didn't mean that,* she tried to convince herself.

Paula came in, wheeled TJ out to the van, and drove her home. Not a word came from the woman in spite of several attempts at conversation by Paula. *Lord, she's worse now than before she went in. Are we doing the right thing? Let's hope that seeing Flag cheers her up; it's remarkable what that animal can do for her.*

* * * * * * * * * *

Mare pushed her front door open and trudged through, letting the screen slam shut behind her. The heat inside was almost as oppressive as it had been outside. Mare mentally kicked herself for not leaving the air-conditioning switched on. She threw her bag on the floor, took off her hat and jammed it on the hook near the door then headed to the kitchen.

She flipped the switch by the side of the refrigerator and listened as the air-conditioner rattled to life. In a few minutes the rooms were noticeably cooler. Opening the fridge door, she grabbed a beer then slumped tiredly into a chair at the kitchen table.

Gods, what a day. When a day starts out bad it stays that way, doesn't it? She was exhausted. The call to the Meridian Ranch this morning had been a hellishly perfect start to a hellishly nasty day. She had been on call, after call, after call. The animals in the area were suffering badly from the heat, and if it didn't break soon, some of the ranches would be losing livestock.

Mare loved working outside, but today the heat had been a formidable challenge. She had to admit, though, that she had put herself in a bad mood, mulling over this morning's argument with TJ Meridian. Not that she particularly regretted storming into the woman's office and telling her what she thought; but her conversation with Erin afterwards weighed heavily on her mind.

The woman had been right: she didn't know TJ Meridian. She only knew of the father's reputation and, yes, she had judged the daughter on it. And yes, she didn't like that the Meridian family had made money from the town when they had left the town with none. And yes, in an ideal world, turning that money over to the town would solve its current problems. But this wasn't an ideal world. Mare knew that throwing money at the problems wasn't the solution and she knew that it wasn't likely to happen anyway. So now she was feeling a little bit guilty about her outburst to Erin, and maybe just the tiniest bit guilty that she had invaded Miss Meridian's home.

The shrill sound of a ringing phone startled Mare from her thoughts. She climbed to her feet and reached for the wall phone. *Oh lord, I hope this isn't work. Don't think I have the energy to restock the truck tonight.* Summoning enough energy to keep the weariness from her voice, she answered, "Dr. Gillespie."

"Hey, Mare." The vet smiled as she recognized Jess' voice.

"Hi, Jess." She pulled the chair over from the table and sat back down. "What are you up to?"

"Well, I was hoping I could persuade the local vet to come out to dinner with me?"

Mare sat back, relaxing and sipping her beer. "Jess, that's a lovely idea but I'm beat and honestly just don't have the energy. I'm going to have a bath and crawl into bed."

"Hmm, did you stop for lunch today?" Jess' concerned voice inquired. Silence greeted his question. "I thought not; Rochelle said she hadn't seen you. Tell you what. While you hop in the bath, I'll hop over to the diner, get 'Chelle to pack us something up and I'll bring it over with a bottle of wine."

Mare thought for a second. She hadn't eaten much today, just the sandwich that Mabel Stirkle had brought out to her while she was looking at their cattle. And she hadn't seen much of Jess recently. He'd been away on business and she hadn't had the time to sit and talk since he returned. It was about time they caught up with each other. Besides, she could find out if he knew anything about the Meridian Ranch. "Sure, Jess, that's a great idea. See if they have any of that blueberry pie, will you?"

"No problem. See you in about an hour, okay?"

"Yep. An hour is fine."

Mare didn't bother to get dressed up for Jess' visit; she jumped into a pair of old sweats and a T-shirt. He arrived promptly at eight with a couple of roast beef platters, a red wine and blueberry pie. They ate in the kitchen, chatting about how the Astros were fighting for a playoff berth. Jess proudly announced that his company had just won a big contract to design a web site and graphics for a major manufacturing firm. He was in a good mood because the job would pay handsomely and allow him to buy the new truck he wanted.

After they had cleared the table and done the dishes they retired to the living room and settled at either end of the couch.

"Where were you rushing off to this morning?" inquired Jess as he lounged back onto the comfortable, plump cushions.

Mare looked over at him, wondering whether to tell him the Meridians were back. She knew whatever she said within these walls would stay here. After all, Jess hadn't gone blurting out the fact that she was gay when she told him. He'd realize that letting everybody know that TJ Meridian was at the ranch would only create trouble. While that family deserved all it got as far as Mare was concerned, they could still cause an awful lot of problems for the town, if they wanted to.

"I was going up to the Meridian Ranch. They had a sick horse up there." She looked over, expecting to see shock on Jess' face and seeing none. "Did you know it had been reopened?"

"Not really. But we knew someone was up there; we've made a few deliveries."

Mare raised her eyebrows at that. "Didn't think your dad would approve of that."

Jess shrugged his shoulders. "The store needs the money just like everyone else. Some woman named Scott opened an account and paid a whole stack of money in advance. Dad couldn't afford to turn it down."

I guess the whole town is in the same position, thought Mare. *They have to take what they can, from wherever they can get it, to survive.*

"So," said Jess, "what's it like up there? It was a bit of a mess when I went up about a month ago."

"It looks good. They've put a lot of money into it. Did you meet the owner when you went up?"

Jess shook his head. "Nope, just the Scott woman."

"I met the owner today. It's one of the Meridians—the daughter."

"Really? I thought they were all dead. Some car accident, or something. But hell, if they are back, the folks around town aren't going to like that."

"Yeah, I know; I told her that."

"You told her?" prompted Jess, knowing already that there was more to the story. Mare's temper was famous in town.

"Actually, I stormed into the house and yelled it at her."

Jess started laughing. "Oh, boy. Bet she loved that."

Mare sat and considered TJ's reaction to her invasion. "She really didn't seem that surprised. It was Miss Scott who lit into me as she was escorting me out of the premises."

"What's she like?"

"Who? The daughter?" Jess nodded. "Long black hair, really intense blue eyes, great bone structure." *And she looked like death warmed up.* "And now that I think about it she was very pale, as though she was just getting over an illness or something. She had a real quiet voice; didn't raise it once to me, even though, technically, I was trespassing." Mare's voice trailed off as her conscious mind took note of what her subconscious had observed earlier in the day... the slump to TJ's shoulders, the listlessness in her eyes. Something she couldn't quite put her finger on was wrong with that picture.

"Tall or short?" asked Jess, watching Mare carefully. "The Meridian woman—was she tall or short?"

How the hell would I know? She was sitting down. "I couldn't really tell; she didn't stand up while I was there. Just sat in her chair and presided over it all." Mare stood up and started toward the kitchen. "You want a beer?"

"Yeah, please." As soon as Mare returned with the beer, Jess continued his friendly inquisition. He had noticed the tone of Mare's voice as she spoke of the woman. "So Miss Meridian is pretty good looking?"

"Beautiful," came Mare's instant reply. Jess chuckled as Mare blushed when she realized what she had said.

"You found her attractive then?"

"Physically? Yeah. But inside she's just another Meridian."

"It's unlike you to make a knee-jerk diagnosis, Mare." *Besides, you liked her; I can tell.* "She might not be what you think she is."

Mare looked over at Jess but his face was expression-less, and the conversation had turned uncomfortable. "So, how's your mom?" *Yeah, change the subject... before he gets you to admit to something you don't want to admit to yourself.*

A huge grin split Jess' face as Mare's question gave away her attempt to hurriedly change the topic of conver-sation. He was tempted to pursue the subject, but he relented. "Mom's just about the same as she was when she talked to you day before yesterday." Mare made a face at him and he chuckled. "She's a little disappointed that I have to go away again so soon."

Mare's eyebrows lifted. "Go away? But you just got home."

"Yeah, but this new contract means I have to spend quite a bit of time at the manufacturer's headquarters find-ing out just what each department wants on their web site. Management intends to use a lot of on-site pictures and have asked me to advise them what will work the best. I figure I'll be there a month or more."

"So tonight's dinner was a going away party?" Mare teased, but she was disappointed, too. She missed having Jess to talk to.

"You could call it that, I guess. And now it's time for me to go home. I know you're tired and I want to get an early start tomorrow." Jess stood up and pulled her up with him. The two friends said their good-byes and hugged at the door, and Mare watched Jess drive away before she locked up. As she headed upstairs, one sentence of Jess' surfaced in her mind and nagged at her until she fell asleep. *She might not be what you think she is.*

* * * * * * * * * *

Some people woke up at the same time every morning, rain or shine. Mare had never been one of those people. The alarm clock had to drag her awake every day, that is on the days when she was asleep in the morning. Vets didn't always have that luxury. But this day the insistent clang pulled her from the depths and she sat up groggily. The last few days had been a hell of activity with so many heat-stroke cases mixed in with the normal, everyday, sicknesses and injuries. And hell was the right word. *If this heat doesn't break soon, I just might. Thank whatever gods may be for air conditioning.*

But the barns weren't air-conditioned and neither were the fields or ranges. Mare was out in the heat more than she was inside, and the heat drained her energy like a swift siphon.

As she almost sleepwalked through her shower, breakfast and restocking medicines and supplies in her pickup and bag, Mare's thoughts centered on her trip back to the Meridian ranch today. She wondered what her reception might be. She hadn't been especially tactful with either Erin or TJ Meridian, to put it mildly. Or Paula, for that matter.

She mused about the three women. Erin seemed pretty nice. Paula seemed pretty tough. And TJ? Mare wasn't

sure how to categorize TJ or how she felt about her.
Maybe mostly still angry with her as a Meridian, but also
partly apologetic for bursting into her home and lambast-
ing her the way she had.

Finally, bag and truck were restocked and Mare
embarked for the Meridian ranch.   She drove slowly
through town with her windows down. She hit the accelerator more forcefully when she reached the open spaces,
hoping in vain to grab a breath of cooler air. Even so early
in the morning, the sun drew shimmering heat waves from
the asphalt road surface, distorting the horizon. Snorting
in defeat, she wound up the windows and turned on the air
conditioner.

Through the undulating distortion, Mare saw the boy
bicycling some distance ahead of her. He looked to be
about 10 years old and she thought she recognized his
shock of red hair. He pedaled furiously then heard her
truck and turned to glance behind him. As he did, the
bicycle swerved a bit, ran off the road, hit a large stone and
catapulted the rider into the dry ditch that ran alongside.
Mare slammed on squealing brakes, turned off the motor,
grabbed her bag and ran to the boy's side.

Besides unfortunate, but relatively harmless, brush
burns, he had received a nasty cut on one leg where it had
skidded across a piece of broken glass. He sat up and was
trying hard not to cry, but tears rolled from his pale blue
eyes, down across his freckled cheeks.

Mare squatted down, checked to make sure there was
no glass embedded in the wound and applied pressure to
stop the spurt of blood from a damaged artery. "Aren't you
Johnny Robertson?" Mare knew that speaking to the boy
would help to ease his pain. She knew that he was one of
the sons of George Robertson who owned a nearby farm.
The boy nodded his head and sniffled. "You'll be okay,
Johnny. Just let me clean this up and get a bandage on it
and I'll take you in to Dr. Samuels."

At the sound of hoofbeats, Mare looked up and saw TJ
Meridian approaching on a sleek, black mare. The woman

slowed her mount and guided it up to the fence near the accident scene, her cool blue eyes observing the boy's predicament.

Resentment momentarily locked Mare's tongue, but for the boy's sake she swallowed her pride and asked for assistance. "Miss Meridian, we could use some help here. I have a cell phone in the pickup. Could you call for the ambulance? Then we'll try Johnny's family."

Mare saw unexpected compassion in TJ's expression as she looked at the youngster. She reached to the belt encircling her long, blue tunic and unclipped a cell phone that Mare hadn't noticed. When the blue eyes turned to Mare, the compassion had disappeared to be replaced by the usual cool disinterest. "9-1-1?"

"Yes, we have 9-1-1 here."

TJ made the call. "They're coming." Her terseness eased as she spoke to the boy. "What's your phone number, Johnny?" TJ punched in the stated number. "Sorry, there's no answer at your house."

The timbre of TJ's low, soft voice unexpectedly resonated with something in Mare's emotions, astonishing her. She quickly returned her attention to the boy's wound. "If you would come down here and hold Johnny's leg, I could get a pressure bandage on it." When there was no answer, Mare looked up at TJ and caught the slight twitch that flitted across one side of her face.

"I...don't think so."

Mare strained to hear the soft voice and was dumbfounded when TJ turned the horse's head, clucked to it and trotted off, pulling the phone again from her belt. The trot soon changed to a gallop, and horse and rider rode out of sight.

I can't believe it! You'd think even a Meridian would want to help an injured child. But I guess I already knew they were a pretty heartless bunch. Mare turned her attention back to Johnny who hadn't taken his eyes off of TJ until she rode away. "That lady is beautiful!" he said almost reverently.

Mare smiled at the wonder shining from his eyes. "Yeah, she is." *At least on the outside.*

"Who is she?"

"She's a new neighbor, Johnny. She owns the ranch across from your farm."

Mare heard a vehicle approaching. Looking toward the sound, she saw a Land Rover come toward them, then pull over to the side of the road right near them. Erin Scott jumped out and hurried to Mare's side.

"TJ called, said you needed some help." Erin squatted down next to the boy and smiled at him. "How do you feel?"

Johnny blushed at this attention from a stranger. "I'm okay. The doc's taking care of me."

"Erin, this is Johnny Robertson from one of the farms across from the ranch. Johnny, this is Miss Scott. She works for the lady who was on the horse."

"Glad to meet you, Johnny." Erin offered her hand to the boy and he sat up straighter and shook it respectfully. "I expect we'll be staying at the ranch for a long while, so I hope to meet your family one of these days."

Another pickup slowed to pass them, then zoomed to the side of the road and a big, redheaded man leaped from the cab. "Johnny! Are you okay?" He ran to the boy and grasped his shoulder.

"I'm okay, Dad. Doc Gillespie helped me."

The man's eyes turned to the vet. "Thanks, Doc. What happened?"

Mare told George Robertson about his son's mishap. As she finished, the ambulance arrived and the EMT's took over. Mare picked up her bag and walked back to her pickup with Erin following her. "You on your way out to the ranch?" Erin asked.

"Yes, I was. I'll be right along." Mare turned to meet Erin's eyes and saw that she felt rebuffed by Mare's atti-tude. *I shouldn't give her a hard time. After all, she's not TJ.* "Thanks for offering to help." She smiled at the blonde and got a tentative return smile. "TJ wouldn't help, but she sends you to. I don't get it. What motivates that woman?" *She thinks she's too good to dirty her hands with us little people?*

Erin looked earnestly at the vet. "As you get to know her, you'll find she's a very complex woman, Doctor. Many times even I don't know what motivates her. But I respect her. She has a noble heart."

"Humph! I doubt if I'll ever get to know her that well." Mare opened the pickup door and stepped in. "Shall we go take care of her horse?"

"I'll turn around and be right behind you." A sad little smile curved Erin's lips. "Give her a chance, Doc. You might be surprised at what you find."

"Right." Mare used one of her favorite words, but her derisive tone negated any sense of agreement. She turned the key and started up the pickup as Erin walked away.

****

After asking Erin to come and help the doctor, TJ spoke to Paula. "I'm coming in. Meet me at the barn." She closed the phone before Paula answered and concentrated on balancing herself on Ebonair's back. The straps that were connected to the front of the saddle came across her thighs and buckled to the back flaps. These gave her enough stability to ride with little difficulty if she went slowly, but on horseback TJ wanted to fly.

With Flag, TJ became such a unit with the palomino that Flag's legs became her legs and there was never any question of sliding off. Ebonair, however, wasn't Flag and TJ had to stay constantly alert when she galloped her. She slowed the animal to a walk as she got nearer to the barn, giving it a chance to cool down.

Finally, she reached the barn where Paula was dutifully waiting outside on the ramp, with the wheelchair next to her. A lift, made of a T-shaped piece of metal connected to a chain, dangled overhead from a makeshift roof. An electrical wire was threaded through the chain and ended at a 2-button box that was connected to the underside of the T-bar.

TJ pulled Ebonair alongside the ramp and Paula hooked the horse to a lead rope attached to the side of the ramp. Then she undid the straps on one side of the saddle while TJ worked on the other side. TJ reached up, grasped the T-shaped bar with both hands, and with sheer strength pulled herself up out of the saddle, swinging her upper body to free her legs. With one hand, Paula guided her friend's body and legs into proper position over the wheelchair. TJ thumbed one of the buttons on the electrical box and the T-bar slowly descended and lowered her into the chair. Ebonair skittered a little at the noise, but her rider was well out of harm's way.

"Why didn't you use the lift to pick you out of the saddle?"

TJ shrugged. "Just felt like doing it myself."

TJ hooked herself into the chair, reached into a pocket of cloth hanging from the chair arm and pulled out a towel. Briskly, she scrubbed the perspiration from her face while Paula unlocked the wheels and maneuvered the chair into the tack room. Paula opened the fridge and pulled out a couple of the sodas. Handing one to TJ, she popped one for herself and sipped at it. TJ popped hers, tilted it back and drank it down without stopping.

Paula frowned at her. "You okay? I still don't think it was a good idea for you to be out in this heat."

"It's still early morning, Paula. I'm fine, just a little thirsty from sucking in all that dry air."

"What happened out there?" Paula tilted her head and frowned. "Erin goes flying outta here, then you come flying in."

"A boy from one of the farms fell from his bike and the doc was on the road and, apparently, saw it happen. She was taking care of him and needed some help." TJ dropped her head and a grimace gave a quick tug at her lips. She took a deep breath, then lifted her head and her ice-blue eyes swept up to meet Paula's nearly black ones.

"But I couldn't do a damn thing except make a couple phone calls." The pained eyes moved away.

Paula's frown was still there, but her eyes softened and she grasped TJ's shoulder and squeezed it. "Hey, you did what you could, okay? Calling Erin was the smart thing to do." When there was no response from TJ, Paula walked behind the chair and started pushing her. "C'mon, let's get you in the house."

"And to the bathroom."

That wasn't meant to be funny, but Paula grinned. At least TJ had something else to occupy her for a little while. Might help take her mind off her latest bout with her disability. "And to the bathroom," she agreed.

Chapter
5

The bathroom that was part of her personal suite of rooms was the first place that TJ had ordered remodeled. It contained every contrivance she needed to take care of her own needs without assistance.

The second remodeling done was the wooden ramps: one into the sunken living room for convenience, and the one behind the barn to enable TJ to get on and off a horse. TJ was tall and solid and neither Paula nor Erin, alone, was strong enough to help her in mounting and dismounting. The ramp had been a lifesaver for her.

Once Paula was sure her help wasn't required, she went back to the barn to unsaddle Ebonair. She carried the saddle into the tack room and placed it on the saddle rack, then went back to remove Ebonair's bridle and replace it with a woven halter.

She looked into Flag's stall as she went by and thought how glad she was the doc was coming out today. TJ's pride and joy seemed a bit better, but she wanted to hear that from the vet.

Paula sprayed Ebonair off with a hose, then turned her into the corral with her own horse, a chestnut mare named Running For Fun, called Runny, for short. Ebonair was

Erin's horse and every time Paula saw her friend aboard the mare, she thought how perfect it was that the curly-headed blonde had chosen such a sleek, black horse. The contrast between the two made a gorgeous picture.

Paula took the bridle into the tack room and hung it on the wall. As she walked out, she heard two vehicles come to a stop outside the barn, one after another. *Probably Erin and the doc.* A short moment later, her guess proved correct as the two women walked side by side into the barn, chattering about the injured youngster.

They stopped when they saw Paula, who stepped forward and offered her hand. "Dr. Gillespie, I'm Paula Tanner. We...ah...weren't exactly formally introduced." A light blush warmed Paula's tanned cheeks as she recalled just how they did meet.

A slow, sardonic grin worked its way across the vet's lips as she noticed the blush. *Maybe not so tough as I thought.* "Glad to meet you, Paula." She held the taller woman's hand for a moment, lifting it up with hers. "I have to admit I like your hand better here than clutched around my arm."

"Yeah. Sorry about that." Paula spoke brusquely, a bit put off by Mare's sarcasm, and Erin lifted an eyebrow at her friend. "When TJ says jump, I jump. If you're the one in the way, you're the one I land on."

Erin spoke quickly. "Maybe we can get off to a better start, now that things have calmed down."

Neither the doctor nor Paula committed themselves, each eyeing the other warily.

Finally, Erin broke the silence that had fallen. "C'mon, Doc, take a look at Flag. She looks a little better, doesn't she?"

Mare went through the usual routine, taking Flag's temperature and checking her heart rate. "She does seem to be improving. Let me get some more Ringer's in her." Mare went to the truck to get what she needed while the other two waited for her in the barn.

"What's wrong with you, Paula? You about bit her head off." Erin poked her friend's ribs with her elbow.

"I'm not too happy with anyone who upsets TJ and she sure as hell did upset her. Mouthy little son of a bum."

"Whoa! Is this the pot calling the kettle black? You've done your share of mouthing off at TJ. You wouldn't have dared to say some of those things before her injury." They could see the vet searching through the various compartments of the camper.

"Some of those things I've said purposely to get some kind of reaction from her. TJ scares me when she pulls that I-don't-give-a-damn act. I'm afraid it might become real."

"Well, her anger at the doc looked a lot healthier to me than that fury she gets into when she's frustrated."

Paula's face lost some of its sternness and her eyes changed from stubborn to interested. "You know, I think you might be right. I know the doc's words hurt her; I could see it in the way her jaw clamped together. But, later, when I took her in to her therapy session, she actually teased me about the bath we gave each other." Paula slowly nodded her head. "Maybe the doc woke something up in TJ. I sure hope so."

Mare came back in waving a drip clamp. "The darn clamp broke and I had a heck of a time finding another one. Guess I know one thing to put on my shopping list."

Paula put a lead on Flag and held onto her while Mare again put a catheter in Flag's jugular vein, set up the IV of Ringer's solution, and ran it in. "You have three beautiful horses here." Mare had gotten a better look at the other two today, especially the black one.

Erin smiled and nodded. "Runny, the chestnut, is Paula's, Ebonair is mine and Flag is TJ's." She reached over and patted Flag's flank. "TJ is crazy about this horse; she's like a member of her family."

Paula snorted. "Better than her family." Then she realized her indiscretion and clammed up.

"She's a jumper. That was a sight to see. Flag and TJ looked like they were one solid animal instead of two separate ones. TJ won a lot of medals with her, before..." Erin's reminiscence came to an abrupt halt and she seemed flustered. Mare gave her a questioning look. "Before we came here," she finished lamely.

"Why don't you write the doc's check, Erin, while she's finishing up?" Paula looked pointedly at her friend.

"I left the checkbook in TJ's office. We can get it when everything's finished here. Give the doc a chance to cool off, too."

Mare asked a question that had been bugging her all along. Flag was a valuable horse, yet its owner hadn't stepped foot in the barn while Mare was here. "If TJ's so crazy about Flag, why isn't she out here?

Erin looked at Paula, who gazed placidly back but didn't say a word. "I think it bothers her a lot that Flag isn't well. Maybe she just can't stand to see her in this condition."

"Ummmm. So she lets you two worry about it." The sardonic smile was back.

"Look, Doc," Paula nearly growled, "you don't know a thing about TJ, so just keep your mouth off of her and we'll all get along a lot better."

When anyone attacked her with words, Mare's first inclination was to strike back. Her mind was quick and she had a wit that could turn a nasty phrase with the best of them. But something made her pause. Maybe it was the softness she saw in Paula and Erin's eyes when they mentioned their employer. TJ obviously was not just their employer, but their friend. And for some reason, they both felt protective of her. It was a puzzle to Mare, and she loved the challenge of a puzzle. She determined that sooner or later she would discover for herself how TJ had been able to deceive two intelligent women.

Mare didn't answer Paula. She gathered the plastic bags emptied of their Ringer's solution, and unhooked the IV apparatus. She picked up her bag and walked into the tack room to clean the IV equipment out in the sink, tossing the plastic bags in the trashcan located there. More wide awake this time than when she had first been in here, she looked curiously around the whole room. Other than the table, sink, cupboards, and refrigerator she had seen on her earlier visit, she saw three Western saddles on racks, bridles dangling from wall hooks, a couple of space heaters stuck back out of the way, and a couple of fans standing out ready for use.

One of the saddles, partially blocked from view by another, appeared to have extra leather straps attached, possibly for decoration. *Or maybe to attach extra saddle-bags. That one's so fancy I would guess it's TJ's.* A closed can of saddle soap with a rag lying next to it was sitting on the rack as though its user had been interrupted in the midst of attending to one of the saddles.

Mare finished her cleaning, set out some more supplies on the worktable for Flag's continuing care, put new medication in the fridge, and went out of the tack room. Erin stood there alone. "Paula just went up to the house to get the checkbook. I'll help you with your stuff."

"I left the same supplies for you as last time. Flag's care will remain the same and I'll come back again in a couple of days to check her again. If she gets any worse, call me."

Paula entered the barn. "TJ says, would you please come to her office. She will pay you for your services, but she wants to speak with you about Flag."

This is different. Usually an owner cares enough to come to the barn and watch me treat the animal. But this one can't be bothered; I have to go to her. Just about the time I think, well, she isn't her father, maybe I'm being too hard on her, she pulls something arrogant like this. Mare took her bag and IV apparatus outside and dropped them off at her camper then followed Paula and Erin into the house.

Paula stayed in the kitchen, while Erin escorted Mare to the office. Erin knocked on the closed office door then, after a slight hesitation, opened it and walked in. Mare's eyes met a pair of blue eyes that reflected her own non-committal attitude.   *The woman certainly does exude power, and not just from her manner. You can see it in her eyes and feel it from the deference of her two friends.*

Erin motioned Mare to a seat in front of the oversize desk. "Would either of you care for some iced tea?" She looked from one to the other but both women declined.

In a calmer mood now, compared to her first visit, Mare took closer notice of the office. The room was large, with a random hardwood floor of a slightly darker shade than the honey-oak furniture. A large, square, deep-blue rug held the desk, its attached computer wing, and several comfortable chairs covered in milk-chocolate-colored leather. The desk was bare except for the usual caddy of pens, pencils, paper clips and rubber bands; a telephone with built-in intercom; a console covered with labeled buttons; an appointment book and two pictures. One picture was of a young man, with the same black hair and unforgettable blue eyes as TJ's; the other was of Faithful Flag.

Broad, arched, floor-to-ceiling windows graced two sides of the room. Wide, vertical, jalousie-style shades made of ecru cotton covered the windows, enabling one to adjust the light streaming through them and adding an airiness that complemented the eggshell walls. Honey-brown drapes, woven to simulate burlap, hung to each side of the windows to provide room darkening if desired.

There were two other doors. One, in the wall to the left, probably went to another part of the house, or possibly to a bathroom. The other, wider, door apparently gave egress to a screened porch, which could be seen through one window.

One set of bookshelves stood immediately behind the desk. Another, more informal looking set, stood in a corner to the left of the door Mare had come through. In front of it, a couch, two stuffed chairs, and a television sat atop a dark blue and cream oval rug. The juxtaposition of the ensemble, complete with reading lamps, made a cozy nook.

A giant television screen covered part of the wall directly opposite the honey-oak desk. In the two corners of the wall behind the desk, Mare saw the oak cabinets that displayed trophies, medals and ribbons. On one shelf of the right-hand cabinet lay a hat, quirt, and white gloves.

To the right of the entrance door, a five-tiered corner shelf fitted snugly against the walls and held framed photographs. Without turning around, Mare wasn't able to see whom the photos depicted.

On the eggshell walls, several painting rested, over-hung with display lights. Outdoor scenes, featuring at least one horse, were accentuated with various shades of blue skies and burnt sienna earth tones.

"Do you need us for anything else, TJ?"

"No, just one of you stay by the intercom. I'll call you when we're finished."

"Sure enough." Erin patted Mare on the shoulder as she turned away, a friendly touch that brought an answering smile from the vet.

The smile still lingered as she brought her attention back to TJ. "Hi. You had some questions about Flag?"

This time TJ picked up a pen to play with. Her checkbook lay on the desk, unopened. She seemed uncomfortable, shifting several times in her chair. A jacket hung on the back of the chair, just as before.

Mare realized that because she had blown off steam the first time they met, TJ probably wasn't sure of Mare's attitude now or how to start the conversation. Never one to sit quietly unless she was concentrating on her job, Mare spoke up. "Flag's coming along very nicely. I expect she will start sweating by tomorrow or the next day; that's usually the course of heatstroke. One more visit, day after tomorrow, will probably be enough. Erin and Paula have done their job well."

TJ cleared her throat. "Erin and Paula always do a good job. They've been keeping me apprised of Flag's care and recovery." She hesitated, took a deep breath and let it out slowly. "I thank you for that." The remarkable eyes dropped to her fiddling hands. "I've had Paula and Erin asking around about you. By all reports, you're a very competent vet." The eyes swept back up and locked on Mare's.

Great gods, woman! Those eyes are a weapon, aren't they? This time, a little miffed, Mare didn't say anything and the silence drew out. *Asking about me, huh? I could have given you references. I refuse to say another word until you do. I will sit here forever, if I have to.*

As they sat there staring at each other, Mare saw something flicker in the depths of TJ's eyes. *Is that amusement?* One dark brow barely twitched. Finally the dark-haired woman spoke.

"I'm planning on making Meridian ranch a working cattle ranch again and eventually reopening the meatpacking plant. That should give a shot in the arm to the economy around here. I'm going to need the services of a good vet and I'd like you to think about accepting a retainer to take care of the livestock, both horses and cattle."

Mare still didn't answer. *Think I'll let her stew for a while. She knows I'm the only vet within 50 miles of this place. She'll be in dire straits if I say no. Of course, I will be, too, since I'm just barely providing for myself as it is now.*

TJ waited, but when Mare didn't answer she opened the checkbook and riffled back to the previous stub for the vet. "Paula said your fee for today would be the same as last time?" She looked up again, and Mare nodded. TJ wrote the check and handed it toward Mare. Mare stood up and accepted the payment, folding it and stuffing it into the breast pocket of her gold-and-brown-plaid shirt.

"Will you think about the retainer offer? If you decide in favor of it, we can discuss remuneration on your next visit."

Remuneration? Holy Hannah! The word alone ought to be worth a hefty price. Trying not to let her expression give away her thinking, Mare kept a blank face and nodded. "I'll let you know."

TJ picked up the phone, pushed a couple of buttons and asked the one who answered to come to her office. She reached out her hand and Mare shook it. The large hand engulfed Mare's smaller one but there was no undue display of strength, just a firm grip that hinted at it. "Thanks again."

"Right."

Erin came in and walked Mare to her truck. The taller blonde looked down at the doc. "Thanks."

"Taking care of Flag is part of my job." Mare patted her pocket. "My fee is thanks enough."

Erin grinned. "I meant thanks for being nicer to TJ. Paula and I were kind of nervous about it, but you two actually looked civilized this time."

Mare laughed. "You suggested I give her a chance and I decided you were right. I'm going to give her plenty of rope and see which one of us gets hung."

Erin shivered dramatically. "That's not a very pleasant figure of speech."

The vet threw back her head and laughed again. "Maybe not pleasant, but probably appropriate!" She got in the truck. "See you day after tomorrow."

"I'm looking forward to it." Erin waved as Mare closed the door, started the engine and left.

Erin went back to TJ's office. Paula had just brought in some iced tea and the two women sat down. "Well, how did it go?" Erin inquired after she took a sip of tea.

"She's going to think about the retainer and let me know when she comes back out."

"TJ," Erin said firmly, feigning exasperation, "I meant how did you two get along. Paula and I were nervous wrecks."

TJ looked down at her hands, which were quiet for a change. A small lift of one side of her lips made Paula surreptitiously stick her elbow into Erin's ribs.

"She has a mind of her own, that's for sure," she said as she looked up. Seeing the tiny seed of amusement that struggled to sprout in her eyes warmed the hearts of both of her friends.

"She sounds perfect then, TJ." Paula surprised Erin with her quick endorsement of Mare. "You wouldn't want anybody working for you who didn't have a mind of her own," Paula grinned wickedly. "Would you?"

The small lift of TJ's lips turned into a bona fide lop-sided grin. She shook a finger at her pesky friend. "You're gonna get it one of these days..."

"Yeah, promises, promises," laughed the audacious Paula while Erin blushed and hid the grin that came unbidden to her lips.

"Get out of here, you two, and let me get some work done." TJ waved her hands to shoo them out, but the grin stayed on her face. "Come get me when supper's ready."

The two women got up and left the office. "Yesssssssssssssss!" Paula threw her fist in the air. "I knew that little doc was having a good influence on her. I don't know what it is, but I hope it keeps up."

"Yeah, Polly, and you managed to get a smile out of her." Erin's eyes were bright and shining. She grabbed her friend's shoulder and shook it as they entered the kitchen.

"She's even going to join us for supper instead of sitting there by herself in that office eating off a damn tray. I tell you, Erin, I am one happy camper. I'll even help you make supper!"

This earned her a quick kiss from Erin. "Offering to cook? You must be happy!" The two friends laughed and started preparing the meal.

Chapter 6

Mare entered her kitchen, tossed her bag on the floor next to the door, and grabbed a soda from the fridge. Drinking it quickly, she examined the contents of the fridge for dinner possibilities and decided on cold, sliced ham and the potato salad still left from the weekend. *But first, a shower.* Rinsing the empty can and tossing it in the container used for recyclable discards, she headed for liquid refreshment for the outside of her body.

After her shower and dinner, Mare went into the sitting room and sat at the piano. *Everyone else would call this a living room, but Mom always called it a sitting room and that's what it will always be to me ...the sitting room where my Muse appears.* She dropped her eyes to the familiar keys as her hands lifted to touch them.

The Steinway, purchased second-hand for Mare's first music lessons, still possessed a mellow tone. As soon as Mare could play a simple tune, the piano became an ardent companion. Through the years, she turned to it in joy or sorrow, serenity or disruption, triumph or defeat. When her fingers transmitted these emotions through the piano's keys, the cherished instrument reverberated with a resonance that nourished her spirit. Magically, this transformation enhanced any happiness Mare was experiencing, and soothed any discord. Music served not only to express her emotions but also to balance them.

With little conscious thought, her caressing fingers ran up and down the keyboard for a few minutes of loosening up, then leaped of their own accord into George Gershwin's *Rhapsody in Blue.*

The strong chords, intricate melodies, and fast fingering spoke for the disturbance within Mare and she lost herself in the music. "Why am I disturbed?" she finally asked herself, aloud, when she finished the composition. For a long moment, she truly puzzled over what had caused a strong enough impression on her to lead her to the keyboard for solace. Then the title of the piece struck her brain and immediately conjured up a familiar pair of blue eyes.

She replayed the rhapsody, thinking this time of the woman sitting in the office of the ranch and reliving their words and actions from their first meeting. Finally, her fingers finished and came to a rest. *Yep, that's her all right—a rhapsody in blue.*

Why can't I get her out of my mind? The fascination of this woman has awakened my thoughts in a way nothing has ever done before. I have to find out more about her and the Meridian family. Maybe once I have all the facts I can lay the mystery to rest.

Mare got up, went into the kitchen, and checked her appointment book. *Nothing on my schedule for tomorrow that can't be put off one more day. I'm taking tomorrow off and going to the library in Sharlesburg on a fishing expedition. Fishing for information about TJ Meridian and her family. Maybe that will help make up my mind about the retainer, too.*

At first the offer of a retainer had sounded repugnant to Mare, coming from the daughter of the reviled Thomas Meridian, and her inclination had been to refuse. Then Erin had told her that saying about giving someone a fish or teaching him to fish and her resolve had wavered. Then today, TJ herself had recounted her intention of rebuilding the town by rebuilding the ranch and meatpacking plant.

If she does as she plans, that would pick this town right up. And if she builds up her cattle herd, she will need a vet, so, by helping her I would also be helping the town. I'll make sure that rebuilding the town is spelled out in the retainer agreement.

The doctor nodded, satisfied that signing a retainer with the Meridian ranch would help the town as well as herself. She got a second soda and sat at the table to finish it. Another thought sprung into her mind and she had to chuckle at the persistence of whatever had touched her subconscious. *If you sign a retainer, you'll get to see the mysterious TJ more often.*

Mare turned and spoke to her reflection in the wall mirror. "Get yourself to bed, Doctor, and give your soppy brain a rest."

The golden-haired vet did go to bed, but her brain wasn't cooperating with the idea of rest; it wouldn't shut down. Mare couldn't get TJ out of her mind. Something just didn't ring true, and it nagged at her. *Okay, look at this like you are trying to diagnose an illness. What do you know that doesn't seem to fit? First, here's a powerful, independent woman with two employee/friends who watch over her and are as protective of her as mother hens with their chick. They're the ones looking after the horse she's so crazy about, and she hasn't been out to the barn to check on Flag either time that I've been there.*

Second, she stops at an accident, seems concerned, makes phone calls, but doesn't get off the horse to help. Something started to work its way forward from the back of Mare's mind. *Matter of fact, except for the one time on the horse, at the accident scene, I haven't seen her outside of that office. She's never moved from behind the desk. I've never seen her on her feet!*

Mare bolted straight up in bed and tucked her legs up close to her body. Her long, pale-yellow, cotton T-shirt draped in soft folds against the tops of her thighs. Images of two ramps and a saddle with extra straps leaped to her mind. *Of course! How stupid I've been. The ramps are for wheelchair access and those saddle straps aren't decorations, they hold her on the horse. TJ Meridian can't walk!*

The vet sucked in a breath as though someone had kicked her. She tapped fisted hands against the sides of her head, none too gently, as another image came to mind—TJ's expression when Mare first burst into her office. *She had no expression. Her face was pale and those gorgeous eyes were lifeless, dejected. What on earth has happened to her? Maybe I can find out tomorrow at the library.*

Remembrance of her heartless remarks landed on Mare's conscience like a load of building stones, each one pelting her with guilt. *I feel so bad. I judged where I shouldn't have and I judged with a mean spirit. Why didn't Erin tell me?*

But Mare guessed the answer to that was pride—TJ's pride. *She's afraid people will feel sorry for her.* Then Mare had another insight into the mysterious woman's feelings. *Somehow, she's slipped into feeling sorry for herself. That seems so out of character; she must be tearing herself up. I wish I could help her.*

Nearly exhausted by this emotional upheaval, Mare lay back down, mulling over that last thought. *Get real, Mare. TJ Meridian has everything money can buy. Just how the heck can a vet from the sticks help her? Only thing I know how to take care of is animals.*

Finally, mind and body gave up and she drifted to sleep.

* * * * * * * * * *

Mare got out of her pickup and stretched. Today had been a long day. Old man Thomas had phoned her at the ungodly hour of 4:30 a.m., saying some of his cattle had been spooked and got caught up in some barbed wire and could she come out and patch them up. That took the better part of two hours. Although the cattle weren't seriously injured, they had still needed suturing.

She got home just after seven and didn't see the point in returning to bed. Her morning clinic was unusually busy, with several of the local children bringing in their pets. That finished up just before lunch, allowing her to grab a bite to eat, then she was on to her rounds of the local farms and ranches. Now it was late afternoon and she had saved the Meridian ranch for her last call.

Mare still had mixed feelings about this place and its owner, but the research she had done at the main library in Sharlesburg had given her a new perspective on TJ Meridian. And, yes, she had to admit to herself that she had been a little harsh in her assumptions.

It was likely that this would be her last trip to the ranch. Flag was well on the way to recovery. It would probably be safe to let her back out into the corral, either this evening or tomorrow. But now that she had some facts, Mare was sorely tempted to take the retainer that TJ had offered for care of the livestock, once they arrived. Reaching back into the pickup, she grabbed her bag and headed into the barn.

It was quiet, which was unusual. By now, normally Paula, Erin or both, would have come out to greet her. She had a quick look through the barn and the tack room; just to be sure they weren't around. All three horses were in their stalls, out of the heat of the day and relishing the coolness the fans provided. Mare put her bag down and stepped inside Flag's stall, giving her a brief check over. Flag was sweating easily now and her breathing had stabilized. Satisfied with what she saw, she decided to look for Erin and Paula up at the house.

Leaving her bag behind, she left the barn and walked toward the house. She noted that the van and Land Rover were still parked by the side of the house. From her previous trip here, she knew that Erin and Paula could likely be found in the large kitchen when they weren't in the barn. She was debating with herself whether to use the side entrance or go around to the front when she heard a loud crash emanate from the kitchen. She ran the last few feet and bounded up the steps, opening the kitchen door and going straight in.

At first, she couldn't see what had caused the commotion and then she heard TJ cursing from behind the island.

"Hello? Miss Meridian? You okay?" she inquired, not really wanting to startle the woman by just appearing in front of her.

TJ froze as she heard the vet's voice. She was sprawled on the floor, her chair tipped over on its side where it had fallen when she had reached into the cupboard above her. "I'm fine," she hurriedly replied, pulling herself over to right her chair.

"You sure? I thought I heard you fall." Mare stepped closer to the island.

Ah hell, she's going to come in. TJ was starting to feel a little panicked. "I said, I'm fine. Would you just leave me alone?" she snapped.

Mare was leaning on the island now, and could see TJ's legs and her fallen chair. *So do I call her bluff or do I let her get away with it? She might have hurt herself. She hasn't fallen far, but she wouldn't be able to tell if she'd broken something.* Taking a deep breath, not sure how she was going to be received, Mare walked around the island. "You look fine, as well. I take it that studying the kitchen floor from such close range is one of your normal pastimes?"

TJ closed her eyes, not wanting to see the pity in the vet's eyes, and struggled to push herself into a seated position. She felt hands on her arms, and she froze. "I can do it by myself," TJ snapped angrily.

"I'm sure you can, but I'm here, so why not let me help?" Mare suggested gently. From what she had read, TJ Meridian had once been an excellent all-around athlete and superb horsewoman. Seeing her in this condition, after the video footage she'd watched of her and Flag, was shocking. Still, if she let the proud woman know that, there was no way she'd accept her help. Mare's hand was batted away as TJ opened her eyes.

"I'm not asking; I'm telling you. Leave me alone." TJ's body trembled with the effort of trying to rein in her anger and fear. She hated anyone seeing her in her chair, but to have this woman discover her on the floor, so help-less, was more than she was willing to take.

Mare let go and stood back, staying quiet, but keeping a close eye on the woman. When she got herself into a seated position, TJ grabbed hold of her chair and pulled it towards her, setting it upright. She checked the brakes, making sure they were set, pulled the footrests up, then pushed herself in front of it. She powered down on the armrests and levered herself upwards.

Mare, seeing the sweat break out on the woman, stepped forward to help but narrowed blue eyes held her in place. "Stay back," TJ reinforced with words.

A creak of the door turned Mare's head. Paula and Erin walked in and stopped, staring at her. "Dr. Gillespie." Paula nodded at Mare in greeting. Both sets of eyes then turned to TJ who had pushed herself back into her chair and was pulling her legs onto the foot rests. "TJ, you okay?"

TJ didn't answer, just turned her chair around, and wheeled out of the kitchen.

"What happened?" Erin stepped around her partner and placed a bag of groceries on the island.

Mare let out a shaky breath; still worried that TJ may have hurt herself. "Came out to check on Flag, but couldn't find either of you in the barn, so thought I'd come over to the house. I heard a crash as I got near the door, came in, and TJ was on the floor. Somebody really ought to go check if she's all right. She didn't fall far, but this floor is hard. She might have hurt herself." Erin and Paula looked at each other and then Erin left the kitchen, following TJ.

Paula stared at Mare intently. "You already knew, didn't you?"

"Yeah, I did," replied Mare softly.

"How did you find out?" Paula walked over to the fridge and brought out a pitcher of iced tea.

"It was a few things really: her saddle with the extra straps, the way you and Erin keep an eye on her, the ramps—one in the barn and another in the living room. The day she saw me helping Johnny Robertson and refused to get off the horse. I began to put two and two together." Mare hesitated briefly, running Johnny's accident through her mind, remembering the wrong conclusions she had jumped to about TJ.

"Then someone in town said they thought that all the Meridians were dead. I was in Sharlesburg the other day and thought I'd check it out. So, I went to the library there, pulled up some back issues of several newspapers on the computer, and read all that I could find about the Meridian family."

"I guess you know everything you need to know, then."

Paula handed Mare a glass of iced tea and indicated that she should sit. "So, what did you find out?"

Mare blew her hair off of her forehead. "Where to start? I found out that TJ went to Harvard and graduated summa cum laude. From there she went on to work in one of her father's companies and eventually took it over, but she never worked directly for her father. In fact, Business World magazine reported that she personally financed the campaign to turn the land—which he'd wanted to develop into a leisure complex—into part of a national park. Now that took guts, and plenty of money." Mare took a sip of the chilled tea and looked up at Paula who was grinning.

"Oh yeah, I remember that. Boy, was he pissed at her. Even more when he realized that she had convinced the board to sponsor the park, and that he'd paid for most of the publicity. Still, he'd signed the company over to her;

couldn't even get his buddy boys to vote her out, their stock options had shot up so much."

Mare just stared at her. "You're kidding, right?"

"Nope. She can be unbelievably devious when she wants to be."

"Considering who her father is, that doesn't surprise me," Mare replied tartly.

Paula felt the smile slip from her face and then quickly replaced it. *Well, at least that's one thing she didn't find out.* "So, you found out that TJ doesn't follow the work practices of her father. Does that mean you're willing to give her the benefit of the doubt, now?" Mare shrugged, not yet willing to admit to anybody but herself that maybe there was more to TJ Meridian than met the eye. Paula sighed. "Did you find anything else out, or was that it?"

"No." Mare drew the word out. "I found out she is...was...an excellent athlete who excelled in track and field and equestrian events. That four years ago her parents were killed in a car accident and that she took over her father's holdings. And if Business World can be believed for a second time, she pissed a load more people off then. Then, eighteen months ago, she and her brother were mugged as they left a charity event. Her brother was killed and she was seriously injured. There wasn't much more information available."

"There isn't that much more to get."

"I know a lot more than I did. I still don't know everything. But you and Erin were right; she isn't her father."

"TJ was a complex person before her injury, now she has more twists and turns in her psyche than a mountain road. Time bombs just waiting to go off. It will be days before we get her over you seeing her in the chair; it will be ten times worse because she'd fallen."

Paula took a drink of the tea and looked over at the vet, wondering how much to tell her. There seemed to be something between the vet and her enigmatic employer, but she wasn't sure how far that went. *Maybe Erin will have a better idea how much the doc should know.*

"Days? Ten times worse? It's hard to believe that someone like TJ would get that upset." Mare looked skeptical but sounded as though she were pondering it rather than arguing about it. *She sure sounded upset, though. She scooted out of here as fast as she could, hardly even looking at me... and too proud to let me help her.*

"What do you mean 'someone like TJ'?" Paula made an effort to keep the naturally blunt edge from her voice. She was seriously trying to gauge the doc's reaction.

"You know. Beautiful, rich, intelligent, top of the world. She could have almost anything money can buy. Unless this is one of those 'the bigger they are, the harder they fall' kind of things." *Maybe it is. Could be that everything important to her was snatched away in seconds. Except the money; and that won't keep you from hurting.*

"Might be, Doc. Money can't replace what TJ has lost, and it can't buy what she needs."

Chapter
7

Erin hurried through the house, looking for TJ. She wasn't in the living room, and a quick glance in her office didn't yield the woman. She walked further up the hall until she reached TJ's room and knocked on the door. "TJ?" She got no reply, but she could hear movement behind the door. "TJ, can I come in?" Still no reply, though the movement stopped. "TJ?" Erin rested her head against the cool oak door and made her decision. She dropped her hand to the knob and pushed the door open.

TJ heard the door open, and Erin enter, but refused to turn around and face her, eyes fixed pointedly on a framed photograph of her brother. *What would you think of all this, Lance? Would you be sitting here if it were you?*

She felt a hand gently squeeze her shoulder then Erin's face came into view as she knelt in front of her. TJ tried to turn her head, but Erin moved her hand to her cheek and wouldn't let her. "You okay?" her friend asked. TJ clenched her jaw and just nodded. "I need to check your legs and hips to make sure you didn't hurt yourself." Pulling her head away from Erin's cupped hand, TJ pushed herself away from the woman.

"I told you, I'm fine."

Erin sighed quietly and dropped her head. She knew this was hard for TJ; her back injury meant that some bodily functions had to be taken care of with tubes and bags. TJ was highly self-conscious about it and refused all help in that area of her care. For Erin to insist on inspecting her lower extremities would mean exposing the equipment and TJ's pride.

"Honey, you can't know that. I need to check. Come on. The quicker you let me see, the quicker it will be over with." Erin got to her feet and stepped up behind TJ, wrapping her arms around the proud shoulders, pulling her into a hug, and kissing the raven hair. "Please, TJ, don't make this hard; it's only me." She felt her friend let out a long sigh. TJ's shoulders slumped even more and she nodded her head. Erin hugged her tighter for a few seconds, then stepped back to give TJ room to maneuver herself around to the frame that allowed her to pull herself in and out of the bed.

TJ had refused to sit back and allow people to do anything for her, even after she had tried to take her life in the hospital, which was why everyone was so shocked that she even made the attempt. To the outside world, TJ had come to terms with her injury remarkably quickly. Not even her closest friends knew what was going on in her mind. The doctors, unable to unearth the reasons for her attempted suicide, had made her therapy sessions a condition of her being released from their care.

Erin watched as TJ raised one of the chair arms out of the way, grabbed hold of a grip attached just above the bed, and lifted herself out of the chair and over onto the bed. Erin moved the chair and waited for TJ to loosen her jeans, then pulled them down, taking care not to dislodge the catheter bag or the tubing that was strapped to her leg.

TJ, still avoiding looking at Erin, had her hands clasped behind her resting head. "So, what's the prognosis? Will I survive?"

Erin continued her exam. TJ had a nicely purpling bruise about the size of her fist on her right hip. "Well, you have some excellent bruising but I don't think you've done any serious damage. Still, it might be worth getting an x-ray done on it."

TJ's stomach rolled at the idea. "Uh-uh, no way." She pushed herself up onto her elbows so that she could see Erin. *If she thinks she's getting me to go to the hospital, she has another think coming. If there is the slightest chance of having to stay at that place, I'm not going. Hell can freeze over first.*

"And I thought you liked Dr. Hamilton. Or was it his assistant you liked? She was kind of cute." Erin raised her eyebrow and smothered a grin. She knew TJ hated the local hospital. Dr. Hamilton had been recommended to take over TJ's care, and even TJ had to admit that he was an excellent doctor. But he had taken a shine to TJ the first time he'd laid eyes on her and he pestered her every time she went in for her checkups and physical therapy. For some reason the good doctor wouldn't take no for an answer, no matter how glacial TJ acted.

Still, if TJ had fractured something in her fall, she would have to be admitted but it would take all of hell's horses to achieve that feat.

TJ just scowled at her friend. "No way."

"Okay, I'll make a deal with you. Your next physical therapy session is two days away. Let me bring it forward to tomorrow, and if Sacha says it's okay, then we won't go see Hamilton. But if she says you need an x-ray and it shows something, then you have to behave and do as the doctor decides. Otherwise, I'll go get Paula and maybe Doc Gillespie to give me a hand and we'll take you up now."

TJ's heart thudded in overtime. *She'll do it; you know she will. And do you really want to embarrass yourself any more in front of Dr. Gillespie? Wasn't it bad enough that a woman who obviously detests your family saw you sprawled on the floor like a child? Think of the field day she is going to have when she gets back into town and gets to tell them all that TJ Meridian is a cripple.* "Okay, if Sacha says it needs an x-ray I'll have one."

"And follow doctor's orders if there is anything wrong." Erin stared hard, letting TJ know she wouldn't get away with anything less than full cooperation.

Blue eyes looked up from beneath raven bangs, gauging how far she could push but the determined look on Erin's face assured her that it wouldn't be worth it. She nodded, feeling tears come to her eyes but blinked rapidly to prevent them falling.

"Good. Let's get you dressed again. Are you going to come out and join us?" Erin already knew what the answer would be but hoped for a different one, nonetheless.

"I'm a little tired. I think I'll stay here and have a nap," TJ replied, knowing that she was avoiding seeing the vet again and that Erin knew what she was up to. Erin nodded and helped TJ pull her jeans back into place, then gently pushed her hair off of her forehead and kissed her softly before leaving.

* * * * * * * * * *

Erin walked back into the kitchen and made straight for the fridge and a cold drink, before sitting across from Paula and Mare at the island.

"How is she?" Mare asked as Erin sipped her drink. The blonde looked over at Paula who nodded.

"About how I expected her to be, a little withdrawn."

"Has she hurt herself?" inquired Paula.

Erin shrugged. "She has a nice bruise on her right hip which should probably be x-rayed just to be on the safe side. But a tank couldn't drag her to that hospital today."

Mare was shocked that TJ's friends weren't more concerned. If the woman had hurt herself then shouldn't they make her go to the hospital and get it checked out? "Are you just going to leave it?"

Erin smiled and chuckled. "No, but if I pushed, TJ would just dig her heels in and refuse. Even if we got her to the hospital, she'd refuse there and it would be a wasted trip. You have to know how to deal with her to get anything done."

"So, what are you going to do?" Mare was curious now. Both of these women had obviously learned how to take care of TJ well and experience had taught them harsh lessons. It seemed to Mare, though, that Erin and Paula were just as devious as TJ when it came to getting their way.

"TJ is due in physical therapy in two days' time. Her therapist, Sacha, is about the only person in the medical world that TJ will listen to. So I'll phone Sacha and move the session up to tomorrow and if Sacha thinks it needs an x-ray, TJ will get it done."

"Yeah, but getting her to stay in, if there is a fracture, is going to be hell," remarked Paula.

"Nope, I settled that; if the doctor thinks she needs to stay, she will."

"And just what did you bribe her with to achieve that?"

Erin glanced over at the vet before looking back at Paula. "I didn't exactly bribe her. Besides, TJ is an intelligent woman and although she may be belligerent at times, she knows what's best."

"Come on, there is more to it than that."

A small grin appeared on Erin's face. "Well, I did threaten to get you and the doc here to help get her dressed and to the hospital if she refused."

Paula raised both her eyebrows and smiled. "Yeah, that would have done it. On the more serious side, though, how is she?" Paula knew that TJ was very adept at hiding her feelings, but Erin had developed a sixth sense about what was going on with her.

"And why would Paula and I, helping get her to the hospital, be a threat?" asked the vet. Mare leaned forward, placing folded arms on the island surface.

Erin and Paula looked at their drinks, avoiding the vet's gaze for several seconds before Paula spoke up.

"Let's just say that TJ understands that some people, especially in this area, would have great pleasure at knowing that one of the Meridians was less than capable."

"You mean she thinks that I'm going to go running back to town and announce to them all that she is a cripple? Like it was something to ridicule her for?" Mare was angry at the thought that the two women would actually believe she'd do that.

"Bluntly?" asked Erin. Mare nodded. "Yes, that is exactly what she believes."

"But I wouldn't do that. I haven't even told anybody yet that TJ was here at the ranch. I may not like the woman but I don't get any pleasure out of her condition. Ridiculing anyone because of a disability is not in my nature."

"Well, the people that TJ is used to associating with would think nothing of it. Most of the people in this town would think nothing of it. You assume that she is like her father and the rest of his kind, why shouldn't she assume the same about you?"

Mare already had her next hot protest ready when the pure logic of this statement left her dumbfounded. She suddenly realized her mouth had gaped open and she closed her teeth with a click. Sitting back in the chair and sighing, she looked at each woman and a self-effacing smile wound its way onto her guileless face. "That makes such perfect sense, you've stopped me in my tracks."

The expression on Mare's face and in her eyes so obviously attested to her sincerity that it was Erin and Paula's turn to be surprised. *Here is a genuinely caring, thinking person. Maybe that's the spark that has ignited TJ's interest. Erin's liked her from the start, too, and she's usually a pretty good judge of character.* Paula glanced toward her friend and smiled in answer to the smile on Erin's lips.

"But, please," Mare continued with pronounced earnestness, "be assured that I would never, ever do that. I couldn't, even if I hated someone. TJ doesn't have to worry about me. Convince her of that for me, would you?"

"We'll try." Erin wasn't too sure of how convinced TJ would be, but she knew she would make the attempt.

Mare stood up. "Look, TJ and I were supposed to have a talk today about retaining my services. I don't want to bother her after this... unsettlement, but tell her I will stop back tomorrow morning."

Paula stood, too. "Wait a minute, I'll get your check."

Mare waved a hand. "That's okay, I'll pick that up tomorrow, too."

The vet moved to the door and Erin accompanied her out to the barn to pick up her bag, then they walked to her truck. Opening the door, Mare tossed her bag in then turned with raised brows as Erin put a hand on her shoulder. "In the world of big business, sincerity is in short supply. I apologize for not recognizing yours."

Mare's attractive eyes crinkled and her lips turned up. She reached up and patted Erin's hand. "No problem. I didn't exactly cut any of you a break, either. We were strangers and it's just taking us a little work to get to know each other."

Slipping her hand from the doc's shoulder, Erin grinned. "Well, I, for one, am beginning to think it's worth the effort."

"Me, too." Mare got in the truck and nodded to the friendly woman. "See you tomorrow, first thing." She started the motor and reached for the gearshift.

"Doc?"

"Yeah?"

"You might have some trouble getting to see TJ tomorrow. Just wanted you to know that you might be on a wild goose chase."

Mare snorted. "You get her in that office and leave the rest to me. I'm an expert at catching wild geese."

With a chuckle and a wave, Mare took off.

Erin stood watching, a smile stealing its way onto her lips. *I wonder...? She seems feisty enough to do it, but how would TJ react?* The smile stayed in place as she returned to the ranch house to let Paula in on Mare's last remark.

* * * * * * * * * *

CRASH! Erin's eyes flew open as her dreams disappeared, to be replaced by visions of TJ lying on the floor. "TJ!" The woman's curly-blonde head lifted from the pillow and she leaped from the bed, grabbing a robe and putting it on. As she reached the doorway and hunted for the light switch, Paula caught her arm.

"No lights," she growled. "And put your shoes on." Another loud crash sounded, then another, and another. Erin realized that it wasn't TJ who had made the first noise; someone was breaking windows. Erin could barely see her shoes. She stuck her feet in them and followed her partner.

"What's going on?" Erin whispered as the two of them ran down the steps to the first floor to check on their friend.

"You deaf? Someone's breaking the damn windows." Paula's snarl was enough to cut off any other questions Erin might have asked.

They reached the bottom of the stairs as several more crashes were heard. "Go see if TJ's okay." Paula ran toward the enclosed gun rack that stood in the living room. Erin heard her curse as she stumbled over the ramp and she was torn between checking on TJ and staying with Paula to make sure she didn't do anything rash. Her friend's nasty mood didn't bode well for the trespassers. But TJ might need her.

Erin raced to TJ's door, rapped, and opened it at the same time. "TJ, you all right?" TJ had managed to pull herself to the headboard and was sitting up against it.

"Yeah, I'm okay." TJ answered dejectedly. The light sheet that still lay over the bottom half of her legs was covered with glass. A large rock had been flung through the deep-set window in the wall across from one side of the bed. Erin picked up the sheet, dropped it onto the floor, and got TJ a new one. In the dim light, she saw a piece of paper had been fastened to the rock and she untied it.

"Take it in the bathroom and read it." The flatness in TJ's voice worried Erin, but she did as directed. When she came back out, being sure to turn out the light before opening the door, TJ asked, "What did it say?"

Erin hesitated, but she knew TJ would have to be answered. "Something to the effect of telling the 'effing' Meridians to go back where they came from."

Erin heard a puff of breath being expelled from TJ's nose. "Guess our little doctor didn't waste any time telling them who was out here and siccing them on us."

"TJ, she wouldn't do that, she..."

"Who the hell else knew, Erin? All the utilities, the post office...everything's in your name." TJ's reasonable tone worried Erin more than an explosion would. She was hurt and it showed. *But she's right, no one else knew a Meridian was here. It's a darn shame; TJ seemed to like the doc. So much for trust.*

Just then a shotgun was heard firing several times. There were shouts, then a motor revved up and moved away, its sound diminishing down the road toward town. A few minutes later, a patrol car pulled in, siren dying as it came to a stop.

"Go see what's up, Erin, and see if the horses are okay. Come back and let me know."

TJ sounded so woebegone that Erin put a hand against her face and kissed her cheek. "I'll be right back. Be careful of the glass, there might be some in the bed."

Erin hurried out to where she saw Paula speaking with an officer. "Erin, this is Chief Jackson. The alarm company called him. Chief, Erin Scott." Erin and the police chief shook hands. The chief was a tall, heavy-set man in his fifties, with graying hair.

"Paula, did you see if the horses are all right?"

"The lowlifes did knock down the corral, but they left the barn alone, so the horses are okay. We just can't put them out till the corral is fixed."

"We heard some gunshots."

"Yeah." Paula sounded disgruntled. "I shot a couple of barrels over their heads to scare them off, then I put a load of buckshot into the side of the pickup they were in."

All the outside lights had been broken, too. The chief had left his car lights on so he could see to write in his notebook. "That should help identify them, Miss Tanner. I'll just take a look around, if you'll accompany me?"

"I'm going back in with TJ." Erin got a nod from Paula and she left.

"T. J.?" The chief looked up from his note taking. "T. J. Meridian? I thought he was dead."

"He is. This is his daughter, Taylor Jade Meridian. She's called TJ."

"So, the news was right; there really is a Meridian out here." The chief's jaw clenched. He stopped writing and put his notebook in his breast pocket. His face looked like he'd smelled a polecat.

"Yeah, there is." Paula's voice grated. "But last time I looked, our laws protect everyone."

"That they do, Miss Tanner, and I'll sure check this out. If we can find the vandals, they'll be made to pay for the damage they've done." Somehow Paula wasn't reassured, but she figured getting on the wrong side of the local law wasn't a good idea, so she kept silent about it.

"You know a glazier who might fix our windows?"

Chief Jackson hesitated for a minute and then gave a slight shrug. He pulled his notebook back out and wrote a name and number on it. "You might try this fella, he's kinda new in these parts, never knew the Meridians. He's got a big shop in Sharlesburg, but lives out here and runs a small operation from his house."

"Thanks." Paula stuck the paper in her pocket. "C'mon, I'll show you the rest of the damage."

Chapter
8

Mare finished her cereal and coffee and stacked the dirty dishes and spoon in the dishwasher. No emergencies had come in during the night, so her plan for an early visit to the Meridian ranch was still a go.

She had taken some time last night to write down the points she would insist be placed in the retainer agreement. Pulling the list from the yellow tablet, she stuck it in her pocket, picked up her bag, and got on her way.

Neither Paula nor Erin had gone back to sleep. They each quickly showered and dressed and started cleaning up. Erin cleaned TJ's room, double-checked her bed for glass, and got her comfortably resettled. Then she sat with TJ until her morose friend fell asleep.

After hours of sweeping and cleaning, Erin and Paula finally stopped. "Time for TJ to get up. I'll go wake her while you set out breakfast. Cereal's fine for me." Paula stretched and yawned, cracking her back and her jaw, one right after the other. Paula went off and Erin set out bowls, spoons, mugs, cereal, milk, and sugar. As she finished, Paula returned.

"TJ asked to have a tray in her office." Erin cut a cha-grined look at her partner, who shrugged. "I couldn't talk her into coming to the kitchen. She's really out of sorts. Only good thing about today so far is the weather isn't ter-ribly hot and it's not raining. With all these windows out, it's bad enough we can't use the air conditioning, but rain would be a real pain."

Erin herself felt a bit down. That Mare could have seemed so nice, yet have fooled her so thoroughly, dis-turbed her. But that the vet could have hurt TJ so badly made her downright angry. "I know what's bothering TJ." When she explained to Paula that Mare had to be the one who spread the word of TJ's presence and indirectly caused the night's troubles, Paula got angry, too.

"She musta run right home and told everybody in sight that the Meridians had returned and were looking for trou-ble. Then sat here like Little Miss Innocent, swearing she hadn't told anyone that TJ was here. I think we've been played for a couple of suckers." Paula's lip curled as she berated herself for her own foolishness in trusting the doc. "Look, here she comes now."

The first thing Mare noticed was the shards of glass from the outside lights that were lying all around the edge of the parking area. Then she saw the broken corral gate and ran into the barn. She breathed a sigh of relief when she saw all three horses in their stalls with no apparent problems. She jogged out of the barn and turned toward the house. That's when she saw the damaged windows. Sprinting onto the side porch, she knocked on the kitchen door, which was promptly opened by Paula.

"What in tarnation happened out here?" Mare turned a puzzled look on Paula as she stepped in, then swung her eyes around, seeing that all three windows in the kitchen were broken.

"Why don't you tell us?" Paula's demanded coldly.

"Me? What do I know about this?" Mare, frowning comically, looked from one to the other of the two women.

Erin's voice dripped with disappointment. "You were the only one who knew that TJ was here; all the utilities and the post office records are in my name. Only you could have told anyone. Obviously, her presence angered a certain element in the town and a bunch of them came out here last night and broke all the windows and all the outside lights and the corral fence."

"Is TJ all right?" Mare demanded loudly. Her heart thudded in her chest until Paula answered.

"Yeah, no thanks to you. She could have been badly hurt."

The little vet walked right up to Paula, stuck her face into the taller woman's, and shouted, "If you think, for one minute, that I would condone anything like this, let alone cause it, then you don't know me very well. In fact, you don't know me at all."

Paula's nostrils flared and her fist closed, but Erin grabbed her arm. She looked at Mare, unhappiness showing in her face. "I think you better leave."

"I am not leaving. I came out here to see TJ and I am going to see TJ." Just as she had on her first visit, before anyone could stop her, Mare swung away and marched out of the kitchen, into the hallway, and up to and through TJ's office door, not bothering to knock.

TJ had heard the raised voices, yet Mare's barging in, unannounced, startled her. The vet strode over to the huge desk and placed her hands, fingers splayed, palms down on its surface, leaning in toward TJ. TJ jerked back away from the desk, huddled into the chair, and hunched her shoulders as if warding off a blow.

Erin and Paula came running in right behind Mare. Erin intended to stop Mare, but Paula grabbed Erin's arm and pulled her back with a small shake of her head. "Let them fight it out," she whispered into her partner's ear as the vet started shouting.

Sparks flew from Mare. "You really think I had anything to do with this vandalism?" TJ's eyes shot daggers that answered the question better than any words could.

The jolt of hurt that ran through Mare astounded her. She took a deep breath and poured out her anger. "I don't know who the hell you people think you are. You come here outta nowhere. You don't use the Meridian name, like it's a big secret. Then somebody finds out you're here, there's some trouble, and right away I'm the culprit—the terrible person who let out a secret that I didn't even know was supposed to be a secret! Did anyone ask me not to mention your name? No. But I got news for you, I didn't mention it in town, anyway." *Except to Jess and he left town the next morning and wouldn't have said anything anyway.* Irate, Mare picked up one hand and slammed her fist on the desk. "My life does not revolve around the Meridian ranch."

She stopped talking and glared at TJ. The slamming fist seemed to have awakened the dark-headed woman from whatever funk she had been in. She suddenly grasped the chair handles, leaned forward, and glared back.

"Then how did they find out...Doctor?" sneered TJ, biting off the title like it was a dirty word.

"How the hell do I know? I'm not your personal protector; I'm a vet. I came out here to treat a horse, and that's what I've done. I didn't expect to be tried and found guilty of causing an attack on the high-and-mighty Meridians without even a chance to speak in my own defense."

"High-and-mighty Meridians?" TJ inquired through clenched teeth.

Mare stepped back from the desk, cocked her head, and put her fists on her hips. "Yeah. Look at you. Do you think just being a Meridian makes you better than the rest of us?" The vet knew she was skating on thin ice but the dangerous chill growing in those ice-blue eyes aroused a curious excitement in her breast and she charged on, recklessly. "What do you do with that oh-so-superior intelligence you possess, besides sit and stare at a computer screen all day... while the hired help does your work for you? Does it take an attack against the precious Meridian name for you to stop feeling sorry for yourself and start rising to life's challenge?"

TJ's jaw worked to force the words out. "How dare you come into my house and start preaching to me! All the evidence points to you as being the instigator of the attack. Shifting attention to my problems won't change that."

Unable to ignore Mare's taunts, her voice rose. "And what the hell would you know about it anyway? You're not the one sitting in this chair, are you? You can get up in the morning, do what you please, run your own life. I have to rely on my friends, on machines and, yes, on hired help, to come even close to matching the freedom you take for granted. I have the right to feel sorry for myself if I want to."

Punctured by the poignant truth of TJ's statements, Mare's anger flattened to exasperation. "Sure, you do... if that's what you want your life's goal to be. So you're disabled! So what? Susanne Wallers was born blind, but she learned to do everything around a busy house that a sighted person can do. She got married and raised three children and her oldest boy just won an art scholarship. He's proficient in a field she'll never be able to appreciate, but she's as proud and happy as any other mother would be."

The vet stood up straighter, crossed her arms, and said softly, "And I'm wondering where your heart is."

TJ's eyes narrowed. "What's that supposed to mean?"

Mare waved an arm toward a corner trophy case. "All those trophies had to be won by someone with heart and courage. I'm wondering where you parked yours while you indulged your 'right' to feel sorry for yourself."

TJ's head jerked as though she had been slapped and her lips twisted. Erin grimaced at TJ's expression of pain and made a move to come forward, but Paula, still hanging onto her arm, frowned and shook her head again.

The blue eyes dropped to stare at the desktop. *You know she's right, TJ. You have parked your heart and courage. You've buried life so deep down inside yourself, you can barely find it anymore, let alone steer it in a satis-*

fying direction. And your pride? What's happened to your pride? You think Lance would approve of the way you've been acting?

After a slight pause, Mare continued. "Stan Birsek was paralyzed in a farming accident when he was fourteen. Fourteen! He took an in-home writing course and now he produces a national newsletter for farmers. I could go on and on. Plenty of people have had to overcome serious handicaps. And they have, because they never gave up. They set their goals higher than just sitting around saying 'poor me.'"

TJ's eyes swept up and met Mare's and an electric current sparked through the vet's heart. *Here come those damn eyes again. No fair.*

The two women stared at each other for a long moment, seemingly mesmerized. TJ dragged her eyes back down to the desktop, searched for a pencil, and picked one out of the desk caddy. Several unidentifiable expressions fought their way across her face, while she began to spin the pencil through her fingers. Finally, she regained some calm. She looked back up at Mare and spoke quietly, not really understanding why she felt obligated to explain herself to this reproachful woman. Or how the tables had so rapidly turned from accusations against the doctor to criticism of herself. "I don't sit here saying 'poor me.' I sit in front of the computer screen running a multinational company... and you still didn't answer my question about how the town found out I was here."

The question was so far afield from Mare's current focus that it confounded her. She weakly waved a hand and shrugged. "I...er..." Suddenly she threw both palms against her face and dropped into the nearest chair. "Oh, hell. You're right. It was me."

Mare's pained expression opened a tiny wedge in TJ's reserve and curiosity got the better of her. Ignoring the fact that Mare's admission should have renewed her anger, she frowned and tilted her head inquisitively. "What are you saying?"

"Johnny Robertson. Remember at the accident? I called your name." TJ started to shake her head, but Mare saw the recollection dawn on her face and the two women both said the same thing at the same time. "Miss Meridian."

The embarrassed vet nodded. "Then I told him you lived on the ranch across from his farm." She hid her face in her hands momentarily and then looked back up. "I come charging in here popping off to you and I was wrong the whole time."

A self-deprecating grin edged a corner of TJ's sculpted lips. Her rich, low-pitched voice disagreed. "Not the whole time."

When her meaning struck Mare, the contrite vet impulsively reached across the desk and laid her hand on top of one of TJ's, quieting them. "I had no right to say those things to you. I apologize."

TJ dropped the pencil, turned her hand up, and clasped Mare's within both of hers. "Don't apologize. It's about time someone kicked me in the butt and got me jumpstarted."

Paula and Erin quietly left the room, large smiles rimming their faces.

TJ looked down at their entwined hands, then back up at Mare and felt the vet's captured hand twitch. She let go of the hand and Mare hastily withdrew it, a faint blush rising on her cheeks.

"You could be good for me, Doc. Most people tiptoe around my feelings, scared to make me angry. With good reason, I might add. I do have a somewhat volatile temper." A lopsided grin and cocked eyebrow accompanied the remark. "Think you can keep an eye on me and give me an occasional boot when I need one?"

"I'd be happy to!" Mare blurted, then her green eyes twinkled and met an answering gleam from TJ's breathtaking blue ones. "And... uh... my friends call me Mare."

"Great. And mine call me TJ," she smiled. For the first time in months a heavy load had shifted from her

heart and life had started to look interesting again. She
pulled a sheaf of papers from a drawer. "Now let's talk
about that retainer."

* * * * * * * * * *

Erin lifted one end of the wooden rail and rested it
against the post, then turned and looked at her partner,
sighing. "Paula, honey, wipe the grin off of your face and
help will you?"

"Hmm? Oh sorry." Paula quickly lifted her end so
that Erin could hammer in the nails. "I was miles away."

"No, actually, I think you were about a hundred feet
away. But I have a lot of work to do around here today and
I'd like to get the corral patched up so we can get the
horses out of the barn." Erin finished securing her end of
the rail and quickly walked over to Paula and started on
hers.

"So what do you think?" Paula asked her partner as
she watched her hammer away at the post.

"About what?"

"Come on, don't give me that. You know exactly what
I mean."

"Okay, you can let go now," Erin replied. Standing
back from the mended fence, she reached forward and
shook it, testing its sturdiness. "I don't know, but I think
TJ likes her," she said with a smile on her face. "Wonder
how she feels about TJ?"

"Guess we'll just have to wait and see."

Erin chuckled. "At least we know she's not intimidated by her."

"Are we done here?"

"Yep, all fixed. Let's go and let the horses out." The
two women turned and walked toward the barn.

Paula, the taller of the two, draped her arm around her
partner's waist and pulled her close. "What do you think
they are talking about up there?"

Erin smiled up at Paula. "Don't know, and don't really

care. It's just nice to have her talking to someone other than us."

"Yeah, that is good to see. What time did you rear-range her therapy for?" asked Paula as they stepped into the cool shade of the barn.

"Sacha couldn't fit her in until six this evening, but she has arranged for TJ to get an x-ray when we get there so we don't have to hang around."

"Great. Mr. Thorton said that fixing the windows was too big a job for what he had at the house but said he'd have a crew out here this morning from Sharlesburg to get things fixed. And I also gave Adam a ring. Asked him to send out a crew to get an expanded security system installed. If feelings around here are that inflamed about TJ being here, I don't want anybody to be able to get up the drive without us knowing about it; especially since we're not always nearby. I wish TJ would reconsider get-ting some help in here. I'd rest easier, knowing she wasn't in the house alone when we're not around."

Erin stopped at Flag's stall. "You think TJ is going to agree with expanding the system?"

"I doubt it, but I'm not going to give her the chance to say no. We've got a busy time coming up. You need to get out and inspect the fences, outbuildings, and water sources. I need to start interviewing and getting the staff for here and the plant, which is going to take me off of the ranch. After last night, if TJ won't get a housekeeper or something, then I'm having it installed for my own peace of mind."

"You won't mind if I make sure I'm out of the country when you tell her, will you?" Erin said with a raised eye-brow.

Paula grinned as she snapped on Flag's lead rope. "Oh no, my pretty one, you're going to be standing right next to me, catching the flak and telling her you agree with me. Besides, if I tell her it's to make sure that Flag and the horses are safe, she won't say a word."

"She's going to see right through that, but you might get away with it," Erin replied, getting Runny and Ebonair and leading them out of the barn to the corral. "Why don't you come into the city with TJ and me this evening? We could all get a bite to eat and maybe catch a movie."

"You buying?" Paula let Flag go and watched as the horse playfully bolted into the freedom of the corral, quickly followed by the other two. Feeling Erin's arms wrap around her waist, she turned toward her.

"Only if you make it worth my while," laughed Erin as she pulled her taller partner into a kiss.

****

The trip to the city turned out to be better than either Erin or Paula had imagined. TJ was given a clean bill of health by Sacha and, in way of celebration, the three friends invited the physical therapist to eat with them. Paula picked out the wildest restaurant she could find and they never made it to the movie.

Both Erin and TJ imbibed more than they should have, knowing that Paula was driving home. The women weren't about to tell TJ she wasn't supposed to overindulge, it was the first she'd relaxed fully in a long time. They finally made it home just after midnight and Paula and Erin, with happy smiles on their faces, put the tipsy TJ to bed.

From then on, life at the ranch moved at a startling pace. Despite the damage that Paula did to the vandals' truck, the chief was unable to apprehend them, which didn't surprise Paula or Erin.

There were no more direct attacks on the house, but fences were broken along the road and slogans were daubed in red paint on the gates. TJ seemed unaffected by the events. Not even a thrown bottle, which shattered the van's windshield as they drove out of town, upset her.

Surprising Paula and Erin, TJ agreed wholeheartedly with the installation of the expanded security system. Adam and his team visited shortly after the initial attack.

They began to survey the property and design the system, and the ranch house put up its first visitors. The ranch gates were to be replaced with electronic ones, which could be opened and closed from the house. Cameras were installed so that they could see who was at the main entrance. Cameras were also placed in strategic areas around the ranch buildings, including the barn and corral.

That week, the engineers turned up and installed the stair lift so that TJ had free rein of the house. Shortly afterwards, builders arrived to construct the ramp for the porch and several walkways around the rougher areas of the land near the house.

Erin made a thorough survey of the whole of the ranch lands and its associated buildings. Luckily, the bunkhouse didn't need much more than a cleanup and minor repairs. A few of the family houses needed more done to them but, on the whole, the accommodations for workers were in pretty good condition.

Next, Erin took to surveying the water sources and outlying barns and feed drops. She did all of this from horseback, occasionally taking a sleeping bag and food to camp out overnight.

Despite Erin's claims to Mare that Paula could hire away angels from heaven, she was having a tough time organizing workers for the ranch and packing plant. She had spent several days in Sharlesburg, and at the factory, with a consulting firm, finding out what was needed to bring the factory up-to-date. With that in mind, she hired another firm to computerize and update the machinery within the plant.

Once that was well in hand, she turned to the task of buying livestock to start the herds up at the ranch. Again, she had to resort to hiring outside of Meridianville. She had traveled around with Bill Jacobs, whom she had hired away from a ranch in Porter Valley. Bill would be the fore-man of the ranch once it was up and running. He was selecting prime livestock direct from ranches he knew and

later, when the cattle auctions started, he'd be buying there
as well.

Mare became a frequent visitor to the ranch. Even
when her schedule didn't call for her to drop in on the
ranch, she made the effort to stop off and see the three
women. As she had expected, even though TJ had made
overtures of friendship, at first things were still quite
strained. While Mare found it hard to give up her precon-
ceived ideas of who TJ Meridian was, TJ had erected protective barriers around herself and found it hard to let the
friendly vet in. But Mare worked on the woman, refusing
to let her sometimes gruff and occasionally openly hostile
attitude dissuade her. The more she was around TJ, the
more she realized that the woman's volatile demeanor was
probably a reaction to her insecurities rather than a personal attack.

Mare made sure to check in more often if she knew
Erin and Paula were out of the house. Slowly but surely
she was able to build a friendship with TJ. She knew that
it would take time for her to break down all the barriers
that the enigmatic woman had built between herself and
the world. Still, she persisted. By degrees she learned
how to pull a begrudging smile from the reserved woman's
face and how to cajole her into relaxing a little more often.

On the other hand, when the occasion called for it, she
practically grabbed TJ by the scruff of her neck and told
her to buck up. Sometimes it worked and TJ would rise to
the challenge, and sometimes she fell afoul of TJ's horren-
dous temper. Although occasionally frightened by it, Mare
was unwavering in her determination to stand up to the
woman—even when an enraged TJ sent objects flying
about the office.

As the feisty vet pulled TJ out of the depression she
had fallen into, TJ slowly began to take control of her life
again. The companies soon realized that their commander-
in-chief was back, and where she had once hidden in her
office, TJ now directed from it. The phone rang inces-
santly, at all times of the day and night, as various depart-

ments and offices demanded her attention. Her computer was constantly busy, receiving and sending data and mail across the globe.

TJ seemed happier as her plans for the ranch and packing plant began to take on momentum. The only thorn in the plan was the attitude of the town she was trying to help.

Chapter
9

Mare finished clipping the blades of grass that were too close to the tombstone for the mowers to reach. She wiped the hand shears on the carpet of mown grass she was kneeling on and returned them to the tote bag at her side. Reaching over, she brushed her fingers across the letters chiseled into the granite monument. Jane Arnold Gillespie. *Hi, Mom.*

Mare often marveled at the cemetery's quiet beauty. Jane's gravesite sat atop one of the softly undulating hills, resting just beneath a sheltering tree that spread its branches over several graves in peaceful guardianship. Mare had planted colorful petunias, remembering how her mother loved many different flowers, but petunias were her favorite. This past spring, she had planted them again.

Today marked the first anniversary of her mother's death. In defiance of her terminal cancer, Jane had clung to life long enough to see Mare graduate and open her practice. A month afterwards, as though those two events were the milestones marking the end of her earthly journey, Jane succumbed.

Mare, bereft not only of her mother, but also of the closest friend she had ever known, buried herself in her work. Many late evenings had been spent at her piano, seeking solace in her music. On the first Sunday of each month, Mare visited her mother's gravesite and recounted the month's activities, believing that, somewhere, her mother was listening and watching over her.

Guess what, Mom? I've met one of the Meridians and she's not at all what I expected. No, that's not completely accurate and I know you are particular about accuracy. She is a powerful woman, with powerful emotions that she keeps damped behind a cold exterior. Don't ask me how I know that, I can just feel it. It's almost like there is some invisible thread linking us together and, though I can't tell what she's thinking, I can feel her emotions. Does that sound crazy?

Anyhow, Mom, she's having a real problem with low self-esteem. She's had an accident that has paralyzed her legs and she's lost confidence in herself. Sort of like an eagle with a broken wing that thinks it's not an eagle anymore just because it can't fly. But penguins don't fly, or ostriches or turkeys (hardly, anyway) and they are still birds. Someone's got to make her see that. And I think that someone just might be me.

Rising and picking up her tote bag, Mare kissed her fingers and touched them to the stone. *I gotta go, Mom. I'll keep you posted.* She walked slowly to her truck, drinking in the peace and tranquility, storing it away in her heart. Climbing into her pickup, she drove home, musing over a woman with unforgettable blue eyes, unaware of a particular event about to unfold that would drastically affect her life.

* * * * * * * * *

And they call Sunday a day of rest! Mare stood up and stripped off the sterile latex gloves that had all but turned her hands into prunes. She sighed and wiped at the sweat threatening to run down her face. With one last dejected glance toward the dead animal, she turned and looked at the worried face of Abner Stirkle who leased the small ranch she had been on for the last four hours. "Sorry, Abner, there wasn't anything I could do. The others should recover okay, though. I think I got to them in time." The man nodded and scuffed the dirt with his booted feet. "Are you sure you haven't changed their diet or introduced something they might be reacting to?"

"Nope, Mare. It's like I said. They were fine yesterday but I came up to put out their feed this morning and those three were down. I've racked my brain trying to think what it could be but I really haven't got any idea."

"Maybe you ought to keep the cattle nearer to the homestead for a while. Don Holland had a few of his come down with similar symptoms the other day. To be honest, it looks as though they have been poisoned in some way. I'm still waiting on the results from Don's livestock. I'll send bloods off on yours as well but it will be a few days until I get the results. Keep a close eye on the herd and if any of the others start to show signs give me a call. If I'm not at the house then page me, or call my car phone. That card I gave you has all the numbers on it."

"Thanks, Mare. I sure appreciate you getting out here so quick, I can't afford to lose cattle like this." Abner lifted his hat and scrubbed at his hair with his hand. He looked at the perky blonde standing before him, considering his next words. "Rumor has it, you're gonna be working up at the Meridian ranch. That true?"

Mare sighed, knowing that it would soon start to spread around and that questions were going to be asked. At some point, she would have to answer them. She just hadn't thought they would be so quick about it. Taking a deep breath, she decided to be up front about it; after all they were all going to benefit from her association. The signing fee that TJ had insisted she take had enabled her to get hold of some of the more expensive medications she had wanted to use in this area but had not been able to afford; and she had been able to update a lot of her equipment already. "Yeah, it's true. They're gonna have a lot of livestock arriving soon and they needed a vet."

"Lot of folks around these parts aren't going to be too happy about that. The Meridians aren't liked around here. Mare, you should know that; you've lived here long enough."

"Yeah, I do know that, Abner, but let me ask you a question. Can you afford the $400 medication I just gave your cattle?" The rancher looked at her unhappily. "I didn't think so, but the monthly payment I get from the contract I've signed means you don't have to, until you can. People may not like it, Abner, but it gives me options I didn't have before. We have all been living on the very edge the last few years, me as much as any of you, and I've tried to keep costs down. But some things can't be treated without money. People are just going to have to get used to it if they expect me to be able to keep treating their livestock, in the way I have, for the amount they are able to afford. Sorry, but that's just how it is." Mare looked over at Abner, waiting for a reply, but the rancher just nodded at her. "I'll come back tomorrow to check on them."

"Sure. Thanks, Mare." The vet collected her things, thankful that no one else required her services this evening. She climbed into her truck, dreaming of a nice, relaxing evening at the piano followed by a soothing bubble bath and topped off by snuggling up in her sitting room with a good book.

****

Music filled the house as Mare's fingers moved confidently across the piano keyboard. She halted their movement as she heard a banging at the front door. The vet hurried to answer it, pulled open the door, and smiled apologetically at Lew Sturgess. "Sorry, Lew, I didn't hear the bell."

The silver-haired gentleman's eyes crinkled and a friendly smile lit his face. "No problem, Mare. I could hear the music and knew I'd have to bang on the door to get your attention." Following Mare into the house, he took a seat at the kitchen table. Mare opened the fridge and poured two glasses of lemonade as she wondered what had prompted the lawyer's visit on a Sunday evening.

Medium height, slim and tanned, Lew had been a friend of her mother's for a long time and took care of her legal work for her, including her will.

After he and Mare had chatted for a while, finishing their lemonade, he came to the point of his visit. "Mare, before your mother died, she called me to the house and handed me a sealed envelope. She didn't tell me what was in it, she just asked me to put it in my office safe and give it to you on the first anniversary of her death. I know it's Sunday, but I stopped by the office this evening and I had this lying on my desk to bring to you tomorrow. When I saw it, I thought, today is the actual first anniversary and since I was coming right by here on my way home, I brought it over." He reached into the inside pocket of his suit jacket, pulled a buff envelope out and handed it to the young doctor.

"To Mary Theresa Gillespie, My Daughter." Mare's eyes misted as she read aloud the words scripted onto the envelope in her mother's strong hand. She turned the envelope over and started to open it and Lew stood up. "I'll show myself out, Mare. I think you may want to read it privately."

Mare's dampened green eyes smiled up at the man and she sniffled. "Thanks, Lew. And I appreciate your loyalty to my mother's wishes." The vet heard the front door shut as her fingers closed on the letter. *Mom's last words to me. What could she possibly have wanted to wait a year to tell me?*

Before she started reading, Mare laid the letter flat on the table. She ran her fingers over some of the words, then pressed her hands against it and closed her eyes. *Oh, Mom.*

You made these letters, you touched this same paper; if only I could touch you! Why did you have to die? The past year's loneliness gripped her heart with an almost physical force. Her hands slipped from the letter and she hugged her arms to her body, rocking back and forth. *I am so alone.* But directly on the heels of that thought came another: *Except for TJ.* That unexpected thought surprised Mare enough that she opened her eyes and gradually stopped rocking.

Except for TJ? she asked herself, then reflected on it. *Well, yes. In a very short time, TJ has helped to dispel some of my loneliness. I've started thinking about someone beside myself. I was even playing happy music for a change!*

With a small smile, Mare picked up the letter and started reading. The beginning discussed Mare's adjustment to living without her mother and Jane's undying love for her daughter. But the next part dropped a bombshell.

Mare, my darling, please try not to be too angry with me for what I am about to reveal. When you were a youngster, I told you that your father, my husband, had died in an accident before your birth. I made that story up, Mare, so you would believe you had a father just like your little friends had. And to prevent your searching him out and raising embarrassing questions.

Your father and I loved each other very much, but we never married. We had an affair in our last year of college and you were conceived. Your father was planning to go on with his studies, he had a very bright future ahead of him that could have been ruined by the presence of a wife and child. So, I broke off with him shortly after graduation, and moved away. He never knew that he had a daughter and I was too proud to hold him to supporting us. I vowed to take care of you myself, without his help, and I managed to do that.

I never intended to reveal this to you until years from now, but when I found I was dying, I realized that to withhold it from you forever would be needlessly selfish. Perhaps it was selfish from the beginning, but I can't go back and change that.

I'm not going to tell you his name. If you insist on searching for him, the time and trouble it takes you to discover who he is will afford you an opportunity to decide what you will do when you find him. He may be a happy family man who would be appalled to find that he had a daughter he never knew, and perhaps shouldn't be told. Or, he may be happy to meet you. That is something you will have to decide for yourself.

Please forgive me if I have hurt you. You know I would never have hidden this from you without good reason. I love you more than words can ever say.

Good-bye, my dear daughter, please don't think too harshly of me.

Your loving Mother.

Mare put her head down on the kitchen table, stretched her arms out past her head—still holding the letter in both hands—and groaned. Her hands laid the letter down and started patting it. *A father. I might have had a living father all this time and I never knew him. I have to find him. I have to.*

The sudden revelation that could possibly cause a dramatic shifting of Mare's whole life overwhelmed her and tears dripped from her eyes, gradually becoming a torrent. She cried for the mother she had loved and lost and for the father she had lost before she had a chance to love him. She cried for what had been and for what might have been. Finally, she cried herself to sleep, there at a kitchen table in Meridianville, Texas, in a turmoil over what her search for a missing father might uncover.

Unfortunately for Mare's peace of mind, unfolding events would hinder that search before it even got started.

****

Two days later, as she neared her destination, Erin slowed Ebonair's gallop to a canter, then a walk, giving the animal a chance to cool down from the hard ride. She guided her into the barn, a look of concern apparent on her face. Jumping down from Ebonair's back, Erin grabbed her travel pack from the saddle, then undid the girth and pulled the heavy leather off of the black mare's back, resting it on a nearby box. She then removed the bit and bridle, put a halter on Ebonair and closed her into the stall to await her grooming.

Paula had obviously been in the kitchen and not her office when she rode in, because she could now hear her footsteps approaching from behind.

"Hi, love, everything okay?" Erin felt her tall lover's arms slip around her waist and moist lips press against the side of her neck, and she relaxed back into her embrace.

Despite her seemingly carefree attitude, Paula knew something was wrong. Her normally assertive mate was a little too docile for her tastes. When she felt the tense bunching of muscles, she knew it was more than a small problem.

Erin turned in Paula's embrace and hugged her back. "I missed you," she said as she snuggled into Paula's chest. "And no, everything isn't okay. We have a pretty big problem. I need to talk to TJ."

Paula's arms gave Erin an extra squeeze and she kissed her hair. "I missed you, too." Then she chuckled. "I haven't even kicked her out of bed yet."

Erin frowned. TJ was known for rising early in the morning. "She okay?"

"Oh yeah, she's fine. A certain vet came over last night and they spent the evening talking horses in the living room. Which, of course, progressed to watching TJ's videos of Flag in the nationals. Think Mare finally got out of here just after two."

Paula laughed again. "I don't think the poor woman knew what hit her. She hasn't exactly seen TJ's best side has she? I did try to warn her that she would be out of her depth when it came to talking horseflesh with TJ; but you know what she's like, she steamed right in there without any thought of the consequences."

"What did TJ make of the visit?" Erin had now torn herself from Paula's loving hold and started to groom Ebonair.

"Don't think I've seen her smile so much since Lance told her he'd got Harvard Med. That vet has caught TJ's eye, that's for sure."

"Yeah, Mare seems to be enjoying herself, too."

Erin smiled. "You think you could kick TJ out of bed? She ought to hear what I've found, as quickly as possible."

"You got it, honey. See you in the kitchen in a few minutes. I'll have breakfast waiting for you." Paula picked up Ebonair's saddle and bridle and put them in the tack room on her way out, bringing a tickle of warmth to Erin's heart for her thoughtfulness. *We've been together for eight years and she's still a sweetheart.*

Paula had breakfast laid out and coffee poured. Erin sat at the island, still in dusty jeans and shirt, looking tired. TJ was rocking back and forth in her wheelchair, mulling over what Erin had just told her.

"How many streams did you say were affected?" TJ stopped for a second.

"Looks like all of the southwest sector." Erin took a swig from her mug and watched, as TJ turned her chair and wheeled herself from the kitchen.

"Be back in a second." True to her word, a few minutes later she appeared with a rolled map across her knees. She handed the map to Paula who unrolled it and flattened it out, using the condiments as holders. TJ handed Erin a red marker. "Can you mark the affected areas for me?"

"Yep." Erin took the marker and studied the map, marking it in several places before clicking the red cylinder's top back on. Paula then picked the map up and folded it so that TJ could see where Erin had marked. TJ studied it, tracing the streams that Erin had marked back through to their sources.

"They all originate outside of our land. Do you think someone has deliberately poisoned the water?"

Erin considered TJ's question. "I doubt it. Even if we did have livestock on the land they wouldn't be down in that area. Our best grazing is to the north by the lake and river. It would make more sense to poison that supply if it were deliberate."

"And the river and lake are okay?"

"They were when I checked three days ago. From the amount of dead fish I saw in the streams in the southwest, it has been that way for longer than three days. I backtracked as far as I could up the streams but I couldn't find an obvious source or cause for the contamination."

The room descended into silence. Then Paula spoke up. "So, what are we going to do?"

TJ started rocking back and forth in her chair again. "Paula, I want you to drive into Sharlesburg and send Erin's sample to our biochemical division. They should be able to figure out what it is and how to get rid of it. I'll phone them and tell them it is on the way and to assemble a cleanup team ASAP.

"Erin, see if you can find somebody around these parts who does aerial photography and get them to do some visuals of all the water sources on the property. Let's make sure that the southwest range is the only area affected. Then go into town; see if you can find out who else is having problems. Mare said she would try to stop by today. I'll get an update from her, too."

Now that they had something to do, the kitchen soon emptied. Erin went to grab a shower and get changed; Paula got hold of her partner's bag and left with the sample to be shipped to the biochemical division. TJ retired to her office. She got on the phone, booted her computer and got the resources of her vast empire working on a solution to their current problem.

Erin popped her head around the door before she left for town. "You want anything while I'm there?"

"No, thanks," replied TJ, frowning in concentration at the computer screen. Then her head raised. "Unless we're out of cookies. I think Mare and I finished the last of them off last night."

"You and the doc seem to be getting friendly," said Erin, perching on the side of the desk. "I take it you like her?"

A smile unconsciously spread across TJ's face. *Do I like her? Yeah, you could say that. She is always smiling, she knows how to kick my butt and make me forget about my problems. The mere thought of her brightens my day and I count the hours between one visit and the next.* "Yeah, I like her. She's feisty and won't take any crap, not even from me. I like that; I respect it. She isn't someone who lets life get on top of her, no matter how bad it seems." TJ's face fell. "She's the exact opposite of me."

Erin was touched that TJ had obviously spent so much time thinking about the woman. In the past, her affairs had been short, and not all that sweet. No one had been able to get past that wall around her heart. When her father was alive, her love life had been non-existent. And thinking about it, she honestly couldn't remember anybody having this sort of effect on her friend, at all.

"Well, it isn't as if Paula and I aren't like night and day now, is it? If you were the same it wouldn't be interesting." Erin looked out of the window as she heard the rumble of an engine coming to a rest. "Speak of the devil." TJ looked, and the smile swiftly returned as she saw Mare step from her vehicle.

Oh yeah, my friend. You have got it bad, thought Erin as she stood up from the desk. *Just hope the little doc reciprocates.* "I'll send her on in, shall I?" TJ just nodded, her eyes still glued to the slim and perfectly defined body of the vet.

Mare grinned as she stepped into the now familiar kitchen and saw Erin walking toward her. "Hi, how is everyone today?"

Everyone's just peachy now that you've turned up. "We're fine. TJ's in her office if you want to go on in."

"Okay. I'll see you later, then." Mare walked past as Erin grabbed her keys and made for the door.

"Hey, Mare?" called Erin before she stepped through. The vet turned. "You know anybody who does aerial photography?"

"There isn't anybody in town, but if you drive out to Bancroft they have a small airstrip there. Some guy out there does it. Don't know how good he is, though."

"Great. That will save me a bit of time. See ya later."

"Bye."

The door to TJ's office was open. As Mare approached she looked in but couldn't see TJ. "Hey, TJ, you here?" she yelled.

"Be right with you!" TJ shouted from further up the hallway. "Go on in and make yourself at home."

Mare went into the office and sat in one of the more comfortable chairs, leaning her head back and relaxing for the first time since a five a.m. wake-up call. *Uh...Less than three hours' sleep and no end in sight. I should be out checking the other ranches, making sure they haven't got any cattle down. But, to be honest, an hour of relaxation here will be as good as a couple of hours' sleep.* She heard the door and struggled to open tired eyes, but still managed a grin for her friend. "Hi ya."

"Hi!" TJ smiled as she wheeled herself into the office. "You okay? You look a little tired. I didn't keep you up too late last night, did I?" Her voice didn't hold the slightest bit of remorse for the previous evening's marathon video session. It wasn't often she got to indulge in her obsession with horses and she had thoroughly enjoyed last night.

"Of course, you kept me up too late last night, but that was my fault. I could have gone at any time; I was just having too much fun." *Actually, I was having too much fun watching you rave on about that horse of yours, and that smile on your face was worth the loss of sleep.* "But I also got called out to the MacMasters ranch. Some of their cattle decided they couldn't wait until office hours to become ill."

"You want some iced tea? I could rustle you up something to eat as well, if you'd like." TJ raised an eyebrow, wanting to do nothing more than make her tired friend a little more comfortable.

"Sure, that would be great," replied Mare.

"Come on, then." TJ turned her chair around and proceeded out of the door. "So," she said over her shoulder, "what's wrong with the cattle?"

"Not too sure. I'm still waiting on test results from a load of cattle I saw the other day, but whatever it is it seems to be spreading. This is the third ranch to be affected." Mare rested her hand on the handles of TJ's chair but didn't push. She'd already seen how her friend reacted to what she saw as coddling.

TJ frowned as she listened to Mare, wondering whether her problem might be the same as the other ranches except she didn't have cattle. "Mare? Could the cattle be ill because of some sort of contaminant in the water?"

Mare felt her heart rate pick up. *Oh, TJ, please don't tell me this is something else the Meridians are caught up in.* "Yes," she said cautiously. "Why do you ask?"

"Where are the ranches that are affected in relation to us?" asked TJ as they entered the kitchen

"The MacMasters ranch is the next one over to yours. The other two are to the south. Why?"

"Erin's been out checking over the fencing and water supply for the last couple of days. She came back in today; most of our water supply in the southwest section of the ranch seems to have been poisoned with something. Erin says the streams have dead fish in them. I wondered whether the same thing could have affected the cattle," she replied, pulling open the fridge and getting the pitcher of iced tea that was constantly kept full.

Mare let out a silent sigh of relief. "Well, it sure could. The cattle weren't found particularly near to water but that doesn't mean they hadn't drunk it. I'll need to go out and get some samples."

"Erin already did that. Paula's on her way to Sharlesburg. She's sending a sample to my biochemical division and we should have an answer by tomorrow. There's a map on my desk in the office. If you go get it, I can show you what we know is contaminated and you can figure out whether the ranches affected are on the same water source as our streams."

Mare spent the next hour studying the map, seeing where the streams had started and following where they headed. As far as she could tell, there were two more ranches likely to be affected and then the contamination would hit Meridianville.

"You think that the town's water supply could be hit with this?" Mare asked as she finished the last of the croissants that TJ had placed before her.

"Depends where you pull your water from and whether it goes through a treatment works first."

"We have natural aquifers and it isn't treated. There hasn't been any need."

"Then, yes." TJ responded seriously. "If the aquifers become contaminated, the town could have a big problem on its hands. I'm having some aerial photographs of the area done to see if any of my other water sources are involved. We have a massive lake up in the northern sector. If that is affected, we could be in bigger trouble since it's supplied from the river."

"I need to get back to town and let someone know about this. I hate to run out on you, especially after the effort you just put into feeding me."

TJ smiled. "No problem. You go. I should have the photos tomorrow and the results from the labs."

"Okay, I'll drop in tomorrow and see what you have."
Mare jumped down from her seat and pulled her keys from
her pocket. She bent down, impulsively kissed TJ on the
cheek and was out the door, leaving a rather stunned TJ
behind.

* * * * * * * * * *

Erin slumped back in the seat and switched the engine
off, enjoying the calm silence that enfolded her. She had
been up as the sun rose above the horizon this morning;
now it was well past midday. The drive out to the airfield
at Bancroft had proved fruitful and at this time Paul Will-
iams and his partner, Jenny, were readying their helicopter
to photograph the ranch's water resources. Erin had also
asked them to fly as far up the contaminated streams as
they could, to see if they could locate the source of the
contamination.

She pushed the door open and got out of the van,
stretching tired muscles and noting with a little disappointment that Paula hadn't yet returned from Sharlesburg.
Trudging slowly up to the house, she removed her Stetson,
and plodded into the kitchen.

"Hi, TJ," she said as she saw her friend and employer
sitting cradling a glass of something cold. "Photos will be
done this afternoon and the photographer is going to drop
off the prints tomorrow." She opened the fridge and
grabbed a cold beer, forsaking the iced tea for something a
little stronger. She frowned, not getting an answer, and
turned to take a closer look at her friend. TJ sat near the
island rocking back and forth in her chair, as was her habit
when thinking. She was flushed and had the weirdest look
on her face. Erin walked over to her, placing her hand on
TJ's forehead, checking for a temperature. "You okay?
You look a little flushed."

TJ's smile grew wider. "Oh yeah, I'm fine."

Erin removed her hand, still studying her friend.
"Okay, if you say so. Mare gone?" Erin swore that TJ's

face lit at the mention of the vet's name, her flush becoming a full-blown blush. *Well, well, well, our TJ is well and truly smitten.*

"Yeah," replied TJ, coming back to her senses from the dream world she'd been floating in since Mare had left. "She's been having a few problems with cattle becoming mysteriously ill. I think some of the other ranches in the area are affected, too, which makes it unlikely that it is anything against us specifically. She's gone to inform the town that their water supply may be hit since they are about ten miles further down the water course affected."

"Is she coming back?" She saw TJ's face fall slightly.

"Not till tomorrow. I said I'd give her whatever the labs come up with."

Oh yeah, Cupid's arrow was certainly well aimed when he got those two. Just wait till I tell Paula that TJ was mooning over Mare. Ha! This is going to be so much fun. Let's just hope that TJ's notorious bad luck doesn't decide to stick its nose in.

Paula returned to the Meridian household later that evening. She'd spent the day in Sharlesburg, conferring with several of TJ's companies on how to tackle the problem they had on the ranch. Whether the contaminant could be cleaned up quickly would depend on what it was. Of course, TJ had already alerted them to her emissary's imminent arrival in the city; all Paula had to do was sort out the details.

The biochemical division had already received the sample that Erin had brought back with her and had identified it as an industrial byproduct. They would have a proper breakdown of its components in the morning. They also had started to gather a cleanup team, which would arrive on the ranch tomorrow afternoon. *Another disaster averted. Let's go see what else has happened today.*

Nobody was in the kitchen when Paula entered. Music was coming from the living room so she headed that way, spotting her lover sprawled on the couch listening to Shania Twain on the stereo. Erin looked completely relaxed, with bare feet resting on one arm of the couch and both forearms folded across her face.

Paula crept over and tickled the bottoms of the exposed feet. "Yo!" Erin yanked her feet back and pulled both arms down. She half-lifted her head, but it quickly flopped back onto the couch as her yelp turned into a groan.

Paula sniggered, pleased with the results of her tormenting. "What are you groaning about?"

"While you were out having yourself a good old time all day, I came back and unloaded a load of hay. Then I mucked the stalls, which were a bit overdue. How can just three horses produce so much... fertilizer? Yuck." Erin made a face. "Wonder when TJ's going to let us hire some extra help? That is one job that is going to the top of my 'To Be Delegated' list." She started giggling. "Gives a whole new meaning to the word 'pooped.'"

Paula grinned and sauntered slowly alongside the couch, bending over several times to twitch her nose and sniff loudly at Erin's body. Finally, nearing Erin's head, she remarked in a mockingly supercilious tone, "There seems to be a suspicious absence of unpleasant odors for someone who claims to have engaged in such an aromatic pursuit."

"Well, cutie," Erin said dryly, "that's because I did exactly what you would have done when finished. I made a mad dash for the shower."

Paula tousled her lover's blonde curls. "Yep, you are a little damp."

A saucy smile slowly curved Erin's lips.

Chuckling, Paula leaned over to place a kiss on Erin's forehead only to find herself pulled down on top of her partner. "So, feeling frisky, are we?" she said as her lips closed over the soft sweetness of her partner's.

"Hmmmm, that would be a 'yes,'" replied Erin as their kiss ended, wrapping her arms around Paula and pulling her closer.

"Where is TJ?"

"In the barn, fixing something on her saddle and talking to Flag, knowing her."

"Soooo.." Paula snuggled into Erin's embrace, her
fingers walking slowly down Erin's chest. "We have the
house all to ourselves?" Her eyebrows rose and her fingers
began to undo the buttons of Erin's shirt.

"Yep, all to ourselves..."

Chapter
10

The next day Erin was on kitchen duty when she saw the vet pull up outside the house. Her thoughts immediately turned to the conversation she had had with Paula on the couch last night, or rather lack of it. *Yep, love is definitely in the air.* As Mare walked into the kitchen, Erin turned from the counter with a welcoming grin, and waved the knife she was using to slice tomatoes onto sandwiches. "Hi, Mare. You're just in time for lunch... almost. TJ's still in her office. I'll get you when it's ready." *You go enjoy yourself and cheer up TJ who's been moping after you all morning.*

"Hi, Erin. Thanks. Everything okay?"

Erin's smile dimpled. "Everything's fine." She'd been thinking about something for a while and figured she might as well say it. "Your coming here to visit with TJ sure has given her a boost. Which gives Paula and me a boost, too. Thanks a lot." *And that cute smile of yours cheers us all up.* Erin chuckled to herself as Mare grinned in acknowledgement and headed toward the office. *I know it does a little more than that for TJ. You brought that woman back to life.*

With their friendship now firmly established, TJ filled Mare in on the plans for the ranch and the plant and often asked Mare's opinions on various phases as they were implemented. Now they were trading thoughts about if, and how, the water was poisoned, and what to do about it. The town council had already notified District 6's Clean Water branch of the EPA about possible problems and they were to send a team to investigate.

Mare rapped on the office door and stepped in.

TJ smiled and waved her in. "C'mere. The photographer just brought the aerial photos of the ranch." The desktop was covered with 8-1/2 x 11" pictures, in color. "Those show the two streams where Erin found the dead fish, but, look, here's the lake I was telling you about."

The golden-haired vet walked behind the desk, to the left of TJ, and leaned her elbows onto one of the few bare spaces on the oaken surface. She swung her right arm forward and rested her fingers on the bottom edge of the picture TJ was pointing to. "That is breathtaking!" Mare tilted her head and looked at TJ's profile as the dark-haired woman concentrated on the photo. *And so are you.*

Mare didn't have the courage to say the words aloud. She recognized that her feelings for TJ were growing stronger day by day. Once she had gotten past her unfair antagonism toward the woman, she had embarked on discovering who she was. The more she learned about this complex and intriguing person, the closer she wanted to be to her. Both as a friend and... *Do I dare imagine being any closer? How do I know if she even would want to be close in that way? I know Erin and Paula are a couple, but would TJ be open to that? Hell, I'm afraid to even take the chance. I'm willing to settle for friendship if nothing more ever develops. I just want to be near her.*

TJ reached up to slide the picture closer to Mare and her arm touched Mare's arm. The contact sent a jolt through the vet and she snatched her arm away before she could stop herself.

TJ's words froze in the middle of a sentence. Her lips twisted and her shoulders slumped. *She can't even stand for me to touch her. Then, what the hell did that kiss mean? Just when I think maybe I can safely lower some barriers, I get a "reality check" slap in the face. Maybe I've read her wrong. Sure wouldn't be the first time. Let's face it, most of the world leans the other way. Or maybe it's because I'm crippled. That would be tough for anyone to handle.*

Mare was suddenly aware that snatching her arm away had somehow hurt TJ. Without a word, she slid her left hand under TJ's palm and put her right hand on top of the long fingers. TJ stared at their hands and forced a rasp through her tight throat. "Is my touch so repulsive to you?"

Wounded blue eyes swung toward the vet, who gasped when they struck her, and startled green eyes brimmed with sudden tears. *Oh, TJ, if you only knew...when you are so near, I yearn for you to touch me. I'm just not sure of what you want, or whether you're even attracted to me.*

Mare turned around, facing straight at the side of the wheelchair. She lifted the strong hand she was holding and placed it over her thudding heart. "Repulsive?" A tear trickled down her face, and she half laughed and half cried as she struggled to talk. The door she thought she had closed on her emotions sprung open and so unhinged Mare that she threw caution to the winds. "Don't you know I'm falling in love with you?" Leaning down, she pressed her lips to a surprised TJ's slightly parted mouth, then just as quickly she drew back in embarrassment. "Look, I'm sorry... maybe I'm presuming something I shouldn't..." *Mare, you idiot! You've shocked the woman. You'll be lucky if she doesn't throw you out.*

Wide blue eyes stared at her, giving nothing away. Mare couldn't tell that TJ's heart was hammering even harder than her own, or that her mind was going a mile a minute. *That's twice she's kissed me. Maybe she's just flirting. Do I dare hope? She has no idea what loving me means. Would she turn away in disgust from the tubes and bags that are part of my life now? Could she handle that? Damn it, could I handle it?*

But how can I turn my back on this woman? I think I'm falling in love with her, too. If I'm ever going to have any kind of relationship with her, I will have to learn to handle it... and hope that she can learn, too. These thoughts charged through TJ's mind in a matter of seconds and she made her decision. She chose to take a chance on love right now and leave worries to be tended to later.

Mare still held TJ's hand against her heart. Entwining her long fingers in the material of Mare's shirt, TJ gently pulled her back into a longer kiss... and ice turned to fire.

Mare was a lightning rod and TJ's tongue was the bolt. Unprepared for the strength of her own reaction, or that of TJ's, Mare pulled her lips away to draw a ragged breathe. *That sure killed any of my doubts!* She released TJ's hand, which moved to push the side handle of the wheelchair out of the way. Then TJ looked up at Mare and raised her arms in invitation. The golden-haired woman slipped into the open arms and gently sat on her lap.

TJ's magnificent eyes caressed the young vet's face. *Is it safe to believe that she enjoyed that as much as I did?*

Mare raised her fingers to the gorgeous face, stroking along the perfect cheekbone, the strong jaw. She smiled a little self-consciously then took the plunge. "Can we try that again?" So they did. In the circle of each other's arms, their bodies alight with the warmth of touching for the first time, they shed their reticence and lost themselves in the sweet passion of the kiss. Mare tilted her head back as she surrendered to the pressure of TJ's searching mouth. *Oh, TJ, I want to stay right here in your arms forever.*

The dark-haired woman's long-dormant aggressiveness was slowly awakening. She was elated, and her hands yearned to show Mare the pleasure she knew she was capable of giving her, but she held back. *Careful, TJ. Don't scare her away. She's too precious to risk losing because of your eagerness. Let her needs dictate the pace.*

As they interrupted the exploring of their kiss, Erin knocked and opened the door. Her eyebrows shot up and a delighted smile stretched across her face. "Er... do you uh... still want lunch?"

TJ waggled an eyebrow and beamed. "I think we'll eat in here if you..."

Mare put a hand over TJ's mouth and shook her head, her passion still evident in her breathless voice. "No, I have to make some calls right after lunch. We better go to the kitchen," she said with a low laugh, "or I might never get out of here." Erin nodded and hurried back to the kitchen, eager to pass some happy news on to Paula.

TJ kissed Mare's fingers then the vet stood up and made an attempt to calm herself while TJ resettled the chair arm. Walking behind the chair to escort her to the kitchen, Mare thought a neutral subject might be in order, so she asked a question that had been on her mind for a while. "How come you don't use an electric wheelchair?"

TJ felt as if her heart had grown too large for her chest and she grinned, understanding Mare's obvious move to quiet her emotions. "Well, when you gals aren't pushing my chair around, my pushing it gives me a lot of upper body exercise and I want to keep strong. I have an electric one in the garage that I use in the city. Besides, this one is absolutely quiet."

"Oh, so you like quiet, huh?" Mare knew she herself was anything but quiet.

TJ's long arm reached behind her, laying her hand on Mare's as it rested on the chair back. "Not always."

The vet blew a small laugh through her nose. "Glad to hear that." With a singing heart, she bent down and dropped a quick kiss on TJ's hand, then pushed her on into the kitchen for lunch.

* * * * * * * * * *

Lunch started off as a quiet affair, Erin and Paula trying desperately to hide their amusement at TJ and Mare

who were constantly looking at each other from the corners
of their eyes. Fleeting smiles crossed their faces whenever
their eyes connected, but they eventually settled down and
conversation picked up. Mare asked about the results on
the water samples that had been e-mailed to TJ that morning.

"So, what is it in the water supplies?" *Good idea. Ask
a question. It gives you a great excuse to look at that
beautiful face a little longer*

TJ sat back, chewing absently on her bread roll before
answering. "Bit of a mixture of stuff: industrial slurry
from some production process, various types of oil. The
boys at the lab seem to think it can be cleaned up if we can
find the source of the contamination, though it may take a
few weeks. I have a cleanup team coming in today.
They'll work up the watercourse and find what's causing
it. Chances are it's someone dumping illegally out of
Sharlesburg."

"You know there's a meeting in the town hall tonight?
The Mayor is going to tell us what the EPA is going to do."
Mare looked at Paula and Erin to see if they knew about it,
but from the blank looks on their faces she knew they
didn't. "It might be a good idea if you came to it."

* * * * * * * * *

The meeting had been going on for an hour and nothing had been sorted out yet. Mare was getting bored. All
they were doing was going round in circles. The EPA had
sent out its scientists and samples had been taken. *Big
deal. TJ already has the results. I was kinda hoping she
would turn up for this. Still, I doubt she would have had a
good reception.* Apart from the fact that they were going
to monitor the town's water supply, they couldn't do much
more.

Resources were in short supply. The agency said if the
contamination turned out to be a threat then maybe a
cleanup team would arrive within the next few days. *And*

TJ's is already at the ranch. Though I guess if her team finds the source of the problem and removes it, she'll solve the town's problem for them without the agency knowing about it. As the meeting dragged on and the ranchers realized nothing was going to be done about the problem, they got louder and louder. Mare sighed as another of the more vocal antagonists spoke up yet again. This time, though, she sat up.

"Who's to say that the Meridians aren't behind this? They dumped this town before. Doesn't mean they won't do it now that we're getting back on our feet." There were a few yells of agreement and laughter at the statement. But Mare was infuriated. TJ had been in Meridianville for several weeks now and yes, at first Mare had been suspicious of her motives, but she knew better now. She was about to get up and tell them exactly what she thought of the statement when someone beat her to it.

"Nah, don't hold with that," a strong voice said from the back of the hall. Mare turned her head to see who had spoken and Chuck MacMasters strode forward. "Her ranch lies between mine and Abner's so she must be affected as well. Now the Meridians may have all but bankrupted the town before but they never did anything to harm themselves. If Miss Meridian wants to make a go of that ranch, and all signs point to it, then I can't see her poisoning her own water sources. Can you?"

Mare wanted to get up and cheer but instead got up to speak. "Chuck's right. Water in the southwest section of the Meridian ranch has been affected."

"Yeah, and you would know that, seeing as how you work for her!" jeered an unknown source. Mare didn't know quite how to respond to that and she didn't have to.

"No, she knows because I told her and asked for her opinion. Do you have a problem with that?"

The vet turned to see TJ in the doorway. *Wow!* thought Mare. *She sure knows how to make an appearance—and when to make it.*

The hall was stunned as TJ wheeled herself through the crowd, closely followed by Paula and Erin. None of them had known she was in a wheelchair, since Mare hadn't thought to tell anyone. Now the hall stood in silence, as even those who had been so vocal a few moments before were loath to harangue a cripple.

TJ let her eyes scan the crowd, putting all the menace her father was known for into the gaze, quickly turning away anyone who was staring. "What? Now that I'm here in person and you see that I'm not the mighty Tom Meridian, but a cripple, do you think I'm not capable of doing exactly what you suggested?" taunted TJ, her steely voice full of implied power. Mare had never quite heard that tone before but she didn't want to argue with it and neither, did it seem, did anyone else.

TJ brought herself to a halt several feet from the front of the hall, barely ten feet away from where Mare was sitting. "However, we find ourselves in a similar situation, do we not? And it may be beneficial to help each other out."

"We don't need your kind of help!" There was that voice again. Mare wished she could see who it was; she'd shut him up on a semi-permanent basis.

"Fine," said TJ without inflection. "I'll take my cleanup team and go. You can wait for the EPA to figure out what it is. However, I should inform you that I'm cleaning my section of land and until the time that all sections upstream of me are cleaned I'll be diverting the contaminated streams off of my land."

That brought shocked gasps from everyone including Mare. *She wouldn't do that, would she?*

TJ was enjoying herself immensely. It had been a long time since she had gotten to play the bad guy. Paula and Erin knew her too well and even her company employees had learned that her bark was worse than her bite. But this town remembered only her father. It wasn't often she got to play like this. She turned her gaze to Mare and gave her a wink.

Did she just wink at me? She did. I can't believe this; she's enjoying herself. Mare saw the glint of amusement in the blue eyes that had for several seconds locked with hers.

"You can't do that!"

"Try me," was TJ's quick response to the yell. "Now do you want to talk about this, or shall I leave?"

There was a buzz of conversation through the hall then the Mayor spoke up. "The thing is, Miss Meridian, the town and its people don't want to be beholden to the Meridians ever again."

"Good." TJ smiled and that, Mare realized, was actually more frightening than if she'd been angry. "Because I'm not offering this for free. I'm a businessperson and as all businesspeople know there is always a deal to be done. Now, I can have a cleanup team working within hours sorting this problem out or you can wait for the EPA. Shall we talk?" TJ's eyes locked with the Mayor's who nodded his consent, then the cool, sky blue windows to the soul swept around those gathered in the hall, seeing their begrudging agreement. "Okay, then let's get to work."

This woman is remarkable. Here she is, sitting in a room full of people who essentially hate her, and she's just taken over the whole meeting. Ha! Mare relaxed back into her seat and watched the woman she was slowly coming to think of as more than a friend, in her element.

"The first thing I need to know is who else is likely to be affected by this pollution and what type of water source the domestic supply comes from."

"Why?" interrupted Abner

"So that my teams can fit a filtration unit so that your home supply won't be affected," replied TJ.

"Er, Miss Meridian," the Mayor spoke again.

"Please, call me TJ." TJ grinned, knowing that the use of her first name would put them off their stride even more.

There's that smile again, thought Mare. *Boy, they have no idea what they are letting themselves in for.*

"Right, TJ. Well we have a small problem with the town's water supply. We don't know whether it is contaminated, or if it can be."

"That's okay. My team is all ready to fit filtration units to the pump house with the council's approval; the town won't be affected." The mayor looked stunned. "What?" TJ raised her eyebrow. "You really think I'd sit back and watch people become ill because of this? I may be a Meridian, but I'm not my father."

* * * * * * * * * *

Mare took a quick glance at her watch as she stepped into the cool, fresh air the night had brought with it. The meeting had started at six and TJ had arrived just after seven. It was now just before eleven and they were still going strong. TJ was a wonder to behold; every time someone threw up a problem, she had an answer, no matter how stupid or petty the concern was. The whole town was rapidly coming to realize that Tom Meridian had been a reasonable businessman, who'd just happened to be a total bastard. His daughter, though, was a genius. She got things done; not because she had to use threats, though they had all seen she was good at that as well, but because she knew exactly what to do.

When TJ told them what she wanted in payment for her help, the Mayor and the town folk had been taken off guard. Mare had to admit to being a little surprised herself, though when she thought about it she knew that money wasn't TJ's main concern; however, getting the ranch and eventually the packing plant up and running was. So, for payment, she told them that she wanted all those unemployed, who had any farming, carpentry, or mechanical skill, to work for her at the ranch and the packing plant on a minimum one-year contract.

There had been another silence at that, but Paula had brought a copy of the contract with her and passed it around. They could see right away that it was a good deal.

Those being employed would get a reasonable wage and extremely good benefits, including the building of a medical center in Meridianville. It would take time for the town to accept that TJ was different from her father, but she had made a very good start.

Now Mare was on a mission for coffee and food as she walked over to the diner; TJ had obviously been going nonstop since Mare had spoken to her earlier in the day. Paula and Erin both tried to persuade her to finish for the day, to no avail. She was on a roll and had no intention of stopping while there were things still to be sorted out.

Paula had then been dispatched back to the ranch to coordinate the cleanup team. Most of the team were visiting the ranches affected, and those likely to be, to install filtration units to protect domestic supplies. As a precaution, filtration units were being placed on every water supply, whether or not there was a current need. A smaller, four-man team had already started to backtrack up the stream to find the source of contamination.

The door of the diner swung open easily as Mare stepped into its brightly lit domain. "Hey, honey." Rochelle had been a waitress at the Pot-o-Gold Diner for as long as Mare could remember. "They still going at it over there?"

"Hi, Rochelle," said Mare as she slid onto a seat at the counter. "Yep, they're still at it. Can I get three coffees to go?"

"Sure can," replied the plump waitress. "Anything else?"

"You got anything to eat I can take back across?"

"Brad can make you up some sandwiches and I have some pastries left. Will that do?"

"Thanks. Ham and cheese on white with mustard will be fine." Mare propped her head on her hand and watched as Rochelle called the sandwich order in to the kitchen, then busied herself taking care of the coffee and pastries.

****

Erin sighed as she sat back and stretched. She was more than ready for bed; the day had been long and hard. But TJ looked as though she'd be going for a couple more hours. When she had the bit between her teeth she rarely stopped until she'd finished; they could be here most of the night. A light nudge to her side prompted her from the doze she had been falling into and a steaming cup was held in front of her. The waft of coffee woke her and she grinned. "Thanks, Mare, you're a life saver." She sat up and took the coffee and the proffered sandwich.

"Does she ever stop?" Mare nodded her head toward TJ who sat at a table with several other ranchers, arranging for their cattle to be herded over to the sections of Meridian land where water sources were clean.

"Not until it's finished, she won't." Erin took a hearty bite out of the sandwich. "It's how she gets things done."

"She's so focused, she didn't even realize who put the food and coffee in front of her," replied Mare, sitting back and watching TJ.

"I know. It used to worry me when I first got to know her. When she was studying, if you didn't stop her and put food in front of her she could go for days without eating. She was a full-time job all by herself."

"That I can believe," grinned Mare. "You okay? You look a little tired. I guess she's been working you hard."

"TJ works hard, we work hard. It used to be she'd do all the legwork herself but now, well, she lets us help out more."

"I was surprised she came tonight. I thought she might send you or Paula, but I didn't think she'd come herself."

"Yeah, we were pretty surprised at that as well. But she knew that she couldn't get anywhere with these guys unless she came down here herself and got in their faces. Besides," Erin grinned, "she knew you would be here."

A smile sprung on Mare's face. "It's about time this town got to find out who TJ Meridian is, and not who they think she is. But it's late and I need to get to bed and so do you and, even if she won't admit it, so does our friend over there. Do you want to tell her it's time to go home or do you want me to?"

"I think you have more chance of surviving than I do."

"We'll just have to find that out, won't we?" Finishing her coffee, Mare got to her feet and wandered over to the table where the discussions were taking place. The men all smiled as she approached. TJ had her head buried in papers so didn't realize Mare was near until she placed her hand on her shoulder. "Gentlemen, I know you still have a lot of questions for Miss Meridian but I think it's about time you let her get home. She's been working on this since early morning." The men immediately began making their apologies.

TJ was stunned. She couldn't remember the last time someone had had the nerve to actually interrupt one of her business meetings. She was about to say something when she caught the stern look on Mare's face and immediately thought better of it.

Erin wanted to laugh but managed to stop herself, knowing that TJ surely wouldn't appreciate it; it might just anger her enough to make her change her mind and stay a lot longer.

Chapter
11

Mare became so busy attending to poisoned cattle and being involved with the contamination problem that her quest for her father had to be postponed. The frustration of not being able to search for him, and the uncertainty of how he would react to her, were playing havoc with her nervous system.

Until she could discover something definite about him, Mare decided to keep quiet about her parentage...even with TJ. It surprised her how quickly telling TJ had come to mind... almost an automatic response. *But TJ already has enough on her mind without having my problems added to it. Besides, I don't know if he'll even want to acknowledge me and I don't want anyone to witness my humiliation if that happens.* For the same reason, she decided against using a detective agency, except as a last resort.

Finally, Mare was able to free up at least part of a day by rearranging several of her calls and coaxing a vet acquaintance in Sharlesburg into covering emergencies. The night before her time off, she tried to come up with an organized plan. *I know my birth certificate doesn't show anything, so where do I start? At the college?*

Going to the bookcase, she looked through her mother's yearbooks, which stood right next to her own. She removed the fourth year one and took it to the couch. Sitting in the corner of the couch, under the floor lamp, Mare pulled her legs up under her and started leafing through the pages. Contrary to the usual custom, no flowery sentiments were handwritten across the pictures. That brought a smile of chagrin to Mare's face. *Mom, I know you always hated to see people write in books, but couldn't you have bent a little this time? I mean, come on, everybody writes in yearbooks.* But not in this one. Mare's hope that a message would give away her father, or even a friend of her mother's, was useless.

The graduates were displayed according to their major field of study. *What could he have majored in if he had this outstanding opportunity where a wife and child would be a hindrance? Maybe looking toward a medical career? Chemistry? Biology? I guess those are good places to start.* Mare found the appropriate pages and pored over each picture, hoping to see some familiarity to her own looks. Moving from major to major, she spent two hours in a fruitless pursuit. *I have no idea what he looked like. Why am I wasting my time?* In frustration, she slammed the book shut and tossed it onto the low table next to the couch.

Just then the phone rang. Mare snatched it up and snapped out her name, regretting it within the second. "Doctor Gillespie." No one said anything and her frustration spoke again. "Look, if this is a joke, go play somewhere else."

"Mare?" The velvety richness of TJ's voice came through even though she spoke tentatively.

Mare's face softened as her heart speeded up. "TJ! I thought someone was trying to be funny. Sorry I didn't get by there today. Just didn't have the time. Are you okay?" *I should have called her.* Mare closed her eyes, picturing the beautiful face that found constant display in the gallery of her mind.

"I'm fine now. I won't keep you; I know it's late. I wanted to make sure you were all right and...I guess I...just wanted to hear your voice."

This touching revelation from such a proud woman filled Mare with a sense of awe. When she could find the words, she answered TJ. "It's good to hear yours, too. Any further news on the water problems?"

"I'll fill you in when I see you. Think you'll make it by here tomorrow?"

The vet frowned at having to hide the truth. "I might not, TJ. I have some business to take care of out of town and I'm going to try to see to it tomorrow. If I'm not too late returning, I'll give you a call, okay?"

"Two days without seeing you? I'll be getting Mare Withdrawal Syndrome." The vet heard a soft laugh that melted her insides. "Sounds like you have another busy day coming up, so I'll say goodnight."

"Goodnight, TJ. Sweet dreams." Mare hung up and sat savoring the call. Then her mind turned back to her search.

A thought occurred to her and she retrieved the year-book. Turning to the back pages, sure enough, an address was given for each graduate. Mare didn't really know much about her mother's early life. Jane's parents had both died before Mare was born and Jane never talked about her home, leaving there after graduation and never returning.

So an address was a start, something tangible to work with. Mare got up and wrote the address down on her appointment pad. She stretched, yawned, and went to bed, satisfied to have found another avenue of approach.

****

The day had been a waste. After hours of searching through the neighborhood, Mare had found only one

woman, a grandmotherly type, who remembered her
mother as a young girl. She recalled that Jane had gone to
college, but she wasn't able to shed any light on her boy
friends. "Jane was a friendly person, but she was very discreet about her own concerns. If you tried to trade tidbits
with her, it was mostly all one-way."

Mare listened to the few tales the neighbor remembered then graciously thanked her and left.

It was late when the vet returned home, dejected with
the futility of her search. She flopped on the couch and
reached for the phone then realized it was much too late to
call TJ. She looked yearningly at the instrument that could
connect her with the woman whose mere voice made her
heart sing. *I'll call her first thing in the morning.*

Now what? Try as she might, Mare could come up
with no solution other than to hunt down and call each and
every male in Jane's graduating class. The only bright side
she could see to that was that their names more than likely
wouldn't have changed. Jotting down a note to pick up a
computer program that listed current names, addresses and
phone numbers on CD-ROMs, she decided she would set a
regimen of making 20 calls a night.

*You might be out there somewhere, Father, and if you
are, I'm determined to find you.*

****

The Meridian ranch had virtually changed overnight.
The day after the town meeting cattle started to arrive from
the ranches that were affected by the contaminated
streams. Keeping the cattle from the various herds separate had been a problem at first. But that had become easier when a truckload of men drove up from the town to
give a hand getting the herds into the correct pastures.

Those same ten men also became the first to be hired
by Paula and by the end of the day the ranch was once
again fully operational. Of course, with the hiring of
hands came a few more problems. The cookhouse needed a

cook, which was soon settled as two of the new hands' wives offered to do those duties. Paula immediately hired them on the same terms as the hands.

Most of the men and their families lived in the town and a few of them opted to stay there. Most of them, however, once they had gotten a look at the accommodations, decided to move onto the ranch. The bunkhouse initially would be home to the single ranch hands, and the families would have the houses. However, TJ planned to have new houses built for single ranch hands on the basis of two sharing each house. The bunkhouse then would be converted to a gym and leisure center, complete with a pool.

The day after the arrival of the cattle from the other ranches, Bill Jacobs, Meridian ranch's new foreman, arrived with his wife and they settled into their new home. The first thing on Bill's agenda was to get the hired hands together and find out what experience they had. Most of them at one time or another had worked on ranches, though few had been permanent hands due to the economic situation in the area.

The next thing was to ensure that each of the men had a horse. Several of the men had their own which they would bring with them; the others, though, were without a mount. On any other ranch this might have caused a major problem; horses weren't exactly inexpensive. However, after a short discussion with Erin, Bill had found himself with a bank account and budget to provide quality horseflesh for the ranch hands.

A barn near the bunkhouse provided sufficient stalls for the animals for the current work crew. Adjacent to the barn, a large, fenced pasture held a run-in shed that could be used for feeding and shelter for a larger herd of horses when necessary.

With the limited amount of work hands available, Paula hired several local teenagers to tend to the cleaning duties in both barns and to help with getting up the hay. The kids met at the local high school and were picked up in the van and driven to the ranch. After work had finished they were all taken back. They were all paid and given the opportunity to ride and learn about the running of the ranch. The only condition of their employment was that when they returned to school in the fall, their grades must remain at a 'C' or above. TJ didn't want any complaints that working at the ranch after school or on weekends was in any way detrimental to their studies.

Apart from helping Bill with buying the horses, Erin also kept an eye on the cleanup operation. Their main concern was to ensure that the streams no longer caused harm to the environment. The cleanup team backtracked the streams to within ten miles of Sharlesburg. There they had found an area of wetlands where containers of industrial waste had been dumped. Erin passed the information on to the EPA and left it to deal with the investigation of who was responsible for it.

TJ's cleanup teams worked with a team from the EPA to clean the wetlands and prevent further damage being done. Then they had moved back toward the ranches, cleaning the streambed. That process was going to take at least a week to complete, then they would bring in pumps and oxidizing agents to re-oxygenate the streams. The final stage would be the reintroduction of fish stocks and placement of monitors to prevent contamination from occurring to that extent again.

With Erin and Paula so busy with the ranch, TJ immersed herself in running her companies. She had found it limiting to be so far away from her headquarters and had two more computers and ISDN lines installed into the house, one in her bedroom and the other in her office. She directed her administrative assistant, Teresa, to field all her calls from the head office, routing only those that required TJ's personal attention. Business meetings were conducted via videoconferencing; those who didn't know better had no idea that TJ wasn't sitting in her office in downtown Atlanta.

All in all, it was a busy time for all three women. They rarely got a chance to sit down together for meals.

TJ's outings on Flag were almost non-existent, due to being snowed under with work or there being no one available to assist her. Erin had offered to ask Bill to keep one of the hands near, but TJ had quashed that idea. They were still shorthanded, and keeping someone at the house just so she could go riding was a waste of resources. However, all work, no play, and no Mare began to take its toll on TJ's moods.

Paula and Erin noticed that Mare hadn't been around in sometime and that her phone calls had been scarce. The times that TJ had called her she was rebuffed with flimsy excuses. Still, the whole area was busy recovering from the near disaster and Mare was the only vet in the area. It was hard not to be judgmental, but she had to be as busy as the ranch, if not busier.

****

Mare forcibly devoted herself to achieving her target of 20 calls per night. Unfortunately, it cut heavily into her time visiting with TJ. Her last visit to the ranch had been brief and somewhat upsetting. Neither Paula nor Erin had been at the house when Mare stopped by.

She was surprised when TJ answered her knock. "TJ! Are you here by yourself?" Mare's heart fluttered, but the joy of seeing TJ couldn't override the guilt she felt. She had almost totally neglected her friend for the past week.

"Yeah, I am. Come on in," TJ answered, straining to sound cheerful.

TJ seemed drawn in on herself; her whole attitude was tense. Mare bent down and kissed warm lips that quivered beneath hers. The sensation was arousing, but she realized TJ was upset and her guilt returned, making her highly uncomfortable. Parting from TJ's lips, Mare looked into, then pulled her eyes away from, the intense blue gaze that was scrutinizing her. She let her eyes drop to the strong hands that were starting to twist a pen around and around.

"I'm really sorry I haven't been able to get by any sooner."

"That's okay," TJ said with a shrug, pretending that it hadn't hurt. "Sit down, I'll get you something to drink."

Mare shook her head. "I can't stay." Her insides squirmed as she saw disappointment flicker across TJ's features. "I'm sorry. I have a call at the MacMasters farm and I was so close, I just wanted to stop in and see you."

Mare reached out and caressed the side of the strong jaw. "I've missed you, TJ." *And I'm so, so sorry I've hurt you. I swear I'll make it up to you.*

TJ sighed. "You've been really busy lately, huh?" *What's going on, Mare? Change your mind about me? Trying to let me down easy?*

"Yeah, I have. Too many things going on that I have to take care of. Too many sick animals." Mare gave a short, dry laugh. "I feel like I'm on a roller coaster and it won't stop to let me off.

"I've tried to phone you during the day, but the line has always been busy." *At least that's the truth.* "And by the time I get home, all I want to do is flop in bed. Sometimes I even take the phone off the hook." *Well, I do, don't I? I have to, in order to make the calls.*

TJ quirked a half-smile, half grimace. *I'm not stupid, Mare. I recognize a lie when I hear one.*

Mare glanced at her watch. "I have to run." She bent and brushed a kiss on TJ's lips then turned quickly and opened the door. Catching the odd expression on TJ's face almost made her turn back but another pang of guilt propelled her through the door and she shut it firmly behind her. She ran to the truck, hopped in, revved it up, and pulled quickly away.

The tears started as soon as she left the house area. *Am I making a mistake? I can see that TJ is hurting. And so am I.* Mare shook her head and wiped her eyes. *I have to put this behind me for right now. I have to find my father! TJ will understand when I finally explain it to her.* "If you ever get a chance to," a small voice whispered inside her head, "if you ever find your father." *No! I will find my father! I will!*

****

As the days stretched into two weeks, Mare's frustration continued building on both fronts: missing opportunities to see TJ, and having no success with her search for her father. So far, her calls had been in vain. The few men who remembered Jane as a classmate had no recollection of her boyfriend.

The vet felt overwhelmed. An already heavy caseload of animals that needed her attention had been stretched to the limit with the addition of the ones that had been poisoned and, although the poisonings had slacked off, she had had to play catch up. That, together with the buildup of nervous tension from not finding her father and another kind of tension from not seeing TJ as often as she wished to, had made her extremely irritable. Mare recognized this and fought to control it, but that was just one more weight on her back.

Finally, she squeezed in time to spend a morning at TJ's, having no idea what kind of reception she would receive. *Will she even still talk to me?* When Mare entered the kitchen, Erin handed her a steaming mug. "Hi, stranger. Guess you've been as busy as we have."

"Yeah." Mare avoided elaborating. She threw a quick smile and saluted with her mug. "Boy, it can be the hottest day in the summer and I still need a cup of coffee to start my day... thanks. TJ in her office already?"

"No, she's not finished her morning wake-up routine yet. She has exercises she has to do three mornings a week. Paula's giving her a hand. She'll be in soon." She added an extra dish and place setting for Mare on the island.

Mare sat at the island and Erin joined her. "Erin, just what happened to cause TJ's paralysis? Would you mind telling me? I mean, I read about the mugging where her brother was killed, but it didn't mention exactly what happened to TJ." Erin didn't hesitate when she saw the loving concern in the vet's eyes. *If she's as in love with TJ as she seems to be, she needs to hear this.*

"Soon after Lance graduated from medical school, TJ and her brother were returning to their car after a theater performance. A gang of thugs stopped them and demanded their money. TJ handed over her purse and encouraged Lance to give them his wallet, which he did. They were trying to avoid trouble." Erin pushed the bagels and cream cheese within the doc's reach.

"A couple of them had been eyeing up TJ and decided they wanted a little more than just money, so they grabbed her. She fought back. TJ wasn't someone you wanted to mess with in those days; the muggers should have left while they had the chance. Then Lance joined the fray. TJ and Lance were making some headway against them when one of them pulled a gun. He shot Lance in the chest. He was killed instantly. TJ went berserk and had plowed through four of them—did a lot of damage, too—before the guy with the gun decided she had to go, too. He shot her in the back and the ones who were still able to, beat her senseless. Then they took off, leaving her for dead." Erin's gaze dropped to the island surface and her lips twisted.

Mare stopped in mid-bite, laid the bagel down, and shook her head. Her green eyes deepened with pain. "Please go on," she whispered.

"You wouldn't have recognized her in the hospital; she was a total mess. Her face was battered. Her nose was bloodied, her lip cut, her eyes blackened and swollen shut. She had bruises all over her body and her hands were covered with cuts and scrapes. When she came to, she never even moaned. The first words out of her mouth were, 'How's Lance?'" Erin reached across to a shelf and pulled a tissue from a porcelain box, using it to wipe the tears that trickled down her face.

"She went berserk again when they told her he was dead. She screamed like a wounded animal and probably would have thrashed around had she been able to. But she was strapped down. The bullet had entered her spine and was pressing against the cord. They couldn't even operate on it. She's still carrying it around in her back. And I guess she'll be paralyzed for the rest of her life, unless there is some miraculous breakthrough."

Mare had sucked her lips in between her teeth.

"You should have seen her before. She was majestic, like royalty. People would stop and stare at her." Erin's face had been distressed but now it lit up and her eyes revived. "But, my God, Doc, look at her, she's still magnificent. Paula and I are half in love with her ourselves."

Then her face darkened again. "But TJ didn't see it that way. She blamed herself for Lance's death. She dropped into a spiraling depression and tried to kill herself. That's why, besides her physical therapy sessions, she goes to a counselor regularly. She wasn't allowed to leave the hospital until she agreed to see one."

"She sees a counselor?"

"Yeah, not that he's doing much good. If he'd get off of the subject of her father, he might have more chance at helping her out."

"Her father?" Mare asked.

"Yeah, she has some bad hang ups about her father and she won't talk about them to anybody, not even Paula and me, even though we've seen..."

"What's going on here, show and tell?" TJ wheeled furiously into the kitchen, her face contorted. Paula came in right behind her, her face ashen. She looked at Erin with a stricken expression on her face and shook her head.

"I thought I'd made it quite clear that nobody was to speak of my father in this house." White heat shimmered from TJ's body as she flung her low-voiced castigation at Erin. "It's not enough my father had to mess with my life while he was alive, now you're helping him do it while he's dead."

The words stung. Erin's pale face matched Paula's. "I only told Mare what I thought she deserved to know. I didn't tell her anything about your father."

TJ's lips pulled back from her teeth in an ugly grimace. "I make the decisions who knows about my life and who doesn't, get that? No one... tells anybody... anything... about my father, but me." TJ threw her shoulder forward, resisting Paula's attempt to clasp it. "Is that crystal clear?"

Erin nodded.

TJ wheeled around to leave the kitchen.

Mare had been watching this exchange with surprise that Erin and Paula seemed to be so afraid of TJ's wrath. When TJ swiveled her wheelchair, Mare quickly rose and blocked her exit. Erin threw a half-shocked glance at Paula who also looked startled.

The wheelchair accidentally bumped into the vet's shins. "Get out of my way, Mare." TJ still seethed, but she wouldn't meet the vet's eyes.

The golden-haired woman didn't budge. Her voice was firm and forceful. "Talk to me, TJ."

TJ's eyes narrowed and her nostrils flared, but she still kept her gaze down. "I don't want to talk with you right now, Mare." Then the eyes came up to meet Mare's and the anger and pain pouring from them made her breath catch. TJ's voice was harsh. "You think you can just waltz in here whenever you please and pry into my family relationships?"

Mare's voice had lost some of its forcefulness. "We weren't having a discussion about your father, TJ. Erin just barely mentioned him."

"You don't know a damn thing about my father except the gossip you've heard. Is that why you made a show of getting into my good graces? So you could hang around and get some juicy tidbits to feed the gossip mills? But once I made some headway into changing the town's thinking about me, I wasn't as much use to you anymore, was I? So now you need something stronger to pass around?"

TJ's tone turned venomous and her eyes seemed to bore holes into Mare's. "Get... out... of my... way." The vet was shocked into immobility. Erin got up, took hold of Mare's arm and led her, without protest, away from the doorway. TJ propelled the chair through into the hallway like a torpedo.

The vet threw herself down on a chair, put her elbows on the island and placed her hands on either side of her pale face. She closed her eyes for a minute to regain her composure. Dropping her hands, she turned hurting eyes toward Erin and Paula who stood together at the edge of the island. "What is she talking about? Does she really think I came here just to get some gossip to tell? I thought we settled this once."

Erin looked down at her hands then back up at Mare. "Mare, I know you've been busy, but what would you think if someone hung around almost every day, waited till you fell in love with them, then just practically disappeared?"

"With only a few hurried phone calls making blatantly false excuses?" Paula added.

With a pained expression on her face, Mare put her fist to her mouth and looked into space. Then her eyes came back to Paula's. "There's a reason for that." She sniffled, fighting back the tears that threatened to start. *TJ hates me. TJ hates me. I've hurt her badly and now she hates me.* The terrible refrain tore at her heart.

"Oh, yeah," Paula sneered. "Let's see what excuse you come up with this time." *I gotta hand it to her; she sure can look pitiful.*

"I thought my father died before I was born, but I just found out he might be alive. Every bit of free time I've had, I've been searching for him."

"What?" Both women ridiculed the answer at the same time.

"It's true, honest." Mare reached into the hip pocket of her jeans and pulled out a wallet that was chained to a belt loop. She reached into the wallet and pulled out a buff piece of folded paper. Handing it to Erin, she said, "Read it. It's from my mother. It's all there." While Erin and Paula read the letter, Mare made use of the tissues in the porcelain box to wipe her face and blow her nose.

She looked at the two women and saw their expressions turn to belief as they finished reading. "I've been calling the men in my mother's graduating class. Every night I call 20 people. That's why I couldn't stay on the phone. And those excuses were so bad because I never was very good at lying." She wiped her face again. "Now, TJ hates me." She bowed her head and the tears came in earnest.

"You've hurt her pretty badly, Doc. She took all this as your turning your back on her. Abandonment, I guess. Maybe even betrayal." Paula started to hand the letter back to Mare, but Erin intercepted it.

"TJ's a proud woman, Mare. You do something that attacks that pride and she writes you off." Erin's face was filled with concern. "I'll go talk to her."

Paula raised both brows. "You sure? Want me to go with you?"

Erin smiled and shook her head. "No sense in both of us stepping into the line of fire." She patted her partner on the arm and left the kitchen.

Mare listened to this exchange with interest in spite of her upset. "Why are you two so afraid of TJ?"

Paula sat down in the chair next to Mare and grinned. "I guess it looks that way to you but we're not so much afraid of her as afraid for her."

"You mean because of the suicide attempt?"

"So, Erin has been talking too much, huh? Partly that, but mostly because TJ has an unbelievable temper. She keeps a pretty tight rein on it most of the time, but when she lets loose, run for cover! When she's that angry, sometimes she does things that physically hurt her or someone else. We try to keep that from happening by giving into her when she's on edge."

"Or by moving people away from doorways."

Paula grinned. "You got it."

* * * * * * * * * *

Erin looked into the office and there was TJ, her head pillowed on her arms on the desk, her shoulders shaking. As soon as she stepped through the door, TJ rasped, "Get out." The curly-headed blonde kept moving toward the desk.

Picking up a square, solid bronze paperweight and without even raising her head to look, TJ flung it straight at Erin. Knowing TJ's aim was unerring, Erin was already stepping to the left and the paperweight, thankfully, sailed past her. *Damn! That was a half-arm throw. I keep forgetting how strong she is.*

Erin walked up next to TJ and put her hand over her friend's. TJ jerked her hand back. "I said, get out!"

"TJ, honey, we shouldn't jump to conclusions about Mare. Again." Erin put a hand out and caressed the raven head.

"You think I'll believe another of her excuses?" TJ's voice broke.

Erin leaned over and put her head next to TJ's and laid her body up against TJ's back. "Oh, honey, love hurts, sometimes."

"How would you know? You have Paula."

A laugh rumbled through Erin, startling TJ. "Yeah, thank goodness. And you have Mare, honest. I have proof."

Erin could sense a subtle change in TJ and she lifted away from her, pulling her upright at the same time. "Read this. It's from Mare's mother." Erin reached in her breast pocket and handed TJ the letter. She watched as the cloud lifted from the beautiful face. She grabbed a couple of tissues and wiped TJ's cheeks and daubed at her eyes. "Mare's been on the phone for hours each night, trying to find her father. She's working her way through all the men in her mother's college yearbook."

"Why didn't she come to me about it?" Puzzled blue eyes sought Erin's.

"Why don't you come back to the kitchen and ask her that?"

"She's still here?" The light of hope coming back to those eyes was a magnificent sight and Erin marveled at their splendor.

Erin chuckled. "You know the doc. Takes more than a few mean words to scare her away. But she is upset."

TJ pulled in her lips and frowned at that news. She lowered her arms to the wheels and backed away from the desk. "How do I look?"

Even with red-rimmed eyes you look beautiful. "You look like you care."

TJ started wheeling toward the door with her friend walking beside her. "Erin?"

"Yeah?"

"I'm sorry about the paperweight."

"At least it missed me."

"Yeah, I must need more practice." Erin's slap against her shoulder brought a tiny grin to TJ's face.

Mare's eyes lifted as she heard the wheelchair come in, but she dropped them again as the wheels receded. Almost at once, TJ's body appeared right alongside her, wheelchair turned backwards. She raised her eyes to the blue ones she loved, now rimmed with red, but still able to stir her heart.

TJ reached in her lap and handed Mare's letter back to her. Mare accepted it and took the time to put it back into her wallet with TJ watching her every move. Paula and Erin slipped unnoticed out of the room.

Finished, Mare looked back up at TJ whose eyes had gotten intense. "Mare, I'm sorry. I..."

Mare reached forward and put her fingers against the sculpted lips. "No apology necessary."

TJ clasped her hand, kissed the fingers and removed them. "I want to say this, Mare, I need to. You are the last person I would ever want to hurt, but I keep doing it, because I find it hard to trust people. I'm sorry. I don't ever want to hurt you again. I love you." TJ leaned forward and kissed her gently.

Then she leaned back. "But I do have a question for you. Why didn't you come to me to search for your father? I have resources all over the world, half of them sitting around waiting for me to put them to work. You shouldn't have to be doing this by yourself."

Mare looked down at her hands and a blush crept up her face. "What if you find him and he doesn't want me? I would be humiliated." Mare's voice got tiny. "I didn't want you to see that."

TJ leaned her elbow on the arm of the wheelchair, put her chin on her fist, smiled and waited. Finally, Mare, curious as to why TJ hadn't said anything, looked up. TJ's smile broadened. "You are trying to tell a woman in a wheelchair that you are afraid of being humiliated?" One raven eyebrow lifted higher and higher. "I've taken lessons in how to be humiliated."

At first, Mare seemed surprised, then embarrassed. Then a laugh burst from her throat and she grinned. "Okay, I get the message. When can you start the search?"

"As soon as you give me as much information as you can about your mother and your father. I'll email it to the central office in Atlanta and a team will get on it right away."

"I can give you that information right now. I've memorized every detail of my mother's history, as much as I know of it. And I reached up to the P's in my calls."

"Okay, c'mon in the office and you can tell it to me while I put it in the computer. By the time you stop by here tomorrow evening I can let you know what progress they've made."

"Let's go." Mare jumped up to start toward the door, then turned quickly, grabbed TJ's face between her hands and kissed her hungrily. TJ threw her arms around Mare, pulled her close to feel the warmth of their bodies mingling, and kissed her back.

When they finally separated, Mare sighed. "I've waited too long for that." Then she chuckled. "But it sure was worth the wait."

TJ just grinned like she would never stop and they headed into the office.

Chapter
12

Mare got a phone call from TJ first thing in the morning. "Hi, Mare. When you come out this evening, could you bring the picture of your mother that's in the yearbook? The office wants me to scan it and send it."

"Sure, TJ. I have a couple of late calls so I'll be out around eight. Is that okay?"

TJ's voice dropped to a lower tone and Mare closed her eyes, enjoying it. "Fine. I don't care how late you come, just come, okay?"

"Wild horses couldn't keep me away." The laugh in Mare's voice lifted TJ's spirit.

"Good girl. Bye, Mare." *I love you.*

"Bye, TJ." *I love you.*

When the vet got to Meridian ranch that evening, she spied TJ at her desk, poring over some figures on a printout and waving Mare to come in. TJ's head lifted for Mare's kiss then the dark-haired woman playfully pushed her away. "Hang in for a minute, okay? Just let me finish this bit."

"No problem." Mare laid her mother's yearbook on the desk then noticed that the door to the left of the office was open. Curious about where it led, she walked over and stuck her head through the doorway. The hall it opened into started at the living room, came toward Mare, then continued on to a dead-end wall. There were two doors to Mare's left and one to her right. These she knew went to the dining room, kitchen and porch. Three doors graced the opposite wall; two were open and one closed. There was one more door at the dead-end. "Where do all these other doors go?" Mare pulled her head back in from the doorway and aimed questioning eyes at TJ who was so engrossed in the paperwork on her desk that she didn't seem to hear her.

Mare repeated the question and TJ answered without raising her head from her work. "Those are mine. Exercise room, bedroom, bathroom."

Mare stuck her head back into the hallway and pointed toward the fourth door. "How about that one?"

TJ hadn't heard Mare clearly, but her eyes closed and she said rather impatiently. "Wait... a... minute." Her eyes reopened and fell to the papers. "Please," she added as an afterthought.

"Oops, sorry." Mare walked over, pulled one of the chairs around behind the desk, and sat down next to TJ. She put an elbow on the oak surface, leaned her chin on her hand, and gazed at TJ's beautiful profile with a tantalizing grin.

After a minute under this adoring scrutiny, TJ's lips twisted up, trying to suppress a smile. Finally, with a snort of laughter, she set her pencil down and turned toward the irrepressible vet. "What?"

"Oh, nothing that can't wait. Please, finish your work. I wouldn't dream of interrupting you." Mare batted innocent green eyes at TJ.

"Look, woman." TJ snarled the words, reached out a long arm and grabbed the front of the startled vet's shirt. With a fierce look, she yanked Mare toward the edge of her seat until they were nose to nose. "You've already interrupted me and now you'll pay the consequences."

Omigosh, Erin did say she has a lightning temper! Mare opened her lips to apologize and TJ swung her other hand behind her head, pulled it nearer, and closed her mouth on Mare's. TJ's pouncing lips felt and savored every split second of Mare's change from surprise to surrender.

Releasing Mare's head and shirt, TJ drew back with a grin and cocked an eyebrow. "What was that question, again?"

The vet's brows raised, too, and her voice stammered. "Ah...er...give me a minute, now. I'll remember." She rolled her shining eyes at TJ and laughed at her own stumbling. "Okay, okay, I remember! I asked you what the other door at the end of the hallway is for."

A rapid change overtook TJ's expression, puzzling the vet. Laughter deserted her face and she spoke between clamped teeth. "That's my father's office." Long fingers retrieved the pencil and started twirling it over and over between her hands.

Whoa! Problems about her father surfacing again? Would just his dominance cause this strong a reaction? "Why didn't you use his office?"

The pencil broke. "Bad memories." TJ got a faraway look in her eyes. She turned her right arm up and absently rubbed at the underside of it.

Mare's eyes dropped to the arm and saw three scars. The first, a thready one at TJ's wrist, shouted suicide attempt, which Erin had referred to. But the other two captured Mare's eyes. Each an inch long and slightly curved, they were spaced about three inches apart, farther up TJ's arm.

A feeling of horror spread through Mare's being as she realized the probable significance of TJ's words. She moved her hand to TJ's arm, pulling the dark-haired woman's thoughts back to the present and generating tremors in her muscles. Distress closed Mare's throat but she forced the words out. "These scars...your father did this to you?" A carved-stone face jerked into a nod. "But how?

Why?" Mare lifted her eyes from the scars and searched TJ's frozen face.

TJ's nostrils flared and her glacial eyes turned to raging flame. "I hate him."

She spit the words out of her mouth with such fury that Mare cringed. *What can I say? What can I do? She is in such pain. Maybe I can at least hold her.* "Can I sit on your lap, TJ?"

TJ stared almost vacantly at Mare for a moment, but she pushed away from the desk and lifted the nearer chair arm. Mare moved onto her lap, sliding both arms around her and moving her body close. They sat there together for a while in silence, then TJ's body began shuddering. Slowly, TJ lifted her arms to embrace Mare and started to cry. Mare cried with her, moving TJ's body slowly back and forth in a tiny rocking motion. After a while, TJ quieted, then said with trembling voice, "There's a box of tissues in the desk drawer."

Mare, tears still creeping down her cheeks, almost laughed out loud at the unexpected remark. She reached to the drawer, pulled it open and felt for the tissues. Her hand closed on the box and she brought it out and sat it on her lap. Pulling several tissues from it, she dried TJ's eyes and face, then her own. She tossed the damp tissues in the trash basket under the desk and wrapped her arms back around TJ, pulling the dark head against her and kissing her cheek. "Do you want to talk about it?"

"No!" The abruptness of the answer left no room for doubt. TJ's arms tightened around Mare.

Mare patted her head. "That's okay, sweetheart, you don't have to. Just relax. I'll hold you for a while. Just relax."

They sat together for so long that Mare was beginning to wonder if maybe her sitting on TJ's lap might tire her. Then TJ spoke into the base of Mare's throat. Her low, toneless voice began to pour like a river breaking through a dam. "The scars are from a belt buckle. He used to beat me all the time: sometimes because I antagonized him, sometimes because he didn't like how I acted, or what I said, or who my friends were... he could always find some reason." Mare pressed her lips to TJ's forehead and slowly caressed her hair with her hand.

"He was a big man, that's where I get my size from. And he was strong. Mostly he beat me with the strap end of the belt, but one time he got insanely angry and beat me with the buckle end. I have some scars on my back, too."

Oh, TJ, how could anyone be that cruel to you? Mare's tears started running again, even imagining this torture.

"My mother wouldn't stop him. She wanted the life of wealth and ease he provided her. She said he hated me because I was supposed to be a boy, an heir for his companies, and my father never forgave me, nor her, for my being a girl. I don't think he beat her, he just ignored her, other than insisting that she turn me into some kind of showpiece that his friends would admire. But she said she didn't love him anyway. Never had. She had the advantage over me, there. I started out loving him." TJ's monotone broke, and long-damped emotions crept into her voice.

"I longed for him to love me back. But he told me my birth was a mistake, that I was no use to anybody. He would scream that at me while he beat me. He was the grownup and I was only a child, so I thought he must be right; I was a mistake, a failure, not worth anybody's love. My father. My father was telling me this. And I believed it. All those years I hated myself for not being the son he wanted. I still hate myself, only now it's because I hate him so much! I wanted him dead and he is, but I'm still tied to that hatred. It eats my insides. I'm more crippled inside than I am outside."

The bitterness of these words dragged at Mare's heart. "Didn't Lance satisfy his desire for a son?" Mare asked quietly.

At mention of her brother's name, TJ's tone softened. "He loved Lance. We all did, even Mother. But knowing that he was loved gave Lance the courage to tell Father he had no interest in the business world. He wanted to be a doctor. Father was as furious as I've ever seen him, but he didn't strike Lance, he browbeat him with constant nagging. Lance got so depressed that Father had turned against him that he couldn't eat or sleep properly. He was in agony. So I went to Father and made him an offer. I convinced him that Lance would never be able to run the companies, his heart wasn't in it. I promised him I would concentrate my studies on business and economics and let him groom me to head Meridian Corporation, if he would give his permission for Lance to pursue a medical career.

"Well, Father finally admitted to himself that no matter how much he wanted Lance to take charge, it would never work. Whoever led the companies needed to be driven by a love of power or by greed and neither one motivated Lance. I, on the other hand, not only loved power, I thrived on it. So the deal was made. In order to keep the leadership of Meridian Corporation in the family, Father accepted a daughter as his heir. But he made me pay.

"He knew I loved this ranch, and horses were close to being an obsession with me. In my second year at Harvard, he became fanatically determined that nothing should interfere with my studies. So, he shut down everything in Meridianville, without a care for the people whose lives he was disrupting, and moved us to Connecticut."

TJ reached for another tissue and blew her nose. Mare gave her an extra squeeze and continued to caress her head.

"I got furious when I found he had sold the place. Both my parents had manipulated me all my life, until I didn't even have a life of my own anymore. The horses were my only solace and from pure meanness, he ripped that away from me." TJ's lips curled in distaste. "We got into a terrible screaming match and he went completely berserk. He grabbed the wrong end of the belt and beat and beat me with the buckle end. He stood in front of the door, so I couldn't get past him. I could feel my back was cut and bleeding in several places and I put my arm up to ward off some of his blows. So my arm got cut, too." TJ started rubbing her arm again.

"Erin and Paula had come home with me for spring break. Paula was out, but Erin heard the screaming all the way upstairs and she came running." TJ's face and voice turned ugly. "She dashed into his office and saw him beating me. She yelled at him but that had no effect, he just kept beating me. So she picked up a bronze statuette and hit him over the forearm with it. She broke his damn arm and still he tried again to hit me, but he couldn't." TJ smirked at this, then a touch of admiration entered her voice. "Paula showed up then. She didn't know what was happening, but she knew it was trouble. She shoved him away from blocking the door and she and Erin grabbed me and hauled me out of there." TJ shook her head. "Those women have some kind of guts."

Mare could feel the tension in TJ's body start to slack off at this point.

"They took me to the hospital emergency room and had my cuts sutured and the welts treated." A tiny smile crept into TJ's voice. "They also had the sense to have the injuries photographed and a hospital report sent to the police station. My father never beat me again. In fact, because of their quick thinking and support, I was able to 'persuade' him to give me one of his companies, lock, stock and barrel. And I built it into three times the company it was before...and finished at the head of my class...and got Lance into premed. You might say Erin and Paula were my guardian angels."

TJ lifted her head from Mare's shoulder, brought her arms back in front of her and sat up straight. Mare dropped her arms from around TJ, and smiled. "You could still say Erin and Paula are your guardian angels."

The dark head nodded, but her eyes were cast down and her face wore a troubled, almost embarrassed look. *I can't believe I told her all that. What's she going to think of Meridians now?*

Mare lifted TJ's chin with her finger, and waited. Finally, guarded blue eyes swept up to confident green ones. Mare smiled endearingly into those lovely eyes and put her other hand on TJ's cheek. "That makes three of us who love you to pieces." She leaned forward and entered into a kiss of unconditional love. Both sets of arms came up and gathered each other into a warm, comforting embrace.

Afterwards, Mare sat back against TJ's long arms and gazed into a somewhat happier face. "TJ, I want you to do a big favor for me."

"Another kiss? I guess I can force myself." TJ leaned forward, with a small grin.

Mare pushed her back with one hand and gave a little laugh. "Not yet. First, you have to promise me something."

TJ stayed leaning against the hand and could feel its warmth spreading over her chest. "Anything."

Mare's eyes grew impish. "Hmmmm. I'll keep that in mind. But, really, I want you to promise me that you will talk about all this with your counselor."

"Mare!" TJ threw herself back against the chair, turned her head away and frowned.

Mare wrapped her hands around TJ's arms and shook her. "Listen to me a minute, TJ. Please?" She waited until the dark head turned back toward her. "I can listen to you, I can sympathize with you and I can love you. But I am not professionally trained to help you, and that's what you need. Professional help. You've carried this hurt and bitterness and hatred around for a long time and you need to deal with it."

Mare could see TJ was wavering, but unconvinced. "You say you thrive on power. Well, you have the power to change your life, to rid yourself of all the demons that are fighting to hold onto you. And the decision is completely yours...no one else's. Will you decide to fight for possible love and happiness for the future? Or will you surrender to the proven hatred and defeat from the past?" The golden head tilted and brows raised.

Mare was fascinated by the way TJ could signal a smile without actually smiling. The corners of her lips would quirk ever so slightly, just as they were doing now, and her eyes would grow warmer. "You do have a way with words, Mare."

The emerald green eyes sparkled. "Is that a promise, then? You'll tell your counselor?"

"Okay, okay, I'll tell him." TJ didn't sound convincing.

"Say you promise."

With a sigh, TJ put her hands halfway up in surrender and her voice was firm. "I promise. On one condition."

"What's that?"

"That you come with me?" TJ's voice was quiet, small.

That voice touched Mare to the depths of her soul. She smiled and hugged TJ, bringing her close again. "Of course, I will." Then Mare grinned mischievously. "Now, before we get to work, let's see if you can still force yourself into another kiss."

It really wasn't much of a struggle.

Chapter
13

TJ and Mare were still waiting for a positive word about the search for Mare's father. TJ's team had finished contacting the men in the rest of the alphabet and when that was unsuccessful, they started back at the beginning, figuring some small clue might have been missed.

In the meantime, Mare had come over this evening to help TJ go over the mountains of paperwork involved with the contamination cleanup, including the legal paperwork required to prosecute the company that had been dumping the waste. The EPA had finally found the company responsible and was prosecuting. TJ was handling a private prosecution for the ranches that had lost livestock.

Finally, TJ put away the pen she had been holding and slapped her long hands down on the table. "We've been working hard all evening. Time to call a halt and have a little recreation."

Mare leaned her head on her fist and swung her twinkling green eyes toward the dark-haired woman. "Really? Like what did you have in mind?"

TJ didn't answer with words. She slid the side of the wheelchair up out of the way and opened her arms. Her ever-present desire to hold and kiss and caress Mare had been growing all evening and, by now, she was bursting with it.

"Oh, yeah!" Mare laughed. Jumping up, she stepped over to TJ and sat on her lap, putting her arms around TJ's neck.

TJ slipped her arm around Mare's shoulders and gazed at the emerald eyes and delicate face. *She is so beautiful and loving, she just takes my breath away.* Laying her free hand against Mare's face, she kissed her forehead, eyes, cheeks and nose. Then their lips met: soft pillows of warm, moist flesh, sliding, slipping, opening, and surrendering to two eager tongues. Mare's hand reached out to TJ's shoulder and started to lower the thin strap that held up her loose silk top; then she hesitated and moved the strap back to its original spot.

TJ pulled her lips away from Mare's and disappointment flooded her expression.

Mare's heart thumped. "What? What did I do? Was I wrong to think of doing that? I know you never seem to want…" *Oh, Lord, forgive me, what did I do to put that look on her face?* She stopped, unsure of how to finish the sentence. Unsure of herself.

For a long time, Mare had wanted desperately to make love to TJ, but she had been shy, especially since TJ made no move to explore beyond kissing and hugging. She didn't know what to expect from TJ or what TJ might expect from her. Now the look on that lovely face confused her. *Is she disappointed that I tried, or disappointed that I didn't do it?*

TJ's cheek twitched and her eyes looked stormy. "No, you weren't wrong. I wanted you to do it." *How I have longed to take you in my arms and never let you go.* The emotion vibrating in TJ's words struck an answering resonance in Mare. "But I want you to be sure of what you're getting into. I don't want us starting something you don't intend to someday complete." *I don't want you to do this out of some misguided sense of pity.*

"Don't intend to someday complete?" Mare smiled softly and shook her head. *She's just as confused as I am.* "I love you, TJ. I want you. I need you. Sometimes you are so sure of yourself and other times..."

"I'm not exactly a whole woman, Mare," TJ interrupted hoarsely, tearing the admission from the depths of her being. "That could cause some problems with my... satisfying... your physical needs."

"Oh, but you are a whole woman to me, my love." The sincerity coming from Mare's eyes and voice couldn't be mistaken. "I know you can fill my every need, TJ. I just feel inadequate to fill yours. I want to, so badly, but I'm not sure what would feel really good to you." She lifted her hand and caressed the strong face before her that hid such a vulnerable heart.

TJ's lips twisted and her eyes filled as she finally came to believe. This woman she loved more than she had ever loved anyone else, really loved her in return. She took hold of Mare's hand, returning it to the strap of the silk top. Mare's eyes softened as she brushed the straps from her soon-to-be-lover's shoulders, barely breathing as the clinging material glided slowly downward, gradually revealing the sweet treasure it had concealed. TJ's desire flamed higher as she watched Mare drinking in the vision unfolding before her. Her mouth curved into a lopsided smile and her eyebrow shot up. "Suppose I give you a few lessons?" she suggested, her voice low and sultry.

Mare raised her eyes to the blue pools that she wanted to drown in forever. "You are so beautiful," she breathed.

"So are you, my love." The dark-haired woman pulled her again into an embrace and she and Mare melded their mouths together.

Mare felt her shirt lift. Her body jerked as a strong, hot hand moved sinuously against her quivering skin, then clutched her bare stomach. Like a pebble dropped into a pond, TJ's touch sent circles of desire rippling into every crevice of Mare's being. Her breathing deepened and quickened, and her whole body became incredibly attuned to every touch, every caress.

Mare's hands glided over TJ's muscular stomach sketching every ridge and valley, then proceeded to mimic, on TJ's body, every move TJ made on hers. The hands of the two women stroked slowly, sensuously upward, coming to, and cupping against, the softness of a breast. Searching fingers found their swollen targets, twisting them back and forth in agonizing slowness.

In perfect timing with this movement, a tantalizing tongue ran its curved tip against the tender roof of Mare's succulent mouth, alternately probing and retreating. In a battle of love, Mare's tongue challenged TJ's, making her push hard for every tiny taste of hotly defended territory.

Waves of sensation thrummed across Mare's skin from mouth to breast. Elsewhere, an indescribably sweet ache suddenly expanded into a hungry, throbbing demand. Mare, groaning into TJ's mouth, couldn't stand it anymore. Reluctantly disengaging her fingers from their teasing task, she twined both hands in the raven hair, pulling TJ's head away from hers and gasping for breath as their lips separated.

TJ's chest heaved and questioning blue eyes, deepened by passion, opened upon yearning green ones. "Take me to your room," Mare requested in a shaky voice.

TJ sucked in a hissing breath as incredible delight expanded within her. Sprouting a small, almost reverent smile, she watched the play of emotions crossing Mare's expressive face, as she slowly withdrew her stroking fingers down the burning skin of her ribs and stomach.

Finally, she moved her hand out onto the top edge of one wheel. Releasing her other arm from its hold on Mare's shoulders, she dropped it to the opposite wheel. Her low, passion-laden voice vaulted Mare's hunger a notch higher. "Hold on tight."

Mare drew both arms closer around her love's neck. She leaned her golden head against TJ's dark one, and murmured a warm breath into her ear, "I'm never letting go."

The two wheeled down the hallway and into TJ's room, eager to explore the intoxicating joys of their love's fulfillment.

* * * * * * * * * *

Erin's head rested in Paula's lap as they sat in the living room watching TV. Paula reached for another chip from the bowl balanced on Erin's stomach and crunched it between her teeth. "Hey, watch the crumbs, will you?" Erin smacked her partner on the thigh.

"Hmmmm. Sorry, I was just thinking about this show. You think those two really are lovers?"

"I think the producers very wisely left that up to the viewer. We can think of them any way we want."

"I guess. But I know if I traveled through the forest with you all day, our nights would be times to remember." Paula leered at Erin and grabbed a handful of a strategic body part.

"Whoa, woman!" Erin laughed and caught the bowl of chips that had bounced off her stomach and was about to dump on the floor. "Is that all you think of?"

"Only with you, honey." Paula slipped her arm beneath the curly head and lifted it up into her kiss.

"Ummm. Is it bedtime yet?" Erin set the bowl on the floor and put her arms around her lover.

They kissed again, then Paula answered. "Not till you help TJ get ready for bed." She lifted Erin's shoulders all the way up and the blonde swung her legs around onto the floor.

Erin picked up the chips then stood up and patted Paula on the cheek. "Keep those warm thoughts, baby."

"Yeah? It's not just my thoughts that are warm."

Erin chuckled and started toward the kitchen. Paula's voice brought her to a halt. "Hey, Erin, did you see Mare leave?" Erin raised her eyebrows, shook her head and bypassed the kitchen to look in TJ's office. It was empty.

Paula had gotten up, too, and she headed into the kitchen and looked out the window. Mare's truck was still sitting in the well-lit parking lot.

Erin set the bowl by the sink and walked over behind Paula. She smiled when her eyes fell on the truck. "What do you think?"

"If it means what we think it means, I'm really happy for both of them, but especially TJ."

"Yeah, she was really broken up when she thought Mare had been playing with her. I'm so glad she has someone to love her. Have you ever noticed the wistful expression she gets sometimes when she looks at us?"

"Yeah, I have." Paula nodded. "Always made me feel bad that we couldn't help her find someone."

"So what would you suggest I do about helping her tonight?" Erin lifted Paula's hair and nuzzled the back of her neck with her lips and tongue.

Paula shivered from the tickling lips, turned around and grinned. "I think you should wait till TJ buzzes you, if she ever does." Paula reached down and picked a surprised Erin up in her arms. "I'm the one who needs your help tonight." Paula strode out of the kitchen, into the living room and over to the bottom of the staircase, where she stopped and eyed the steps.

Erin started giggling. "Put me down, honey. You'll hurt yourself."

Paula began to giggle, too. "You're probably right." She set Erin onto her feet. "Okay...race you to bed!" Laughing, the two dashed up the steps, shoving against each other. Still jostling, they ran down the hall to their room and dove onto the bed. Where they had a great time arguing about who won and who lost the race and what penalty the loser had to pay.

TJ never did buzz them.

****

Mare's thoughts were floating up through a filmy cloud, halfway between sleep and waking. The sudden realization that she was in a skin-to-skin encounter jolted her completely awake. *I'm lying on top of a naked body!* Her eyes flew open and her head jerked up and she looked into the most beautiful face she had ever seen. *TJ.*

The peaceful features were relaxed, eyes closed; the calmness of sleep suited her. In slumber all her worries disappeared from her face, the emotional pain that was her constant companion was soothed.

Mare lowered her head back down into the sweet valley where she had awakened, basking in the movement of TJ's slow, gentle breathing.

She sighed in contentment and with a feather-light touch caressed the strong arm that lay just to the side of her face, a long-fingered hand resting on her back. She had been worried last night when they reached TJ's room, unsure of how to proceed, or even if they should. It wasn't as if she hadn't been with a woman before, or that she wasn't overwhelmingly attracted to TJ. But from what she had been told about her injuries she wasn't sure how much TJ was capable of feeling, or if she could feel at all.

She found out that TJ also had fears. The woman became almost shy when they entered the room and Mare soon realized that jumping into bed with TJ on the spur of the moment wasn't quite possible. TJ had been so self-conscious as she explained to Mare that intimate details had to be taken care of before they could proceed beneath the covers. Mare was touched at the gentle explanations TJ gave and her heart melted further as she saw the proud woman reveal all the limitations of her injury. But contrary to TJ's worries, Mare had taken the tubes and bags in her stride.

What bothered Mare more was that she wasn't comfortable with the thought that their lovemaking would be an entirely one-sided affair. TJ had tried to reassure her that she would be happy giving everything she had to Mare and that her love and affection were enough in return. Mare hadn't been satisfied with that and had come up with some inventive ways to ensure that TJ enjoyed the experience as much as she did.

And, in the process of their mutual explorations, something unbelievably wondrous happened. They discovered that TJ's response, once awakened by Mare's imaginative touch, left nothing to be desired. Both women found complete satisfaction. When it first happened, after they had lifted into the stratosphere of consummated passion, TJ cried. Their tears blended and Mare kissed every available surface of TJ's face as the awed woman struggled to speak.

"They told me I might be able to have some sexual response, other women had reported it. But I didn't believe them; I felt dead inside. As much as I wanted to make love to you, I had lost hope that I would ever even come close to feeling the way you just made me feel. My God, Mare, you've given me a new life."

They had cried together for a while, then eager hands and mouths renewed their quest to revisit the delights they had just become acquainted with. Again and again they soared above the mundane world until a glorious exhaustion finally quieted their loving frenzy and they slept in each other's arms.

Remembering each delicious moment, Mare sighed once more, pressing her lips to the warm body beneath her, savoring the still-salty taste of her lover, before her lips languidly made their way up her torso. She looked up and stilled as crystal-blue eyes connected with emerald green.

A slow smile curved TJ's lips as she watched the changes of expression flicker across her lover's beautiful face.

Mare, filled with a need to kiss that seductive mouth, slithered her body up along TJ's without considering the fire it would rekindle in both of them. The skin around TJ's eyes tightened and her mouth opened, hungry for the kiss that Mare offered her. Wrapping her arms around the awakened body, TJ pulled her up, dragging skin against skin, until the golden head was even with the raven one. While their mouths tasted each other, TJ's hands started a journey of love down Mare's tantalized flesh. Mare slipped her mouth sideways and began her own voyage, fingers finding and mouth sampling. Time had no meaning as, borne on the wings of tongue and touch, they ascended once more through the realm of passion.

****

Mare and TJ finally made it into the kitchen to join Erin and Paula for breakfast. Erin set a steaming mug of coffee in front of the vet and a glass of iced tea in front of TJ. Everyone sat eating bagels and cream cheese for a moment without a sound. But everyone was smiling, and the new lovers absolutely glowed. Finally, Erin got up, came over to Mare and kissed her on the cheek. "Welcome to our family, Mare. We're really glad to have you. Really glad." The blonde's warm brown eyes twinkled. "Now maybe Paula and I will get an occasional rest from trying to keep TJ entertained."

TJ gave her a shove and laughed. "Keep your day job, Erin. You gals will never make it as entertainers." Then TJ waggled her eyebrows and grinned wickedly. "Except maybe for each other. What the heck was that racket on the stairs last night?"

Paula and Erin both blushed as TJ kept her grin on them. "Uh...we had a race to the bedroom," Erin admitted.

"Oh, yeah? Who won?"

Now Paula waggled her eyebrows and grinned wickedly. "Neither one of us. We both had to pay up."

Mare and TJ both chuckled at the look on Erin's face when she tried to shush Paula, then realizing the futility of it, just rolled her eyes.

Chapter
14

Erin helped Paula with the dishes before they both disappeared to work and left TJ and Mare sitting at the island. Mare looked over at TJ, seeing that she was a little subdued.

"So, Abner tells me that they are moving all the cattle back to their own ranches today. The ranch is gonna be a little quiet without them here, isn't it?"

"Yeah, they go back today, but Bill and the boys will have their hands full. Our cattle will start arriving the day after tomorrow. And Paula has a few more hands for Bill to break in." *Just ask her. The worst she can do is say no. You can't expect her to play hooky just because you can.*

"Are you okay? You seem a little quiet." Mare leaned closer, trying to see TJ's face.

"I'm fine." TJ lifted her head and decided to go for it. "You busy today?" she inquired.

"Not especially, why?"

TJ grinned. "Want to go for a ride? We could go up to the lake. It's only about an hour or so on horseback."

"Sure, but shouldn't we have told Erin or Paula where we're going?"

Yesssss. "Nah, I'll take the cell phone with me and we can leave a note. Besides, if they see Flag and Runny aren't in the stable they'll know we're out riding."

"Let's get going, then. Do you need to take anything with you?"

"Nothing special, but we can take a rucksack with a few drinks and snacks with us." TJ pushed herself over to the fridge and began grabbing soda and snacks. "You'll find a bag on the hook over there."

Mare watched in frank admiration as TJ instructed her on how to assist with Flag and the lift they had installed so that TJ could mount her horse. Within thirty minutes they were on their way, Mare trailing behind TJ and Flag as she became used to the gait of Paula's horse, Runny. They made their way at a steady pace and eventually left the buildings of the homestead behind. Once in the open fields, Mare pulled abreast of TJ.

TJ smiled as Mare pulled alongside, savoring her presence. Ever since she was a child and her father had given her first horse, she had loved to ride. Her first horse had also been her first love. She had spent every minute of the day with it that she had been able to. She had named it Artemis, after the Greek Goddess of the Hunt, and they had been thoroughly devoted to each other.

Around then TJ had begun to realize that her parents' attitude toward her wasn't like that of other families. She had thought it normal for her father to hit her; after all it was her fault, wasn't it? Hadn't she been late? Hadn't she upset her mother? Weren't her school grades lower than they expected? She had done everything within her power to please them, and still it wasn't enough.

Her saving grace was Lance. He excelled at school and achieved 'A's across the board. His success sometimes managed to deflect their father's anger away from her, though not all the time. And, like Artemis, his love of his sister had been unconditional.

There was something liberating about being on top of such a powerful creature, even more so now that it gave

her a sense of freedom that was denied to her by her wheelchair. "Come on, Mare, let's pick up the pace and let these
two run off a bit of their energy."

Mare had been observing TJ closely. Her whole body
language changed when she was on a horse. She hadn't
noticed it when she'd seen her before, but she was much
more relaxed, the constant tension that could be found in
her shoulders was gone. She was free and it was a sight to
behold. "You go on ahead, I'm not so hot on a horse." She
leaned down and patted Runny on the neck. "Let me get
used to the big guy before I start running him ragged."

TJ smiled indulgently down at her friend and lover.
"And there was me, thinking you were a vet. Runny is a
girl."

Mare laughed. "I know that; it was just a figure of
speech. Now you go play on that horse of yours and I'll be
right behind you."

"Okay. I won't go too far, just enough to settle Flag
down some. I haven't been able to take her out much
recently." With that she turned Flag and with a flick of the
reins and a quick yell urged her golden steed forward.
Mare brought Runny to a halt so that she could concentrate
on watching TJ and Flag rather than staying on Runny.
She wasn't kidding when she told TJ that she didn't have
much experience on horses. She knew TJ had, though.
You could tell that without having any knowledge of
horses or riding. Watching her as she charged away on
Flag was electrifying. *Lord, she must have been something
else before her injury.*

TJ was in heaven. There was no other way of describ-
ing what she was feeling. She was on her horse for the
first time in days, riding like the wind, feeling its fingers
lifting her hair. Not only that, but she was in the company
of a woman who she now believed could love her like no
other ever had. She let out a whoop of joy as she crested
the small rise she had urged Flag up.

The view from the rise was unhindered and though it
wasn't a mountain she could see for miles. On the whole,

the Meridian ranch was rolling prairie that was criss-crossed by streams and a river. Up to the north the land became hilly and a whole section was wooded as it stretched to the mountains which were some miles distant.

She brought Flag to a stop and looked out over her domain. As a child she had never really considered how precious this land was. Only when her father denied it to her had she truly understood what was being lost all over the world to development and urban sprawl. That was one of the reasons she had fought so hard to deny her father the land he had wanted in Colorado. It was also the reason she had funded a national park taking over the management of it.

As a businessperson she had been taught figures and numbers, geographical thresholds, what people would put up with and what they wouldn't. The business world had thought she was mad when she bought that land and handed it over. But TJ had learned from her father's mistakes. Tom Meridian didn't think anything of alienating whole communities and sections of the public. TJ, on the other hand, courted them. She went to the area and listened to what the people were saying, heard their worries and concerns.

They didn't want a major industrial development sitting on their back porch. Unemployment was low in the area, so they weren't so concerned about jobs. What they did worry about, however, was the area they were bringing their children up in, the crime that a new development would attract, the pollution it would create. After spending a week in the area, TJ went back to the board of her company and told them she was buying the land and wouldn't take "no" for an answer.

TJ's company bought the land and public awareness of the company grew. It became known as a company that considered the environment and heeded public concern. The company began to specialize in low-impact industries. Communities that hadn't been too welcoming to other big businesses opened their arms to them. TJ's company grew to three times its former size. The profit margin had risen, the stockholders were happy and so was the public. The only person who had been furious was TJ's father, and that had made the venture even more worthwhile.

TJ inhaled the clean air and relaxed, enjoying the scenery in front of her. She twisted in her saddle as she heard Mare and Runny approach. "Beautiful, isn't it?" she asked, waving across the land.

Mare nodded as she pulled up alongside. "Yeah, it is. You enjoy your run?" It amused Mare to see how much pleasure the ride invoked in TJ; the woman was positively glowing.

"Yep!" grinned TJ. "I haven't been able to get out much in the last week or so. Been too busy or there hasn't been anyone to spare to give me a hand. But it's great to be out here now, even if it is a little cloudy." Her grin widened. "Thanks for coming with me. Come on, it's about another hour or so."

They started off again at a more leisurely pace now that TJ had rid herself of her excess energy. The ride was pleasant. TJ knew a lot about the land she owned and took great delight in showing Mare where she had played as a child. Her favorite places recalled fond memories of the time before she had known her father's hate and punishment; a time when she had believed she had a loving relationship with her parents.

It was nearly midday when they eventually reached the lake that TJ had wanted to show her, though you couldn't have told that from the sky. They had started out under a cloudy sky and the clouds had built as they neared the lake. The air was warm and dry but the clouds were now dark and ominous. Still, Mare was enjoying herself and TJ certainly was, too.

The lake was larger than Mare had realized and curved away to the right of where they stopped. On the far side, trees grew down to the water's edge, but here a pebble beach stretched before them.

"It's gorgeous. Did you spend much time here when you were a kid?" Mare handed a soda and candy bar over to the raven-haired woman and took some for herself.

"As much as I could. If things got too tense at home, I'd sneak out on Artemis and come here." TJ pointed. "I had a hideout in the trees over there. Nobody ever found it."

"You want to go over, see if we can find it now?"

TJ shook her head. "Nah, another time maybe. If we go up this way we can circle back and head for home. How are you holding up? Ride not too much for you, is it?"

"I'll no doubt suffer for it tomorrow, but right now I'm fine. You mind if I get down and stretch for a while?" TJ shook her head and Mare slowly dismounted from Runny. She clutched hold of the bridle, letting her feet become readjusted to the ground. Then she took the reins over Runny's head and began a slow walk along the lakeside. "Are there fish in here?"

"I would imagine there still are. My father liked to bring his associates out here. An invitation to the ranch for the weekend was an indication that you were on your way up in the company." TJ leaned on her saddle horn. "Of course, he never brought Lance or me out here. I do remember him taking Lance to a ball game once or twice."

"Did Lance get on with your father?"

"You mean did Lance know what a bastard he was?" Mare nodded, pleased that she was getting TJ to talk to her. She remembered that she had promised to go to her counseling session with her, but so far TJ hadn't mentioned it.

"Not at first, no. I never told him that Father beat me and I didn't even try to make him see what a cruel person he could be. For a long time Lance believed he was a good person. Even if it was an illusion, I couldn't take that away from him."

Mare brushed her hair from her face and bent down, picking up a brightly colored and perfectly rounded pebble. "What changed that for him?"

"A number of things. Lance wasn't an in-your-face type of person, but when it came to what he wanted he had a will of steel. If he wanted something, he put his mind to it and didn't waver until he got it. Father thought it was a particularly brilliant facet of his personality... until it was turned on him. Lance wanted medical school; Father wanted him to go into business. Lance took all the sciences in school; Father wanted him to take mathematics and business ethics. When Father realized that he wouldn't win with persuasion, he tried browbeating him into it. All it did was make Lance hate being at home or around him, but eventually it got bad enough that he was getting depressed about it. He didn't really understand why Father turned on him, but I put a stop to that as soon as I could."

Yeah, you did, didn't you? Didn't think twice about sacrificing your own happiness to ensure him of his. "Did he ever find out about what your father did to you?" Mare picked up another pebble, this time a flat one. She sent it skimming and bouncing across the water, keeping her back to TJ, allowing her to sort through her emotions without the pressure of her watching. Behind her, Mare heard the sigh and the sadness in TJ's voice.

"I never told him but, yeah, I think he did. He was smart and he saw the bruises occasionally... when they were too prominent to hide."

A forbidding rumble echoed overhead and both women looked up. While they had been talking the sky had turned a threatening shade of dark gray. Mare readjusted Runny's reins and bridle before she remounted. "Guess we ought to head home before the skies decide to open on us."

TJ assessed the sky. "We better go back the way we came, it's the quicker route. Will you be okay if we go a little faster? We might be able to make it back to the house before the rain starts."

"No problem. I think I've gotten used to Runny here."

"Come on, then. We can come back here another time." TJ turned Flag, urged Mare to take the lead and they started home at a canter.

Big, fat, wet drops of rain started falling as soon as they had made their decision to return to the house. Mare clenched her legs around the barreled belly of her horse, concentrating on staying in her seat. She was comforted that TJ was close by her side; the constant rumble of thunder was starting to unnerve both her and the horse.

The rain began to fall more heavily, rapidly soaking her cotton shirt and jeans. She wished she had brought her hat with her, at least that would have kept the rain from her face. The wind had picked up and now had a decided chill to it. With the water and all, she'd be surprised if she got out of this without catching a cold. It suddenly occurred to her that catching a cold might not be in TJ's best interests either. She had no idea how illness might affect her.

While Mare was worrying over TJ, TJ was worrying over Mare. With each rumble of thunder the vet's form tensed even more and TJ was questioning her wisdom in bringing the inexperienced vet on such a ride. A trickle of cool water was now a permanent feature running down her back and she already knew that Erin and Paula were going to throw a fit over this little excursion. If she got ill from it, as well, it would only be worse.

She was a little concerned about the storm, too. It was raining hard enough that it was difficult to see the ground and TJ was loath to push the horses any faster when she couldn't see where they were going. The wind was picking up at a steady pace and lightning was striking over to the west of them. TJ urged Flag a little bit faster so that she was alongside Mare. She made a signal with her hand, asking if the vet were okay and got an affirmative answer. TJ thought hard, trying to remember if there were anywhere nearby that they could find shelter until the storm passed, but nothing sprang to mind. They were still thirty minutes away from the ranch and TJ decided they should carry on and hope that it didn't get any worse.

* * * * * * * * * *

Paula bounded into the house with a soaked Erin hot on her trail. "Whew, where did that storm spring up from?" She went into the laundry room, grabbed two towels from the clean pile and threw one across to her partner.

"I have no idea, but it looks as though it has set in for the afternoon. Did you notice that Mare's truck is still outside?" she asked as she towel-dried her hair, leaving the blonde locks in frizzy disarray.

"I did. Wonder what they are up to? You'd think they could at least have had the coffee on for us, considering the weather."

"Hmm. Well, they may be a little involved and didn't notice the rain. Why don't you go on up and run us a hot bath? I'll make us a couple of hot chocolates and join you in a few minutes."

Paula leaned over and placed a kiss firmly on Erin's slightly parted lips, while her hand blazed a trail of pure flame across a damp and sensitive breast. "You got it, babe." She smirked at her lover, knowing she had just ignited a fire of desire within her... and how much fun it was going to be to put it out.

Erin sighed and wet her lips as Paula turned and slowly made her way from the kitchen with a pronounced sway to her hips. The day was a washout and she hoped there would be many more of them if it put Paula in this type of mood. She heard the door close upstairs and quickly moved to prepare the hot drink she had promised.

In her haste to get upstairs to the now hopefully naked form of her lover, she almost missed the folded piece of paper that had been left on the counter. She was tempted to ignore it, but she knew TJ wouldn't have left it lying around for no reason. It then occurred to her that TJ wouldn't have left it at all, if she were in the house. She unfolded it and read the short note:

Taking Mare out to show her some of the
sights on the ranch. Should be back early
afternoon. I've got the phone if you want
me. See ya later.
Love,
TJ

"Hell!" Erin looked out of the window again, staring
into the rain. *The only way she could have taken her out is*
on one of the horses. Flag is okay in this sort of weather.
I doubt she would have let Mare ride Ebonair, she's too
big; but Runny is about Mare's size. She put the note down
and forgot about the hot drink she was supposed to be making. She dashed out of the kitchen and up the stairs.

Erin flung the bedroom door open, barely registering
the fact that Paula was sprawled on the bed buck-naked.
"Paula, what's Runny like in this sort of weather?"

Paula frowned and looked pointedly down at herself
then at Erin. "I'm here in my birthday suit and you want to
talk about horses?"

"TJ took Mare out to see the sights of the ranch. I
know Flag won't have a problem with this weather and TJ
is too good on a horse to worry about. But I don't know
how good Mare is. Chances are she's on Runny, since
she's smaller than Ebonair."

Paula sat up. "Runny's okay as long as you keep a
firm hand on her. Otherwise, she can be a little skittish. I
can't believe TJ would go out without letting one of us
know."

"She left us a note and she's got the phone. Mare's
with her so why would she let us know? I know we act like
her mother sometimes, but she is an adult."

"You think they are okay out there? Maybe you ought
to give her a ring and make sure." Paula had gone to stand
by the window, gazing out into the sky. "This storm is in
for the rest of the day."

"Yeah, I know, but it's lightning out there and ringing
the cell phone might be a mistake. The last thing she

needs is to be struck by lightning just because we wanted to check up on her. Besides, I'm sure she'll ring if she needs us." Erin walked over and curled her arms around Paula's waist, cuddling her close to her body and absorbing her warmth. "They'll be fine. TJ knows what she's doing."

"Yeah," replied Paula, patting Erin's hand.

****

The lightning was getting awfully close and TJ wasn't too happy about being on top of Flag, or Mare being on Runny at this moment, but she didn't see what choice they had. Mare was keeping up well and Runny was behaving herself. Neither of the two horses was showing a great strain at the pace TJ demanded they keep. They weren't that far away now from the safety of the barn. She looked over to Mare's bedraggled form and smiled. Even soaked through and looking like a drowned rat, she was beautiful.

Mare knew immediately that something was wrong and tried to shift her seat to compensate for the horse's movement. Runny was having none of it as she pulled back on the reins to slow the horse down. Another flash of lightning and Runny again shied, this time over to the left almost unseating Mare.

She looked frantically across to TJ, seeing that the woman had already noticed Runny's panicked movements and brought Flag alongside to help calm the horse down. She relaxed as she saw TJ lean across the small gap between them and give Runny a slap on her shoulder. The horse shook her head in the direction of the slap, seemed to take reassurance from Flag's presence and calmed down.

Mare smiled through the rain at TJ and nodded when she saw her indicate that they should slow down. After all, it wasn't as if they could get any wetter. She pulled back firmly on the reins and Runny obeyed the command, slowing her speed. They would have been perfectly all right if lightning hadn't struck a small outcropping of rock about twenty feet away from them. Runny immediately reared as she was showered with fragments of rock that had been blasted by the lightning.

Mare held on for all she was worth but could feel herself slipping as Runny rose into the air. She felt her balance being thrown backward and clenched hold of the reins but they slipped through her hand and she was in flight, heading for the ground.

Flag charged past Runny as the horse brought herself to a complete stop and reared in fright from the lightning. TJ pulled the reins tight against the left side of Flag's neck, turning her into a tight circle so that she was heading back towards Mare and Runny.

She watched in horror as Mare fell from the back of Paula's chestnut. TJ's heart was in her throat as she rode up to the still form. "Mare? Mare!" she got no response. TJ looked around and saw that Runny had come to a halt not too far away, scared it seemed, to leave the presence of Flag. TJ guided Flag to walk in a small circle around the prone Mare. She leaned down, looking for any sign of injury. She couldn't see any blood or anything that looked as though it was broken.

"Mare, can you hear me?" she yelled again. Instinctively she went to get off of Flag but remembered the straps holding her to the saddle. She almost yelled out in frustration. The trip out, and the time spent on her beloved horse, had for those few precious hours made her forget her limitations. They were in trouble and she knew it. She looked anxiously around, again trying to gauge the distance from the house. Even if she rode at the fastest speed she and Flag could manage it would take at least another fifteen minutes, which would mean at least thirty before help would arrive.

She pulled the phone from its carrying case and although she knew it was stupid to use it in this weather she called the ranch, praying that Paula or Erin were home.

Chapter
15

Erin had her eyes closed and was lying back, snuggled in Paula's loving embrace, up to her chin in warm water and bubbles. She couldn't think of anything more heavenly than where she was now. Paula's arms were wrapped around her, one hand caressing her inner thigh, the other cupping her breast, teasing her with tantalizingly gentle touches. She groaned as Paula's hand once again shied away from the need she was stirring. "Tease," she whispered as her lover bent her head and kissed her lightly, before sucking her earlobe and sending a shiver down her spine. "God, you are so good at that," she sighed. The ringing of the phone went unnoticed.

God damn it! Where are you? TJ silently screamed as the phone continued to ring without answer. She broke the connection and rapidly punched in another number, hoping that one of them at least had their own cell phone switched on despite the weather.

Paula jerked from the languid place she was in as a shrill warble echoed from the bedroom. "Leave it," Erin murmured lazily.

"Can't, might be important. Just because you can laze the rest of the day away doesn't mean that I can, you know." Erin tightened her grip in protest as Paula began to climb out of the tub. Paula grinned and kissed her soundly on the lips and was about to give in to her love when a thought crossed her mind. *What if it's TJ?* "Sugar, Erin, move. It might be TJ." All sexual tension left the room as both women bolted from the tub.

TJ nearly cried with relief as the phone was answered. "Paula! Paula, I need help. Mare's fallen, she's unconscious and I can't..."

"TJ, honey, calm down. Tell me where you are," came Paula's disembodied voice.

TJ took a deep breath, struggling to calm herself. Frustration at not being able to help Mare tore at her, coupled with attacks of fear and guilt. "We decided to take a ride to the lake. We're about a mile and a half away. Runny reared and Mare fell. I think she hit her head or something because I can't wake her up."

Paula repeated TJ's message aloud and stared urgently over at Erin who was scrambling into her clothes. She had already picked up the house phone and started dialing. "Bill? It's Erin. Get a couple of the men together and meet me in front of the bunkhouse, right away. TJ and Mare were out riding when the storm hit and Mare's been thrown and is hurt." She paused for a second. "Great. See you in a minute." She put the phone down quickly, kissed Paula good-bye and was out the door.

"Honey, Erin and some of the men are on their way. Just stay by Mare and if she wakes up don't let her do anything stupid like move. They'll be with you in a few minutes, okay?"

TJ sat anxiously on Flag, already staring off into the distance, hoping to see the Land Rover even though they had only just set out. One hand nervously rubbed her wet jeans, the other clutched the phone she held to her ear. "She doesn't look like she's gonna come around."

"She will, TJ. Don't you worry about that. She's too tough to let a horse get the better of her." Paula walked over to the house phone that Erin had recently used and picked it up, trying to figure out whether she ought to call 911 or the doctor. She settled on phoning Jon Hunt who ran the local doctors' service. "TJ, I'm just going to get Doc Hunt to come out to the ranch to take a look at Mare when you guys get back. You hang in there; Erin isn't far away."

Erin skidded to a watery stop outside the bunkhouse and waited as Bill and two of the men Paula had recently hired ran from the building and piled into the vehicle. "This is Mark and Burt." Erin nodded to them.

"Thanks, Bill." As soon as the doors were closed Erin floored the accelerator and they were off. With the windshield wipers on high she roared through the pools of water that had accumulated in the downpour. Going at a much faster speed than was safe, she fought to keep the Rover under control, fear pushing her onwards. Several minutes later a tall figure appeared in the distance. TJ had been right; they weren't that far from the ranch.

TJ heard the deep rumble of Erin's Rover before it came into sight. "Stay with me, Mare, Erin is nearly here." TJ had positioned Flag so that she sheltered Mare from the worst of the rain. When she hadn't been searching for signs of Erin, she had concentrated on Mare, looking for signs of life. She could see her lover's chest moving so she knew she was breathing.

TJ had never been so glad to hear such a painful groan as the one that rumbled from Mare at that second. The vet's arms lifted her hands towards her head and TJ could tell she was coming around. "Mare, you need to stay still. You fell when Runny shied." Emerald eyes cracked open and TJ sobbed with relief. "Stay still. Erin is nearly here. Are you okay?"

Mare nodded and immediately regretted it, closing her eyes again. "I feel like I've been thrown off a ten-story building." Both hands were now holding her head. "And TJ?"

"What?" TJ's voice was full of fear.

"I'm lying in a puddle." Mare's voice held the petulant tone of a two-year-old child.

"What?" TJ couldn't quite believe her ears.

"I said I'm lying in a puddle. Couldn't you have at least trained Runny to throw me somewhere dry?" Mare tried to smile, but the pounding of her head wouldn't let her.

I can't believe she's joking about this. Doesn't she have any idea how serious this could be? Hell, she only has to look at me to see what the consequences of a back injury could be. "This is serious, Mare. You could be badly hurt." TJ looked up from Mare. The roar of the engine was closer and she could see Erin's Rover. She'd be here in a minute.

"Nope, I'm just a little banged up. I hurt way too much for it to be anything more serious." Mare draped one of her arms across her eyes to stop the rain from hitting them.

Erin slammed the brakes on and slid to a halt barely ten feet from where TJ had stationed Flag. Bill and his two hands jumped from the vehicle. Burt headed off to get Runny, Bill and Mark headed straight for Mare and TJ. Erin grabbed a blanket from the rear seat and jumped from the Rover, sloshing through the mud over to where Bill was now crouched.

"Hey, there, little Missy, what ya doing lying in a puddle?" Bill's voice was deep and rough from the years spent bellowing at cowhands, but it also held a gentle lilt to it.

Mare giggled and smiled up at the ranch foreman. "Ask TJ. She's the one who trained her horses to throw people in the wettest place possible."

Well, Erin thought, *at least she sounds okay.* "Hi Mare, you hurt anywhere?" she asked as she knelt down by Bill in the mud.

"You mean besides my pride?" Mare raised her eyebrow then remembered nobody could see it with her arm draped over her face. "No I don't think so. Took a pretty good bang to the head but nothing else seems to be hurting me. Though I can't say I will feel the same tomorrow."

Erin looked up into TJ's stony face. Mare might not have lost her sense of humor over this but TJ obviously didn't feel the same. Her whole body was rigid with tension and it was agitating even Flag. "Okay, let me just quickly check you out, then we'll get you two adventurers home." Erin quickly ran her fingers through Mare's hair, finding a nasty bump on the back of her head but it hadn't split and bled. *Thank the Lord for small mercies.* Then she carefully felt down her neck, looking for any deformities or lumps that shouldn't be there. "Any neck pain at all, Mare?"

"Nope, just a little stiff from where the rain and wind were attacking it."

"Okay." Erin continued with her inspection. "Any pain in your arms and shoulders?" Again Mare replied in the negative. "Wiggle your fingers for me?" Erin watched as Mare complied. "Okay, what about your legs? Any pain?"

"Nope."

"Can you wiggle your toes and bend your knees for me?" Erin watched closely and sighed in relief. It didn't look as though Mare had done any major damage. "Well, it looks as though you survived. Come on, Bill, let's get her up." Bill and Erin both took hold of Mare's arms and slowly lifted her into a sitting position. "Feel okay?" Mare nodded gently. "Bill and Mark here," she nodded at the ranch hand near Bill, "are going to get you into the Rover. I'm just going to make sure TJ's okay." Erin passed Mare's arm over to the ranch hand and stood back as Bill and Mark lifted Mare to her feet and slowly walked her over to the vehicle. Erin turned and faced TJ. "You okay?"

"Fine," she replied tersely; her voice strained with barely controlled anger.

Erin walked over and ducked beneath Flag's neck, patting TJ's faithful steed. "You sure?" TJ nodded this time. "Okay then, once Bill and Mark have Mare settled we'll get you off Flag and back to the house. Burt can bring Flag in."

"I'll ride."

Ah hell, TJ. Now is not the time for an argument. "TJ, be sensible. You are soaked through to the skin. If you ride, it will take you at least another twenty minutes or so to get back to the house. Besides, I'm sure Mare would rather have you with her."

TJ stared down at Erin whose blonde hair was now plastered to her head by the rain that showed no sign of letting up. And if TJ had been thinking rationally, she would have known that Erin had only her best interests at heart. But right now TJ wasn't thinking rationally. All she could see was that once again she had been unable to help someone she cared about. *Yeah, use emotional blackmail to get Lance to go to that stupid play with you, just so the damned magazines and newspapers would have somebody beside yourself to write about, and get him killed. Take Mare out on a simple horse ride and almost do the same. You could have gotten her killed or seriously injured and what could you have done about it? Well, you proved that you couldn't do a damned thing. That's what you get for thinking you can live a normal life, for forgetting you're not a whole person. You're inferior just like father kept telling you were.* "I said, I'll ride." TJ pulled on Flags reins and moved the horse off in the direction of the house.

Erin stood drenched, silently watching TJ's rigid form ride slowly into the distance on her horse. She sighed and trudged back through the mud to the Rover. Getting in, she slammed the door and turned the defroster on full blast to clear the steamed windows. Mare was sitting in the back wrapped in a blanket with Mark sitting by her side and Bill sitting in the front.

"Where is TJ?" Mare asked.

"She decided to ride Flag back."

"What!" yelled Mare. "Is she nuts?"

Bill cleared his throat and looked over at Erin, whom he was slowly coming to admire. She had a good business head and was prepared to get her hands dirty to get the job done, and better yet, she didn't question him. He said he needed something then she trusted him and made sure he got it. "You sure it's wise to let her ride back?"

Erin looked over at Bill. "No, it's not wise to let her ride back, but are you gonna tell her she can't?" Erin turned on the engine, put the vehicle into gear and started the journey home.

"Erin, is she okay?" Mare leaned forward so that she could see Erin's face.

"Let's just say that I think she's feeling a little inadequate right now. And my treating her like a two year old and telling her she couldn't ride Flag home was only going to make it worse." Mare sighed and sat back, staring out of the window, hoping to catch a glimpse of TJ as they drove past.

* * * * * * * * * *

TJ was miserable. She was wet, cold, and angry. Not even the joy at being on Flag was going to shake her from this mood. It had been stupid and reckless to think that she and Mare could spend a normal day together. And her stupidity could have cost Mare her life. She should have asked Mare about her riding skills, instead of just assuming she was comfortable, and she shouldn't have taken her so far away from help. If she had been thinking, instead of mooning over a day out with Mare, she would have realized that the gray skies only meant trouble.

If she had thought about it at all she would have known it was impossible to do anything on the spur of the moment. Everything she did had to be planned down to the last detail so that all eventualities were covered. She had to remember that she couldn't simply do things anymore.

TJ urged Flag to a greater speed, needing to work out her frustration, trying to run from the desolation that was building inside her. She had thought that she had adjusted to her injuries but days like today just forced her to realize that she would never be able to forget them.

****

Paula stood anxiously waiting at the front door when Erin and Mare finally drove up in the Rover. Erin had dropped Bill and Mark back at the bunkhouse, knowing that Paula would be able to help if Mare became unsteady on her feet. Erin jumped out and ran around to open the door for Mare. Paula ran down the steps with an older gentleman by her side. Erin and Mare recognized him as Doctor Hunt from Meridianville. Paula and the doctor escorted Mare into the house while Erin parked the vehicle.

As soon as she had settled Mare on the couch in the living room, in Dr. Hunt's care, Paula ran upstairs to find some of Erin's clothes that would fit the vet. "Well, Doc, what's the prognosis?" she asked as she came back down.

"We've always known that Mare had a tough head on her shoulders; she has a mild concussion and should rest for the next couple of days." The doctor put his stethoscope away and turned his pen light off. "I'd like you to keep her awake for the next few hours, but there should be no complications. I'll leave you a checklist of signs and symptoms to watch out for—any problems, give me a ring. And you, young lady," he turned to Mare, "should know better than to give an old man a fright like that."

Mare grinned at him. "Think I gave myself a bigger one, Doc."

"Lucky for you that you didn't break an arm or a finger. That sure would have played havoc with your piano playing! You just take it easy for the next couple of days.

I'll leave some painkillers for the headache you will no doubt develop in the next hour or so. Next time don't make it an accident that brings you to see me, okay?"

"You got it, Doc. Thanks for coming all the way out here."

"No problem. I'll see you soon. Take care of yourself." He picked up his bag and nodded to Paula who followed him out of the door.

Mare closed her eyes as Doctor Hunt left the room. Her head did hurt more than she had let on, but she knew that complaining about it too much would have provoked a trip to the hospital in Sharlesburg. She was worried, not about herself but about TJ. Erin had implied that TJ wouldn't take this little incident well and thinking about it, Mare knew she was right. She had heard the barely restrained panic and frustration in her lover's voice as she had come around and knew that TJ had felt helpless in the situation. TJ was a proud woman and Mare knew that not being able to help her would have hit her pride pretty badly.

"Hey." Erin's voice broke into her reverie. "Paula stole some of my clothes for you. Let's get you out of these wet things. You want to take a quick bath or something to warm up?"

"Thanks for the offer, Erin, but I'd rather get changed and wait for TJ to get back."

Erin nodded her understanding. "Okay. I'll take you down to TJ's bathroom and you can wash up and get changed. There is a buzzer in there if you need any help. I'll start a fire and bring one of the spare quilts in here and you can snuggle on the couch."

Erin helped Mare down the hall to the bathroom and left her to change, walking back into the living room just as Paula closed the front door. They looked at each other with concern. "Mare okay?" asked Paula.

"Yeah, just getting herself changed," replied Erin as she strode over to the fireplace and began to build a fire.

"Where is TJ?" Paula moved over to her side and started to pass pieces of kindling and wood.

"Riding Flag home. She wouldn't accept me bringing her back in the Rover even though the hands would have brought the horses back." Erin started to twist paper wicks to use to light the fire.

Paula sat back, watching her partner. "I take it she isn't handling this as well as Mare is?"

Erin gave a sad chuckle. "Paula, she isn't handling it at all. She's putting one almighty guilt trip on herself. I could see it; she hardly said a word when we arrived. She sat up on that horse proud as you like and anybody looking at her could have told you it was a show."

"So, I take it we aren't going to tell her that she should have told us where she was going?"

"No, we aren't. Her self-confidence has just taken one hell of a thump and us pointing it out to her isn't going to help one iota. Besides, she's an adult and okay, she's an adult with special needs, but we have to let her have a life of her own. We can't control everything for her."

"Yeah, I know." Paula leaned her head on Erin's shoulder. "But it's hard not to be protective when things like this happen."

Erin turned and kissed the side of Paula's head. "Come on, let's light this, get Mare settled then go over to the barn and wait for TJ to get back."

"I heard the doctor say something interesting to Mare. Something about her piano playing." Paula looked at Erin and smiled. "Bet TJ will like to hear that."

"Yeah," Erin agreed. "But let's wait till she's in better shape."

* * * * * * * * *

TJ saw Erin and Paula waiting for her when she rode into the barn. She hadn't called ahead because she had the other ranch hand not far behind her on Runny. Still, she should have known better. Paula and Erin weren't likely to leave her by herself after something like this; they knew her too well.

They didn't speak as she pulled Flag to a stop near the ramp, and in silence they unbuckled TJ's legs. TJ reached up for the T-bar and took her weight on her arms as Paula led Flag away to be walked and rubbed down. Burt had brought Runny in right behind TJ and he made a welcome offer to take care of the two horses. While TJ manipulated the lift controls, Erin steered her into her chair. She handed her a towel and wrapped a blanket around her shoulders then wheeled her out of the barn to the house.

Mare was wrapped up tightly in the quilt that Erin had provided. After calling her vet friend in Sharlesburg to cover for her for a few days, she had closed her eyes and lay back on the couch, listening to the crackle and hiss of the fire that the girls had lit before they left for the barn. The faint scent of hickory smoke battled with that of the hot chocolate that was on the table by her side. Her head was pounding and she felt slightly nauseous, the results of a mild concussion. The tension building in her shoulders from TJ's continued absence wasn't helping either.

She heard footsteps on the ramp outside and pushed herself into a seated position so that she could look over the top of the couch. The door creaked open and she could see the front wheels of TJ's chair progress through. Mare was unable to keep a grin of relief off of her face. Her grin slipped a bit when the bedraggled form of her lover was pushed into the room. "Hey!" she said with cheerfulness that she didn't really feel, instinctively knowing that TJ would need her reassurance. The lack of reply and the sullen look on TJ's face reinforced that instinct.

Erin wheeled TJ into the living room and down the small ramp there so that she was near Mare and the now roaring fire. "I'll leave you here while I go run you a bath," said Erin as she pushed the brakes on. TJ nodded but didn't say anything. Erin looked over TJ's shoulder, catching Mare's attention. "Help?" she mouthed to the vet who gave a small nod. Erin left the two women to go draw TJ's bath.

There was silence for a few minutes and Mare was concerned that TJ didn't seem to be able to look at her. She swung her legs off of the couch and reached over, taking TJ's hand into her own. She didn't speak, just held tightly to the deeply chilled hand, her thumb unconsciously stroking along the back of it.

TJ stared down at the entwined hands, then looked up into Mare's green eyes, and took a deep breath. "You okay?" she asked quietly

A smile lit up Mare's face. "I'm fine. A small knock on the head but the doc has given me a clean bill of health."

"Really?" TJ inquired, her mood brightening a bit.

"Really. So what's the long face for? Huh?"

TJ looked away again, before answering. "I should never have taken you out today."

"Nonsense. Why not?"

"Oh, please!" TJ slammed the brakes off, pushed herself backward, and turned away. "You could have been killed today."

Mare stood up and walked to her side. "I could be killed walking down the street." She ran her fingers through the dark hair on the bowed head. "What was different about today?"

"I was different today, Mare. You walk down a street at least someone could help you. What could I do today? Nothing, that's what. I shouldn't have taken you out, at least not before making sure you were happy on the horse and then I should only have taken you out into the corral where I couldn't put you in any danger."

"TJ, honey," Mare moved to where TJ could see her. "You didn't put me in any danger." TJ opened her mouth to speak but Mare put her finger across it. "No! Now listen to me. Am I an adult?" TJ nodded her head. "Okay, that's good. Do you consider me an intelligent adult?"

TJ looked up sharply. "Of course."

Mare smiled at her indignation. "Well, that's nice to hear." She lifted her hand and caressed TJ's face. "So considering all this do you not think I'm capable of making a decision all by myself?"

"I guess," TJ said begrudgingly, a pout appearing on her face.

God, she's cute when she's like this. "Then, if anything, it wasn't you putting me in a dangerous position, I put myself in one. But honestly, TJ, all we did was go for a ride. So I fell off the dumb horse. You were prepared, you had the phone, and you'd left a note so the girls knew where we were. What more could you have done?"

"I could have got down off my horse and helped, that's what," she huffed.

"Oh, sweetie." Mare leaned forward and kissed her brow. "No, you couldn't, and I knew that before I went out with you. You did everything you could. You got Erin and the boys out to me; you even had Flag keep the rain off me. Nobody could have done better whether they could walk or not." She stood up and walked behind TJ's chair. "Now I love that cute look on your face but you can stop pouting. You're cold, wet and we need to get you into a bath."

This at least got a grin from TJ. "You gonna come with me?" she asked as Mare pushed her up the ramp.

"Oh, I might be persuaded to get a little wet." Mare looked up. Seeing Erin in the shadows of the hallway, she grinned and gave her a wink.

Chapter 16

It was still dark when Mare opened her eyes. A soft breeze gently ruffled the drapes through TJ's open window before entering the warmth of the bedroom. Yesterday had been a demanding day for both of the women, but they had come through it together. It had surprised Mare how insecure TJ had been. She thought that they had come further in their relationship, that her disability wasn't an issue.

It also brought home a frightening reality that TJ wasn't as strong and tough as she appeared to the outside world; her emotional state was incredibly fragile. Hopefully, last night had been a big step in allaying her fears and insecurities.

Erin had done a great job in drawing the bath. The bathroom, which had been specially modified for TJ, had been hot and steamy. The bath was scented with exotic oils; the tub filled to the brim with bubbles. Mare had been looking forward to a long, sensuous soak, reassuring her lover of their growing bond in her warm embrace. It would be a chance to ease Mare's bruised and battered body at the same time as healing TJ's bruised emotions.

Mare had assisted TJ in the use of her hoist and then climbed in behind her, pulling her backward until she rested comfortably in her arms. But Mare hadn't been able to resist the close proximity of TJ's bare skin. Her gentle caress had been maddening to her love and what started out as a seductive tease rapidly disintegrated into an all-out tickle fest and water fight.

Somehow TJ had managed to turn herself around in the water so that they were face-to-face, and at the first possible chance had claimed Mare's lips for her own. For what seemed like hours they reacquainted themselves with each other's body, touching, tasting, holding. They then left the steamy warmth of the bathroom for TJ's bed. Mare delighted in TJ's attentions; for someone who was disabled from the waist down she was surprisingly agile.

****

Although Mare loved TJ's caresses and cries of passion, she enjoyed these quiet times in the middle of the night more. TJ's head rested on her stomach, her left arm wrapped possessively around Mare's waist, her other splayed up by her head. The worries of yesterday had been driven away, she was at peace. Mare would never tire of seeing her like this.

She dropped her hand and softly ran her fingers through the somewhat bedraggled hair, frowning slightly at the heat coming off of her companion. She tried to move without disturbing the slumbering TJ, but TJ only tightened her grip and fussed. Mare returned to her gentling caress and let her hand drop to TJ's forehead, once she had settled again.

Yep, sweetie, you have a fever. With all that wind and rain yesterday, you must have caught a chill. Her temperature wasn't that high, just enough to cause a sheen of perspiration across the brow and make her hot to the touch. *Hmm. I guess that will give me a good excuse to pamper you in the morning.* She grinned as TJ seemed to sense her thoughts and snuggled in closer. Mare tightened her embrace and settled back down, closing her eyes and basking in the sensation of affection and love emanating from her sleeping lover.

The next time Mare opened her eyes bright sunshine was pouring in through the windows. She groaned as every muscle and bruise on her body made itself known, despite the bath and loving touch of TJ the night before. She lifted her head and searched around for her lover. TJ had migrated during the night and was now sprawled on her back by Mare's side. Mare ran her hand over TJ's head checking for signs of the fever that she had noticed when she woke up during the night. *Still warmer than I'd like, love.*

Mare checked her watch, surprised to find that it was after ten in the morning. *Unusual for you, love, considering Erin and Paula were complaining about how early you get up. Is this because I wore you out last night or is this fever of yours to blame? Huh?* Now that she was free of TJ's nocturnal octopus-like grasp, she decided to get up. Her stomach was demanding to be fed. After yesterday's ordeal and last night's strenuous activities they hadn't gotten the chance to eat. She left the bed, managing not to disturb TJ, grabbed hold of one of TJ's T-shirts which fell almost to her knees and went in search of food and coffee.

The house was quiet as Mare walked through its rooms. As it was a weekday morning she assumed the girls were out working. The kitchen was empty when she entered but either Paula or Erin had left coffee in the coffee maker. She opened the fridge and took out the milk, diving back in to grab a grapefruit. While she was busy pottering around she heard a phone ring several times before it was picked up. She faintly heard Paula's voice deal with the inquiry. Several seconds later footsteps could be heard approaching the kitchen. Mare grabbed another mug and poured a second coffee.

Paula smiled as she saw Mare standing by the counter dressed in one of TJ's T-shirts. "Hey, there. How's the wounded soldier today?" She reached out and took the mug that Mare offered her.

"Sore. I feel like I've been run over by a truck," Mare replied ruefully. "On the plus side, my head feels better."

"I'm glad you're feeling better. You look better, too. You were a little pale yesterday. TJ getting up?"

"No, she's still asleep." Mare took a sip from her mug.

Paula grinned evilly. "You wear her out last night, Doc?"

Mare grinned back. "Maybe, but I think yesterday took a lot out of her, and she's running a slight fever. I think maybe she caught a chill or something."

Paula frowned. "That doesn't sound good. I'll give her doc a ring and see whether we need to take her in to see him."

"Well, I plan on keeping her right where she is for the rest of the day."

"Did I hear Doc Hunt say something to you about playing the piano?"

"Yeah, I've been playing since I was knee high to a grasshopper. Calms me down when nothing else will."

"I'd like to hear you sometime."

"Stop by my house anytime I'm home. I love an audience."

After another half an hour of chatting with Paula, Mare was ready to return to TJ. Paula told her to yell out if they needed anything since she was working from TJ's office just across the hall.

TJ was still deeply asleep. She was in the same position as when Mare had left except she was now hugging a pillow. Smiling at the childlike scene before her, Mare crept quietly onto the bed, trying not to disturb the slumbering woman. She was leaning over to place a kiss on TJ's cheek when two blue eyes popped open. TJ turned her head, capturing Mare's lips on her own. She released her hold on the pillow, wrapped her arms around Mare and pulled her down on top of her.

"Morning," whispered TJ as they broke.

"Good morning, sweetheart," replied Mare, lifting her hand to TJ's face. "How are you feeling?"

"Great, now that you're here. I woke up earlier; where were you?"

"Kitchen. Food and coffee were required. You're running a temperature."

"I know. My throat hurts and I have a headache," she said, pulling Mare down for another kiss. "But I'll be fine. Will you give me a hand to do my exercises?"

"And what exercises would you like to do?" asked Mare as she ran her finger down TJ's bare chest, delighting in the instant reaction her caress provoked.

TJ took a deep, shuddering breath as the sensation caused by Mare's inquisitive fingers raced through her. Her body woke with a vengeance, craving more than a simple caress from the beauty who lay with her on the bed.

Mare let her fingers wander lower, pulling the sheet from TJ's body as she went. She could see the goose bumps ripple along her lover's body, the downy hairs on her arms stand to attention. She sent a smoldering gaze into TJ's eyes as her hand found its destination.

TJ stopped breathing altogether, her whole body taut with sensual tension. She couldn't feel it exactly, but she knew where Mare's hand rested, and knew that her body was reacting to it. After her accident she had never believed that she would ever feel this way again. Now that she knew that she could, she couldn't get enough of it, especially with the blonde who had brought her body back from the dead and was invoking the response right this second.

"Don't tease," gasped TJ, her voice low and urgent with desire.

Mare leaned closer and ran her tongue along the valley between TJ's breasts. "Who said anything about teasing?"

****

TJ lay with her arm around Mare's sweat-slicked skin, her hand stroking the waist it rested on. Her breathing had now returned to normal after her early morning "exercises." *I sure liked those better than the regular ones.* Mare had curled her panting body into TJ's side and sleep had found her as her breathing calmed.

TJ was listening to the sounds of the house; it was past lunchtime. She had heard Erin return from her morning activities and greet Paula with a loud yell until she had been shushed. She hadn't heard the phone ring, so Paula either had turned the ringer off or had calls diverted to her cell phone. The silence was heaven and she was enjoying the relaxation far too much for it to last.

How long had she known Mare now? Six? Eight weeks? Never before had she moved so fast into a relationship and never had she felt so comfortable in one. Mare fit perfectly. All of TJ's bad moods and tantrums just bounced right off of her; she was stubborn and refused to take anything sitting down. She was a challenge and TJ knew already that she loved her from the bottom of her soul. Just being around the green-eyed blonde gave TJ hope and enthusiasm for life. *Would it feel like this if I could walk? Is the reason she likes to be around me because I'm no threat to her? She can up and walk out at anytime and there would be no way for me to stop her.*

She took a deep, steadying breath and let it out slowly, letting it release the tension that had been building with her thoughts. She turned her head and nuzzled the blonde locks, inhaling the heady aroma of her lover, and smiled. *No, stop thinking she would act like the others who thought having a relationship with you would be easy money. So far, she has put up with all the crap you have thrown at her and still come back for more. And admit it, you love that no-nonsense look she gets on her face when she's about to tell you off. And, boy, do you love the way she cheers you up. How many people in this world have you known, besides Lance, who have ever been able to make you smile like she does? Hmm? Yeah, that's right, none. So it is*

time to stop feeling sorry for yourself and to show this
woman exactly what she means to you. Time for you to
show her a little romance, I think. Oh yeah, she grinned, *I*
love a little romance.

* * * * * * * * * *

Erin stood and stared at Paula who had her hand
clamped over her mouth. "Shhhhh," whispered her partner.
"TJ and Mare are still in bed. And Mare said TJ had a bit
of a fever." Paula pulled her hand away.

"Paula, it is nearly one o'clock in the afternoon. Even
if they are still in bed, I doubt they are sleeping." Erin had
a wicked grin on her face and looked down the hallway to
TJ's bedroom door. Paula slapped her soundly on the
shoulder and pulled her toward the kitchen.

"What was that for?" she asked, rubbing her shoulder.

"That, Miss Scott, was for the obvious look of jeal-
ousy on your face. Besides, I know they are asleep
because ten minutes beforehand they were making enough
noise to make a saint blush."

"Eavesdropping, were you?"

"Hard not to. I have never heard that tone of voice
from TJ before. Whatever Mare was up to sure sounded
good."

"Hmm." Erin smiled slyly. "Maybe I'll ask for a few
pointers."

"Oh, hush up, and don't you tease them when you see
them next." Paula began pottering about, grabbing the
makings of a sandwich and pulling a couple of cans of soda
out of the fridge. "How is it going out there? They nearly
finished?"

"Just re-oxygenating the streams now." Erin reached
over, snagging a piece of celery from the salad Paula had
put on the table. "Couple more days at the most and
they'll be finished."

"Is everything set for the arrival of the cattle tomorrow?"

"Yep. Bill and the boys are just getting the holding area in order. Then all we need is for Mare to check them out before we let them loose. That is, if I can pry her away from TJ." The women smiled at each other, hoping that TJ had finally found someone to pour her love into.

*   *   *   *   *   *   *   *   *

It was after three when Paula decided enough was enough and caved in to her desire to make sure the two lovers were all right. Mare had seemed fine that morning but the doctor had told her to take it easy. And although TJ's doctor had said that a slight fever wouldn't be too much of a problem, Paula still needed to see for herself.

Besides, TJ hadn't eaten at all today and both of them could probably do with a drink. So she made up a tray of iced tea and some fruit and knocked quietly on the door to TJ's room. She got no reply but cautiously opened the door and entered. Wide-awake blue eyes greeted her and she smiled, holding up the tray. TJ nodded and Paula walked into the room, placing the tray within TJ's reach. Mare was snuggled tight underneath TJ's right arm, her own clasped possessively around TJ.

Paula reached over and placed her hand on TJ's glowing face and frowned slightly. "You feeling okay?" she whispered.

"Yeah, just a little achy."

"You still have a fever so you need to drink lots of fluids to bring your temperature down." Paula crouched down so that she was near TJ's head and wouldn't disturb Mare with her questions. "When did you last catheterize yourself?"

TJ sighed. "Last night."

"You'll need to get up and see to yourself soon, love. You don't need a kidney infection on top of everything else."

"You sure know how to spoil the mood, don't you?"

Paula grinned cheekily. "That's what you hired me for. But seriously, Dr. Hammond said you needed to drink plenty of fluids and you can't do that for any period of time unless you..."

"I know, I know. But jeez, Paula, it sorta gets in the way."

"What does?" Mare mumbled.

"Nothing. Go back to sleep," replied TJ, a little embarrassed.

Mare's head poked up from where it was nestled on TJ's breast, blushing slightly as she saw Paula in the room. "Hi."

"I was just reminding TJ she has to look after a few personal issues." Paula was conscious that TJ didn't really like to talk about this aspect of her disability, but it was unlikely that Mare knew what the consequences would be if TJ neglected them.

"Oh," said Mare uncertainly, watching TJ who was now shooting daggers at Paula.

"And I thought you might like a snack and something to drink."

"Oh, yeah. I could do with a drink. However, first things first; I need to get cleaned up. My bed warmer here did too good a job last night. Paula, could you grab me the robe from the bathroom?"

"Sure, be right back." Paula stood and walked into the bathroom.

Mare gazed up at TJ's face, a small smile appearing on her lips. "I'd suggest we take a bath but I don't think we'd get very clean, do you?"

TJ grinned back at her. "No, I doubt we would. Besides, I really need to do my exercises. Sacha gets really pissed at me if I miss out on too many sessions. Bearing in mind that I only have to see her once a month now, I like to keep on her good side."

"Here you go, Mare. I dug a load of TJ's shampoo and stuff out of the cabinet for you to use." Paula handed over the terry cloth robe.

"Thanks." Mare leaned up and kissed TJ on the cheek. "See you soon." She slipped the robe on and made a dash for the bathroom.

"All right, boss-lady, you want to get your exercises done?" TJ nodded and pushed herself flat in the bed. "Here's a towel to cover your modesty, though after this morning's racket I don't know how you can profess to having any."

"Well, that'll teach you to work in my office, won't it?" TJ laid the towel over her middle so that her breasts and pelvic area were both covered before Paula started her lower leg exercises.

Paula took hold of TJ's right foot and slowly started to rotate the ankle to limber it up and help stop the joints from freezing due to disuse. Her skillful hands massaged TJ's foot before moving up to her calf. "I found out something interesting yesterday."

"Hmm?" inquired TJ who had her hands behind her head and was staring at the ceiling.

"Yeah, apparently Mare plays the piano." That got TJ's attention.

"Really?" TJ pushed herself upward so that she was resting on her elbows.

"Really."

TJ grinned. "I guess she might like the music room then." She let herself fall back to the bed, as Paula started to bend her knee to stretch the hamstrings.

"I guess she might at that." Paula could already see TJ's mind ticking over the possibilities.

Chapter 17

Wham! An arm came down across the side of Mare's face and bumped her nose, sending jolts of pain to her brain and waking her from a sound sleep. It took a couple of seconds for her to remember where she was as she threw her own arm over her head defensively. Then she remembered and jumped out of the bed that was vibrating from movement.

Moonlight shone through the double window, painting silver patches on everything it touched, and illuminating the body thrashing about on the bed. As Mare watched, aghast, TJ flopped over onto her side and raised her arms alongside her head, crossing her forearms toward the back of her head, cowering in a protective mode. "No, stop, stop!" TJ's pleading voice activated Mare and she ran around the bed and knelt at TJ's head, in front of the window.

"TJ, sweetheart, what's wrong?" Mare reached a tentative hand to caress her lover's head, but TJ shrank back from the touch.

"No! Stop! Please, stop!"

The light lay full on TJ's face and Mare could see that she still slept. She reached her hand to a shoulder and gently shook it. Suddenly, TJ's face changed from fear to anger and her voice from pleading to venomous.

"Stop it, you rotten bastard, stop it, or I'll kill you. I wish you were dead!" TJ started gasping and Mare ducked barely in time to avoid the fist that punched out at her.

She quickly took a stronger grasp of TJ's shoulder and shook her much harder, laying her hand along her beloved's face. "TJ, wake up. It's Mare. Wake up."

Blue eyes seething with hatred snapped open. Mare flinched and pulled her hand back, then, hesitating, she returned it to TJ's cheek. The eyes passed from hatred to confusion, to anguish. TJ saw a tiny trickle of blood coming from Mare's nose. "My God, I've hurt you," she whispered.

"No, no, I'm fine. Don't worry. Can you roll over and let me get back in bed?" TJ nodded and moved to make room. Mare climbed back in and scooted just a little higher than TJ so she could hold the raven head against her chest. She pulled TJ to her, kissed her hair and forehead and caressed her cheek and TJ put her arm across Mare's hip and up the side of her body.

"Do you have these nightmares very often?" Mare's soft voice conveyed so much concern that TJ felt an ache start in her chest as she barely nodded.

"Mare, your nose is bleeding. What did I do to you?"

The vet lifted a hand and wiped at her nose. She saw there was hardly any blood. "I'm perfectly all right, TJ. A wayward arm just kinda smacked me. But I'm okay. Now tell me about these nightmares. You were pleading for someone to stop. Then you were yelling and hollering. At your father?"

"Yeah." TJ's dry word puffed warm air against Mare's skin. "That was the only place I would plead with him... in my dreams. I wouldn't give him the satisfaction in real life. For a long time, I didn't yell, either. When I was about 14 I started yelling at him and threatening him. He only beat me harder and longer, but at least I had that small moment of satisfaction."

TJ could hear Mare's breathing getting ragged and the ache in her chest hurt even more. "Mare?"

"Yes, TJ?"

TJ took several deep breaths and then spoke in what Mare thought of as her "small" voice. A proud woman, TJ obviously found it uncomfortable to ask even minor favors. "I don't want to talk about my father. Can't we just go back to sleep? I'll be all right, now."

"We can do that. But tomorrow, you are going to call your counselor and set up an appointment for us to see him. Right?"

TJ knew that Mare had promised to go with her but she was touched to hear how readily she said "us." "Right." The dark head moved just enough to touch full lips to deep pink flesh. "Goodnight," she murmured against it. "I love you."

The soft contact sent a warmly pleasant flush through Mare and she tightened her arms and rested her chin against TJ's head. "Goodnight, my love."

****

Dawn's rays stole quietly in through the window, spread silently across the floor and crept upwards to raven-lashed eyes that opened to greet them. Meeting a blue unmatched in the early morning sky, they moved on to brighten golden threads in the head just above, before completing their task of bringing light to the entire room.

TJ lay without moving, her head still resting where she had pillowed it during the night's interrupted sleep, her lips a hairsbreadth away from a tempting morsel. She forced herself to ignore temptation, relishing the simple act of waking with her love beside her. *How many times have I wakened in the middle of the night, stressed out and sweating from that nightmare, only to lie here until morn-ing without rest? Last night, Mare changed all that. Her*

*presence soothed me and allowed me to beat it back from
my conscious mind. How wonderful it would be if she
could be here always. I wish I had the guts to ask her to
live here with me. Don't know if I could handle her saying
no. Maybe I better wait.*

"What's that serious look for?" Mare's still sleepy
voice rumbled against TJ's ear. The dark head tilted back
and smiling blue eyes sought the half-lidded green ones.

"Aha, you're awake!"

Mare reached her arms above her head and stretched
putting the object of TJ's temptation in motion. TJ's will
power evaporated and her mouth swooped down, accom-
plishing its aim.

"TJ!" Mare gasped, then laughed, and grabbed the
raven head, shaking it. "Let go!" By the second shake,
she realized she was helping TJ, not dissuading her, and
she dropped her arms in surrender.

TJ put her hands to good use and Mare's voice
sounded breathless. "Don't you think we're being a little
decadent, here?" Without releasing the hold her mouth
had, TJ nodded up and down vigorously and Mare got the
giggles. Starting to giggle, too, TJ let go and the two
women collapsed beside each other, laughing out loud until
they couldn't laugh any more.

"Aahhh," TJ breathed, wiping her eyes then grabbing
her sides. "I haven't laughed that hard in years."

"Neither have I, not since college." Mare reached for
a tissue from the bedside table and wiped TJ's eyes, then
her own.

"Let's get up. I have a surprise to show you after
breakfast."

Mare cocked her head and grimaced. "You know I
don't like to be teased."

"Oh, yeah? That's not how you acted yesterday," TJ
grinned.

"Well... that was different." Mare got up off the bed
and walked toward the bathroom. "There's a time and
place for that kind of teasing. I'll run us a bath." She

turned around and grinned. "Now there's a perfect pairing of sentences if I ever heard one."

TJ, thoroughly enjoying watching Mare's progress to the bathroom, shook her head. "And you called me decadent."

* * * * * * * * * *

TJ and Mare got to the kitchen in time to have breakfast with Erin and Paula. They took a little kidding about hibernating out of season then TJ brought up a few stories from Erin and Paula's past and breakfast was a lively time. Everyone was smiling by the time the two partners went off to their duties.

At one point during the meal, TJ had whispered something to Erin and she had nodded. Mare's curiosity was at fever pitch and her patience was being sorely tried. As soon as the other two had departed, she asked TJ what the surprise was.

TJ rubbed her chin and furrowed her brow as if in deep thought. "I don't know if it's time to show you, yet."

"TJ, you are going to be in big, big trouble if you don't tell me what it is." Mare tried to look fierce, but it wasn't working. After a day and a half of a wall-to-wall love-in, every time she looked at TJ she saw her gorgeous unclothed body. Which was absolutely marvelous, but also absolutely disconcerting. *Wonder if she's having the same problem?* The thought made a blush move up Mare's cheeks. TJ ran her tongue from one side of her lips to the other and back again, a glint of pleasure showing in the depths of her eyes. *Oh, you betcha,* thought Mare and rolled her eyes.

Laughter spurted from TJ's throat. "Come on, I can't tell you the surprise; I'll have to show you. Follow me." She took off toward the living room with Mare behind her.

On the far side of the living room was a double set of French doors, heavily curtained. TJ opened them and pushed them forward, then wheeled into the exposed room, stopped and turned the chair toward Mare so she could watch her expression.

Mare's whole face lit up as she walked to the grand piano sitting near the center of a room 30 feet long and 30 feet wide. The keyboard cover receded into the piano as she lifted it. The top of the piano had already been raised and she ran her fingers reverently along the keys, filled with a sensual pleasure by their melodious tones. She turned her awed gaze to a smiling TJ. "May I?"

TJ found she couldn't talk past the lump that suddenly formed in her throat. *She looks like a kid in a candy factory.* She twisted her lips into a smile and nodded.

Mare sat at the piano and, as was her usual custom, ran through some light pieces and exercises to limber her fingers. Then she played in earnest. This was the finest piano she had ever played and she lost herself in enjoyment of it.

TJ closed her eyes and let herself float with the music. They sat for hours, transported together to an area of the mind that resonated with beautiful sounds, one leading with nimble fingers, the other following with sensual delight. Finally, coming back to earth, Mare halted.

TJ wheeled over next to her and engaged her eyes with intense blue. "How come you never told me you played the piano? That was magnificent." *I can see we're going to have fun getting to know each other, Mare, in more ways than one.*

Mare smiled, her face suffused with peaceful energy. "Thank you, TJ. What a pleasure it is to perform on such a fine instrument. How did you find out I played?"

"Paula had to hear it from Doc Hunt. Remember he said something to you about a broken arm or finger hurting your piano playing?"

"Yeah, now I remember. And Paula picked right up on that, huh?"

"She and Erin play guitar. Guess that struck a chord with her."

Mare wrinkled her nose. "Bad, TJ. Really bad."

"Sorry, I couldn't resist."

"Do you play an instrument?"

"Uh... no, I don't."

Mare never missed a trick. "What's the "Uh" for?"

Paula had come back from her journey to town. She walked into the room from the doorway where she had been standing for a minute. "TJ sings. And don't let her tell you she doesn't. She has a gorgeous voice."

Mare's eyes widened and she inclined her head toward TJ with a smile. "So, Miss Meridian, what would you like to sing for us? Hum a few bars and I'll pick it up."

"C'mon, ladies, give me a break. I'm just getting over a sore throat."

Mare looked at Paula and raised her eyebrows. Paula shrugged. "She's right, I guess we have to hear her another time."

"But she called us ladies. Are we gonna let her get away with that?"

Paula shook her head. "How about when she does sing, she has to sing at least eight songs?"

"Sounds good to me. Think her throat should be more than okay in about a week?"

"Yeah, that sounds good. Same day next week, in the evening."

TJ's head was swinging back and forth from Paula to Mare as this conversation progressed. "You two are worse than a hanging judge. At least he makes a show of being fair before he condemns the prisoner."

Paula smiled wickedly. "Yeah, but we aren't gonna hang you."

Mare snorted. "I'm not making that promise. I haven't heard her sing, yet."

"On that note, I think we better break for lunch." TJ laughed as the other two groaned.

****

After a spirited lunch, Mare insisted that TJ call the counselor for an appointment. The dark-haired woman sighed, but she followed through on her promise and an appointment was made for four days away.

That evening, Paula and Erin had propped TJ in the corner of the couch before going to their own quarters and Mare was lying there with her head in TJ's lap, luxuriating in her nearness. TJ played with her love's golden hair, wrapping and unwrapping it around her fingers, as she gazed into Mare's face, appreciating her beauty.

"I'll have to be going home, soon." Mare's disappointment sounded in her words.

"Mare, how hard would it be to run your practice from somewhere besides your home?"

Mare was totally relaxed and missed the significance of the question. "Why would I want to do that? Everything I need is there."

"I was... sort of... that is..."

TJ's stumbling caused the light to dawn. "Are you suggesting that I operate my practice from here?"

"Uh... well... only if you wanted to." *TJ, you were going to wait to ask her, remember?*

Mare saw that TJ was embarrassed and she certainly didn't want to hurt her feelings, but she couldn't see how that could be done without a lot of problems.

Mare sat up and edged as close to her love as she could get, putting her shoulder against TJ's and taking hold of her near hand. "TJ, if I didn't have any other responsibilities, I wouldn't hesitate to take you up on that offer." She raised the strong hand and kissed it. "But I don't see how I can right now. Maybe when everything gets going and the economy improves, I can afford to get an assistant. Until that happens, I have to stay home."

She held TJ's hand against her face and looked into those blue, blue eyes. "No one's any sorrier about that than I am."

"I could lend you the money to hire someone."

"Thanks, but you know I can't do that. I want to pay my own way. You know what pride is. My pride won't let me do it." That was the perfect choice of words to explain her decision without hurting TJ. The head of Meridian Corporation did know what pride is, and she accepted that as a valid reason.

TJ reached her other hand up to Mare's cheek. "I want to kiss you, but you are going to have to come to me. If I lean over, I will fall for you, literally."

Mare laughed at the little joke, knowing that TJ used it to hide her disappointment. The vet moved so that her body pinned TJ against the corner and made it possible for them to kiss. The push of one body against the other was like kicking embers into flame, a flame that was fed by the meeting of their mouths and the movements of their hands. Time ceased to exist.

Chapter
18

Mare had heard both Paula and Erin speak of TJ's dislike of the counseling sessions but she hadn't realized what a profound effect the mere notion of going to one had on the woman. The days leading up to the session were a lesson that Mare wouldn't soon forget. TJ was a kaleidoscope of mood swings; one moment she was on a high, the next she was a brooding recluse. Even Mare had a hard time shaking her out of the depressive attitude. Paula and Erin, however, assured her that this was the normal build-up to her meetings with Peter. Mare had to wonder whether her therapist wasn't a big part of TJ's reluctance to talk about her problems.

Mare suggested that she drive TJ to the session by herself, but Erin said that it probably would be better if she drove. Mare would be free to concentrate on TJ, especially if Peter actually got TJ to open up about her father. Though Mare was under the increasing impression that Peter wasn't going to get much enlightenment out of the resistant TJ, she agreed.

Mare spent the night at the ranch prior to the appointment. TJ was in a quiet mood and they retired to bed early, where the two women were content to lay in each other's arms, savoring the closeness their relationship had brought them.

The drive into Sharlesburg the next morning was a subdued affair. TJ sat and stared out of the window for most of the drive, giving one-word answers to the questions she was asked as Mare and Erin tried to draw her into the conversation.

Erin jumped out of the van and grabbed TJ's chair from the back. Mare clambered out and looked at the imposing building before her. An old, red brick building four floors high, it had a small well-kept lawn in the front. Steps led up to the main entrance and to the side was a ramp for disabled users. Mare frowned at this. The ramp, though advertised for use by the disabled, was quite steep and Mare knew that even with TJ's incredible upper body strength, she would have difficulty negotiating it by herself. *I dislike this place already and I don't even have to be here; no wonder TJ hates it. I hope Peter is better than he sounds.* Mare looked over at TJ as Erin wheeled her around the van. She reached over and squeezed her hand.

"You okay?" she asked with concern.

TJ squeezed her hand back. "Yeah. Come on, let's just get this over with." Erin, taking the hint, turned TJ's chair and pushed her up the ramp to the building.

Mare's first impressions of Peter's waiting room were good. His secretary was a discreet distance from where his patients sat, allowing them reasonable privacy to talk, and the room was brightly decorated with various scenes painted on the walls. Mare especially liked the one of the sailboat on the ocean at sunset; it had a soothing quality to it. The chairs were comfortable and gracefully spaced. These touches, together with the varying plant life and the light from the large windows, made the room quite pleasant.

Peter's secretary was a white-haired lady, mid fifties in age by Mare's guess. She greeted both TJ and Erin by name. She asked the usual pleasantries and informed Peter that they were waiting. TJ immediately wheeled herself over to the window that looked out the back of the building towards the nearby park.

The park was a field of grass and walkways hidden within large stands of trees. The residents of the city were making the most of the warm and sunny day, playing ball and lying around the recreational areas.

Erin stayed by the desk, chatting with the secretary, while Mare went to keep TJ company, sliding into the seat nearest to the tense, brooding woman. Mare knew that anything she said wasn't going to ease the tension and trepidation that TJ was feeling, only her continued presence could do that. She let her hand rest on TJ's arm, just letting her know she was nearby.

A door opened and Mare turned to see a medium-sized gentleman with short, brown hair, beard and wire-rimmed spectacles walk from the inner room. He glanced over toward her and TJ but made no greeting, walking immediately to Erin. They had a quiet conversation and Mare saw Erin gesture across toward them.

Mare's hackles rose. From the description that TJ had given during one of their midnight chats she knew that this was Peter. The fact that he hadn't even bothered to say anything to TJ but had headed straight to Erin spoke volumes about his attitude towards his patient. Mare patted TJ's arm then stood and walked over to where Erin and the doctor were talking, catching the tail end of the conversation.

"...well, I don't really think that is appropriate," said the therapist as Mare approached.

Erin looked over his shoulder and beckoned Mare forward. "Peter, I'd like you to meet Mare Gillespie."

Mare strode forward and held her hand out. "Doctor," she said as she shook his hand, which totally enveloped hers.

"Miss Gillespie," he said in return.

"I was just explaining to Peter why I thought he might make more headway with TJ if you were with her today," said Erin.

"And I was just explaining to Miss Scott why I thought that wouldn't be a good idea," replied Peter.

"And why would that be?" inquired Mare, raising her eyebrow in imitation of TJ's favored expression.

"Because, Miss Gillespie..."

"Please call me Mare," interrupted the vet.   Erin grinned, seeing another of TJ's tactics in action.

"Because, Mare, patients often feel inhibited when close friends or members of the family are included in this type of session. I'm trying to get TJ to open up about feelings that obviously cause her some distress." Peter had a placating look on his face.

"I see," said Mare, seemingly pondering his words. "And it makes no difference to you that I already know the details you are trying to get TJ to tell you? Or the fact that I wouldn't be here unless TJ had requested my presence?" Peter opened his mouth to reply but Mare wouldn't let him speak. "In fact, why don't we ask your patient exactly what she'd prefer?" Mare paused in her tirade. "It occurs to me, Doctor, that you would get a lot further in your sessions if TJ felt at ease with you, but she obviously doesn't. I really can't say I blame her seeing as you haven't even acknowledged her presence yet." Mare ended pointedly, staring Peter in the face.   Erin had to hide her mouth behind her hand to prevent Peter from seeing the grin that was spreading.

"There is no need to be confrontational, Miss Gillespie..."

"Mare," interrupted the vet once again.

"Yes, Mare. As I said there is no need to be confrontational..."

"I don't believe I was being confrontational at all; I was merely stating a fact. Because, let me tell you, Peter, if I were the one sitting in that chair and the first thing you did when you walked into the room was to walk over and talk to my caregiver, and not to me, I'd be a little put out. In fact I might even think that you were checking up on me, or maybe I'd be paranoid enough to think that you actually had her watching me. Tell me, just how would that help me to trust you?"

"Do you have any idea why Miss Meridian is in therapy?"

Mare opened her mouth to speak, but a familiar voice answered for her. "Of course she does, Peter. Why do you think I asked her along?" All eyes turned to TJ as she wheeled herself across to them. "Now, shall we get on with this session or can I leave this hellhole and go home?"

Peter stood and watched TJ, weighing the pros and cons of arguing the matter with her. He knew from past experience that if TJ decided she was going, then nobody was going to be able to stop her. She had even managed it when he persuaded Paula to leave TJ here while she dealt with a business meeting in town. He thought he had TJ cornered and unable to leave, since Paula wasn't around. How wrong he had been. She pulled out her cell phone and within minutes had a limousine and driver outside waiting for her. If he expected her to stay, he had come to learn that challenging TJ's authority over her own life and decisions was a mistake.

"Okay, then. Let's go into the office." He swept his arm before him, indicating that Mare should precede him.

The small entourage entered the room and Erin watched the door closing firmly behind them. She looked over to the secretary and smiled. "I'll just wait here, then."

Mare studied the office as she entered, noting Peter's impressive display of diplomas from varying schools of medicine and psychology. *Shame his bedside manner isn't as impressive.* TJ wheeled herself over near the window as Peter sat behind the desk. The positioning of the players intrigued Mare. TJ was subtly telling everybody that she didn't want to be here, that the room felt as though it was imprisoning her, hence the window positioning. And Peter was obviously intimidated by TJ. His sitting behind the desk immediately put a barrier between him and her. For someone supposed to be breaking down TJ's emotional barriers, putting a physical one in the way didn't seem too wise. *I wonder why these two are so uncomfortable with each other?*

"So, TJ," said Peter, trying to get the session started, "how have you been since we last spoke?"

"Fine," she replied, still looking out of the window. Mare walked over to her and put a hand on her shoulder. TJ looked up and smiled, feeling Mare's welcome caress.

"You gonna stop dreaming out the window and come join us?" asked Mare, gently reminding TJ that she was supposed to take an active part in the session, not just give one-word answers. TJ sighed but took off the brakes and wheeled away from the window, closer to Peter's desk. Mare took a seat nearby.

"Sorry. I'm fine, thank you, Peter," TJ said, shooting a quick glance at Mare.

Peter sat back in his chair, not quite knowing what to make of the exchange between the two women. There was certainly a dynamic working between them. And he hadn't seen TJ Meridian respond that benignly to anybody before. Maybe having Mare Gillespie here was a good idea, after all. "Do you have anything in particular you'd like to discuss today?"

TJ remained silent till she heard Mare start to move behind her. *Go on spit it out. You know Mare is gonna hit you with those eyes, if you don't.* "Well," she spared another look at Mare, seeing her loving support. "You've wanted to know about my father, so I guess we can start there today." TJ felt her hand creep in Mare's direction, needing more than her gaze to bolster her courage, now that she had said it. She felt the strong, yet gentle, squeeze of her lover's hand as she grasped hold.

TJ's statement astonished Peter. After months of trying to get TJ to open up about her father and finally giving up on it, here she was offering the information

The next hour and a half flew by for Mare as she sat supporting her lover through the ordeal of telling Peter what her father had done to her through her life. Mare's perception of Peter changed over the session as well. It wasn't that he wasn't good at his job, he just had no idea of how to handle TJ. He obviously thought of TJ as an emotionally vulnerable and fragile person. While in some ways that was true, TJ reacted badly to anybody treating her that way.

Now that he had something to work with, though, he wasn't letting TJ get away with skirting around the issues of her father. Although TJ didn't particularly like that he wouldn't let her hide, neither did she try to be obstructive. Throughout the session, Mare felt TJ's hold on her emotions waver; the tense grip on her hand didn't loosen at all. Mare kept her eyes on her partner's face, so that whenever she looked over she saw her love looking back.

For TJ the session was the longest she'd ever been in. Even when she had been in the hospital and physically unable to get away from the sessions, she had been able to tune them out of her mind. Now, though, with Mare by her side, she wasn't able to leave the office when things started to hurt and Mare's constant grip on her hand kept her mind grounded in reality.

She spoke of life in the Meridian household and the constant battle to be true to herself in the midst of her father's abuse. She spoke about things that she hadn't wanted to remember. She told of the times she had ended up in her father's doctor's office, being patched up from the vicious beatings; the concerned look in the doctor's eyes, while refusing to report her father; the time she had been hit so hard that her arm had been broken.

When the hospital inquired how it happened, her mother told them she fell off of her horse. The strange looks and whispers of the nursing staff told a different story, but this was the all-powerful Tom Meridian they were talking about, he wouldn't beat his daughter, would he?

When TJ felt her emotional resolve weaken at the constant onslaught of memories, she felt Mare's presence and continued on.

Peter was having a similar reaction to the session; his whole demeanor toward TJ was changing. When he had taken on the case referral he thought that her attempt at suicide was nothing more than a rich girl's being unable to cope with what life had thrown at her. But from what he was finding out now, it was clear to him that he had completely misjudged the situation. To survive the abuse she suffered at the hands of her father, TJ had built an incredible strength of will. When that was added to her need to protect her brother from similar abuse, her suicide attempt was painted in an entirely different light.

TJ's attempt hadn't really been a cry for help; it was a desperate need to rejoin the one person in her life who had shown her unconditional love. He looked over at Mare and adjusted that thought. *One person till now, that is. We may have a long road ahead of us, TJ, but at least now we are headed in the right direction.*

* * * * * * * * *

The drive home was another silent study of contemplation. This time, TJ had insisted on riding in the back with Mare. Legs on the back seat, torso enclosed, she felt safe after pouring out her innermost secrets.

Mare sat with her arms lovingly wrapped around her, accepting TJ's need for silence. Concentrating on TJ's need for comfort.

Erin drove, her eyes occasionally straying to the rear-view mirror, smiling at the sight of the two lovers embraced.

* * * * * * * * *

Mare had just dropped her bag in its nook in the kitchen when the phone rang. She grabbed it and spouted her usual greeting. "Doctor Gillespie."

The caller's slight hesitation told the vet at once who it was and a smile broke out as warmth spread through her.

"Hi, Mare. Are you going to be home in the next half hour?" TJ's voice oozed into her body like oil into a wick, ready to be set aflame.

"For you, anytime, anywhere."

"Sure, tell me that sometime when you have a sick cow to take care of," TJ kidded. "I want to stop by; I have some information about your father."

The vet came quickly back to earth. "What? Have they found him? Who is he? Where..."

"Yes, we found him. I'll tell you all about it as soon as I get there."

"TJ! I don't have a lot of patience."

The low chuckle sent a shiver of yearning through Mare. "I know, my love, but I don't want to give it to you in bits and pieces over the phone. I'll be right over as fast as I can."

"Okay, but hurry, please?"

"You know I will."

After she hung up, Mare got a ready-made salad and a soda from the fridge and had a quick supper, too fidgety to even taste what she ate. *They found him! My father's alive!*

Afterwards, a need to find some respite from her jangling nerves led her to the piano. She ran through a few light pieces to limber up her fingers, then launched into more robust compositions. Engrossed in her music, she didn't hear the door opening or wheels coming through the kitchen.

Mare finished the piece she was playing and stopped. Clapping hands from behind startled her and she swiveled around rapidly on the piano seat. TJ and Erin both wore large smiles and were clapping vigorously. Mare blushed self-consciously. "Hi, TJ, Erin." She walked over to TJ and kissed her welcoming lips. "C'mon into the kitchen. What would you like to drink, Erin? Soda, lemonade, beer?"

"TJ, tell me what you've heard about my father before I have a nervous breakdown!" While she talked, Mare held a pitcher of lemonade up and raised her eyebrows to Erin. The curly-headed blonde mouthed the word "beer" and the vet opened a bottle, handed it to her and opened two more for TJ and herself. She pulled a chair out of the way so TJ could wheel close to the table. Then she sat in the chair, scooted up next to TJ, and Erin took a seat across from them.

TJ pulled a large envelope from the pocket on the side of the chair and laid it in front of Mare. "Take a look."

With trembling hands, the vet pulled out the contents of the envelope and put them on the table. She grabbed the picture that was lying on top and stared at it for several long moments. It was a professional portrait of a distinguished looking, sandy-haired man with emerald-green eyes exactly like Mare's. Even the shape of their faces was the same except the man's was a little longer than Mare's.

"He looks like me. I mean, I look like him. I looked at every male in that graduating class and I didn't see him." Mare ran her fingers over the picture as if she could feel the face whose paper replica she touched. Her questioning eyes looked up at TJ. "Why couldn't I find him?"

"Your mother didn't lie to you, but she didn't tell you the whole truth, either. Your father and mother didn't go to the same college. My people ran through everybody at her college, then started on every college within 50 miles of it and finally found him."

Moving the picture off to the side, Mare's eyes fell on the name at the top of the first paper beneath it. "Michael Thomas Gillis, MD. My father." Mare gazed up at TJ and smiled through the tears that trickled down her cheeks. "He's a doctor! And look at his name... same initials as mine and a very similar last name. I guess Mother really did love him."

While Mare shuffled through the papers and pictures, Erin finished her beer and got up. She whispered something into TJ's ear and the dark head nodded. The she picked up a box of tissues from a counter and brought them to Mare, taking several out and handing them to her before setting the box within easy reach. Erin bent down and kissed her on the cheek. "I'm going home for a while. I'll stop back about 10 o'clock for TJ. I'm really happy for you, Mare. I hope things work out well for you and your father." Mare smiled her thanks. Erin patted her on the shoulder and left.

The investigators had taken numerous photos of the doctor, his office, his home, even pictures of him entering and leaving the hospital where he practiced. TJ looked on with an affectionate smile as Mare's face lit with excitement at every new picture she saw. *You have such an expressive face, my love. I delight in watching it reveal the poetry of your heart.* TJ's mouth curled higher. *You even bring out the poetry in me!*

Mare picked up the sheaf of papers and made an attempt to read them. She shook her head and turned toward the eyes watching her so tenderly. "I'm too nervous. Would you read it to me, please?" She placed the papers in the extended hand, sat back and listened to TJ's warm voice fill her in on her father's life history.

TJ read through Dr. Gillis' medical school attendance, internship, and specialization. As she narrated the report on the doctor's specialization, three words jumped out at her. They had startled her at her first reading of the report and she still stumbled over them. "Dr. Gillis specialized in neurosurgery and has won many awards. He is a recognized authority in the field of... spi... spinal cord injury."

Mare put an arm on the table and leaned forward to look into TJ's face. "Did you say spinal cord injury?"

"Yes. Kind of eerie, isn't it?" Her wide-eyed look swept to meet Mare's inquiring gaze. "SCI. Your father is a recognized authority in the field of spinal cord injury."

"My gosh, TJ, I'm getting goose bumps."

"Yeah, I did, too."

The two women sat looking at each other for a moment, then Mare patted TJ's arm. "Keep reading, okay? I want to hear everything there is to hear. We can follow up on that later."

TJ finished the career investigation and proceeded to the personal history. Mare's father had made his career his life. He had never married and lived in a large, well-appointed house in an elite area bordering Dorburton Lakes, just outside Springerly, the city of his practice.

"Springerly's only a couple hours' drive from here." Mare's face and voice turned wistful. "All these years, my father's been just a couple of hours away."

Mare's expression tore at TJ's heart and she returned the pat on the arm. "But you've found him now, Mare. You know what they say, 'Better late than never.'" Then she grinned. "And he's wealthy, too."

Mare mused about that for all of three seconds. "Lucky me," she scoffed.

"And listen to this, Mare." TJ handed her a flyer as she continued to read aloud. "A student of classical music, Dr. Gillis gives semi-annual piano recitals on behalf of SCI patients who need financial assistance."

Mare's eyes beamed as she looked up from the flyer. "And his next recital is only a couple of days away. I have to go. Just think, he's a doctor, he plays the piano, and we look just alike. I can hardly believe it."

Looking to TJ for advice, she asked. "Now what do I do? Do you think he would want to know that he has a daughter?"

TJ's sweet smile wrapped itself around Mare's heart. "I guarantee that once he knows you, he will love you. But I don't think you should drop in on him unannounced; it's safer not to presume anything." Picking up the loose papers, TJ jogged them together, laid them on top of the envelope they came in and placed the pictures on top of them.

"I think going to the recital might help you find a little more comfort with the idea of meeting him. But I think he needs that chance, too. How about if I talk with him, show him a report just like this one that explains the highlights of your background and the situation, and let him decide if he wants to meet you?"

Mare, her face a study in serious concern, nodded. "Could you do that before the recital? Then maybe we could meet soon afterwards."

"Do you really think I should approach him right now? This will be an emotional moment; it has to be. That might disturb his recital."

"Oh, no, TJ. Music flows from emotion. The stronger the musician's feelings, the stronger the performance."

"All right, you're the expert. I'll try to set up a meeting as soon as possible. My team has already gathered information on you."

"You've had people checking up on me?" Mare frowned, not entirely comfortable with that idea.

TJ looked away, a little abashed. "It was before you even set foot on the ranch, Mare. Before I knew you. I mean, you were just a name to me and we knew the people in Meridianville wouldn't be happy to see me here." She glanced sideways at Mare whose eyes were still on TJ's face. "Look, I told you I'm not an especially trusting person, okay?"

Mare's frown slowly lightened and she nodded. Then she poked TJ's side. "Just don't ever do it again."

TJ threw a hand down to protect her ribs, and quirked an eyebrow. "But the report didn't tell me half what I've learned through personal contact." Then she grinned, turning it into a leer. "Especially how emotion strengthens a musician's performance."

Mollified, Mare wrinkled her nose and grinned back. "Very funny."

TJ looked at her watch. "Hey, it's nine-fifty, Erin will be here in about ten minutes. Do you want to play?"

"Umm. I thought you'd never ask." In one continuous motion, Mare swung around, pulled the wheelchair arm out of the way, reached under TJ's shirt and zeroed in on her intended objective.

TJ gasped, startled by her body's unhesitating response. "I meant the piano."

Transferring to a seat on TJ's lap, Mare growled in pleasure at her lover's reaction. "Quiet, woman, we only have nine more minutes." A moist mouth smothered TJ's laugh.

Chapter
19

The nurse came through the waiting room door, holding it open with one hand. "TJ Meridian?"

TJ laid down the book she had been leafing through and steered the electric wheelchair through the doorway. The nurse went ahead of her and held open an office door. Smiling at TJ, she said, "Dr. Gillis will be with you soon. Please make yourself comfortable."

Does every office in the world have buff walls? TJ wondered with a grin. But the yellow birch furniture, dark gold rug and dark green upholstery gave the pleasant room a light warmth. Sunny prints of several master works dotted the walls, balancing the black and white austerity of the framed diplomas and awards.

Within minutes, the doctor entered the room. He walked over to TJ and shook her hand. "Miss Meridian, how are you?" TJ was momentarily disconcerted by the direct gaze of the emerald green eyes of her lover, ensconced in a different face.

"I'm just fine, Doctor." TJ laid a large envelope on the desk as the doctor moved behind it and sat down.

"Your message intrigued me. I do remember Jane Arnold, very well. I was saddened to hear that she died last year. You said you had a letter from her that you wished to give me?"

"Actually, Doctor, I have a copy of a letter from her. It's not addressed to you, but when you read it, you will understand why I've brought it to you." TJ handed the copy to the sandy-haired man and watched as he read it.

At first he looked naturally puzzled. As he read a small smile appeared, then his face went slack and his jaw dropped. When he finished he set the letter on the desk and sat back in his chair, his eyes still down and his breathing rapid. After a minute, he looked up at TJ and his eyes showed the struggle he was having to comprehend what he had just read. "We had a daughter? Jane and I had a daughter?"

TJ nodded. With his elbow on the desk and his chin resting on his hand, Dr. Gillis sat there thinking. Suddenly his eyes jerked up to TJ's and he asked, "Is it...are you...?"

"No, not me." TJ's soft voice held his attention. Reaching into the envelope, she drew out its contents and laid them in front of the confused man. Mare's picture was on top.

"My God, she looks just like me." He dropped his fingers to the portrait and ran them over its surface, just as his daughter had done to his. "But she's beautiful."

Twisting her lips, TJ managed to get one word out. "Perfectly."

"Where is she? Can I see her? Can we meet? What's her name? Where does she live?"

TJ had a terrible time keeping a straight face. *He even talks like Mare.* "We'll make arrangements for you to meet. I've given you the answers to most of your other questions in the papers you have there, under the picture."

He pulled the papers out and read the name aloud. "Mary Theresa Gillespie." His voice broke a little as he made the same discovery Mare had made. "Same initials... almost the same last name." He put his head down against his hand. "Jane, Jane, Jane." His eyes came up to meet TJ's sympathetic ones. "She always was independent. A remarkable woman. And I know she meant well, but she cheated both of us out of a lifetime together." Then he smiled. "But she left me a daughter. What's she like? Do you know her well?"

TJ finally let her smile break across her face. "Yes, I know her very well. She's a remarkable woman, too, and a special favorite of mine. You'll love her. We all do."

His eyes lit up as he read further. "She's a veterinarian! A doctor, too! And she plays the piano. Amazing." He shook his head at the similarities that were showing up. "When can I meet her?"

"You have a concert tomorrow, right?" The doctor nodded. "She wants to come to the concert, check you out, so to speak. Maybe, if she's willing, you could meet together after the concert."

"Yes! How many will be in your party?"

"Four of us. I have two friends who accompany me to public functions."

"I have a townhouse directly across from the hall. After the concert, a small reception is being held there for a few of my friends. Please bring your whole party and we will have a chance to meet with less pressure on both of us. Having her friends around will, I hope, make her feel more comfortable.

"That's very thoughtful, Doctor. I know Mare will appreciate it."

"Mare? Is that what she's called?" He smiled and nodded to himself. "I'll have to remember that."

"I'll say good-bye, Doctor. We'll see you tomorrow evening at the recital."

Dr. Gillis came around the end of the desk and took TJ's hand in both of his. Instead of shaking it, he raised it to his lips and kissed it. "Thank you, Miss Meridian. You've brought me the happiest news I've ever had."

The nurse appeared, summoned by a silent bell. "Miss Hansen, please show Miss Meridian out. Good-bye."

"Good-bye, Doctor."

The door closed and the doctor sat again at his desk.

Thoughts of Jane wandered through his mind. The only woman he had ever loved. *In all these years, I never met a woman who could chase your memory from my heart. Now I find, too late, that you left me because you loved me.* The tears he had managed to stifle during the meeting now ran down his cheeks, unchecked. *But you gave me a daughter. I have a daughter. Thank you, Jane.*

****

TJ decided to lay on the grand treatment for the occasion of attending Doctor Gillis' recital. She provided one of the company helicopters to fly all four women to Springerly and directed the pilot to wait to take them home. A folding wheelchair, carried at all times by the helicopter, ferried TJ between vehicles. After they arrived at the airfield near Springerly, a Meridian limousine took them to the concert hall where TJ had reserved a box. The light shining forth from Mare's face and eyes when she squeezed TJ's hand in gratitude made every gesture worthwhile.

Paula had arranged for two Meridian employees to be waiting at the concert hall with an electric wheelchair. As the limousine approached their destination, the driver called ahead to alert them to TJ's imminent arrival.

The women being assisted from the limousine drew close attention from the bystanders, people standing behind police barricades who had come to watch the cream of society gather. Each attractive in her own right, together the four made an impressive array. Necks craned to see as first Paula, wearing a deep rose gown, then Erin, in shimmering burgundy, emerged, followed by Mare, resplendent in antique gold. The chair was wheeled to the door of the limo and all eyes watched as the two attendants assisted the last occupant from the limo into the chair. TJ was dressed in a cocktail length sheath, with the bottom two thirds of the material black and the top third of a blue that matched her eyes. Thin, black, spaghetti straps held the top, while the neckline plunged to a diamond shaped opening, tied together above her breasts with a thin, black string that matched the straps.

Once settled in the chair, TJ raised her eyes to Mare's and smiled. She knew the vet was so excited at the prospect of seeing and meeting her father that she could barely stand still, so she steered the chair right up to her. "Ready?"

"As ready as I'll ever be." Paula and Erin moved in behind them and they entered the hall and were escorted to the box. All the extra chairs had been removed to make access easier for TJ so she moved right up to the rail and halted. The others sat and looked out over the assembly.

"How were you able to get this box on such short notice? These have to be the best seats in the hall." Mare marveled at the perfect view of the stage from the box, which slightly overhung one end of it.

TJ's eyes twinkled. "I had Erin check out the person who had it and she found out he's a local horse breeder. I offered to share our box at the Kentucky Derby with him and his guests, in return for letting me rent this one from him. He jumped at the chance and here we are."

Smiling, Mare shook her head. "I'll never get used to how easily you seem to make things happen. Or how you think of every tiny detail." Just as she finished speaking, an usher arrived and handed her a corsage of white orchids. Mare's eyebrows went up as she looked from the flowers to TJ.

The dark head swung back and forth. "That's not my doing. Read the card."

Mare pulled out the card from the envelope that rested on the florist box. "To my dearest daughter from your fa..." Mare stopped as her breath caught. She bit down on her lip and tried to blink back tears but it was a losing battle.

Erin reached in her bag, handed her some tissues and patted her arm. Hearing a suspicious sniff from Paula, she turned to give her some, too.

TJ put a hand on Mare's arm and tried to chuckle. "Hey, cut that out, you'll ruin your makeup." Seeing TJ's brimming eyes, Erin handed her some tissues, too. Then she took one and daubed her own eyes.

The curly-haired blonde reached for the florist box. "Here, Mare, let me pin this on for you." The greenery that nestled against the orchids was the perfect touch, forming a beautiful border against the antique gold gown and deepening the color in Mare's green eyes.

Mare sniffled and tried to laugh. "Boy, we sure look like a happy group." She jumped as the lights dimmed then came back up. A nervous wreck, she grabbed the hand lying on her arm and squeezed it between her own.

Smiling, TJ watched every movement of her love's face as the lights dimmed again, the stage lights came up and Dr. Gillis walked out for his bow. Dressed in a long-tailed tuxedo, he looked handsome and youthful. He walked to the piano and just before he sat down, he looked up at their box, nodded his head and smiled. Had the size of their hands been reversed, TJ would have been suffering some broken bones. *Oh, Mare, I hope your father's a decent man. He certainly seems like one. If he's not, he'll answer to me. No one I know will ever go through what I went through.*

The music filled their minds and hearts as it filled the hall. *My father plays well; really, really well.* Mare couldn't take her eyes from him. She had an irrational feeling that if she looked away, he would disappear.

Because Mare held her hand, TJ found herself in an awkward position. She tried to stay still to avoid inter-rupting Mare's concentration, but finally, just at intermis-sion, a cramping shoulder forced her to move. Mare tore her eyes from her departing father and swept them to TJ. Suddenly, she realized she was crushing TJ's hand, or try-ing to.

She raised the strong hand to her lips for a quick kiss and whispered, "I'm so sorry. I didn't mean to hurt you."

"I'll probably never write again with that hand, but it was worth it." TJ's smile, filled with love, made Mare's heart flip-flop.

"Oh, TJ, he's wonderful, isn't he?"

"Yes, he is. Are you ready to meet him?"

"Oh, yes. I can't wait. And I can't thank you enough for finding him for me." *How was I the lucky one, TJ? What did you see in me that made you fall in love with me? Someday, I'll have to ask you that.*

"I'm just thrilled for you that my people were able to find him. If he had changed his name and moved away, like your mother did, it would have been a lot tougher."

"Poor Mother. She had too much pride for her own good." Mare looked sad for a moment, but then she shook it off. She gave a tug to the hand she still held. "Sort of like you, sometimes."

"Me?" TJ laughed. "Never. And you can stop that snorting, Paula. You're supposed to act like a lady tonight."

Now Erin snorted and all four women laughed.

The lights dimmed again and the hall hushed as Mare's father reentered the stage to complete his performance—and to bring him closer to meeting his daughter.

* * * * * * * * * *

Numerous quiet conversations spread a blanket of warmth through the reception. "This has a good feel to it. The people seem happy and friendly." TJ tried to divert Mare's nervous impatience with small talk. Again, she had latched onto a hand, but this time she stroked it rather than squeezed.

"Yes, yes. I wonder what's taking him so long?"

"I'm sure he had some backstage visitors, Mare. He'll be here soon. Have you thought about what you are going to do when he comes through the door?"

Erin and Paula were just choosing drinks and hors
d'oeuvres from a series of trays brought around by white-
jacketed servers. They handed drinks to TJ and Mare.

"I'm not sure what to do. Have you any suggestions?"
Mare took a reflex sip, totally unaware of what was in the
glass.

"It might be best to wait here and let him come to us in
his own time. You wouldn't want to upset his usual routine. You think?"

Mare sighed. "You're right. I really just want to run
to him and throw my arms around him. But I realize that
isn't quite the thing to do."

TJ took a hefty drink from the glass she held in her
free hand and her eyes swiftly flashed up to Paula's. Paula
had already tasted hers and she grinned at TJ's surprised
face. "Double Manhattan."

"Whew!" TJ chuckled and shook her head. "It's a
wonder the cherry isn't desiccated. Don't hand me anymore, even if I beg you, okay?"

"Darn, guess I'll have to drink your share." A sharp
look from Erin brought a frown of mock disappointment to
her partner's face. "You weren't supposed to hear that."

Erin was just about to answer, when a round of
applause signaled the entrance of their host and the four
women turned toward the doorway.

Dr. Gillis was the epitome of charm and graciousness
as he made his way through his admirers, gathering their
congratulations and accolades. Although his eyes hadn't
made an obvious search for them, TJ saw that he circled
around their group, leaving them for last.

Finally, he arrived. Although he walked to TJ, took
her free hand and nodded, his eyes immediately went to
Mare's. "Miss Meridian, welcome."

TJ smiled brilliantly, tilted her head to see Mare's face
and said, "Dr. Gillis, may I present Erin Scott, Paula Tanner and... Dr. Mare Gillespie?"

Dr. Gillis smiled at Erin and Paula as he shook their
hands and welcomed them. Then he grasped Mare's hand

in both of his and the two just stood there looking into each other's eyes. Mare tried to laugh and talk at the same time, but tears choked her throat. Her father's eyes filled, too, and he gently drew Mare into his arms. The two stood embracing and crying quietly.

At last they parted and Erin handed them tissues from her never-ending supply. "Hello, Mare." Michael Gillis spoke his first words to his daughter.

Mare grinned and her eyes brimmed again. "May I call you Dad?"

No one would have believed that Michael's face could light up any more than it already had, but somehow it managed to. "I would be absolutely thrilled to have you call me Dad." He turned to encompass the other women in his look. "Why don't we sit on the couch and chairs over in that corner and chat?"

"Why don't you and Mare go ahead, Doctor? You must have a lot to talk about and we can mingle for a while." TJ, reveling in Mare's happiness, found herself enthralled by two pairs of emerald green eyes that looked almost exactly alike.

The doctors excused themselves and went to the corner couch. They were laughing and talking even before they reached it.

Erin nudged Paula with her elbow and tilted her head toward TJ. They watched the rapt expression on their friend's face as her eyes followed Mare and her father. After a few moments, she turned and looked up at her two grinning observers. "What?" An eyebrow crooked up and blue eyes struggled to cool down.

"We were just enjoying one of the most beautiful faces in the world," Erin explained.

TJ's eyes swept to Mare and back up to Erin. "She is beautiful, isn't she?"

"She is, TJ, but Erin meant you." Paula tapped TJ's creamy shoulder.

The startling blue eyes widened in surprise, then a blush rose from TJ's neck up over her cheeks. "Cut it out,

you two. You looking for a raise or something?" Her lips
twisted into a mock smile as she taunted her friends in
friendly retaliation for embarrassing her. "Paula, go get us
a couple more Manhattans, will you?"

"Just one more," Erin admonished.

"Why? We're not driving." Paula put on her best
aggrieved look.

Erin looked from one to the other and grinned. "TJ
is."

The co-conspirators looked at each other and frowned.
In a moment, they realized that Erin was teasing about TJ
driving the wheelchair and they chuckled. "Erin, this is
one time when I'll be glad to let you push me around...in
the wheelchair, that is. Go for the Manhattans, Paula."

Erin rolled her eyes but actually she was glad TJ was
enjoying herself. The raven-haired woman had worked
hard to help make Mare's first meeting with her father go
as smoothly as possible and she had earned this small
reward. It also tickled Erin that Paula stood next to her
waiting for her "permission."

She grinned at her partner's hesitation. "Go ahead.
I'll be designated driver for her."

This evening has turned out really, really well. TJ's
heart swelled with happiness for Mare and for her own part
in bringing her lover such delirious joy. *One for the
"Memories" scrapbook.*

* * * * * * * * * *

All the way home, first in the limousine, then the helicopter, then the car that met them at the airport and transported them to the ranch, Mare talked. Her meeting with
her father had been a huge moment in her life and she was
totally wound up over it. TJ, Erin and Paula happily let
her retell, several times over, every word, every nuance of
the conversation she had with Dr. Gillis. Her nervous
energy was finally winding down as they reached the ranch
and piled out of the car.

The driver retrieved TJ's lightweight wheelchair from the porch, brought it to the car and helped her into it. "I can take it from here, Jeff. Thanks for your help."

"My pleasure, Miss Meridian. Just call whenever you need me again." Jeff touched his forehead in an abbreviated salute, climbed back into the car and drove away.

The four women made their way into the house. "I don't know about you gals, but I'm dying to get outta this gown and hit the shower. It's been a wonderful, but tiring night. Thanks, TJ." Paula hugged TJ and kissed her cheek. "Happy for you, Mare." Paula gave the vet's shoulders a quick squeeze.

"Yeah, TJ. Thanks. Everything was lovely. Glad things worked out well for you and your father, Mare." Erin gave each of the women a hug and a kiss and she and Paula went upstairs to prepare for bed.

When she had come to the ranch earlier in the day to dress for her momentous meeting, Mare had brought an overnight bag with clean clothes. Now she followed TJ into her bedroom and lifted the bag onto the chair at the foot of the bed. Unzipping the bag, Mare pulled out a pale green garment.

"What's that?" TJ tilted her head sideways, propping it on her hand and lifting her brows.

"I thought I would slip this on after my shower." Mare grinned at her lover. "At least for a little while."

TJ reached to the console next to her bed and turned a rheostat to dim the lights a little. "Why don't you slip it on now, then help me undress? Forget the shower." TJ's voice had dropped into its seductive lower register that turned Mare's willpower to marshmallow fluff.

Somewhat self-consciously, Mare slipped out of the gown, her shoes, stockings, slip, bra and panties. She thrust her arms and head into the oversized T-shirt, wriggling her body to settle it past her hips, feeling TJ's eyes on her every movement. Finally, she mustered the courage to raise her own eyes and was astounded by the sweet look of adoration spread across that stunning face. In five swift steps she reached the chair and gently melted her lips against the mouth that opened to greet her arrival.

Pulling slowly from the kiss, Mare moved the chair arm out of the way and swung onto TJ's lap. Two long arms wrapped around her. "I've had a wonderful reunion with my father, my love, and it's all been your doing. I'll never be able to thank you enough."

"I was thrilled to do it, Mare. You know that."

"I know, and that made it even better."

The vet's face turned stern and her words became more forceful. "But there is one thing that, no matter how excited I was at meeting my dad, I will never forgive you for."

TJ's eyes widened and she looked dumfounded. "What are you so disturbed about, Mare?"

"This." Mare frowned and her forefinger bounced on the black string bow that held the front of TJ's gown together. "Every time I looked your way, this little black bow rose and fell signaling, 'Untie me. Untie me.' Like it was holding a couple of prisoners, begging for release. Drove me crazy!"

A delicious smile transformed TJ's concerned features. "Well, are you going to listen to it, or not?"

Mare tugged on the bow playfully for a few moments, pretending to untie it, but only rolling it between her fingers. "I really should shower first..." Now she had turned the tables and was driving TJ crazy with anticipation.

"You haven't done any heavy work; will you forget the damn shower! Besides," TJ's tone dipped again, "I want to smell you and taste you and..." A gasp cut off her words as Mare pulled the bow's string and lifted one of the freed prisoners to meet her descending mouth.

Chapter
20

"Mare, the recital was a great experience. Your dad plays beautifully." Erin collected the empty cereal bowls and stacked them in the dishwasher.

"You should hear Mare, she's pretty good, too." Paula cleared the cereal boxes, milk and sugar as Erin finished putting the cups and utensils in the racks.

"I did hear her, when I dropped TJ off the other day. You are outstanding, Mare."

The praise heightened the color on the vet's fair cheeks. "It takes years to play as well as my dad does." Two words replayed in her mind and she grinned at the novelty of them. "My dad." The others smiled at how her face lit up.

"When did you say you will see him again?" Mare had told the women every detail of their conversation, but TJ wanted to watch her say it again.

"He invited me for a late dinner this coming Friday and I'm to stay over and we'll spend Saturday together. We want to see if we can set up some sort of regular visiting schedule." Her eyes, which had brightened as she spoke, now dimmed a little. She put her hand on TJ's arm. "That's going to cut into our time together."

TJ looked down at Mare's hand, reached her own hand over and patted it. Then her eyes swept up and grabbed Mare's heart. "Nothing's ever easy, is it?"

"Maybe we could have you and your dad over here a few times for dinner." *At least TJ would get a chance to see you, and maybe you could stay awhile after your dad leaves.* For confirmation, Erin looked at TJ who nodded vigorously.

"That sounds like a good plan. By the way, don't we have a singing date tomorrow night?" Mare directed the question to Paula who agreed.

"Sure do." She turned to her partner who had missed the by-play last week about TJ's singing. "Mare's coming over and TJ is going to sing. Eight songs."

When Erin saw TJ roll her eyes, she figured the decision had been made for her, but she didn't deny that she would sing. "Wonderful! You haven't sung for quite a while. I miss hearing you."

"Show up in the music room at 6 o'clock. That's performance time." Mare squeezed TJ's arm and got up. "Well, folks, I have to get to work. I'll see you tonight. Thanks for breakfast."

Mare leaned down and kissed TJ's waiting lips. "Ummm...thank you, too." TJ winked at her lover and Mare left.

"You okay, TJ?" Erin had noticed that TJ was a little quieter than usual.

"It has dawned on me that Mare's finding her father may have created a monster."

"What's that supposed to mean?" Erin furrowed her brow and Paula stopped wiping the counter to turn and listen.

"You just heard one problem. Mare has only so much free time so that means we won't see each other as often."

"But...there's something else?"

"Yeah." Anxiety showed in the depths of the blue eyes that swung from Erin to Paula and back. "What if her dad is opposed to...our loving each other?"

A look of consternation passed between Paula and Erin then their eyes came back to TJ's vulnerable expression. "Do you think she would choose me over her new-found father?"

Erin pulled a chair out and sat down next to her friend. "Look, TJ. Granted, Paula and I have been very fortunate that both our families accepted us as lovers. And I know a lot of families have made life miserable for their children who happen to prefer people of the same gender. But let's not borrow trouble, okay? Her dad's a doctor, a famous specialist who's been all over the world. He's probably a lot more tolerant than you seem to be giving him credit for."

"Plus," Paula walked over to stand in front of TJ. She put her hands on her hips in a challenging attitude. "I don't think you're giving Mare enough credit for her own strength of character. I've seen her face when she looks at you, and you're not watching. The woman's in love with you, body, soul, heart, thought, emotions, whatever. You name it, she's offering it to you. So instead of worrying yourself sick over something that might never happen, suck in your gut, TJ, and show some gratitude. The woman is yours."

Paula and Erin watched a bevy of emotions cross the strong-jawed face until one overpowered the others—respect. She reached her hand out to shake Paula's then pulled her close and kissed her firmly on the lips. "Thank you." One side of her mouth quirked up just a little when she saw a flush cross Paula's startled features.

TJ turned to Erin who tried to smother her grin. She wound her fingers in the blonde's tight curls, pulled her forward and kissed her lips, too. "And thank you." Swinging the wheelchair around, TJ left the kitchen.

Ignoring her self-consciousness at the kiss, Erin got up and put her arm around Paula's waist. "I am so proud of you, Polly. You said exactly the right thing."

"Well, I'm more than just a pretty face, you know." Paula basked in the praise. "Hey, Erin..."

"Yeah?"

"Have you ever wondered what it would be like to kiss TJ's gorgeous lips?"

"Maybe. Is this a trick question?"

Paula laughed. "No, I've wondered myself sometimes. Just curious."

"And what's your verdict?"

Paula slipped one arm over Erin's and the other around her waist, bringing her close. "It was very nice, but her lips don't belong to me. I think I'll stick with the ones that do." She dipped her head and met Erin's eager mouth with her own.

"Hmmmm. Me, too." The women parted and scrambled out the door, tickling each other.

****

Mare's ongoing visits with her dad had brought the two to the closeness that both yearned for. Similar tastes in many areas surrounded them with a natural comfort zone. Mare's narration of her life history continued with each visit as Michael added bits and pieces of his own, intertwining segments of his and Jane's time together.

Unfortunately, TJ had proved prophetic in her assessment of Mare's limited free time. Because of the two-hour driving time each way, Mare's visits to the townhouse at Springerly or her dad's main house at Dorburton Lakes generally extended through the weekend. Coverage of her practice by her vet friend in Sharlesburg helped to make this possible.

Ironically, the vet's extra duties related to Meridian ranch's start-up made free time even scarcer. Mare rushed so much to keep on top of those duties and her practice's usual responsibilities that even lunch together was hurried. A late call to a sick animal's side had forced a last-minute postponement of TJ's evening of singing, stealing away that chance for another night together.

Any physical relationship beyond hugging and kissing reached a point of non-existence while Mare concentrated on becoming acquainted with her dad.

Paula and Erin tiptoed around TJ's moodiness, understanding the cause of it, but unable to do anything but sympathize. Contrary to past behavior, though, TJ's moods didn't deteriorate into nastiness, a welcome change they noted and attributed to Mare's influence

They all breathed a combined sigh of relief when, at last, Michael's schedule enabled him to accept the standing invitation to dinner at the ranch. If nothing else, TJ would have her love near for the evening, which might help to soften the edge of her frustration.

On the phone that afternoon, Mare had promised to stay overnight if she could think of a suitable excuse to her father as to why he should follow her to the ranch in his own car. Waiting in the living room for their arrival, TJ's smile threatened to burst the bonds of her face when Erin informed her they had just pulled in with two separate vehicles. *Mare, my love, I can't believe how I've missed you. Telephones just aren't an adequate substitute for your presence.*

Paula had gone out to meet their guests and escort them in the front door. Michael nodded to Erin, "Hello, Miss Scott," and walked briskly to TJ, accepting the hand that she offered as Mare gave Erin a hug. "Miss Meridian, I am so glad I was at last able to accept your generous invitation. I would have been here sooner if my schedule had permitted it."

"I understand that, Doctor and I'm delighted that you are able to be here tonight. But, please, call me TJ and this is Erin... and Paula."

The doctor nodded again to the two women, his eyes crinkling. "I'd be happy to, if you will call me Michael."

TJ inclined her head. "Michael it is."

Erin slipped her arm through Michael's. "Mare has agreed to provide some preprandial music for us, Michael. Please come with me; I'll escort you to the music room." They went on toward the music room with Paula following as Mare stepped up to TJ.

"We'll be with you in just a minute," she called to their departing backs.

Glancing toward the group to make sure they exited the living room, Mare turned back and pressed her lips to her lover's, a darting tongue teasing its adversary into retaliation. Breaking away before she succumbed to total loss of control, Mare whispered, "Till tonight." The yearning felt by the two formed an almost tangible bond. TJ's eyes darkened and her lids lowered as pictures of their past passion played across the screen of her mind.

"Hey." Mare chuckled, pulled a tissue from her jeans and patted the moisture from TJ's upper lip and around her hairline. "You can't go in there looking like this, your face will be a dead giveaway." Mare and TJ had talked it over and decided to let Mare's dad get to know both of them better before revealing to him their relationship.

Sculpted lips twisted into one of TJ's lopsided smiles that Mare found so endearing. "Just how am I supposed to turn myself off?" As Mare anticipated, one raven eyebrow lifted in accompaniment to the question.

Music sounded as Mare's dad apparently was trying out the piano. "I've got to get in there. I'll send Erin out to you. That will give you a little time to regroup." Mare couldn't resist, she had to kiss TJ one more time, then spent a moment quieting her own emotions before moving to the music room. True to her promise, she sent Erin back to TJ.

"Whoa, honey." Erin's eyes danced with merriment when she got a close look at TJ's face. "No wonder Mare said you need help. Maybe a bucket of cold water?"

Both Erin and Paula were enjoying the development of the relationship between TJ and Mare. It even served to

add some extra spice to their own passion by recalling
their first encounters with each other. The two had met in
their second year of college but for months had shied away
from confessing their mutual attraction until TJ had
informed each of them of the other's interest. By their
third year, they realized that theirs was a lifetime commit-
ment and their love had deepened and expanded ever since.

"Funny, funny," TJ said dryly. "Wait until I send
Paula to Europe for several months and see how you feel."

Erin's jaw dropped and her face paled. "You wouldn't
do that to us, would you?"

TJ laughed quietly. "No, but the look on your face is
so comical, it's helping me cool down."

Erin cuffed the dark-haired woman's shoulder. "One
of these days, TJ, you are really going to get it."

"It sure as hell better be tonight," TJ said fervently
and the two of them chuckled. Feeling a lot calmer, TJ
wheeled into the music room with Erin walking beside her.

When they entered the room, they saw Mare and her
dad both sitting at the piano, running through exercises.
Paula sat over to the side with two empty chairs next to
her. Erin settled next to her partner and TJ wheeled alongside her. Paula leaned forward to include TJ in her vision.
"Mare and Michael have a surprise for us."

Hearing a voice, both pianists stopped and turned
toward the women. Mare winked her far eye at TJ who
quickly tightened and released the skin around her eyes in
a surreptitious glare. This brought a broadened smile to
the face that was carved on her heart.

"Are you ready?" Mare asked the double entendre
with feigned innocence and TJ swallowed hard, but managed to nod.

Mare and her dad smiled at each other, turned to the
keyboard and played a duet that swept the three listeners
into their circle, twirled their psyches gloriously around in
a high-stepping routine, then set them sweetly back to
earth, finishing with a charming trill.

The duo rose and moved around past the piano seat to stand together and bow to the applause they heard. When they lifted from the bow, Mare saw that TJ hadn't joined in the applause. She sat with her head lowered, one hand across her eyes.

Mare rushed to her side, with Michael coming over right next to his daughter. "TJ, what's wrong? Are you ill?" Disturbed, Mare rested her hand for a moment on the raven locks.

TJ dropped her hand and lifted her head. She raised her powerful gaze to two sets of green eyes and two hearts lurched. Her voice exuded wonderment and she blinked back moisture that had accumulated in the blue orbs. "You made me walk again. For just a few precious moments, I walked again." A brilliant smile appeared even as Mare wiped away the tear that had overflowed onto her love's cheek. "And not just walked, I danced!"

TJ threw her arms wide and Erin jumped up and hugged her before Mare had a chance to collapse into her embrace. The action brought Mare back to her senses and she turned and hugged her father who had been watching the obviously emotional exchange between Mare and TJ. "I'd say the surprise was a huge success," he remarked with a pleased smile.

Erin stepped away from TJ, smiling at the "Thanks" that had been whispered in her ear.

"Dad composed that piece." Mare's eyes shone with pride and Paula and Erin each remarked on the beauty of the music and how it had moved them.

Martha, one of the women from the ranch's cookhouse, appeared in the doorway. TJ had engaged the two cooks to prepare and serve the dinner. "Dinner's ready, ma'am."

"We'll be right there, Martha." TJ wheeled around and led the group into the dining room.

Dinner was a thoroughly entertaining affair. Michael proved to be a nimble raconteur with a broad repertoire of fascinating anecdotes. With Mare's natural affinity for chatting, and TJ's expertise as an accomplished hostess assuring that each person contributed to the conversation, the time flew by. After the dessert, Paula and Erin excused themselves, allowing the others some private time together as they lingered over coffee.

The conversation had continued without effort. TJ's charming hostess side was new to Mare and she found it very appealing. Her father seemed to be totally captivated, too. *Look at her. She's got him wrapped around her little finger. Hmmph,* she laughed at herself, *just like me.*

"TJ, Dad has made me a marvelously generous offer." The sudden closing of a curtain over TJ's eyes startled Mare.

"Oh? What's that?" *If you tell me you are leaving here, I'll die. Please, God, not that. Anything but that.*

Puzzled by TJ's reaction, Mare halted. Michael picked up where she left off. "Since Mare's my only living relative..."

I knew it! You're going to go live with him! The color blanched from TJ's face, worrying Mare that she might be ill. Michael, too, looked concerned.

"Someday she'll inherit all I own. I've persuaded her to let me settle some of my estate on her now. She was reluctant to take it, but after a long, hard discussion, I convinced her that she would be doing me a favor. I mean, why should she have to wait until I die to use what will be hers one day anyway? I'd rather be here to see her enjoy it."

Mare thought TJ looked a little strange. "Are you all right, TJ?"

TJ took a couple of deep breaths and began to recover her color. One side of her mouth curved into a smile. "I'm fine, Mare. Just a little jolt there for a minute. I think that's a wonderful idea, Michael."

"I told Dad you would handle the transfer from his lawyer. Is that okay?"

Yeah, I'm okay now, TJ's heart sang. "I'd be happy to. Just a minute and I'll give you the names of my lawyers." She pushed a button on the side of the chair arm and Erin appeared with little delay. "Erin, bring Michael a card for my lawyers, will you, please?"

Erin reappeared shortly with the requested card then left.

"This will do fine, TJ. Now," he got up from the chair, "it's time for me to leave this remarkable company." He got up and took TJ's hand, bowing low over it. "I have had a wonderful time and a delicious dinner. Thank you for inviting me."

"We were delighted to have you. And the invitation is still standing. Anytime you can fit us in, we would love to have you."

"Thanks, I'll try my best to take you up on that. May I use your powder room facilities before I leave?"

"Certainly. Mare, there's one in the music room." Michael smiled, then turned to allow Mare to escort him to the music room. As she waited outside the powder room, Mare ran her fingers along the piano's keys, musing over what a good time she had had tonight.

Michael flushed the toilet then moved to the sink to wash his hands. A soft light flickering through the chest-high window drew his curiosity. He stepped close and peered out. The window opened onto a dimly lit courtyard that seemed to contain trees, bushes and benches. A flickering yellow citronella candle sat on a pathway next to one of the benches. Two people on the bench were kissing. The darker head lifted from the kiss, into a beam of light coming from some place along the wall. *It's Paula.* The other person sat up straighter, put an arm around Paula's neck and kissed her again. The blonde curls left little doubt as to who it was. *Erin and Paula kissing?* Their hands started moving and Michael jerked his head back. *What are you, some kind of voyeur? What does it matter to you what they're doing, they're adults, aren't they?*

Still, Michael had been raised with the conventional idea that men are attracted to women and vice versa. He knew that wasn't always the case, but he'd never come face-to-face with the reality before and he was a bit uncomfortable with it. *I wonder if Mare knows? My God, I wonder if Mare...No, I don't even want to think about that possibility.* He could hear Mare's light touch on the piano. Deciding not to make an issue of something that was, after all, none of his business, he walked back into the music room and Mare showed him to his car. They spoke a few minutes, kissed good-bye and Michael got in his car and left.

Mare ran back into the house, her head swiveling, looking for TJ. "TJ? Where are you?" She ran into the hall and saw the light showing through the transom above TJ's bathroom door. She tried the door then knocked on it. "TJ?"

"Just a minute," TJ answered in a singsong voice.

"I'll be right back." Mare dashed to the powder room, made use of it herself, then ran back to TJ's bathroom, just as her wheelchair was coming through the doorway. Mare opened the bedroom door. TJ wheeled in then swung around, lifted the arm and went "oomph" as Mare landed against her stomach. Long arms pulled the supple body as tight as they could against TJ's chest and two mouths joined for a banquet of treats.

They eventually parted and Mare reached for TJ's blouse straps. "Wait," TJ said, "let's get on the bed. I can move better there."

"Just a minute," Mare said in a perfect imitation of TJ's earlier singsong, bringing a smile to her lover's face. Mare slid the straps down and TJ lifted her arms through. The top was cotton and tight enough that it wouldn't fall so Mare sat a little away from TJ, put her hands, palms flat, thumbs down, on the top of her chest and slid them down, pushing the blouse lower in tiny tantalizing increments. This was a purposely slow process, made even slower by the massaging that went on with each lowering of the blouse. As her hands slid against skin, Mare's thumbs played a counterpoint through the blouse material. When her hands almost reached the critical masses, now yearning for a bare touch, Mare stopped. "Now, we'll get on the bed."

TJ clamped her hands on Mare's wrists. "My God, Mare, you can't leave me like this. Stop tormenting me."

"But you are soooo much fun to torment, sweetheart." Mare leaned in till her mouth was next to TJ's ear. "Just wait till you see what we do in the bed," she purred and blew her warm breath into the ear's sensitive opening.

TJ let loose of her wrists and said, in agony, "Okay, okay, let's move to the bed...floor...anywhere. Just doooo something...anything! Help!"

* * * * * * * * * *

Soft light had just entered the room when TJ awoke. Mare's body covered hers, the top of the golden head even with TJ's eyes, which fit the curves and valleys of their breasts perfectly together. TJ closed her eyes and smiled, remembering their escapades of the night before. *Just when I think we've tried about everything, Mare comes up with something new. Well, she's a musician, right? And musicians are creative, right? She sure is that and, boy, does she ever know how to play me. I'm gonna have to work on some way to surprise her.*

"Ummm." The golden head glanced up at open blue eyes then turned to put warm lips against TJ's neck and start nibbling. Then she stopped and TJ felt a puff of breath against the dampness as Mare snorted a laugh. "Believe it or not, I think I'm worn out."

TJ chuckled. "No wonder. You've been working like a madwoman, then you spend half the night working on me, turning me into a begging mound of marshmallow. You should be worn out."

"A mound of marshmallow? Now there's a picture. You're all muscle and you know it." Mare moved her chest back and forth against TJ's. "Well, almost all muscle," she giggled.

"Well, if exercise builds muscle, then you've got them on a strong path to change." Both women laughed.

Mare's voice sobered. "TJ, when my dad gives me that money, I have some plans for it."

"Like what?"

Mare moved off of TJ and onto the bed beside her so she could look into her face. "I've decided I'm going to hire an assistant. I can't stand being away from you for so long."

Delight leaped into her lover's blue eyes. "Mare, that's wonderful news! How soon do you think you could get someone?"

"Hard to tell. How soon do you think I will get the money?"

"Maybe a couple weeks, maybe a month. Depends on how fast these lawyers move. But you could go ahead and advertise, start interviewing. Things are going to be picking up around here, Mare. The area will be expanding. Your assistant will earn his own keep soon." TJ's business mind was gearing up.

Mare recognized this and wanted to bring her back. "Does the offer for me to move out here still stand?"

TJ threw her arms onto the bed above her head, causing an interesting change in her chest. "Pinch me, I'm dreaming!"

So Mare pinched.

"Mare!" TJ's arms came back down in a hurry. "You didn't have to pinch there, for Pete's sake. They're still tender from last night."

"Oh, poor babies. Let me kiss them and make them better." Mare leaned forward and TJ pushed her back, laughing.

"No you don't. You have to get up and go to work and so do I."

"Darn!" Mare grinned and winked, twice. "But I'll be back, you guys."

Chapter
21

Michael sat in his home office staring blankly at the computer screen. He had called up the financial worth file that enumerated all his assets and liabilities, with the intention of choosing how much of his estate to settle on his daughter. He had a problem keeping his mind on the figures in front of him, however; a picture of two women kissing insisted on intruding.

There are three women in that house and two obviously are gay. Doesn't that hint at maybe TJ's being gay, too? Then where does that leave Mare? Erin and Paula appear to be lovers, does that mean that Mare and TJ are? There does seem to be some kind of connection between them, but I assumed that was because of their friendship. Besides, TJ's in a wheelchair!

Come on, Michael, you're the SCI expert. You know that some people with SCI can still have a sexual relationship. Maybe TJ's one of them. But I don't want it to be with Mare!

Some niggling little aggravation behind this thought bothered Michael and he was straightforward enough to examine it honestly. *Am I more worried that Mare might be gay...or that TJ might be?* He turned this question over in his mind searching for the impetus behind it. *The woman is stunningly beautiful, charming, intelligent, poised...and she definitely has an aura... of what? Power? Magnetism? There in the music room, when she swept those remarkable eyes up, she just about bowled me over. I took for granted that her passion was directed at me and I have to admit, it woke up something inside me. But maybe it was directed at Mare.*

Michael had engaged in sporadic relationships through the years, none very long, nor worth pursuing. For the last few years, he had buried himself in his work and his obsession with it had enabled him to learn all the latest procedures in his field and also to make several small breakthroughs. Because of his hermit-like life, his reaction to TJ surprised him. *But she is an extremely attractive woman. And face it, Michael, that question you asked a minute ago has an answer. Don't kid yourself. You are more upset about TJ's sexual preference than you are about Mare's, at least for the moment. And you find that a little embarrassing.*

What if I won't give Mare this money unless she...? Does what? You're sitting here thinking she's the lover of TJ Meridian, an extremely wealthy woman, and you think you can turn her into something false by waving a paltry couple of million at her?

But what will my friends think about Mare? That's a pretty stupid question. What are you planning on doing, hanging a sign on her? How Mare spends her private time is of no concern to your friends or to anyone else. Including you.

But I'm her father. So, who put you in charge of her life? You're her father, not her owner.

What if you're totally wrong and you are making a mountain out of a molehill? This question cheered Michael and brought him out of his self-inquisition. *Right, first things first. Mare's coming over tomorrow night. Let's find out if they are lovers, or not.* Having made this decision, Michael tentatively chose which assets were to be transferred to Mare and sent the information to his attorney to start drawing up the papers.

* * * * * * * * * *

Mare and her dad finished dinner and moved to the den for their coffee. They sat on a comfortable couch with a coffee table immediately in front of them. A grand piano sat at the far end of the room in an area set off by a large archway. Another archway, to the right of the piano, connected the area to the living room in an L-shaped configuration.

At Dorburton Lakes, Michael employed a married couple as housekeeper/cook and butler/chauffeur and they took excellent care of him and his guests. Once they had served the coffee, they retired to the kitchen.

"I had a wonderful time at TJ's the other night." Michael waited until Mare finished with the cream and sugar, then he added some to his coffee and stirred it. "She's a remarkable woman."

He watched as Mare's eyes lit up. "Yes, she is. From her office at the ranch, she directs enterprises that are spread throughout the world."

"I'm not much of a businessman. I have a financial consultant who manages my affairs, but even I have heard of Meridian Corporation. The few times TJ mentioned it at dinner I was impressed with her grasp of what each subsidiary does and how she has meshed them all together into a smooth-running operation." Michael hesitated for a moment then, watching Mare closely, but unobtrusively, he continued. "Tell you the truth, I was more impressed with her as a woman. She's stunningly attractive."

Mare nodded sagely, "Yes, she is." *We sure agree on that count, Dad.*

"In fact, I've met a lot of glamorous women, but she's one of the most beautiful I've ever seen." *I don't believe anybody can argue with that,* Michael thought.

"I think so, too," Mare nodded again, wondering where this paean of praise to TJ was leading. She didn't have long to find out.

"I was thinking about calling her and asking her for a date. Would you have any objection to that?" *Here's where we find out: Is it safe to pursue TJ Meridian, or should my interest remain platonic?*

This had come at Mare unexpectedly and she was speechless. After a moment she found her voice. "No offense, Dad, but there is a difference in your ages."

"That's true, but it might make less difference to TJ than it does to you. I'd like to ask her that myself. As a matter of fact, I think I'll call her tomorrow evening."

"Dad, I..." Mare searched for the right words to say without hurting her dad's feelings. "TJ doesn't date." *Dear God, how do I get around this one?*

"Well, there's always the chance that someone will change her ways, Mare. It can't hurt to ask."

Should I just tell him right out that we're lovers? How will he react? Some parents have disowned their children for less. Do I want to risk that? Will this come down to a choice between my father and TJ? Mare's mind buzzed with all the ramifications of the situation. *I just found him; I can't lose him already!* She never even considered the option of leaving TJ.

I can't just gloss it over. TJ will turn him down and he'll be terribly embarrassed when he eventually discovers why. That could ruin his relationship with me before we've barely had a chance to know each other.

Mare finished the last sip of her coffee, set the cup in its saucer and picked up her father's hand. She took a deep breath and looked him straight in the eye.

"Dad, there's something I have to tell you. Something important. I know you had no way of knowing this and I would have told you at some point, when we got to know each other better..." Mare hesitated, swallowing, her throat suddenly dry. This was a thousand times harder than she had thought it would be.

Her stomach tensed, turning over as she felt a wave of fear run through her. *He needs to know now before we take our relationship any further. I have to allow him the time to make his own decision on this. If he reacts badly, just accept it; you still have TJ.* This situation had never arisen between her and her mother. Jane respected the privacy of others and expected the same from them. Besides, Mare had always thought her mother knew without asking pointed questions. *Will this be the last I see of my dad? Will he hate me?*

Mare gathered her courage. "You know how much you and I are alike, right? In the short time that we've known each other, we've been amazed at how many things we both enjoy, how similar our tastes are, right?"

Michael nodded. His eyes were locked on the ones that so perfectly mirrored his own. He suspected what was coming and braced himself for it.

Mare saw his lips set and her courage slipped, but she seized hold of it and set it upright again. "Well, it so happens that you and I are so much alike that..." Mare gave a quick little nervous smile, "...we have both been attracted to the same woman. I'm gay, Dad, and I'm involved with TJ. We're in love with each other." Mare's eyes were pools of anxiety, pleading for understanding.

Michael's hand moved and Mare, her heart sinking, started to let go of it. But Michael surprised her. He turned his hand over so he could hold hers in both of his. The fear and anguish that had crossed Mare's expressive face, before struggling with and being supplanted by courage, had touched his heart. He looked at the daughter whose existence had been so recently revealed to him and he realized that now she was revealing her heart. *I've been a fool to put her through this distress just because of my own lack of compassion.*

"I have to confess, Mare, that I'm not totally shocked by this revelation. After dinner at TJ's, when I was in the powder room, I noticed a flickering light outside. I looked out the window and I saw Erin and Paula kissing each other. So I wondered about your situation, and TJ's."

A bit startled by this news, Mare raised her eyebrows. *I thought it was a little early for his suspicions; we tried to be discreet.*

He sighed. "I hoped I was wrong. At first I was angry at the possibility that you and TJ were in love. Partly because I didn't want you to be like that, and partly because I really was attracted to TJ and didn't want her to be like that. Do you understand what I'm saying?"

Mare nodded and swallowed, hoping to contain the tears that threatened to flood her eyes.

"Is it stupid to ask if you could ever change?"

Mare forced out a breathless and hoarse voice. "Dad, that would be like asking you to change your green eyes to brown." She tried a tentative smile.

Michael thought about that for a few moments, looking down at their entwined hands. Finally, he nodded a little and looked up. "I haven't been fair to you at all, Mare, and I deeply apologize. You're my daughter and I love you, as you are, not as the person I think you should be, or wish you had been. It might take me a while to adjust and there might be times when we accidentally embarrass each other, but please be patient with me. About the best face I can put on this whole situation is," here Michael offered his own tentative smile, "if I can't date TJ, at least you're keeping her in the family."

Mare started to cry in relief and he took her into his arms, patting her back and soothing her with small shushing sounds.

Finally, Mare calmed down and with the help of some tissues handed to her by Michael she dried her tears. He, too, had to use a few. "I knew Mom would pick a winner," she smiled up at him.

"I am a winner, Mare, since you came into my life." Michael smiled back and gave her an extra squeeze before releasing her. "I just want you to promise me one thing."

"What's that?"

"Not to tell TJ that I was developing a crush on her, okay?" Michael grinned like a shy schoolboy.

Mare reached up and patted his cheek as she returned his smile. "Never, Dad. But crushes are okay, just as long as that's all they are. I think anyone who really knows TJ has a mild crush on her. How could you help it? She's wonderful." Mare's smile twinkled. "Of course, I am prejudiced."

Michael laughed. "No, she is wonderful and I probably always will have a mild crush on her. Beyond that, though, I'd like to see if I could do anything to help her. Do you think she would let me look at her case history, x-rays, MRI's, and so forth? I'd like to keep up on her condition, in case we come across anything that could improve it. That is my field, you know."

"I know, and I thank you for wanting to help. I'll ask TJ. She's kinda close sometimes about her privacy, but in this case I think I can talk my way around her. Like you said, we'll be keeping it in the family."

"Perfect. Now how about if we cap off this evening with my duet that we played for her?" Michael's voice caught for just a moment, remembering TJ's emotional reaction to his original composition. "The one she danced to?"

"Perfect." Mare echoed her father and they rose and walked arm-in-arm to the piano.

Chapter 22

"Hey, TJ, here comes Mare!" Paula stuck her head into the hall and hollered then ducked back into the kitchen and put another glass, plate and setting on the island.

Erin turned from the fridge where she was getting the iced tea and frowned at her partner. "You could have used the intercom."

"Yeah, yeah, yeah. I know you were raised in polite society." Paula gave Erin a light pinch as she passed by her.

The curly-headed blonde swatted at Paula's hand and laughed. "And so were you, though no one would ever suspect it."

The storm door burst open as Mare came through. "Hi, folks! Believe it or not, I have some extra time today; time for a real visit for a change." She hugged each of the women, then her smile broadened as TJ came wheeling into the kitchen, right up to Mare's legs.

Mare leaned forward to kiss her love, but TJ pulled back. "Something wrong?" Mare's eyebrows just about disappeared.

TJ flung up the arm of her chair and patted her thighs.
"Yeah! I haven't seen you for days and you are going to sit
down and let me give you a proper kiss." Long arms
reached out and Mare slipped into them and onto the volunteered lap at the same time, wrapping her arms around
TJ and melting into a kiss of fire.

When their lips finally parted, Mare laid her head
down in the V between TJ's neck and shoulder, kissing her
neck, then snuggling her body into a more comfortable
position. "I want to stay here forever. Can I do that,
please?"

Erin grinned. "Might be a little messy. Lunch is soup
and sandwiches and TJ has to eat; she already skipped
breakfast." As she spoke, Erin ladled soup into a bowl and
set one at each place.

"Oh, darn." Mare slowly slid her tongue up the side of
TJ's neck, across her cheek and into her mouth, sealing its
entrance with her lips against her lover's.

"Ummm." TJ's arms tightened around Mare and they
held the kiss until Paula dropped some ice cubes down
Mare's back.

"Yiiiiii!" she yelled and leaped up, jumping up and
down and pulling at her shirttail until the cubes fell out
onto the floor. Mare threw a mock glare at Paula who was
laughing at the impromptu dance.

"Sorry. I know if you get too hot, you can cool down
with some ice cubes and you looked like you were siz-
zling." Not looking at all contrite, Paula picked the cubes
up from the floor and threatened TJ who shook a fist at her.
Grinning, Paula tossed the cubes in the sink and washed
her hands. "Come on, let's eat. I'm starving." She helped
Erin set the sandwiches out and they all sat down to lunch.

The food disappeared quickly and the group sat around
talking for a while. "By the way," TJ's eyes swept
between Erin and Paula, "did Mare tell you that you two
outed her to her father?"

"What?" Two surprised voices asked together. Two pairs of eyes looked first at each other, frowning, then toward Mare.

"That's right." Mare gazed at them very seriously, nodding her head.

"How did we do that?" Erin queried, slightly flustered.

"You remember the night he had dinner with us?" Both heads nodded. "You remember being in the court-yard?" Both heads nodded again. "You remember what you were doing?" The two looked at each other, then back to Mare.

Erin had a slight blush on her cheeks but Paula looked cocky. "Damn right I do! It's a courtyard. We were court-ing."

Mare sucked in her lips to keep a straight face. TJ twisted her mouth and covered it with a hand.

Mare cleared her throat. "Well, Dad used the powder room next to the music room, and guess what he saw?"

Now even Paula blushed. "Aw, hell, Mare. We didn't know he was there. We're sorry."

"What did he say about you, Mare?" Erin's face was filled with concern.

Mare gave a big sigh and looked really sad. "Well, he put two and two together and figured if you two fooled around with each other, maybe I fooled around with TJ, too."

"And what did you say to that?"

"I said, 'Damn right I do!'" Mare's face cleared and a huge smile split her face. TJ laughed out loud as Erin and Paula frowned at each other then realized a joke was being played on them.

"Funny, funny, funny." Actually, Erin did think it was funny, but Paula took a moment longer to laugh and Erin pulled on her arm. "Come on, Polly, that was a payback for the ice cubes."

"Right," she said gruffly. "But what did your dad say? Was he upset?" Paula remembered the trouble some of her friends had when their families first learned they were gay.

"He was not especially happy about it, but he is determined to love me as I am. And I can live with that." Mare looked toward TJ and smiled just for her. She turned back toward the other two women. "That's enough talk about me. How are things coming along out here?"

Erin smiled. "Things are looking pretty good with the cattle. We culled the sick ones you pointed out and turned the others onto the range and they are doing fine. Bill says the men are all shaping into good, solid hands and at the rate we are getting cattle shipped in we should be up to full capacity in a couple more months."

Paula chimed in. "The plant is being brought on line, the foremen and a skeleton crew are in place, and we should have our first shipment of cattle to be processed by next week. TJ told them we will get scattered shipments so the plant can be brought up to capacity slowly, giving us time to hire and train more and more workers. In the meantime, of the ones already hired, some are being trained to handle the beef and others taught how to take care of the production areas."

Mare clapped her hands together in appreciation. "And I have to tell you there is a noticeable lifting of spirits in town. People are walking with their heads up, nodding to, and chatting with each other with looks of hope on their faces. They are starting to believe that the town is really turning around." She looked at TJ. "And I'm starting to hear Meridian said once in a while without s-o-b accompanying it."

"That is an improvement," TJ chuckled.

"TJ, did you get in touch with your doctor to send your records to Dad?"

The dark-haired woman shifted in her seat and rubbed a hand over her mouth. "Not yet."

Mare looked at her quizzically. She and TJ had discussed this on the phone and she thought TJ was amenable to it, but her body language said otherwise. "Is there a problem?" She frowned. "I mean, this is my father, sweetheart. He's an expert in the field and he wants to keep your records on file in case there is a breakthrough, some treatment that might help you."

"Maybe it's because he's your father, Mare. I feel kinda... exposed."

"Sorry, I don't follow that thinking. It's your insides he's going to see, not your outsides." Mare's eyes twinkled mischievously.

TJ had to grin. "I didn't mean that kind of exposed."

When Mare saw TJ's grin, she knew she had won the argument. "You're going to make me tell my dad that you don't want him to look at your records?" Mare batted her eyes coyly. "Because you're shy?"

TJ closed her eyes, shook her head, and flipped her hands in the air and back again in surrender. "All right! I'll send him the records." Blue eyes opened and fastened on green. "You know, you oughtta work for the government or something. No one would ever get away with anything."

Paula reached behind the wheelchair and gave Mare a thumbs-up sign. Erin smiled to herself. *Sometimes she acts like a little kid, but I sure do love that little tyke. I hope that part of her never grows up.* "Mare, TJ said you were planning on hiring an assistant. Any luck with that yet?"

"Yeah, Erin. I had an applicant almost right away who looks promising; young man with a wife and baby. I have another interview set up with him and if we can get together on a few incidentals, looks like he's the one."

"That'll be great, Mare." Paula sounded sincerely enthused. "It will give you some free time. You keep running around like you have been and you'll soon be nothing but skin and bones."

Mare was touched that the sometimes-gruff Paula was concerned about her workload.

TJ looked at Erin and Paula. "I've asked Mare to come here to live if she can. Having an assistant would be a big step in that direction."

TJ and Mare were happy to see the faces of both women light up. "Wonderful!" they said together.

"Well, nothing's definite yet. I can't be certain until I see how things work out. But I have high hopes."

"Where do you think her office would be, TJ?"

"This is a big place and there are plenty of empty rooms. Mare could have any one she wants."

"Any one?" Mare echoed. She cocked her head at TJ. "Is that a promise?"

"Yeah," TJ smiled, "that's a promise."

"Then I'll take the one that used to be your father's."

TJ's face blanched and then hardened. "No! That's the only one you can't have."

"You just promised me I could have any I wanted. Are you going to go back on your word?" *I've got to get in that office and change it. Even if the counseling helps her, as long as that office is a reminder of her hate, TJ will never be free of her father.*

"If I had any idea that you would choose that one, I would have told you right off that you couldn't have it. But no, you had to trick me and I don't appreciate that, Mare." TJ crossed her arms, held her elbows, and seemed to shrink in on herself. *I don't want you in that room!* her thoughts screamed inside her brain.

"I wasn't trying to trick you, TJ. You should know me better than that. If you had told me right out I couldn't have that room, I would have argued for it anyway. It's at the end of the house with an outside entrance. People could come in and out to see me without disturbing the rest of the house. It has a screened porch adjacent to it that would be ideal for me to work in when the weather is right. It's the perfect room for an office."

What Mare said made sense to Erin. "Mare's right. It sounds like the ideal spot."

TJ threw Erin a nasty glance and then slowly shook her head. Lowered eyes, clamped jaw, and lips pressed firmly together left no doubt as to her mood. *Keep out of this, Erin. None of you understand how I feel about this.*

Mare was becoming agitated at TJ's hardheaded attitude. And when Mare got agitated, her mouth shifted into
another gear. "I didn't think I was coming here as a rental
prospect; I expected to have some say in where my office
would be. It's also the closest room to your office. And
pardon me for thinking this, but I supposed that you and I
would like to see each other occasionally during the day."

Mare hadn't taken her eyes off of TJ. She saw the blue
eyes narrow when she made the rental remark but TJ didn't
respond. "Have you been in the room since you came back
here?"

"No one's been in the room," Paula answered when TJ
kept silent. "It's never been unlocked."

"Who has the key?" Mare glanced at Paula, who tilted
her head toward TJ.

"May I have the key, TJ?" Mare knew she was tread-
ing on dangerous ground. She felt the anxiety coming
from Paula and Erin, and TJ's tension almost crackled
around her. TJ hadn't said anything and that put her two
friends on edge; they had seen some monumental temper
outbursts in the past, most of them preceded by a period of
speechless anger.

TJ huddled in her chair, not moving, not saying anything. *Mare, I love you but I don't want you in that room.
That place is full of hate.* The stillness in the room pressed
against them all, seeming almost to have a life of its own.

Mare's hushed voice nudged the silence, gently edging
it away. "TJ, if we can't even talk about a difference of
opinion, maybe I need to rethink my coming here to live.
It could be a big mistake."

The dark head jerked up and Erin and Paula flinched.
Paula, uneasy, got up and moved to lean against the
counter behind TJ and Mare. Blue eyes, deepened by the
passions of anger and pain, met and grabbed at Mare's
emerald green. As she stared wretchedly at Mare, a cheek
twitched then the beautiful features contorted. TJ opened
her mouth but wasn't able to force the words out. *Can't
you see? I don't want the woman I love to be using the*

room of a man I hate! Why can't you understand that? TJ
tore her eyes away, lowered her head, and covered her face
with both of her hands. Breathing rasped from her throat.

Mare raised a hand to soothe TJ, but Paula stepped
forward, grabbed her hand, and shook her head. Mare's
heart went out to TJ, but she sat still as Paula had signaled,
feeling that she probably was right. No one could predict
TJ's reaction.

After a few minutes TJ's breathing evened out and a
minute later she dropped her hands and raised her head,
eyes still lowered. She rocked back and forth and inter-
laced her fingers but her hands moved anyway, thumbs
rolling over each other, over and over. When she finally
felt composed, she turned and lifted her eyes to Mare's. A
miniscule squiggle of satisfaction soothed a spot in her
soul when she saw Mare's reaction to the impact.

Mare felt like her heart had backed up and restarted.
*She knows those eyes are her most formidable weapon and,
even when I know she's going to use them on me, I'm help-
less to defend myself. I just want to throw myself at her
feet.*

"I don't like to be manipulated, and I don't like emotional blackmail. That was my father's most powerful
tool." Mare flinched at the hurt in TJ's voice and was dismayed to be compared to the monster that TJ's father obviously was. TJ cleared her throat. Her low voice sounded
subdued and hesitant. She looked Mare straight in the eye.
"But for you I'll compromise."

Paula squealed and threw her hands over her heart.
"My God, I'm going to have a heart attack! TJ said the 'C'
word!"

Erin blinked and waited for an outburst and she wasn't
disappointed. TJ turned her head slowly and pinned Paula
with cold, ice blue eyes. "You think this is funny?"

The grin slipped from Paula's face. "I'm sorry, TJ."
TJ stared a moment longer before turning back to Mare.

Mare watched in fascination as TJ's look drained the
blood from Paula's face. She'd heard TJ use that tone

before but not to either of the girls. She needed to take the focus off of Paula before TJ said or did anything that she'd regret later. "What do you propose?"

"You know I hate that room."

"I know you've turned it into a shrine that embodies your hate for your father, TJ, and I don't think that's a healthy situation. I could go in there and redo it and you would never recognize it. Whenever you came in, it would seem like a different room. There'd be nothing left to remind you of the bad times." Mare suddenly realized she was bulldozing her way over TJ's objections before she had heard them. "Er... I'm sorry, what are you proposing?"

After grappling with the terrible threat that Mare might not move to the ranch unless the office battle could be resolved, TJ had capitulated—to a degree. She decided that she could handle Mare taking over the office as long as she didn't have to see her in there. *I can force myself to imagine that door opening into an entirely different room.*

"You can have the room with four conditions. One, everything in the room must go. Throw it out, give it to some charity, I don't care. Just get rid of it so I will never see it again. Two, the door to the hall has to be kept closed at all times, and I mean at all times, unless someone is going in or out. Three, no one will use it as a place to hide from me. Four, I will never step foot in the room and I will not be pestered to," TJ looked around to all three women, "by anybody. Is that clear?"

All three women nodded. "I want to hear each of you say you promise to abide by these conditions." TJ waited expectantly.

"I promise," Mare agreed and the other two added their promise, too.

"Paula, the key's in my bedroom in the bottom drawer of the jewelry chest. Would you get it, please?" Paula was halfway to the bedroom by the time TJ finished. She came back quickly with the key and handed it to her.

TJ reached for Mare's hand, turned it over, and watched her own hand lay the key in Mare's palm. Mare closed her hand around it and smiled at her lover. She slipped the key into a pocket in her jeans.

An errant twitch tugged at TJ's cheek and Mare cupped her hand against it. "I know this has been hard for you, TJ. But someday I think you will feel better for it. Thank you for not letting this turn into a wedge between us."

The anger and pain in TJ's magnificent eyes slowly dissolved as love's passion replaced them. Seeing the change, the other three women began to relax. "I'd give you everything I have if that was the only way to get you here." TJ lifted the chair arm and Mare moved onto her lap. Erin and Paula quietly left the room.

TJ put her arms around Mare who put both hands up to hold the face she loved. She kissed TJ lightly then leaned back against her arms. "I didn't mean that to sound like a threat. I just know we are both pretty hardheaded. If we can't learn to compromise when we disagree then we have a tough road ahead of us." Green eyes smiled into the serious blue ones. "If I lived someplace else, I could always walk out in a huff."

TJ's solemn demeanor began to lighten. "If you get in a huff when you live here, I'll just have to hunt you down and 'unhuff' you."

"Ummm, that sounds pretty intriguing. I'll try to remember that." Mare put her arms around TJ's neck and snuggled closer against her. "Just think, when I move out here we will have lots more time together."

"I'm counting on it." TJ leaned her dark head against the golden one and sat there, peacefully enjoying the feel of Mare's arms around her neck and the warmth of the body pressed against her own. Long-fingered hands, rarely still, contented themselves in gently moving up and down against her beloved's back, sending quiet messages of love.

Mare moaned softly, her heart brimming with the beauty of their companionship.

TJ kissed the golden hair then laid her head back down against it. Mare could feel the soft, velvety voice coming through TJ's chest. "I can't believe how much I love you. You are so much a part of me, it's like we really are just one person."

"I feel the same way," Mare whispered.

They held each other for a while then Mare stirred. "I wish I really could stay here forever. Unfortunately, I have to go back to work." She sat up, treated her senses to one more close-up of her lover's face then leaned into a kiss.

TJ ended the kiss by pulling away with a spurt of laughter. "Don't give me one of those 'light-TJ-up' kind of kisses then walk out the door. Save it for when you're going to stay and cool me off."

"Sorry. You're just soooo much fun to kiss."

"I thought the line was, 'You're just soooo much fun to torment'?"

Mare's eyes twinkled. "Well, sometimes one's the same as the other."

"Humph! You got that right." TJ pushed the button on the chair arm as Mare stood up.

Paula came in to answer the button's summons. "Mare, give Paula the key to the room. She can get started on clearing it out."

Mare retrieved the key from her pocket and handed it to the irrepressible woman. Paula winked and stuck it in her own pocket. "I'll come and help as soon as I can, Paula. Maybe even tonight."

TJ's heart skipped. "Hey, don't go tormenting me with words, now."

Mare grinned and patted her cheek. "You know I can't promise, but I will try."

"Hey, TJ, why not ask Mare to come with us to the plant next week? She might be interested in seeing how it works."

"Good idea, Paula. You might get back in my good graces, yet." Paula splayed her hand against her chest and her brows went up in a supposedly innocent look as Mare and TJ grinned. "How about it, Mare? Think you can make it?"

"You'll have to let me know exactly what day, then I'll have to see what's on my agenda, maybe rearrange a few things, get someone to cover for me. But, yeah, I can probably make it. With a new assistant on the horizon, I can move some things to a later date. Now, I better be going."

"Okay, we'll let you know the exact day as soon as we decide." TJ raised her arms and they kissed once more, then Mare left.

"Wait here, Paula." TJ wheeled over to the window and watched Mare walk to her truck and climb in. Mare felt TJ's eyes on her and she waved before backing up and rolling away.

TJ turned back around with a smile on her face that slowly died as her eyes came back to Paula and an eyebrow cocked up.

"Am I in trouble?"

"You and Erin both. Ganging up on me like that."

"What? We hardly said anything."

"You didn't have to. Mare and I both knew you were on her side."

"Well, she's a lot smaller than you. We think she should be protected." Paula was getting the idea that TJ wasn't really angry, just kidding around. She was sure of it when TJ's expression changed with her next words.

"Oh, that's what you think, huh?" TJ raised both brows and half grinned.

Paula looked at her a bit sheepishly. "Actually when Mare gets her mouth going, I kinda think you're the one who needs protected."

TJ laughed out loud. "Yeah, I think you're right about that." Then her expression sobered. "Listen, I want you to get started on that office, but I don't want to have anything at all to do with it, you understand?"

"I understand. And TJ..."

"Yeah?"

"Thanks. About the office, and for bringing Mare out here. She brightens up the whole place. Erin and I both think she's the greatest."

"Thanks, Paula. I think you two guys are the greatest, too. Where is Erin?"

"She went out to see about the horses being brought into the barn and hosed down. It's getting pretty hot out there."

"Yeah, those early morning rides you thought of were a great idea, for the horses and for us. The afternoons have been pretty nasty. Speaking of nasty, we better get back to work."

TJ and Paula started across the kitchen. Paula looked down at TJ with a wicked look on her face. "I guess when Mare gets here the early morning rides will be out, huh? On the horses, I mean."

TJ's laugh burst from her throat and she slapped Paula in the side. "Erin's right, you are outrageous. We'll worry about that when she gets here." The two left the kitchen, both grinning widely.

Chapter
23

"Aaaaa-chooo!" Mare's sneeze rocked the house as Erin and Paula looked at her in surprise and then laughed. Mare had made it back that afternoon to give Paula a hand clearing the office and Erin joined them shortly afterward. Paula, while working alone, had managed to sift through part of one of the two filing cabinets and had rescued the deeds and plats of the Meridian ranch holdings. She had her fill of paperwork and expressed an opinion that the rest of the files could wait until later, with which the others concurred.

They settled on a system that seemed to be working well. Erin attacked the bookcases, stacking the multicolored, leather-bound tomes in cartons. Paula collected the knick-knacks, trophies, mementos, pictures, wall hangings and other assorted furnishings into other cartons, while Mare investigated the contents of the desk.

The curly-headed blonde, pulling books from one of the bookcases that lined one wall, stopped for a second. "Where the heck did a sneeze that size come from?"

Mare made a face at her. "From all the darn dust you two are stirring up, that's where." The vet rubbed her nose and yanked another drawer from the huge black desk, quickly examining its contents.

"Hey, look at this." Paula pointed to a set of pictures standing on a shelf. Others hung against the wall behind them. She waited until Mare and Erin had come over to join her. "That must be TJ's father when he was a young man. He's not as heavyset there as he was later. Who does he remind you of?"

"He looks something like Peter!" Mare exclaimed.

"Yeah." Erin agreed. "He's taller and slimmer and darker, but give him a beard to go with that moustache and he and Peter could be brothers. That's amazing."

"That might be part of the reason Peter could never get TJ to talk about her father. It would be natural for her to withdraw from someone who reminded her of him. And neither one of them knew why." Mare shook her head at the irony of it. "I think I'll pass this information on to him; he can probably use it."

"Sounds good," Paula said, "but let's get moving with this stuff or we'll never get finished." The women returned to their efforts and worked silently for the next few minutes, each lost in her own thoughts.

Mare, never one to sit quietly, broke the silence. "You know, some of the stuff that was in this desk is valuable. You sure we should throw it all out?" Mare had already emptied three drawers and they were sitting atop the desk. She laid the fourth on the floor and was squatted down, poking through its contents. A carton next to her held what she had emptied from the other drawers.

Erin came over and looked in the carton. She saw several gold pen and pencil sets, sterling silver cups and flasks, old-fashioned cut glass inkwells and paperweights, and assorted other expensive items. "Why don't you put them in a separate carton and we'll donate them to one of the churches? TJ said we could give it away; she didn't insist we throw it out."

Mare nodded her head in agreement. "She sure was determined about not keeping anything from this room.

But it's understandable that those beatings really affected her." Mare's face and eyes grew sad. She stopped and sank cross-legged to the floor next to the drawer, depressed by the very idea of the beatings TJ endured. "It's hard to imagine anyone treating her like that."

Erin's expression turned hard, a drastic change from her usual tranquility. "Paula and I don't have to imagine it, we saw him in action. He was beating TJ like a maniac. She was a grown woman and he was half again her size." Erin's agitation sounded in her voice. "We took her to the hospital and all the way there she shook so hard I couldn't even keep hold of her. At first I thought she was shaking from fear, but then she started talking in a low, nasty voice. I've never heard that tone or those words since. She was shaking from hatred. He'd been beating her like that since she was..." Erin's voice turned hoarse, "It hurts like hell to think of her being abused like that even as a young kid."

Paula came over, put an arm around Erin's shoulders, and gave her a quick squeeze. "Nobody will ever hurt her again, if we have anything to say about it."

Erin gave her a grateful smile. "That's for sure."

Mare's eyes were wet with unshed tears. "Maybe clearing out everything in here that would remind her of him will help. But she's got a long way to go to rid herself of his horrible legacy."

"Well, this is a start." Erin patted the top of Mare's head. "And it's thanks to you. TJ wouldn't have done this for anyone else. Paula and I tried, but never could persuade her."

A silence fell for a minute and then they continued with the cleaning. Erin's eyes had fallen for a second time on the drawer Mare was unloading. Something snicked at the back of her mind, and she hesitated before returning to her task, but nothing surfaced. She went again to the bookcase and began putting books in a carton. Trying to fit a book into an opening between two others, she discovered it was too long, so she searched for and found one that was shorter and fit perfectly. As the book was sliding into place, she shouted, "It's too short!"

Mare and Paula both turned toward her and Paula spoke. "What are you talking about, Airy? Looks to me like it fit perfectly."

Erin raised her eyebrows and pointed her forefinger at her partner. "You better stop calling me that. You know I don't like it."

Paula shook her arms and hands. "Oooooohhh, I'm scared." She laughed at the expression on Erin's face. "Well, it's better than Air-head. Or Mare's initials." She turned to Mare with a grin. "Anybody ever call you MT?"

"No one who ever lived to tell about it," Mare said with such sincerity that all three of them laughed. "What were you talking about, anyway, Erin? What's too short?"

Erin had walked over to where Mare had just finished sorting through the drawer. The curly-headed blonde reached down and picked the drawer up. "This drawer is too short. Look." She laid it on top of one of the other three that were lying on top of the desk. Sure enough, it was about six inches too short. "Look in the opening, Mare. See if there's anything in there."

Mare knelt up and bent over to look in the opening. "Yeah! There is something in there!" She reached in, found an inlaid ring, and pulled it out. It was another, smaller drawer. There were some papers and pictures in the small container and she stood up and dumped them on an open spot on the desk.

Erin stacked the other drawers at the far end of the desk and she and Paula joined Mare in inspecting the contents. Mare spread the pictures out. Most of them seemed to be all of the same person at different ages: a baby, an infant, a boy, and a preteen. The earlier pictures also had a young woman in them, holding the child. The boy had the same black hair and blue eyes that TJ, her father and Lance had.

Mare looked from Erin to Paula. "Do you think this is TJ's father when he was a child? Or maybe Lance?"

Erin had picked up one of the pieces of paper and was reading it. She shook her head. "No, I don't think the answer is that easy. This is a birth certificate. The boy's name is Thomas Joseph Meridian Raphaele. His mother's name is Gloria Raphaele." She looked up at Mare and Paula, then back down at the paper. "His father's name is Thomas Joseph Meridian."

The three stood there, speechless, just staring at each other.

"How old is he now?" Mare managed to ask.

Erin looked at the certificate. "He's sixteen."

"TJ has a half-brother. Wow. Wonder how this is going to hit her?" Paula frowned and put her hands on her hips. "Maybe we shouldn't even tell her. She has this strong, powerful side, but we all know she's still pretty fragile about anything concerning her father."

Mare pondered this for a moment. "I don't see how we can keep it from her. Obviously, these people must know something about her. They could pop up at any time. It would be better for her to be prepared. Besides, she has a right to know she has a brother."

"Yeah, I agree." Erin's face vacillated between anguish and frustration. "Every time something good happens to TJ," Erin squeezed Mare's shoulder, "something else happens to kick her in the gut." She stood a minute, thinking, while the other two waited. "But I don't think we should tell her just yet. I'd like time to investigate this first. That way we can give her the whole story instead of just part of it."

"Sounds good to me. TJ has enough to contend with without someone causing her more problems," Paula growled and Mare nodded in agreement.

Erin put the certificate down and pawed through the remaining papers. "Some of these are copies of letters from Tom Meridian to the boy and his mother." She handed some to Mare and Paula.

The women read through the letters. Mare looked up. "These are pretty sentimental. Sounds like Tom Meridian really loved this boy and his mother."

"Yeah." Erin sounded disgruntled. "Shame he couldn't spare some of that for his daughter." She gathered together the papers, letters and pictures, looked for a rubber band, and encircled them with one. "I'll put these in our bedroom. TJ never goes in there," she addressed Mare, "I'll keep you posted on the investigation. You know who's going to be the one to tell TJ about this, don't you?"

Mare swallowed and agreed. "That's not going to be an easy task. I might need backup. We'll talk about this when you've gotten the information, okay?" Erin and Paula nodded.

Erin stuck the package under her arm. "Time to call a break anyway, it's almost supper time. We can work on this again another day. I'll run this stuff upstairs and be right down. If you two want to wash up and start putting the food out, I'll join you in a few minutes."

"Okay," Paula answered. "Don't forget, we're having our music night tonight. And no excuses from TJ; she is going to sing." That thought lightened everyone's mood and they all went off to their chosen tasks.

****

TJ, lying face down on the bed, sighed with pleasure. She could feel Mare's knees bent alongside her waist and although she had no sensation of Mare, unclothed, sitting across her thighs, she could picture her there with her mind. She grinned. *I always did have a pretty good imagination.* Fingers slathered with perfumed oil massaged the juncture of her neck and shoulders then worked outward and downward, covering every inch of skin.

Each time Mare came to one of the scars on the otherwise unblemished skin, she leaned forward and switched the massage from her fingers to her tongue and lips before resuming her downward journey. After a prolonged trip, Mare reached the point where TJ's feeling stopped.

Mare leaned her upper body against TJ's back and made a request into her ear, "Do you mind if I continue this little expedition? I know you can't feel my hands, but I can feel you."

"Hmmm. You can do anything your little heart desires." TJ had been lying there dreamily luxuriating in every rub and stroke. A soft warmth danced through her when Mare leaned down against her back. When Mare changed position and faced the other way, TJ's body suddenly came to full alert. Now Mare was sitting on TJ's back, her knees bent alongside. Moving back and forth in a rocking motion, she stroked her way down the long-legged half of the prone body.

TJ believed that when she lost feeling in the lower half of her body, the upper half had become more sensitive. Although she had no real basis for this belief, the reaction she was experiencing from Mare's rocking against her back seemed to reinforce it. Twisting her neck to look behind her, the slight glimpse she could manage made her groan and flop her face down again. Exerting enormous will power she waited at least three minutes before licking dry lips and saying hoarsely, "I'll promise you anything if you'll turn me over and do that rocking on my front." Erotic fantasies of sight, touch, and taste blazed through TJ's imagination, deepening her breathing and covering her with a fine sheen of perspiration.

The passionate voice of her lover, accompanied by a low chuckle, pumped her adrenaline up even higher. "Your every wish is my command."

The next hour outdid her wildest dreams.

* * * * * * * * *

Satiated, the two clung together, damp skin slowly cooling. Mare laid in her favorite spot, turned toward TJ, her head in the hollow of her lover's shoulder, one arm spread across her waist. One of TJ's arms wrapped around her while the other moved a softly caressing hand up and down her side and back.

"I am so glad I had only that one appointment this afternoon. I miss you so much when we don't have a chance to get together."

The wandering hand stopped and came to Mare's chin. Long fingers tipped Mare's face up. The dark head, sending a message of love from affectionate eyes, bent down for a sweet kiss. "Me, too."

"Paula and Erin and I got a lot done toward cleaning out the office, too." Mare felt a slight tensing of muscles in the body lying against her. *Oops, that was dumb, Mare. You know she doesn't want to even think about that room. With what we discovered, I don't either, at the moment. Okay, time to get her relaxed again. Glad we had that gathering in the music room before bedtime.*

Mare put an elbow down against the bed and lifted a little to look into TJ's face. "You know, when Paula said you had a beautiful voice, she wasn't kidding."

TJ had closed her eyes. A tiny smile tugged at her lips. "Right."

"You do!" Mare's hand slapped down against the firm belly bringing the blue eyes open. "How about singing me to sleep? Nobody's done that since I was a little girl."

The magnificent eyes slanted down and the smile grew larger. "You still are a little girl."

Mare snorted and nudged TJ with an elbow. "How tall are you, anyway?"

"Just about six foot."

"Wow, no wonder it took me so long to oil your whole body."

Mare's smile grew impish. "Why don't you sing me... 'Rock-a-bye Baby'?"

Newly experienced erotic images suffused TJ's mind this time and she pulled Mare over on top of her, one hand already searching for sweet spots. "Woman, you just don't know when to quit, do you?"

Chapter
24

Mare climbed the ladder out of the pool and accepted the towel Michael handed to her. She dried her face and arms and gave her head a brisk rub, just enough to keep the excess water from running off her hair and down her body. "This is really great, so refreshing. I wonder why Meridian ranch doesn't have a pool? It would be terrific for TJ." She chuckled. "And I don't think Paula or Erin would object, either. I think I'll ask her about that." She walked over and sat at an umbrella table across from Michael.

Her father looked at her and smiled. *There's no doubt she loves the woman. All you have to do is watch her face light up when she mentions her.* "Mare, I finally have finished my examination of TJ's records."

Hope brightened Mare's face even more. "And?"

Michael reached over and patted her hand. "I wish I could be more optimistic, but I'm no miracle worker, Mare. That bullet fragment in TJ's back is wedged against her spinal cord at a level we call T-11. If it could be removed, there are some treatments that might return some feeling and limited use to her legs. But it's in such a precarious position; it is inoperable. There's just no way to get to it without damaging her spinal cord further. I'm sorry."

Mare's face fell. She had harbored some unrealistic hope that her father could help TJ. To find out he couldn't was hard to accept.

"I know you're terribly disappointed and so am I. I'd love to be able to help her—for your sake, too."

"No, Dad, I'm not disappointed for me. I love TJ no matter what. I'm disappointed for her for all the obvious reasons, of course. But also for one that might sound a little crazy. TJ loves horses. I know everything I read about horseback riding mentions the wonderful sensation of wrapping your legs around such a powerful animal. I see her on Faithful Flag and I could cry that she can't feel that sensation anymore."

Mare sighed. "TJ pats her and hugs her and strokes her, but it's not a true substitute. She can't feel her *seat*. It hurts to see these two magnificent animals who belong together and know that TJ can't experience the full pleasure of that."

Michael nodded in sympathy. "I keep abreast of everything having to do with SCI. If anything shows up, I'll jump right on it."

"Thanks, Dad. Just knowing that you are concerned helps a lot." Mare picked her watch up from the table. "Looks like it's about time to get ready to leave."

"Your visit was a little shorter this time. Too bad your latest prospect for an assistant could only be interviewed today."

"Yeah, that is a shame. But he seems like the perfect candidate. I don't want to let him slip through my fingers. If I had my way, he'd start tomorrow." Mare stood up. "Stay out here, Dad. There's no need for you to shepherd me around now. I think I've finally got the house plan down pat."

She leaned down and kissed his cheek, and he kissed hers. "Okay, Mare, if that makes you happy then I'm happy to do it." Michael grinned and waved as she entered the house to prepare to go home. Her mind was already on the logistics of remodeling the office and moving her belongings to the Meridian ranch in time for her about-to-be-hired assistant to move his wife and baby into her house. And making plans for some of the extra time she would free up to spend with her love.

* * * * * * * * * *

"Dr. Gillespie, I had my lawyer look over the contract and the rental agreement and he said everything was in order." Barry Cassel pulled the papers from his briefcase and handed them to Mare. "Here they are, all properly signed." Close to her own age, Barry was tall and muscular with straight, dark brown hair and hazel eyes. He had a friendly, outgoing manner, and he and Mare had liked each other at once.

Although Barry was a native Texan, after graduation from veterinary school he had worked in Idaho with a fellow graduate. He married his childhood sweetheart and he and his wife, Berta, had a two-year-old son, Bobby. The parents decided that they wanted their son, and any future children, to grow up in Texas, so they made plans to move.

He and Mare were in her office seated at the desk. "That's great, Barry. Welcome to the practice." Mare offered her hand and they shook. "From now on, please call me Mare. I know most of the people in this town. They are a pretty good sort. I think you'll be happy you came here."

"I think so, too, Mare. Berta and I have already met a few people and we were impressed by their friendliness. When would you like me to start?"

Mare's smile dimpled her cheeks. "Just as soon as you can. My vet friend in Sharlesburg will be glad to have another person thrown into the mix, too. We've been covering for each other on alternate Sundays and your being here will give us some welcome breathing room. Darn animals don't know what Sunday is." Mare shook her head. Her Sharlesburg friend had been doing extra duty on Saturdays, too, to give Mare a break in getting to know her father. But paybacks would come, sooner or later.

"I assume you will be giving two weeks notice to your current associate?" Barry nodded and Mare continued, "That will give me more than enough time to get moved out. As soon as I am, you can start moving in and I will expect you in the office two weeks from Monday. How's that?"

"That would be fine. The rental agreement doesn't start for two weeks after that, though. Should we prorate the rent for that extra time?"

"No, consider that part of your welcome here." Mare rose and Barry followed her up. They shook hands and Mare walked him to the door. "I'm looking forward to meeting Berta. Anyone married to a vet has to be a very understanding person!"

"She is that. We'll be seeing you soon."

Barry left and Mare leaned against the closed door. "Thank whatever gods that be. An assistant!" Smiling, she put the agreements in her safe, picked up her already packed belongings and went out the door, heading for Meridian ranch. *Heading for TJ,* her heart sang. *I wonder if I'll always have this feeling of being only half a person when I'm not with her? And feeling so perfectly complete when I am? I hope it never stops.*

****

Mare, trying to do too many things in too little time, was exhausted. She crawled into bed and snuggled up to TJ. She lay quietly in her lover's arms, feeling TJ's gentle caress against her back. Gradually, the hand stilled as TJ heard Mare's breathing become slow and deep. *Son of a gun, she fell asleep! Poor kid must be dead tired.* Disappointed, she nevertheless realized that Mare was off the next day and they would have other opportunities. Smiling in anticipation of a whole day together, TJ drifted off to sleep, too.

Mare awoke in the middle of the night. At first, embarrassed that she had fallen asleep after looking forward to lovemaking, she soon realized that she must have been exhausted and the sleep would do her good. She hesitated to move, lest she wake TJ, but she smiled, picturing in her mind the repose that came to her lover's gorgeous face only in sleep.

As often happens when waking during the night, Mare's mind started to think more than she wanted it to, and she fought against it, wanting only to go back to sleep.

I'm so glad Paula and Erin were able to finish clearing the office. Paula said movers will come Monday to haul everything away and she will start painting right after that. Looks like I might be out here within the week! Everything seemed to be falling beautifully into place—a "new" father, a new assistant, a new home, and TJ.

Her smile grew as she recalled the surprise she and Paula had cooked up for TJ for tomorrow. Erin, delighted when they told her, had even offered a few suggestions. *Yeah, my love, tomorrow will be your day.*

Mare kissed TJ's body where her head lay and snuggled closer as TJ's arm reflexively tightened around her. Then the golden-haired vet's mind finally quieted and her breathing slowed to match TJ's as she fell asleep once more.

* * * * * * * * * *

Mare slipped out of TJ's embrace in the morning, and got out of bed, still pleading fatigue. The night before, she really had been too tired, but this morning she was pretending, believing that restraint now would add enjoyment to their planned time together later in the day.

TJ frowned and pouted. "You aren't sick or something are you?"

"No." Mare bent over and planted a swift kiss on the pushed out lip, ducking to avoid TJ's encircling arm. "But don't look so sad. We have a surprise for you."

TJ's face brightened. "What?"

"You'll find out later." Mare laughed at TJ's snort of frustration and dashed into the bathroom. She showered and dressed, fending off any further questions about the surprise other than to tell TJ she could dispense with her tubes and bags for a while.

Mare went in search of Paula, finding her in the kitchen stacking a few items in the dishwasher. "Erin gave me a hand and everything's ready and packed," the dark-haired woman informed her.

"Great." Mare gave her a quick squeeze. "By the time TJ does her exercises and we finish breakfast, we can leave." She grinned wickedly. "I told her we have a surprise for her, so she'll probably try to pump it out of you."

Paula laughed and dried her hands. "She won't get any news from me. I'll go start her on her exercises, now. There's coffee made if you want some."

Mare took a mug from the cupboard and poured a cup. "How do you think TJ's going to react to this? Do you foresee any problems?"

"I hope not. Can't think of a reason for any. I think this is a super idea. That last episode you two went through really shook her up. She needs a good experience to replace that." Paula made a thumb's up sign and went to take care of TJ.

All through breakfast, TJ forced herself not to ask Mare anything about the surprise. She just kept throwing daggered looks at her and Paula and Erin, recognizing that the three were in cahoots and were determined to torment her. And she was just as determined not to let them.

When breakfast was over, Erin went out the door and Mare and Paula, chatting away, cleared the island. After about 10 minutes, Mare took charge of TJ's wheelchair and pushed her out to the barn and up the ramp as Erin brought the saddled Flag toward her. "Mare, what is going on? Where am I supposed to be riding Flag to?"

Mare didn't answer and TJ saw Paula come bounding into the barn, grab a saddle from the tack room and take it over to Runny's stall. "Wait a minute." TJ's jaw set and she frowned at Erin who still held Flag. "Who's supposed to ride Runny?"

"I'm going to." Mare moved to the side of the chair so TJ could see her. "We're going for a ride somewhere to find out the surprise."

TJ's eyes swept up to Mare. "Mare." Her eyebrow hiked up and she looked stern. "Do you really want to ride that horse?"

Mare started to get red and looked away. "Er... I don't... Look, TJ, I want to go riding with you."

"Is riding Runny part of the surprise? Or you just need to go wherever it is on horseback?"

Mare looked at Erin, then at Paula who was still holding Runny's saddle and shrugging. "We just need to go on horseback."

"Okay. Erin, strap me toward the back of the saddle and Mare can ride with me." She glanced from Erin back to Mare and saw her love's beautiful face clear. TJ grinned as she realized the idea appealed to Mare. Erin and Paula were grinning, too.

Erin nodded. "That's a great idea, TJ. Paula and I both are a little leery of Mare riding any more without taking some runs close to home for a while."

Paula, a big grin still on her face, took Runny's saddle back to the tack room while Erin and Mare helped TJ use the hoist to mount Flag. Erin did as TJ asked and strapped her toward the back of the saddle.

Then Mare managed to mount by swinging her leg forward past the saddle horn and settling in front of TJ. Clasping one arm around her, TJ clucked to Flag and they started off.

"You mind telling me which way I should direct Flag to go?"

"We're going to the lake, okay? Just aim her that way."

"The surprise is at the lake?"

"Yep." Mare pushed her lips tight together.

"And you're not telling me until we get there, right?"

"Right." She pushed her lips even tighter together.

TJ reached under Mare's shirt and laid her long hand flat against her lover's bare stomach. Just before her lips locked on the side of Mare's neck, she uttered a throaty laugh. "We might not get to the lake."

Mare grabbed the wandering hand and brought it back outside her shirt. "Uh-uh. No hanky-panky until we get to the lake." *Good grief, the woman's voice turns me on. It's no wonder her touch drives me crazy.*

"Hanky-panky?" TJ raised her eyebrows, mocking the expression. "Okay, no hanky-panky. What do you think about a little necking?" TJ moved Mare's hair from the back of her neck and planted a kiss there.

Mare sighed, closed her eyes, and leaned back against the firm body. "I think we better hurry and get to the lake."

****

At last, they reached their destination and TJ's eyes widened when she saw a blanket spread on the ground with a tablecloth, picnic basket, cooler and several large pillows sitting on it. She gave Mare an extra hug. "So, this is the surprise. A picnic!" She looked around. The spot chosen was a grassy clearing that abutted the lake, just beyond the ring of trees. One solitary old sentinel stood in the clearing, spreading its boughs over the blanket, its branches reaching to the edge of the water.

"This is a perfect spot, Mare. I have just one question."

Mare swung her leg over the saddle horn and slid down to the earth. "What's that?"

"Just how am I supposed to get off of Flag?" Mare looked up for the quirked eyebrow and wasn't disappointed.

"Just hand me your cell phone, baby."

Mare smirked as TJ raised both eyebrows and mouthed "Baby?" But she pulled the phone from her belt holder and passed it to Mare.

The vet punched in some numbers and spoke to the one answering. "We're here."

She handed the phone back to TJ. "Now we have a short wait."

About two minutes later, Erin and Paula showed up in the Rover. They pulled next to Flag and piled out with big grins on their faces. Paula looked up at TJ. "Here we are, boss, ready to bring you back to earth."

Erin poked Paula with an elbow and rolled her eyes. Paula snorted. "Well, it sure as hell doesn't take an hour and a half to ride out here from the ranch, even on a slow horse, and Flag isn't slow."

Mare tried for the innocent approach. "Well, we were checking out the scenery."

"Sure," Paula chortled. "Guess that's why your blouse is buttoned crooked, right?"

Mare looked quickly down at her shirt and saw that it was, indeed, buttoned wrong. A cute little blush started up her cheeks. It turned into a full-fledged red face when she heard TJ's dry response. "She didn't say what scenery."

Everyone laughed, including Mare, and Erin and Paula helped TJ down from Flag. Supporting TJ by draping her arms over their shoulders, they settled their friend on the blanket with her back against the tree. While Erin held TJ steady, Paula moved the cooler against her one side so she would have something to balance against and put a pillow on her other side. Mare tied Flag's reins to a bush, allowing the palomino room to graze the sweet grass, then loosened the saddle girth.

"How's that, TJ? You comfy?" Erin was squatted next to her; not letting go until she made sure TJ could sit with-

out help. When TJ nodded, Erin kissed her on the cheek
and stood up. "Okay, you guys, enjoy. Paula has fixed a
feast for you and there's beer, soda and a bottle of wine in
the cooler. Give us a call when you need us and we'll be
back to help get TJ onto Flag."

"Thanks, both of you. We'll probably be a few hours."
Mare gave them each a hug.

"You know what?" They turned to TJ and waited. "If
someone would loop a wide rope around this limb above
me and tie it off every foot or so, I could probably get on
and off Flag by myself."

The other three looked at each other in chagrin. Then
Mare pointed out something that saved face for them. "We
needed to have the picnic basket and cooler brought out
anyway." Erin and Paula looked a little happier at this
explanation. "But let's get a rope out here for the visits
when we aren't picnicking, okay?"

"Sure thing," Erin pulled a notebook with pencil from
her pocket and added that suggestion. She and Paula
climbed in the Rover, waved and left.

"Mare," TJ's seductive voice climbed across the vet's
heart, "c'mere and let me fix those buttons."

Mare grinned and her eyes twinkled. "Uh... how about
if we eat first?" She walked to the blanket and sat down
next to the basket, opening the lid.

TJ grumbled, but it was a good-natured one, "You and
that stomach! Are you always hungry?"

Mare stopped a moment, seeming to give the question
serious consideration. "Yeah, I think I am always hungry.
But it's not always food that I'm hungry for." She looked
straight into TJ's eyes. "Most of the time it's something...
someone... else." She squealed as TJ rolled onto her side,
then her stomach, got her arms under her, and "walked" to
Mare. She reached for her, but Mare was just a little too
quick. The laughing vet jumped to her feet and stepped
over the picnic basket, settling on the far side of it. "No,
you don't, TJ. Food first! I don't know what you run on,
but this body needs some fuel!"

Joining Mare's laughter, TJ rolled onto her back. "Okay, I give up. I've waited this long, I guess a little longer won't kill me. Food first. Wouldn't want you wasting away to nothing from burnout." She finished laughing and propped herself on one elbow. "This is a great surprise, Mare. Thanks."

"You've been working so hard, trying to keep things moving for the ranch and the packing plant, I figured it was time for you to relax a little." Mare dished out the food onto the china plates Paula had provided and handed one to TJ who rolled up onto her side. "You're the most important person in this mix, sweetheart. We don't want you burning out, either."

"That 'most important person' part is a matter of opinion." TJ's hooded eyes left no doubt as to whom she considered the most important. In answer, Mare tossed a wrapped chicken leg at her, which TJ easily caught and set on her plate.

"Eat!" Mare laughed.

"Yeah, and hurry up about it!" TJ added, eating quickly like she was going to wolf her food.

Mare came back to the other side of the picnic basket to sit cross-legged next to TJ. Reaching for one of the pillows, she handed it to TJ to lean on. "No, slow down and enjoy it. Or..." Mare's face got the impish look that always captivated TJ, "you won't get any dessert."

"Okay, okay, I'm eating slowly. Please notice how well behaved I've been all day, in spite of being mercilessly tormented by a green-eyed vixen." Mare glanced down at the crooked buttoning on her shirt and looked back up with a questioning tilt of her head. TJ grinned and shrugged. "Well, I behaved almost all day. Can't blame a girl for trying."

"Right. So don't go pretending you were the only one being tormented."

TJ's smile burst across her cheeks. "Hehehehe. You loved every minute of it."

A wee smile fought its way onto Mare's lips and her eyes gleamed. "Yeah, I guess I did." She reached for TJ's empty plate, stacked it with hers, and put it into the basket. Then she picked up both sides of the tablecloth, folded them over whatever was left on it, and set it in, too.

Mare reached into the basket with one hand and encircled the stems of two wineglasses. She froze in that position as TJ's arm encircled her waist. Using the hold for leverage, TJ used her other hand to unbutton Mare's shirt. "That was just an appetizer," she murmured, capturing a mound's peak between her teeth and teasing with her tongue. She dropped her hand onto Mare's jeans and began stroking deeply.

Mare let go of the glass stems and entangled one hand in the dark hair to pull it tighter against her. Her other hand loosened her jeans top as she squirmed to straighten her legs to face TJ's body. "Okay, we'll have the wine later," she breathed.

* * * * * * * * * *

They lay together on the blanket, a gentle breeze from the lake serving to cool the vestiges of their lovemaking. Dampness still lingered where their skin touched. Mare lay on her back, fingers lost in raven hair, one hand cupping her lover's cheek. TJ's head rested against Mare's stomach, one long arm wrapped underneath her thighs while the other hand stroked up and down Mare's side and hip.

"Does that hand ever stay still?" Mare's lazy question hung in the air.

The hand stopped. "Do you want it to?"

"No, never."

There was a deep chuckle and the hand returned to its gentle stroking.

"TJ, do you know how to swim?"

"Yeeeeah."

"You want to give the lake a try?"

"You planning on carrying me over there?"

"Come on, it's only about 20 feet. We're practically in it already. You can roll over there. Let go of me and I'll show you." TJ loosened her grasp on Mare's legs and raised her head. Mare scooted out from under her and laid out flat on the ground. She started rolling, traveling right up to the water's edge.

"See?" She waved to TJ. "It's easy. Come on."

TJ turned the upper half of her body and lined it up with the shoreline. She rolled along the ground just as Mare had, a little surprised at how easily her body rolled across the grass. She stopped at the edge of the water and looked up at Mare who was now standing. "Not a bad idea, Mare. But I'm not too sure I can stay afloat. My legs will probably weigh me down."

"In the water you won't weigh anywhere near what you weigh out of the water, so I can help hold you up. I'll support your legs. Come on, give me your hands." Mare took hold of TJ's hands and dragged her the last couple of feet across the grass and into the water. She kept pulling her until the water was up to her chest, then moved TJ's hands to her shoulders and smiled into her eyes. "You okay so far?"

"Yeah, as long as I hold onto you. This feels pretty good. They kept taking me into the pool at the hospital for therapy but I was too depressed to give a damn, then. I don't feel that way now, thanks to you." She pulled herself closer to Mare, encircled her neck with her arms and kissed her soundly.

Hugging TJ's body tightly and holding the kiss, Mare sank below the surface of the water and then rose again to the air. Their lips broke apart and Mare laughed. "You look like a different person with your hair plastered back like that."

"Different? How?" Mare shivered with delight as TJ's velvet voice skittered through her.

"I'm not sure. Younger? More... rakish? Not quite your usual sober self."

"Sober am I?" TJ tickled Mare's ribs.

"Look out, now. Tickling me out in the middle of the water is not a good idea unless you are sure you can swim."

"Mmmm. You have a point. Maybe I should try this instead."

"TJ, stop! I'm warning you, you better stop. You better... ohhhh, don't stop. Don't ever stop." TJ's mouth closed on Mare's as her lover's knees buckled and she and TJ went below the surface again. Mare's hands and body joined TJ's as they locked together in the throes of passion. Mare finally remembered they needed air to live and managed to find enough strength in her legs to straighten up. Their mouths stayed fastened together until their bodies quieted then they pulled their lips apart, panting.

"You could have killed us, woman," Mare gasped.

TJ put her head on Mare's shoulder and clung to her. "I thought we did die. Wasn't that heaven we just visited?"

Mare started to giggle. "Yes, yes, yes! Sure felt like heaven to me! What is it about water that is so sexy?"

TJ snorted a small laugh. "Moments like this, maybe? You know what, Mare? I think we're ready for that wine now. We have a few things to celebrate today."

Mare pulled TJ back to the shore and she helped her to roll back to the blanket. She went to Flag and pulled several towels from the saddlebag. Back at TJ's side, she began to dry her off.

"I can do that, you know." .

Mare's hands froze. "You want me to stop?"

TJ's gorgeous smile spread across her face. "No, never."

Mare grinned and continued, kissing each part as she dried it. When she finished, she helped TJ get dressed, then dried herself and got dressed while TJ, her eyes filled with love, observed her.

"I love to watch you, Mare. Every movement you make is so smooth and graceful. Just like you. What did I ever do to deserve you?"

Mare finished buttoning her shirt—straight, this time—and smiled at her lover as she lifted the wineglasses from the picnic basket and TJ pulled the wine from the cooler. "I asked myself almost that same question the other day. I guess the two of us just got very, very lucky."

TJ had pulled herself up against the tree beside the cooler. Mare sat next to her and held the glasses while TJ filled them, then set the bottle back in the cooler. The dark-haired woman held her glass out to her golden-haired lover. "To us."

Mare clinked her glass against TJ's. "To us."

They sat side by side, shoulders touching, and drank their wine as the mid-afternoon sun reflected from the glassy surface of the lake.

"We'll have more time to spend a day together like this when you get your new assistant and can move to the ranch." TJ glanced down at Mare and smiled.

"Boy, am I looking forward to that. Barry has a great resume, a terrific personality, and talks like a dedicated worker. I know he'll be an asset to the practice and the additional free time that will give me seems almost too good to be true. Running two offices should be a real boost for everybody, too."

"Mare, we have several suites of rooms in the ranch house. I want you to pick out a suite for your own."

Mare sat forward, frowning, and turned to look into TJ's face. "Why, TJ?"

"I want you to stay with me every second, of every minute, of every hour, of every day, forever. But I don't want you ever to stay with me just because you feel obligated to. Or," TJ grinned wryly, "if you're ever in a huff and need someplace to be alone for a while." She looked down and picked up Mare's hand that had been resting on her thigh. "Are you all right with that?"

The blue eyes swept up to Mare's and her heart flip-flopped once again. Mare saw the tiny glint of satisfaction that flickered through them and she punched a slightly startled TJ in the arm. "Yes, I'm all right with that but you know what your eyes do to me and still you pin me with them. Have you no mercy at all?"

The lips started to part in a grin. "Well, I..."

Both the grin and the voice were interrupted by Mare's mouth sealing the lips then forcing them back apart with a tasting tongue. At last the kiss ended and Mare kept her body against TJ's where it seemed to belong.

"Time to call the girls, I guess." Mare sighed and nodded, and TJ made the call.

Touching their heads together, they held hands like young lovers and murmured endearments as they waited for their friends to arrive.

Chapter
25

"Well, boss-lady, what now?" Paula threw the last files onto the desk in front of TJ, a grin pulling itself onto her face. They had just covered every inch of the packing plant work areas and Paula had reason to be proud. The first start-up on the new machinery had gone well and the few workers who were in the plant had no difficulties in using it, or rectifying the simulated breakdowns. As soon as the final inspections were completed, the plant would be operational.

TJ looked up at the grinning woman, pleased to see her so happy. Paula had put an awful lot of work into getting the plant up and running. In fact, without Paula and Erin, the rejuvenation of Meridianville would have been impossible. "Where are Mare and Erin?"

"Hoping I can convince you to call it a day," she suggested.

"Hmm. That might be possible, on one condition." Paula raised her eyebrow in inquiry. "It's late and I think we all deserve to celebrate a little. Let's go to that bar on the road out of town, get a bite to eat and have a few drinks."

"Sounds like a plan to me. Who's driving?"

"You can toss for it," replied TJ, putting the files that Paula had dropped on the table into her briefcase.

"Oh great," moaned the woman, "I never win when we toss for it."

"You could just ask Erin to drive for a change, you know." TJ looked over her shoulder as she wheeled out of the door, "This is your celebration, after all."

"Good point, well presented and you can tell her." Paula smiled sweetly and walked ahead to round up Erin and Mare.

Erin actually took the fact that she had been made designated driver pretty well. They had all piled in the van: Paula and Mare in the rear, TJ and Erin up front. Morale within the quartet was high. Things on the ranch, at the factory and in town were going well; life was treating them all kindly for a change. Erin knew that she would be the only one sober by the end of the evening, but she didn't begrudge Paula her night out.

The bar wasn't that far from the factory site, ten minutes at the most. Since it was still pretty early in the evening, it wasn't that crowded when the girls arrived. It was like most other bars found in smaller towns; dimly lit with smoke-clouded air, the wail of a country singer coming from the jukebox.

The four women immediately found a table that they could fit TJ's chair beneath, and a somewhat tired looking waitress came for their order. TJ dove in first, ordering a jug of beer, and cutting off any remarks by telling them all that they were having a proper drink not some fancy cocktail concoction. She also requested that chips and nuts and whatever else they could lay their hands on be brought. The waitress grinned at the obviously happy group and made to leave but Erin stopped her, asking for a large cola and also telling the waitress that she was setting a limit on the amount of beer that would cross the bar for the table tonight.

TJ scowled across at her but didn't argue. She knew the rules; she was the one who had invented them. They all knew that whoever was driving made the decisions. If Erin told them they were leaving, they left, no arguments, and if she told someone they had had enough then they stopped. Anybody who didn't play by the rules would pay a nasty forfeit when they finally sobered up. If they should get arrested, then they were left for the night in the care of the local law.

They had all paid the forfeit at least once and none of them cared to pay it again. There was the time before TJ's accident when both Erin and Paula had regretted the decision to ignore TJ's "it's time to go" and spent a very uncomfortable night sitting outside their hotel because TJ had told the manager not to let them in. She hadn't even relented when it rained, though she did send out raincoats for them.

But they had got their own back a year later just before TJ's accident. TJ ended up cleaning Erin and Paula's apartment for a week, also doing the laundry and cooking. The cooking had been changed to restaurant or take-out after the initial taste of what TJ had put in front of them that first night. These rules had been carefully explained to Mare and it was up to her to stick to them.

An ice-cold jug of beer and three glasses appeared on the table and Paula did the honors by pouring the first drink. She waited until the waitress got back with Erin's cola and the snacks before she made the first toast of the evening. Paula stood and raised the glass in her hand.

"To the loves of our life and a job well done," she said, looking at her lover and two friends. She took a deep drink as the others repeated the toast.

****

Despite the fact that she was the only sober one sitting at the table, Erin was enjoying the evening. In the two hours that they had been here the bar steadily got busier.

The noise level rose and it became increasingly difficult to see through the layer of smoke that hung in the air. Erin checked her watch again, wondering what time to call it quits on the happy little group. It was just after eight thirty. *I'll give them another half an hour then I'll get them home.*

Mare rose unsteadily to her feet and smiled down at TJ who was gazing lovingly up at her. "I'll be back in a few minutes, sweetie." Even in her inebriated state, Mare managed to hold back her desire to lean down and kiss TJ.

TJ tangled her hand in Mare's and squeezed tightly, knowing that a more overt public display of affection would be appreciated by Mare, but probably not by those around them. "Hurry back, I'll miss you." Her lower lip dropped and Mare grinned at her, loving the cute expression on TJ's face. Mare returned the squeeze then tottered off toward the restrooms, weaving between those who were dancing to the country music with the expertise granted her by the amount of alcohol she had consumed this evening. TJ propped her elbow on the table, placed her head in her hand, and watched Mare's shapely body disappear from sight.

Erin observed TJ with interest. She had never seen her friend so totally taken with someone, not even the few times she had gone out with women in college. It amused her to see TJ so absorbed in the woman.

She felt a heavy weight on her shoulder and looked to her left. Paula, talking to TJ who was still gazing toward where Mare had disappeared, now rested her head on Erin's shoulder. *Time to get this lady home to bed I think.* "TJ! TJ!"

TJ's head slowly turned toward Erin. "Hmm?"

"Last one, then we go. Okay?" TJ nodded and went back to gazing after Mare.

Mare eventually broke through the dancers and spied the facilities she was after. She edged her way around a group of four rather loud men, not recognizing them in the smoky atmosphere. She pushed the restroom door open, squinting at the bright light and groaning to herself. *Boy, am I gonna regret this tomorrow.* A few minutes later she exited the restroom and began to make the trek back to TJ and the girls. She had put one foot on the dance floor when she felt a large hand grab her shoulder and turn her around.

"Hello there, Doc." Mare blearily looked up and recognized Nick Lanson, a local troublemaker. "You gonna let me and my buddies buy you a drink?"

Uh oh. She smiled at the man and then carefully removed his hand. "Thanks for your offer but I'm with friends." She smiled at him again then turned and made a rapid exit across the dance floor.

TJ beamed as she saw Mare appear through the crowd. She grabbed hold of her hand and pulled her down into her chair. "You're back!" Her smile lit up her face. "The big, bad lady over there says we have to go." TJ turned her blue eyes on Erin.

Erin smiled at the pair. "Yes, and the big, bad lady is sticking to her guns."

"No fair," said Mare. "We were just starting to have fun."

"Ah, ah, ah. Remember the rules," Paula said with a pronounced slur to her words.

Nick watched the blonde woman walk away from him and turned back to his friends. Juan was nearly in tears; he was laughing so hard. Miguel wasn't much better. Tony, the youngest of the four, strolled up to him and draped an arm around his shoulders.

"It was a nice try, Nick, but I'd say the doc's brush-off was better." Tony let his gaze wander over in the direction the blonde had disappeared. His eyes fixed as a parting in the crowd showed her sitting down at a table full of beautiful women. "Oh, looky there. I wonder if that's some of her new friends from Meridian ranch." His face turned dark when he thought about the buckshot fired into the side of his truck by some maniac at Meridian ranch. Chief

Jackson had let them off with a warning to stay away from the ranch, but that didn't satisfy Tony.

Nick looked over at the younger man, seeing the look on his face. In the years since they had started hanging around together, Tony had a hundred percent record when it came to the ladies; Nick had a rather less auspicious track record. Juan and Miguel normally kept out of the little competition that had sprung up between the other two. "Twenty says you can't get her to talk to you," Nick said.

Tony let a rakish smile cross his face. "I'll take that bet, but you double it if she walks out of here with me. Why don't you guys come run interference with her girl friends?" *And maybe we can stir up a little trouble for that Meridian crowd.* Nick looked over to the others who nodded agreement.

Erin spotted them first as they crossed the dance floor. She sighed wholeheartedly, wishing she'd suggested they leave earlier. They had had this problem before when they had gone out as a threesome. A lot of men had tried to pick them up, TJ especially. They had come up with inventive ways of dealing with the problem and, of course, there was the direct way of just telling them they were gay. But they had no idea how the town would react to that little tidbit of information, so they couldn't give it out just yet. She sighed again and looked at her companions, trying to figure out whether she would get any assistance from them, but it didn't look hopeful.

Tony walked up behind Mare while his three friends spread themselves around the table. "Ladies," he nodded in greeting.

Mare, smiling, turned to face the person giving the greeting. Her smile changed to a frown when she realized that Nick and his friends had followed her over. She knew this could be trouble. None of them had a love for the Meridian family for starters, and the guys weren't known for their good manners.

TJ saw Mare's frown as she turned to face the man who had walked up to the table. *Wonder what that's all about?*

Now that Tony had the attention of everybody at the table, he smiled and turned his charm on Mare. "I just wanted to apologize for my friend's earlier behavior and wondered whether I could buy you and your group a drink?"

Mare gave him a polite smile, knowing that antagonizing this man and his friends wasn't a good idea. She was rapidly beginning to sober up. "That's a really nice offer, but I'm afraid we were just leaving." With that Erin stood up, pulling the unsteady Paula with her.

Tony was rather shocked with the immediate brush-off he got, but he wasn't known for giving up. "Come on, one more won't make a difference."

Erin decided to take the emphasis off of Mare. "As my friend said, it was a really nice offer but we really do need to get going. Some other time, maybe?"

TJ may have been a little more the worse for wear than was usual, but she could tell that the man questioning Mare wasn't happy. She caught his fleeting glance towards his friends, one of whom was trying to hide a growing smirk. *Uh oh. This might be trouble.*

Tony had now gone beyond shock and was starting to get angry. This had never happened to him before; usually women were falling all over him. His smile faltered slightly, letting his anger show through on his face. "Some other time?" He reached out and put a hand on Mare's shoulder, his hold scarily intimate. "No, we want to buy you a drink now. Just one small one won't hurt."

Mare shuddered as his hand came into contact with her shoulder and she knew that this guy wasn't going to give up easily. "Look, thank you for the offer, but neither my friends nor I are interested."

Nick was grinning openly. He was going to win this one and show Tony up for an idiot, all in one fell swoop. *God, this was going to be good.*

Mare didn't say anything, just continued to look at Tony then down at his hand, which he reluctantly removed. "As I said, thanks for the offer but we were just leaving." Mare stood up, walked behind TJ's chair, and pulled it from beneath the table. "Goodnight."

Erin breathed a sigh of relief. It looked as though they were going to get out of the bar without a major scene. She supported Paula around her waist, and slowly turned her toward the door.

When he saw the wheelchair and recalled the town gossip about the woman who owned Meridian ranch being crippled, Tony's attention switched immediately to TJ. Suddenly, he could taste revenge. His face turned into an ugly mask and he shouted an expletive. "I thought these women were from the Meridian ranch, but I didn't think the owner was here, too, you bitch!"

He said it loud enough that the other patrons in the bar realized that something was happening. "Your family turned this town into a cesspool when you abandoned it." A snarl further marred his countenance. "My old man committed suicide because of you. You took away his livelihood and he couldn't support us no more. You ruined my family's life and you come back here to lord it over us? We're supposed to bow down and kiss your ass? I don't think so."

TJ turned the chair and saw that the man, so engrossed with raving at her, now had a bruising grip on Mare's arm and was actually shaking her. His voice lowered into a growl. "Next time we hit your ranch, I'm gonna put some buckshot into those damn horses of yours, just like some-one did to my truck."

The idiot was threatening three objects of TJ's deepest affection: her lover, her horses, and her ranch. A fierce protectiveness washed over her.

Listening to Tony's tirade, his friends nodded their heads in agreement with his denunciation. Their eyes were glued to him and they didn't seem to be taking any notice of TJ, wrongly assuming that the wheelchair meant she was no threat.

She looked behind her and saw Erin, with a concerned look on her face, holding up Paula. The others in the bar didn't look as though they were going to interfere. *Guess that leaves me to straighten this guy out.* Because all eyes were on Mare and her noisy antagonist, nobody but Tony noticed when TJ rolled up beside him. Reaching up, she took hold of his thumb at the joint where it attached to his hand and twisted, putting pressure on the ligaments and tendons, causing excruciating pain. He let go of Mare's arm and when he felt his thumb pulled downward, he could do nothing but follow.

"Hi," said TJ as brown eyes came down to the level of her blue eyes. Her low, menacing voice spoke to him alone. "The only part of Meridianville that's a cesspool is whatever spot you're standing on, you useless piece of shit." She twisted his thumb again to hammer home her point.

"You do realize I could break this appendage without thinking about it, don't you?" He nodded rapidly and she smiled sweetly. "You come anywhere near anything that belongs to me and it won't be your thumb that gets broken, stud. Your friends will be calling you 'Sally.' You got that?" Another rapid nod jerked his head.

"Now, my friend said we were leaving and we would appreciate it if we could do it without being disturbed." She relaxed her hold a little as though she were moving away. Tony's face took on a look of relief and the pressure eased. He couldn't believe this bitch had brought him to his knees just by grabbing hold of his thumb, but if he tried to move waves of pain surged all the way up his arm.

He squealed in pain as her hold tightened again. "Oh, and when a woman says 'no' that is exactly what she means." She gave one more twist. "Got it?" Tony nodded his head frantically. TJ released his hand, turned her chair, and waited for Mare to continue wheeling her to the exit.

The bar remained quiet until the four women had left, then the absurdity of what they had seen took over. The whole bar roared with laughter at the man who'd been brought to his knees by a cripple holding his thumb. They hadn't heard the interchange of words.

Mare took a deep breath as she walked into the cool night air, relieved to be leaving the tense atmosphere. "My God, TJ. Where the hell did you learn to do that?"

"The boardroom; though I think it looks more impressive now that I'm in the wheelchair." She quirked a smile up at Mare.

"Woman, you are incorrigible," said Mare, lightly slapping her arm.

Erin had already opened up the van and helped Paula into the back. "Hey, you two coming?" she asked. "I'd like to get away from here before you cause any more trouble." She said it with a laugh in her voice, but underneath that she was concerned. The look on the face of the man they had just made a fool of hadn't been that pleasant. She wanted to get out of here before he decided to cause any more trouble.

"Yeah, we're coming, Erin," said Mare, pushing TJ the last few yards to the van.

In the bar, Tony was fuming. He gave Juan a shove. "Go watch them. Let me know when they leave the parking lot." He turned to the other two men. "That Meridian bitch is not getting away with making a fool outta me in front of the whole bar. We already owe her a lesson for messing with our families. Last time didn't hurt her enough. We'll get her good this time."

Nick and Miguel agreed with him. They remembered how miserable life had turned for them when their parents' jobs had disappeared. Nick's father had deteriorated into a typical drunk who beat his wife and kids and finally drank himself to death. Miguel's father had done his best, trying to eke out an existence on a rented parcel of land, but his fun-loving wife, tired of never having any money or the nice things it would buy, deserted her husband and son.

Juan's family stayed together, but his association with the other three led him into always looking for trouble, same as they did. Before long, they had a bad reputation and they gloried in it.

Tony's voice turned even nastier. "And that other one with the dark hair looks like the one who shot at us and messed up my truck. They're both gonna pay." He did the double shot from the round Nick had provided and ordered another round. He saw Juan returning. "They leave?"

Juan hurried over and tossed back both of his double shots before answering. "Yeah. Took off in a van."

****

Erin started the van and looked both ways before driving onto the main road back toward the ranch. She looked over at Mare who was sitting quietly next to her. "You okay?" she inquired.

"Yeah, I'm fine. Just have one hell of a hangover starting. It is amazing how quickly you can sober up when trouble starts, huh?"

"Oh yeah. But I somehow get the feeling that that guy got a little more than he expected."

Mare giggled. "Yep. Don't think he was prepared for the terror on two wheels back there, do you?"

"Uh uh." Erin glanced into the rearview mirror. "Gods, would you look at those two?"

Mare turned and looked over her shoulder. Paula had slumped sideways in the back seat and was now fast asleep, cuddling TJ. TJ was gently snoring, head rested against the cool glass of the window.

"Think our girls had a good night, don't you?"

Erin smiled. "I think we all had a good night till the end, and I think the only person who enjoyed that was TJ."

"Yeah, she did seem to get an inordinate amount of pleasure from bringing that guy down to her level, didn't she?"

"That's our TJ for you." Erin brought her full attention back to the road. The headlights of the van sliced through the thick blackness, letting her know where they were. Another twenty minutes and they would have to wake the sleeping beauties in the back and get them into their own bed.

****

Once the laughter had died Tony had turned back to Nick and the other two, a dark grin on his face. "That Meridian bitch isn't gonna get away with this. Think I'm gonna take the truck for a spin. Anybody coming?"

Nick shook his head. Tony was a hotheaded fool before he'd had a drink, and afterwards he was worse. Going after the women was only gonna cause more trouble in the long run. Things had taken a turn upwards in the town since the Meridian ranch had reopened. Before, the chief had turned a blind eye to their antics, but now his support couldn't be relied on. "Tony, why don't we just forget about it for tonight, have a few beers and enjoy ourselves?"

Tony sneered at the suggestion. "You wimping out on us, Nick? Scared of a group of women?" Miguel and Juan stood next to Tony showing their support for their slighted friend.

"No, just don't see why we should run after them right away, spoiling our night out."

Tony stepped forward and roughly poked Nick in the shoulder. "Because that woman is going to pay for showing me up in front of these guys." He turned and walked over to the door. "You coming?"

Nick sighed, upended his bottle of beer and drained the dregs before placing it on a nearby table and following Tony out of the door.

****

Nearly home, mused Erin in the silence of the van. The road was pretty quiet at this time of night. They had passed only a couple of vehicles traveling in the opposite direction. Bright lights blinded her as she looked in the rearview mirror. She lifted her hand and angled it so that the glare no longer affected her eyes. A minute later and the glare had not dissipated, but now she could make out the dark form of a truck close behind them. A sense of unease settled in her stomach and she sped up slightly. The truck behind sped up, too.

Mare shook herself out of her thoughts as she felt the van pick up speed. She turned toward Erin and saw her looking worriedly at the rearview mirror. "Everything ok?"

"I'm not sure; some jerk behind us is tailgating me."

Mare turned and looked past her sleeping lover and friend out the back window, seeing the truck. "What do you think?" She turned back to the front.

"I think that those guys from the bar couldn't take no for an answer and though TJ's show was pretty good, I bet they didn't appreciate it." A rough jolt threw the van forward. Mare braced her arms on the dash to keep herself in her seat. A startled exclamation erupted from the back. Mare looked and saw Paula picking herself out of the space between the front and back seats.

"What the hell was that?" TJ reached down and hauled Paula the rest of the way into the seat just as another jolt threw them all forward again.

Erin struggled to keep control of the van as the hits from behind crashed into them. "I think those guys from the bar were a little pissed at us." Erin looked to the side as the headlights disappeared from behind them and started to make their way up the left side of the van. Erin slammed on the brakes, hoping that would force the truck in front of them, but a split second later the truck followed suit. "Er, guys, I think we are in trouble." Erin saw it coming this time and swerved, taking the van off of the blacktop to avoid another hit.

Tony filled the truck with a whooping yell as he urged the vehicle forward into the van in front of him. Juan had broken open a case of beer that had been in the back of the truck, and all of the men were drinking.

"Hit them again, Tony," Juan urged, rolling down the window and throwing an empty bottle out, before cracking open another.

Tony complied and put his foot down on the accelerator. Another set of yells echoed through the truck.

"Anybody have any ideas?" a desperate Erin asked as she narrowly avoided the truck again.

"How far are we from the ranch?" TJ asked, leaning forward.

"About five miles," Erin replied shortly.

"In that case," remarked Mare, "the entrance to Abner's ranch is not far away. See if you can swing in. We should be safe up there. I doubt if they want to carry on this game with witnesses."

Paula was digging through her backpack, which they left in the rear of the van under the seat while they were in the bar. With a cry of triumph, she held aloft her cell phone. "I'll get the police." She started to punch in the emergency number.

Tony, grinning, looked out of his side window and faked a swerve at the van. He saw the van move sharply to the right to avoid the implied impact. Then he swerved over as the driver swung back onto the road. The two large vehicles broadsided each other, violently rattling the occupants of both.

Erin resisted the urge to ram the bigger truck back, knowing it was a fight that the van couldn't win.

Now that the two vehicles were side by side, Tony began to force the van off of the road. The dark stretch of blacktop in front of them had a steep embankment to either side.

"Ah hell, hold on tight. I can't keep us on the road," yelled Erin as she strained to turn the steering wheel. For a split second the pressure eased as the truck again swerved away. Erin sighed in relief before it came careening back at high speed and crashed into the van. The shockingly strong impact shook Erin's grip off of the steering wheel. A sharp, agonizing pain washed over her and she realized her wrist had snapped from her effort to keep them on the road. She heard faint screams and recognized that they were hers. Vaguely, she saw Mare reach across her and try to get hold of the steering wheel.

Mare heard Erin's scream and lunged across the woman, attempting to get hold of the steering wheel. She felt the vehicle tip and start to go over the steep embankment.

TJ experienced the same helpless frustration she had felt when Mare fell from the horse. Here she was, yet again, unable to do anything about their situation. Paula got through to the police department and quickly gave them the information they would need to come to their assistance. TJ heard Erin's scream and then felt herself sliding across the back seat as the van tipped. *Oh hell, how many times do you have to be told about putting the blasted seatbelt on?* She grabbed blindly and found the offending item. Knowing she didn't have time to put it on properly, she wrapped it around herself and grabbed a tight hold of Paula, knowing that if she didn't have one on then neither would her friend.

A cackling laugh echoed through the truck as Tony saw the van go over the embankment. "Payback's a bitch, ain't it?" A bright light shone into the truck that was now driving on the wrong side of the road. Tony's eyes widened in shock and he swung the truck to the left to avoid the oncoming vehicle. The truck shot off the other side of the road, rolling forward down the embankment, coming to an abrupt halt against the trunk of a tree.

Silence descended along the midnight-black stretch of road.

****

Mare opened her eyes. There was a full, pounding pain in her head, which she knew had nothing to do with the amount of alcohol she had consumed. She swallowed to get rid of the thick, brackish taste in her mouth and recognized the taste as blood. Her bleary mind began to make sense of her surroundings. The first thing she noticed was grass beneath her hands.

She struggled to push herself up, groaning as the pain from her head worsened. She raised her hand and pushed her hair from her eyes, catching the trickle of blood that ran from a shallow cut on her forehead. Her breathing started to increase and she realized she had been thrown from the van. Frantically she looked about and saw the van twenty feet away where it had come to a stop, lying on its side, facing down the steep embankment

"Oh sweet Jesus, TJ!" She scrambled to her feet, ignoring the multitude of aches and pains she felt her body shout out to her. She heard footsteps above her and gave a startled yell as a hand caught hold of her. At once, she realized she had been falling.

"Hey, hey, take it easy. Sit down, you're hurt." Gentle hands lowered her to the ground.

"My friends are in the van. I have to help them."

"Mare? Is that you?"

Mare looked up into the face of Chuck MacMasters. "Oh, Chuck, thank the Lord. Some idiots ran us off the road."

"Yeah, I know. I saw it happen. They are on the other side of the road. Tree stopped them after I couldn't get out of their way. Missy's called the police and an ambulance."

"Chuck, TJ and her friends are in the van."

The older man nodded his head. "I'll go check it out, make sure they are okay."

"I'm coming with you." Mare's tone of voice assured the rancher that Mare wouldn't take no for an answer. He nodded his head and carefully helped her to her feet.

The police car's siren wailed in the distance. "They got here quickly," remarked Chuck as Mare hobbled along by his side. He kept a wary eye on her as they approached the van.

"Paula phoned them while we were in the van. We were hoping to make it to Abner's place." A deep groaning started off to the side of the van and Mare and Chuck hurried over, trying to find the source in the long grass that hadn't been flattened by the passing of the van. Mare caught sight of the familiar form of Paula, who was now coming around, and she breathed a sigh of relief. *One down, two to go.* "Paula, lay still. Help's on the way."

"Mare?" Paula groaned in reply. "Erin? TJ?"

"We haven't found them yet, sweetie. You just stay here; I'm gonna find them." More rustling footsteps were approaching her through the grass and she looked up, finding Missy, Chuck's wife, approaching.

"How are they?" asked Chuck as she came to his side.

"It was Tony Yarrow and his bunch of rowdies. Tony was driving." She shook her head as Chuck raised an inquiring eyebrow. "But the others are okay, just shook up."

Chuck nodded. "How about if you stay with the lady here, while Mare and I go find the rest of her friends." He had pulled Mare to her feet again and they went straight toward the van. The siren shut off as the police car pulled to the edge of the embankment. The flashing lights illuminated the accident scene somewhat, and the opening and slamming of doors could be heard before two figures appeared at the top.

"Everybody okay down there?" yelled Chief Jackson.

"We got a few injuries down here, Curt."

"Did the truck get away?"

"Nope, came straight at me on my side of the road. Ended up making the acquaintance of a tree over on the other side."

"Okay, I'll go check them out. Ambulance is on the way, shouldn't be too long."

As Chuck spoke to the chief, Mare left his side and
hurried to the van. The back door on the driver's side had
been ripped off of the van, which no doubt is how Paula
ended up outside of the vehicle. She clambered up the
underside of the van, wincing as more bruises made themselves known. Erin's door was intact though the window
was missing. Mare reached over and felt around, coming
into contact with Erin who was still strapped into her seat
by the seatbelt.

The darkness made it impossible to see how badly Erin
might be injured. "Chuck, we need some light down here,"
she yelled over her shoulder. She heard Chuck holler up to
the chief and climbed the rest of the way up until her legs
dangled in the doorway that the back door should have protected. She peered into the deep, dark interior. "TJ?" She
could just make out a dark form huddled at the bottom, but
was loath to jump in when she didn't know what was
beneath her.

Another siren wail throbbed in the distance and Mare
knew that was the ambulance rushing toward them. She
quickly glanced up the embankment and saw that some
other cars and trucks had stopped to offer assistance. Several men made their way down toward the van, and two of
the cars turned in the road so that their headlights shed
light on the scene.

She heard a scrabbling behind her and Chuck appeared
next to her, handing her a long-handled flashlight. Mare
took a deep breath and clicked the light on. She checked
Erin first. Erin was unconscious with a large bump on her
forehead and her swollen right wrist dangling. Another
deep breath and she let the beam of light illuminate the
back of the van. TJ lay crumpled, a dark stain covering her
white shirt on the side on which she was lying. From this
distance, she wasn't even sure that TJ was breathing.

Mare fought hard to keep her emotions under control.
TJ needed her calmness and concentration now. She
needed her expertise in the medical world. Even if she was
more used to animals than humans the principles were the

same. "Chuck, when that ambulance gets here you bring them straight over, you hear me?"

"You got it, Mare," he replied.

Mare braced her arms on either side of the opening and slowly lowered herself in, carefully placing her feet where they would do least damage, until she was surrounded on all sides by the van. She stood still for a moment, letting her weight settle before she crouched down and extended her hand to the neck of her lover, fingers searching for a pulse. She couldn't find one and felt the panic building within her. She forced herself to take another deep breath and felt again, concentrating hard. There it was, a faint flutter against her fingers, but it was there. She quickly made an assessment of TJ's injuries, knowing already that there was some damage to her side, probably from the fractured window on which she was lying. She didn't like the position she was lying in either. Her head was curled toward her chest, cramping her airway, and the arm she was lying on was curled at an unnatural angle.

Another light appeared above her and she gazed upward into a face she didn't recognize, but a uniform that she did. "You need to get Erin, in the front, out first. TJ here has a previous spinal injury and will need an extrication device and collar before we even attempt to move her."

"You a doc?" queried an unknown female voice.

"No, I'm a vet," she replied.

"Better than nothing," murmured the woman before she disappeared.

Mare felt the van move as other people climbed onto it. Another medic, this one male, appeared above her as she leaned over TJ, protecting her from anything that might fall from above. She kept her right hand in constant contact with her lover, reassuring herself that she was still there. She watched the people working above as pieces of equipment were handed into the van. The medic calmly and efficiently directed those helping him to get Erin out of her seat. A stiff neck collar was handed to him, then a

K.E.D. 2000 extraction device which he slipped behind her in the seat to keep her back and neck stable. Within a few minutes, they were ready to lift Erin clear of the vehicle. The van rocked again as they lifted and then for several minutes Mare was left alone with TJ.

"Ma'am?" Mare looked up as the male paramedic reappeared. "I need you to come up here so that I can get down to your friend." Mare nodded and quickly climbed up to allow him to get to TJ. "My partner tells me your friend already has a spinal injury." He looked up at Mare as he checked TJ's pulse. "Can you tell me what level?"

"Um... T-11. She was shot just over twenty months ago, and still has bullet fragments embedded in her spine." She moved herself aside as another medic arrived on the scene.

"Hey there. I've sent Billy and Janice off with the other casualty."

"How was she?" asked Mare.

The man looked over at her with a reassuring smile. "She'll be fine. Has a nasty bump to the head and a fractured wrist."

"Marcus, I need oxygen and an IV line with fluid," said the male medic with TJ. Marcus reached down and hauled up a bag, handing the medic the items he had requested.

Mare refused to get down from the van while they were working on TJ, though several people asked her to. As long as she wasn't in the way of the medics, she wasn't leaving. More and more people arrived at the scene. The local rescue squad had turned up just after the first ambulance and had helped remove Erin from the van.

It seemed an age before they were ready to get TJ out and then Mare stood back with Chuck and his wife. The plan was well orchestrated and the team worked well together. Once they were ready to move TJ, they had her out in minutes.

It broke Mare's heart to see her like this. Her once tan skin was grayish-white, with a sheen of clammy perspiration coating her. Her neck was encased in a collar and strapped tightly to a short backboard. Drip lines ran, one into each arm, and a large pad of gauze was bandaged to her side to slow the bleeding.

As soon as they began to move TJ to the ambulance, Mare felt her legs begin to buckle. Reaction to the crash finally hit home, now that she no longer had to be strong. A wave of darkness tunneled her vision and she felt hands clasping hold of her... then nothing.

Chapter
26

It was the strong, overpowering, antiseptic smell that roused TJ to consciousness, a smell she had come to hate just after the shooting. Four months of immobility in a spinal rotational bed, unable to move even her head, had given her an almost pathological hatred of hospitals. Her dislike of the hospital hadn't lessened when she had been moved into her own room and a normal hospital bed. She knew that this had to be a nightmare, because there was no way on this earth that she would have willingly returned to this setting.

The next thing that assaulted her senses was the humming of electricity and the beeping of machinery—one that kept an annoyingly persistent beat with her heart—the quiet murmur of voices, the gentle squeak of rubber-soled footwear on the highly polished floor.

This nightmare is frighteningly real. Her mind turned that thought over. Was she in bed at the ranch? Now she noticed the pounding of her head and a small groan escaped her mouth. *God, we must have had a good night last night for me to have a hangover like this.* Her eyes were still closed, seemingly glued together. She tried to lift her head into a more comfortable position but found that she couldn't move it. Her eyes flew open and panic gripped her as she realized that this wasn't a nightmare but hard, cold reality. She felt a hand clutch hold of hers and squeeze, but her throat was constricted with the panic that was building within her.

* * * * * * * * *

Mare was sitting curled up in a comfortable chair that had been brought into the room where TJ had been placed after she had been stabilized in the ER. And what an experience that had been....

Mare awoke on the way to the hospital in the back of Chuck's truck, head resting across Missy's thigh. She tried to sit up immediately but Missy prevented that, telling her to rest till they got to the hospital.

"Where are they taking TJ? I need to be there."

Missy gently stroked Mare's golden locks from her face. "Calm down, Mare, honey, we are right behind them. The chief is giving us an escorted run into the hospital. We'll be there soon."

Missy was right; within five minutes they arrived at the Emergency Room entrance. Chuck and Missy took her into the ensuing chaos that was the ER. It wasn't that late at night, but anytime in an ER is busy. Nurses and doctors moved about with controlled speed, dealing with patient inquiries as they sped past.

People surrounded the reception desk. Chuck and Missy were guiding her in that direction but Mare pulled off and went to find the girls and, more importantly, TJ. She wandered the department looking into rooms and curtained-off areas for her partner, unnoticed by the busy staff. She discovered a frantic Paula first, and found herself enveloped in a tight hug. Tears fell in torrents down both faces.

"Do you know how Erin and TJ are?" Paula's voice was hoarse from crying.

"Not yet," Mare said, still holding tight. "I only just got here. Are you okay?"

Paula scrubbed the tears from her face. "Broke my damned leg but apart from that just a few bruises. You?"

"A little roughed up, banged my head, but don't really remember much of the accident. I'm gonna go see if I can find TJ and Erin. You going to be okay by yourself for a while?"

"Yeah, just let me know as soon as you find out what's going on."

"I'll be back as soon as I can." With one last squeeze, Mare left.

Mare found herself outside what looked like a mini operation theater, with several doctors and nurses. One of the nurses rushed out and Mare grabbed her shoulder and swung her around to see her. "Is that one of the victims who was just brought in from the van crash?"

"Yeah. Excuse me, but I need to get these to the labs." And she was gone.

Taking a deep breath, Mare pushed the swinging door open and walked in.

"I'm fine. Now get me off of this damned bed." Mare felt the tears begin again as she heard Erin's gruff voice berating the doctors and nurses.

"Miss Scott," intoned one of the doctors, "we need to make a proper assessment of your condition before we let you up. The more you argue, the longer it will take and the longer you will be on this table."

Mare let a small grin appear on her face. It was great to hear Erin, but she realized that her friend would be anxious for news on Paula, TJ, and herself. "Hey, Erin," she said as she saw the combative look on the woman's face. "Let the doctors do their job."

Several of the doctors and nurses looked up; one walked over to her, a scowl on her face. "Miss, you can't be in here," said the nurse.

"She stays or I get off this damned table now!" yelled Erin, lifting her hand towards Mare.

Mare ignored the nurse and walked straight over to Erin, grabbing the raised hand. "Hey there, Paula sent me on a search mission for you." She smiled seeing the relief cross Erin's bruised face.

"She okay?"

"Yep. Broke her leg, but she is going to be fine. She's in the third cubicle down the hall from this area."

"TJ?"

"Haven't found her in this rabbit warren yet." She felt Erin squeeze her hand supportively

"I'm sure she'll be fine. What about you? You look almost as bad as I feel."

"I just banged my head and I'm a little bruised, but I'll be fine as soon as I find that woman of mine. You going to be good for the doctors while I go find her?"

"Sure. Thanks for letting me know Paula's okay. I'll join her as soon as they finish with me here. You'll come back and let me know how TJ is when you find her?" Erin raised her eyebrow in hope.

"I'll do better than that." Mare bent down and placed a tender kiss on Erin's bruised forehead. "I'll take you to see her."

And she kept that promise. She found TJ in the trauma room next to Erin's. The nurses were more insistent that she stay out of that one, physically restraining her when she had tried to enter. Just over an hour later, a doctor came out looking for TJ's relatives. Mare explained to him that, as far as she knew, TJ had no living relatives and, though she was unsure, she thought that Paula or Erin would be considered her next of kin. That led to a meeting in Paula's curtained-off area. Erin, cleared of any major injury, was already there, wrist in a fiberglass splint.

The doctor was a tallish fellow and, though he must have spoken to relatives before, he had a somewhat nervous disposition. He cleared his throat several times, as Mare sat down in the chair next to Paula's bed. Erin was snuggled up next to her partner, staring intently at the doctor.

"Your friend's condition is quite serious at the moment. As you probably already know, her previous injuries make it difficult to assess the damage done in this accident." The shock must have shown on their faces. He moved closer and ran a hand across his chin. "Please, don't misunderstand me; her life isn't in danger. But we have some decisions that need to be made, and made rather quickly." He pulled out x-ray films and scans from a holder he had brought with him. Walking over to the viewer, he clipped them up and turned on the backlight.

"We thought at first that she might have sustained a new injury to her spinal cord." He carried on hurriedly as he heard Mare's gasp. "But an MRI scan has shown us that that hasn't happened. It looks as though several fragments from her previous injury have moved, causing new symptoms of spinal cord injury to appear."

"What do you mean, new symptoms of injury?" asked Mare, interrupting the doctor.

"By comparing test results to her old notes, several reaction responses have changed, becoming slower, or in one case, disappearing altogether."

Mare couldn't believe what she was hearing. Her gaze traveled to Erin and Paula; they were just as shocked as she was. Paula had turned pasty white and Mare could see the tears brimming in Erin's eyes. "So, what you're saying is that her injury has gotten worse?"

"Essentially, yes; but the reason these fragments weren't removed in the first place was because of their positioning. Now that they've shifted, there might be a chance that they can be removed. That raises another problem—finding someone to perform the operation."

Mare felt as though she had just been given the switch to turn on a light. For the first time since the doctor had started talking, hope began to stir. "That won't be a problem. Call Michael Gillis over in Springerly. He'll do it."

The doctor paused, looking at Mare. "Miss, Dr. Gillis is one of the top surgeons in his field but he won't be able to drop what he's doing and perform the operation. These things cost an incredible amount of money and will need a lot of preparation."

Paula spoke up this time, catching onto the fact that the doctor didn't know whom he was treating. "Money isn't a factor."

Mare got up slowly. "And Dr. Gillis will drop what he's doing and come running. He's my father and he already has copies of TJ's medical records. Now I'd like to see TJ, then I'll phone my father and we'll get this show rolling."

It was obvious that the doctor didn't have a clue what to do now. Mare took hold of his arm and steered him out of the room, back to where TJ was resting.

Of course, it hadn't been as easy as just phoning her father, though Michael had arrived at the hospital within an hour of receiving Mare's call. TJ had other injuries to consider as well. The bleeding that Mare saw when TJ was in the van came from a deep laceration to her side. She lost a lot of blood from that and it had required internal as well as external stitches to close it. She was unconscious, and the reason for that baffled them all. Yes, she had hit her head, but the CT scan hadn't shown a fracture or swelling to the brain. Mare's dad decided to risk moving TJ back to his unit at Springerly. He had better equipment there and the unit was set up for such a patient.

So here they were, three days later, still waiting for TJ to wake up. The only benefit to her continued unconsciousness was that Michael had been able to perform several tests to find out the extent of the newer SCI symptoms.

A moan coming from TJ's bed woke Mare from the doze she had fallen into. She sat bolt upright and, leaning over, took a tight hold of TJ's hand.

"TJ? Sweetie, you back with us?" Mare felt TJ's hand clamp vise-like over her own. TJ's heart rate increased rapidly, as did the beep of the machine recording it. Mare looked closely at her lover who was, at this moment, face down with her chest rising and falling rapidly. Mare got out of the chair and slipped to the floor so that she could see TJ's face. Her lover's eyes were scrunched closed, her mouth slightly open; a cold sweat dripped from her face. *Ah, hell on earth.*

Mare's spare hand scrabbled around for the call button and she pressed it twice, hoping that Dad was close by. That done, she adjusted the bed slightly using the electric controls, so it was inclined instead of horizontal. She gently caressed her lover's face. "TJ, open your eyes for me." She got no response. Continuing to gently stroke her face, Mare carried on. "TJ, I need you to slow your breathing down, honey." The door behind her opened and she looked up to her father's concerned face.

"Everything okay, Mare?" he asked as he got near.

"Dad, she's awake but something's wrong."

Wrong? Something was more than wrong. To TJ's mind she wasn't in this hospital, she wasn't here with Mare at all but in some small, private ward in a hospital two years ago. She was back there, reliving every agonizing minute of the time she discovered not only that she had lost the use of her legs but also that Lance her beautiful, loving brother was dead. She remembered every second of that time in vivid detail, every word in stereo surround-sound, and she couldn't live through it again.

She woke up facing the hospital ceiling, her head, arms, and legs secured to the bed she was lying on. A hand grabbed hold of her and Erin's face came into view. TJ knew from right that second that something was seriously wrong. She hadn't been bothered at the time that she couldn't feel her legs, hadn't been bothered that the parts of her body she could feel were screaming in agony. Her one thought was for her brother. Erin had burst into tears before she could say anything; Paula had barely been able to speak as emotion crowded her throat.

"God, TJ, it is good to see those baby blues again. We thought we might have lost you." Paula had her arms wrapped around the sobbing Erin.

TJ tried to speak but her throat was dry and it took her

*several attempts before she got her croaked question out.
"Lance?" Paula didn't have to say anything. Her head
dropped to Erin's shoulder, fresh tears pouring down her
face.*

*Her life lost all meaning in that one little moment of
time. A black hole opened in her soul and all she had
worked for, all she had ever hoped for herself and Lance
was gone. The desolate cry that erupted from her soul
scarred both Paula and Erin for life.*

Chapter 27

Erin woke, startled from her sleep by the echoing of a nightmare she no longer remembered. She adjusted her position, rolling so that her head was nestled again in the crook of Paula's shoulder. Though Paula was still deeply asleep, her arm wrapped around Erin and pulled her in closer. Erin snuggled a bit more before settling down, but her mind was wide-awake and it refused to let her sleep anymore.

Her finger idly began to paint nonsense patterns on Paula's stomach. They had been let out of the hospital the day before yesterday, after a night of suffering the ministrations of the nursing staff. She'd been on the verge of discharging herself when they relented and made sure she was put in a room with Paula. Erin wasn't sure, but she thought that Mare's father had something to do with that.

They also got to see TJ the morning they were discharged, before she was transferred to Springerly. She looked so small, attached to all the machines monitoring her; it brought back bad memories for both of them. Still they knew that this time TJ had Mare there for her and, hopefully, that would make a difference. Because, if she were going to be honest with herself, she wasn't sure that she or Paula could go through it for a second time.

"Are you going to lay there brooding all night or are you going to tell me what's wrong?"

Erin tilted her head back to see her partner gazing down at her. She strained upwards and felt Paula respond, leaning down to place a gentle, loving kiss on her lips. *God, what would I have done if I had lost her?* Erin dropped her head and hugged Paula tighter, sucking in a tiny breath as she forgot and put pressure on her injured wrist.

"Sweetie, are you okay?" Paula was now getting concerned with Erin's unusual behavior.

"Yeah, I'm fine. Just thinking about things. I want to go see TJ and Mare today. You think Bill will let one of the men drive us up to Springerly?"

"I'm sure that won't be a problem, honey. We'll give him a ring first thing in the morning," replied Paula, rubbing soothing circles on Erin's exposed back. Erin snuggled tighter and Paula smiled indulgently, knowing that within minutes her lover would be asleep, now that her concerns had been addressed. It had been the same the first time TJ was injured. She'd lie awake for hours then ask for the simplest of wishes, like going to see TJ, or going riding, and when Paula agreed she'd be asleep in minutes.

They had talked about it and Erin couldn't explain why these insignificant things bothered her. Paula rather thought that it wasn't them so much as the person they concerned. Ever since TJ had saved her from those thugs in college, Erin had taken it upon herself to look after TJ. And when she couldn't, she needed to be doing something for her. She thought it likely that Erin was feeling responsible for the crash though she had done everything she could to prevent it.

Paula hadn't been able to get her to talk about it yet. *I will though, honey. You won't be able to avoid it for much longer.* Another glance down assured her that Erin was once again in the realms of Morpheus. *A few more hours, sweetheart, then we'll get up and go see if our warrior has decided to rejoin us.*

****

The ride into Springerly was quiet. Bill assigned one of the men to them until they got their casts off. Erin sat in the front next to Mike, while Paula had the whole of the back seat to herself, her leg raised onto it. They phoned the hospital before they left, but were told that Mare was asleep and that her father was attending to a patient and couldn't be disturbed. Although they dug for more information on TJ, all they were told was that she was in stable condition.

Mike parked right in front of the entrance to the hospital, hopped out quickly, and ran around to open the door for Paula. She slid herself forward and took the crutches that Mike lifted from the floor. "Thanks Mike. Go take yourself to the movies or something. We're going to be a few hours. We'll give you a ring when we need to be picked up."

They were a pair to behold as they walked, or in Paula's case hobbled, into the hospital. Bruises proudly worn, they looked as though they had been in the ring with a heavyweight boxer. But they ignored the curious looks they got, and made their way straight to the Gillis Clinic on the sixth floor of the hospital.

The Clinic took up the entire sixth floor. It had its own physical therapy department, its own hydrotherapy pool and its own specialized nurses, therapists and counselors who looked after only those on the unit. And of course the unit had one of the most experienced medical and orthopedic teams dealing with Spinal Cord Injury.

Erin and Paula were impressed when they stepped from the elevator. With a carpeted floor and bright artwork hung from the walls, it didn't look like your average hospital unit. There was an information station directly in front of them. The young woman who sat behind the desk smiled in greeting and asked how she could help.

"We'd like to see TJ Meridian," said Erin.

"Are you relatives?" the woman inquired.

"Not exactly," replied Paula, wondering whether they were going to have an argument about getting in.

"In that case, may I just take your names? I'll make sure Miss Meridian can have visitors." The woman's smile still didn't falter but Paula could tell that she'd defend this desk and admittance to the unit with zeal if challenged. They gave her their names and got an immediate response. "Miss Scott, Miss Tanner, of course, Dr. Gillis has already put you on the admitting list. Sorry to delay you. Miss Meridian is down the corridor, fourth door on the right. Go right on in; no doctors are with her at this time."

"Thanks for your help." Erin smiled back at the woman and moved in the direction she had pointed.

Erin pushed the door open slowly, not wanting to disturb Mare if she were still sleeping, but she needn't have bothered. Mare was wide-awake, sitting in a comfortable chair. Mare turned as Paula swung her crutches through the doorway, followed immediately by Erin.

"Hey, there. How's she doing?" asked Paula as she made her way over to Mare. Erin rushed to pull up another chair for Paula to sit in. TJ had been turned and was now lying on her back, head still securely strapped to prevent movement.

"She woke up last night, but she was a mess—went totally berserk, screaming for Lance. Dad had to sedate her. She's been kind of restless ever since."

Erin sat on the arm of Mare's chair and wrapped an arm around her shoulder. "She was real bad when she woke up and found out about Lance, last time. I guess this brought back too many bad memories for her. What about you? Are you okay?"

Mare lifted her hand and patted Erin's. "Much better, now that I know she's going to wake up. She had me scared there for a minute."

Paula leaned forward and held a hand out to Mare. When Mare took it she squeezed gently. "You do know that this is going to be very hard, don't you? I know it is different this time, TJ has you and something to look forward to... but, and it is a big but, she is not going to handle being in the hospital again very well. From what you said your dad has told you about her condition, she has some very hard decisions to make and it is not going to be easy."

Mare smiled sadly. "I know. Don't worry; I'm here for the long run. She's not getting rid of me that easily."

They sat in relative silence for the next hour, only occasional words being spoken before TJ began to stir. The atmosphere became tense as they waited to see what would happen.

TJ mumbled a few unintelligible words and Mare leaned forward to gently caress her face, keeping a close eye on TJ's fluttering eyelids. As she began to actually open her eyes, Mare stood up and leaned over so that the first thing her lover would see would be her face. Tears began to trickle down her cheeks as the blue eyes stayed open and focused on her. "Hey there, beautiful, good to have you back."

"Mare?" TJ whispered, trying to move.

"Yep, and try not to move just yet, sweetie."

"What happened?"

Mare quickly looked over her shoulder at Erin and Paula then back at TJ. "What is the last thing you remember?"

TJ's eyes left Mare's face and were roaming the ceiling. Mare could actually see her trying to remember. "The bar, I remember the bar."

"Okay, that's good. Well, on the way home we had an accident." Mare saw the buildup of panic in TJ's eyes. "Hey, hey." She leaned closer to TJ. "Everybody's all right. We got a little banged up, but we're fine. You're the one who had us worried." With the hand that wasn't caressing TJ's cheek, she waved Erin and Paula forward.

TJ's face broke into a smile as Erin and Paula appeared above her. "Boy, you two look like crap."

Paula laughed, pleased to see that her friend was calmer than her earlier awakening. "Well, kiddo, you don't look so great yourself. You lose a fight or something?"

"Yeah," said Erin. "Thought we told you to leave the big ones to us."

"So," TJ looked back to Mare, "what's the deal here? And when can I get out of this contraption?"

Her voice was steady but Mare could hear the fear in it. She took a deep breath but didn't hesitate in her answer. "TJ, you got really banged up in the crash. You have a brand new scar on your side, dislocated your shoulder..." Now she did falter slightly.

"And?" TJ asked slowly.

"And, hell, maybe I should get my dad in here; he can explain it better." For some reason Mare didn't want to be the one telling TJ that she would be spending quite a while in the hospital.

TJ pinned her lover with her eyes, sensing her reluctance to tell her the whole truth. "No, tell me now."

"TJ?" Erin stepped forward. "It's complicated. Let Mare get her dad. He'll be able to tell you what your options are."

TJ closed her eyes, feeling the frustration building. It was starting again. People telling her lies, refusing to tell her how bad things were because they were afraid of what her reaction might be. "Tell me what the hell is going on, or I get the nurse in here and sign a discharge form."

She'll do it, too, Mare thought, but she was stopped from having to say anything more because her father opened the door and came in. "Morning, honey, ladies." He nodded to Erin and Paula. "How's my favorite patient this morning?" He walked to Mare's side, wrapping an arm around her and gazed down at TJ. "Good morning, young lady. Good to see you awake. How are you feeling?"

"I'd feel a lot better if somebody would tell me what the hell is wrong and why I'm strapped down to this thing." TJ's anger and frustration clearly showed.

"Okay, that's not a problem. I have all your charts in here. We just need to tilt your bed so that you can see the scans." He pressed the buzzer near the bed and within a minute a nurse walked in.

She smiled at Mare who was now known around the unit. "Well, hello there," she said to TJ when she saw she was awake. TJ just glared back, already fed up with being in the hospital. "Dr. Gillis?"

"Morning, Nancy. Could you adjust TJ's bed to 45 degrees for me?" Michael walked over to the X-ray display and began putting up TJ's scans.

Nancy began moving around the bed, securing extra straps around TJ's body to prevent any movement when they tilted the bed. After a few minutes, TJ was on the move and was tilted so that her only view wasn't of the ceiling. Now, although she was still unable to move her head, she could see most of her room. Erin and Paula were in her peripheral vision, as was Mare. Mare's dad was standing in front of her with the scans displayed for her viewing.

"Okay, your old scans from the original injury are on the left, the ones taken a few days ago after the accident are on the right." Mare pulled a chair closer to TJ's bed so that she could sit and still keep hold of her hand.

TJ was staring hard at the scans; that nervous feeling she always got when she knew something wasn't right started to gnaw at her stomach. "The trauma doctor who dealt with your case in Sharlesburg managed to get your scans and records viewed via a computer linkup with the hospital that treated you originally. I have the actual scans so I can be a little more accurate in my diagnosis." Michael looked over to make sure TJ was following what he was saying, then carried on. "The bullet fragments that remained in your spine are now calcified and show up as white on the later scans, but they are the darker shadows

on the earlier ones. And as you can see they have moved."
He looked over at his daughter and her lover, noticing that
Mare was wincing slightly at the grasp that TJ had on her
hand.

"What does that mean?" asked TJ, though she didn't
really want to hear the reply.

"Your spine from T9 down to just below T12 is unsta-
ble and we will need to operate to stabilize it. But those
fragments have shifted and are now in a position that we
could possibly remove them." He waited to see if TJ
would say anything, but she didn't.

Mare heard TJ's breathing pick up before the monitor's beep registered the change. "You ok? TJ?" She
stood up and cupped TJ's cheek. When TJ opened her
eyes, Mare saw a depth of pain within them that she had
never seen before. Mare felt a hand on her shoulder and
looked up into her father's green eyes.

"TJ, we have to make a decision here. I can go in and
stabilize the spine with rods and leave the fragments. The
residual effects that the doctor in Sharlesburg noticed are
most likely due to bruising, not any further injury. Or I
can remove the fragments and stabilize the spine."

TJ swallowed nervously. "What will removing the
fragments do?"

"I have to say that no matter what decision you make,
it will mean a significant time here at the hospital."

"Just tell me what removing the fragments will do."

"I'm not sure, maybe nothing, but with steroid treatments there is an outside possibility that you may regain
some feeling."

"Would I be able to walk?" TJ's voice was quiet.

"Honestly, I doubt it, though you might be able to with
crutches or a frame. However, we may be able to retrieve
bladder control and some of the lower body functions. But
none of this is guaranteed, TJ, and there are other side
effects you should know about before you make your decision."

"Like?"

"The major side effect we would be likely to see would be pain. If you do regain any feeling it is likely to be a very slow process, and very painful. It is a possibility that you wouldn't regain any feeling at all, and be left with a constant pins-and-needles sensation. If we do go ahead you may be in permanent pain for the rest of your life."

Silence settled in the room. Not even the incessant noise of the machinery disturbed the oppressive atmosphere. Erin had her arm wrapped around Paula, holding her tight. They had known what was coming, as had Mare. What they hadn't known was what TJ's reaction was going to be. Erin was unsure whether the lack of reaction was good or bad. She knew how to deal with TJ's outbursts but had never quite managed the silences. She was beginning to feel uncomfortable, wondering whether she and Paula should have stayed away while TJ was given the news. She looked at her lover's concerned face and saw the same questions echoing in her eyes. She felt Paula shrug slightly. She didn't know what TJ was thinking any more that Erin did.

Mare watched in frustration as TJ once again closed her eyes, denying her those windows to her lover's deepest feelings and thoughts, closing herself off from the support that Mare could provide for her. Mare's emotions were on a roller coaster ride, heading Lord knows where. One second she was overwhelmed with joy that her dad may be able to help TJ. The next she was frightened, her father having explained exactly what TJ would be going through. She knew TJ looked strong, knew that the wall she'd built between herself and everybody, including to some extent Erin and Paula, looked unbreachable to most, but she'd seen the fragile shell that it actually was. If she went through with the operation to remove the fragments, it would be hard and stressful on them all.

TJ couldn't just go out on Flag to forget all her worries—there would be no escape from her situation. Lack of activity would lead to depression no matter how well things were going with her treatment. Mare knew TJ would be thinking of all this and she needed to let her know she wouldn't be alone through whatever trials lay ahead. Right now, though, TJ was closing her out, dealing with it on her own as she always had to before.

"I'd like to be alone, please." TJ's voice, though quiet, echoed through the silence, startling them all from their own thoughts.

Paula moved first, realizing that TJ would need her space. She maneuvered herself to her feet, using the crutches and Erin for support. "We'll be back to see you later. Okay, love?" she said, before hopping to the door. She got no reply from TJ, but then she hadn't expected one.

Mare was more than a little dismayed at TJ's request, and would have argued with her, had it not been for the pressure of her father's hand on her shoulder. "I'll be just outside if you need me," whispered Mare as she placed a loving, gentle kiss on TJ's forehead.

"Can you turn the lights off?" Michael Gillis looked back over his shoulder at his daughter's partner's request, flipped the switch, throwing the room into twilight darkness, and closed the door softly behind him.

TJ opened her eyes as the click of the door signaled that she was alone. She stared up toward the ceiling, her thoughts tumbling over and over. *What do I do? Do I take the risk? Can I go through this all over again? Well, I don't have much choice about that part, do I? Whatever I decide, I'm gonna be here for some time. Weeks and weeks, probably months in the hospital. Just like the last time.*

Suddenly a fierce need for Mare's comforting touch rocked her. *Will you be able to stand to be around me if I do this? Or will I drive you away? Oh, I hope not.* She felt the call button under her finger and pressed it.

Chapter 28

Mare saw Paula and Erin had commandeered one of two small couches at the end of the hall from TJ's room. Paula had her leg propped on the low table in front of her. Mare joined them and sat quietly with her thoughts until her dad appeared with a tray of coffee. "What do you think she'll decide?" Mare took a sip of the hot beverage and looked over at Paula and Erin.

"I have no idea," replied Erin.

Paula shook her head. "I couldn't tell you, either, but I will tell you that whatever decision she makes, she'll need you by her side."

"She'll have that no matter what happens. I'd go to hell and back with TJ."

"It might take that," came Michael's deep voice.

Mare looked sharply at her father, then nodded. "Yeah, but that won't change my mind." She looked up as the buzzer sounded from TJ's room.

"Go on," her father said. "It's you she's calling for."

Mare put her coffee on the table and stood up, taking a deep breath. She smiled reassuringly at Erin and Paula then squeezed her dad's hand. As she walked toward TJ's room the corridor got longer and longer, each step taking those few seconds more until, finally, she reached the door.

* * * * * * * * * *

Michael set his empty cup on the tray and locked his straightforward gaze on Erin's hazel eyes. "How long have you and Paula been with TJ?"

"We've known her since college. She hired us to work for her after she inherited the corporation from her father." Erin leaned her head back against the couch. Paula frowned at Erin's obvious fatigue.

"You've been through this with her before, then, when her brother was killed?"

Head still leaning back, Erin closed her eyes and nodded, strain evident in her drawn face. She reopened her eyes and met Michael's. "And it wasn't pretty. In fact, it was damned ugly—for all of us. She spent months in the hospital, getting more and more depressed. Counseling didn't help her; Paula and I couldn't help her; all she wanted was to join Lance. She tried to commit suicide."

Michael nodded. "The marks on her wrists."

A note of surprise sounded in Paula's voice. "You don't miss much, do you, Doc?"

Michael swung his gaze to the dark-haired woman. "TJ is doubly important to me. She's not only my patient, but also Mare's friend. I'm determined not to miss anything that bears on her recovery. What can you two tell me about her reactions to her first injury that might be helpful now?"

Paula looked toward Erin who began speaking. "Before the accident, TJ sat on top of the world. She'll tell you herself she always loved power and, being in charge of Meridian Corporation, she had both hands full of it. She was a take-charge person and she had broad enough vision to be aware of what each company did and specific enough vision to give bonuses and pats on the back to individuals when they deserved them."

"If she had been the only one injured, I think she would have coped a lot better. She's tough in some ways, not so tough in others, especially when it comes to heavy emotions. She doted on her brother Lance and his death changed her into a different person. She just shut herself down. Whatever anyone at the hospital told her to do, she did, but like a zombie. None of it meant anything to her. For months she was in a deep depression, either screaming and throwing things or totally ignoring us and everybody else."

"And you two suffered, right?" Michael's eyes filled with sympathy.

Erin and Paula nodded without even consulting each other and Erin continued. "You got that right, Michael. For months we were walking on eggshells, reluctant to let TJ get worse, but leery of igniting her anger by pushing her to improve. After a while, the situation affected our own relationship and we had to have a number of heart-to-heart talks between ourselves to even keep trying to help her. I'm not sure we could go through that again." Paula squeezed Erin's forearm and the curly-haired blonde lifted her head from the couch back and, smiling softly, brushed Paula's cheek with the fingers of her good hand. "Some people are too important to risk losing."

Michael quieted, watching the interaction between the two women. That they loved each other was unmistakable and he discovered that he felt happy for them.

After a moment, Paula, her eyes still connected to Erin's, spoke softly as if only to her partner. "TJ's too important to risk, too."

Erin stared deeply into Paula's dark eyes and finally nodded. "You're right, love. We'll be here for her, no matter what. TJ is family."

She took a deep breath and continued. "When TJ tried suicide we convinced her doctors that she needed to go somewhere to get back into life, to become involved again. We knew she had been trying to get people to separate their idea of her from their experiences with her father and

Meridianville was one of the places on her list to be revived. We got the idea that we could bring her out to the ranch with Flag. She's almost obsessed with horses and we thought her interaction with Flag might help to wake up her emotions. But it wasn't really working very well. She stayed depressed."

Michael smiled gently. "Until Mare showed up." This part of the story, he had heard from his daughter.

"Yeah," Erin grinned and Paula smiled in remembrance and their spirits lightened. "Mare brought TJ back to life, got her involved again. You might say she picked us all up from the depths."

Michael leaned forward, putting his elbows on his thighs and interlacing his fingers. "Maybe this time, with Mare to help her, TJ will have a better time of it."

Paula nodded her head vigorously. "Michael, your daughter has TJ in the palm of her hand. If anyone can help her, Mare can."

"Let's just hope TJ lets her," Erin said fervently.

"And we'll be right behind her to back her up, come hell or high water." Paula stated this firmly.

Erin nodded, then smiled wryly. "And with TJ, you can never be sure which is which."

* * * * * * * * * *

Mare pushed the door open and stepped into the darkened room. She walked over to TJ, her hand immediately caressing her face.

"Will you hold me for a while?" TJ's voice almost broke her heart; tears sprung from her eyes even though she smiled.

"Of course I will." She bent and kissed her lover, then altered the bed so that it sank back down to its horizontal position. She climbed onto the bed, wrapped her arm around TJ, and held her as close as the restraints allowed.

They closed their eyes and lay still, surrounded by the shielding armor of their love. But the oppressive silence pummeled them with unanswered questions, unaddressed options—clamoring for satisfaction—until it forced them from their shelter.

TJ sighed, and both women opened reluctant eyes, recognizing that important issues needed to be resolved. "What do you think, Mare?" A furrowed brow indicated TJ's uneasiness. "Should I go ahead with the operation?"

Mare clasped her lover's hand. "TJ, you are the only one who can make that decision. I can only tell you that, no matter what, I'll be here for you. I love you. In my mind—in my soul—you and I are connected forever, and nothing will ever change that."

TJ raised their hands and kissed the small one. "Mare, you have done so much for me. You brought me back to life. Not only through your love, but in allowing me to love you."

Deep affection streamed from Mare's expressive eyes. "You don't have to say anything, sweetheart."

"Please, Mare. I've been thinking and thinking about this. I know you've heard most of it before, in bits and pieces, but I need to put it all together and tell it to you." A wry smile. "Consider yourself my therapist for a few minutes."

"Okay, I can do that." A small smile quirked the corners of Mare's mouth.

TJ dropped her eyes and began to speak in a lower voice. "My parents had smothered any love I had for them: my father through abuse and my mother through just not caring. Lance was the only person in my family whom I truly loved and he was the only one I believed truly loved me. When I lost him my whole world went dark." TJ raised her eyes for a brief moment, lifted her hand from Mare's and placed it on Mare's cheek. Mare pressed her own hand against it for support.

The eyes lowered again. "Being paralyzed at the same time was just one more burden that I couldn't handle. That's when I tried suicide. I just wanted to go wherever Lance was. I ached for that unconditional love that we had for each other." TJ gathered strength from an occasional glance at Mare's concerned face. *Oh, TJ, how I wish I could have been with you then. Maybe I could have helped sustain you through that unbearable loss.*

"This life seemed too cruel, too filled with darkness. Erin and Paula made heroic efforts to chase that darkness but they just weren't able to bring me completely back." The raven head wanted to hide from the terrible truths being told but tight strapping kept the tortured face exposed. "I still yearned to leave this hellhole called life. Most people run from death; I embraced it."

Mare turned her head and kissed the palm of TJ's hand, then brought it down and held it in hers. Tears oozed from her eyes, and she swallowed hard, hoping to contain her emotions. "I love you, TJ," she whispered. *Your pain scores furrows on my heart and, gods, it hurts.*

A softness spread across the strong face, bringing the beginnings of a gentle smile. "Then you came along—this beautiful, caring, generous, feisty person who didn't try to edge cautiously into my life; you jumped in with both feet. No pussyfooting around TJ Meridian's monumental temper; it never even fazed you. That in itself was a miracle of huge proportions. No one else had ever reacted to me that boldly and you piqued my interest right away."

"Mostly I didn't know enough to be scared of you. Thanks for not tossing me out on my ear," Mare murmured. TJ raised her magnificent eyes and her smile brought an answering one to Mare's face.

"After I had spent months looking inward, you forced me to look outward. As naturally as the sun rises everyday, you brought sunshine into my life, and held back the darkness. You captured my heart... my mind... my soul. I fell in love with you." Mare pulled TJ's hand against her pounding heart.

"And, as if that weren't enough of a miracle, you fell in love with me, too." Now TJ's eyes brimmed and her voice thickened. "You taught me to love again and you made me feel worthy of your love. You filled my every need and you let me know that I filled yours. I learned from you that intimacy doesn't mean taking, as I had always thought; it means giving."

The tears slowly spilled over. "I discovered that mutual satisfaction with your lover is the highest form of self-satisfaction in existence. When I learned that from you, I knew I wasn't half a person anymore. I thought my physical disability made me half a person, but I was wrong. My emotional disability was causing that and you freed me from it."

Mare lifted her hand from TJ's for a moment and reached for some tissues from the bedside table. Smiling and sniffling, she wiped TJ's tears, then her own.

"So, no matter what happens...you've made my life as good as it gets." The larger hand, once again clasped with the smaller, tensed. "I'm going to have the operation to remove the bullet fragments and hope for the best." TJ's jaw set with determination. "I will cope with whatever results from it. With you at my side, I can handle any-thing."

Mare released TJ's hand, pushed herself further up the bed, and leaned over. "TJ, you know I'll always be at your side." She worked hard to look mischievous, to give a lift to her lover in this heart-wrenching decision. "I'm grafted there in case you hadn't noticed." Mare's voice went hoarse. "At least my soul is."

Putting a hand on each side of TJ's face, she bathed TJ with the look of love pouring from her eyes and kissed her deeply. TJ's injured side and shoulder prevented her from hugging Mare as she wanted to, but she returned Mare's kiss with abandon.

"Ahhh, Mare, I ache to show my love for you." TJ's seductive voice brought further tears from Mare's eyes. She dried their faces again, patting TJ's as she did so.

"Shush now. We'll have plenty of time together when we get you back home. You just concentrate on that. Paula's got everything just about ready for me to move in at the ranch." Mare chuckled through her tears. "You should see her hobbling around with that cast, supervising the people she hired to help her. I tried telling her she should keep that leg elevated and she said, 'The damn leg's elevated all night long and that should be enough.' You know Paula, there's no slowing her down when she's on a mission."

The change of subject lightened the atmosphere and TJ grinned. "She's a tough cookie, all right. I'm glad Paula and Erin will be there at the ranch to keep you company until I get back."

"They're both wonderful, TJ. We couldn't ask for two better friends." *And Erin has hired detectives to investigate the Raphaeles. You may have a new brother in the wings. I hope he deserves you.*

"That's for sure. They've always stood by me."

A knock came on the hospital room door and a nurse poked her head in. "Miss Meridian, there is a delegation of people here who would like to speak to you for just a moment. They're from," ignoring the fact that Mare was on the bed with TJ, she looked down at the clipboard she held, raised her eyebrows, and smiled, "Meridianville. Will you see them?"

"I'll see them in two minutes," TJ answered and the nurse departed.

"A delegation?" TJ frowned and looked at Mare, who shrugged.

"I don't know anything about it," Mare assured her. "I'm trying to bunch regular calls to free up some time so I've hardly been in town except to sleep."

TJ sighed. "Hope there aren't any problems. How do I look?"

Mare grinned. "You look fine. Of course, you would look fine to me if you were covered with slime."

"Slime? Yuck!" TJ made a face at Mare and chuckled. "You have such a way with words, Dr. Gillespie."

"I try," Mare laughed. "But let's make ourselves presentable." She slipped off the bed and pulled the chair over to TJ's bedside.

Another knock came at the door and the nurse reappeared. "Ready for your visitors?" TJ answered affirmatively and four men from Meridianville entered the room. All were dressed up in white shirts, ties, and suits. Mayor Steve Armando led the group. He and the others nodded to Mare, then he walked to the bed to shake TJ's hand. "Miss Meridian, TJ, I've brought a few people from our town council to visit you. I think you know Abner Stirkle." Abner inclined his head in greeting. "This is Lew Sturgis, the town solicitor and Carlos Sandos, who owns the grocery store." The two men came forward and shook hands with TJ.

Mare's curiosity was in high gear. *What are they doing here? And in such a formal group? I hope they're not bringing TJ any trouble.*

"First, I'd like to say how sorry we all were to hear about your accident. Seems those troublemakers were the same bunch who vandalized your ranch. Chief Jackson looked the other way when that happened because feelings ran so high against the Meridians. He let them off with only a warning. We shouldn't have let him get away with that and we've decided to put him on half pay for six months as a reprimand. We're hoping it will show him that we don't want our police to play favorites."

"I think that's a wise choice. The law should protect everyone, including people you might not like." Lying flat on her back, TJ had a problem seeing everyone. She smiled and politely asked, "Could you all move a little closer, please? I like to see my visitors." At her request, they crowded next to the bed, alongside Mare's chair, where they came into contact with TJ's powerful gaze.

"When we learned of the accident and who was involved, we called a town meeting." Mayor Armando rubbed the back of his neck and his face flushed a bit. "I know when you first came here, we didn't think too highly of you. We were judging you by our dislike of your father and what he had done to the town. But now we know we were wrong. You've done nothing but return our pettiness with generosity. You saved all of us from the contamination spill. You've opened up the ranch and the packing plant and are offering our people honest employment." The mayor looked into the faces of his friends and they nodded their support.

Mare started to breathe easier now that she realized the group was not here to complain.

"You're putting Meridianville back on its feet and you have asked nothing in return except a fair chance to hire people. We spoke about all this at the meeting and we decided we should do something to show our appreciation and gratitude. We don't want you to believe that those young thugs had anything to do with the way the rest of us feel about the Meridian name now."

TJ grinned and quirked an eyebrow. "No more s-o-b connected with it?"

The four men grinned, too, and a couple of them turned red for a moment as Mare choked back a laugh.

"No more s-o-b," the mayor agreed. "Instead, we have a token for you to show our sincerity. Lew?"

Lew Sturgis pulled out a 7" x 14" package that he had been carrying in a plastic bag. "Abner's a bit of a metal craftsman and he made this up for us to present to you, on behalf of the town." He handed the gift to TJ. "We don't want you to think of this as just an object, Miss Meridian. This symbolizes the love and gratitude of the whole town. We all voted for it."

TJ lifted the package in front of her eyes and her hands shook, the only sign of her emotional involvement. "Mare, would you please open this for me?" Mare stood and received the package from TJ's hands. She removed the ribbon and gift-wrap, and handed TJ a plaque. Mounted at the bottom of the mahogany plaque was a large brass key, heavily embellished, with the name "TJ Meridian" engraved on it. Above the key, a brass rectangle, fastened to the wood, was etched with the following message: "This Key to the Town of Meridianville is presented to Taylor

Jade Meridian in recognition of her priceless contributions to our well-being. She is truly our number one citizen."

TJ's lips quivered and her eyes filled with tears. Twisting her lips and putting a hand against them to quiet them, she handed the plaque to Mare to read. Soon two people had tears running down their cheeks and even the men had to blink their eyes and look away. The tissue box got called into duty again.

At last, TJ got some control over her voice. "I don't know how to thank you."

Abner patted TJ's arm. "No need for you to be thanking us, TJ. We're here to thank you. Took us awhile to see who you really were. We want you to know you've opened our eyes to how unfair we were to think you were painted with the same colors your father was. Yours are a helluva lot truer."

"Thanks, Abner." TJ's magnificent eyes acknowledged each man in turn. "Thank you all."

The mayor cleared his throat. "Abner's right, TJ. No need for thanks. We'll be going now. Just remember that key gives you access to anyone, at anytime, for anything you need that we can help you with. We all hope and pray that you recover quickly and get home soon. Good-bye."

Each man shook hands with TJ and Mare, said their good-byes, and left.

Mare stood up, holding the plaque so TJ could see it. "You want me to stand here for an hour or so and just hold this so you can admire it?" Her cheeks dimpled.

"Sure!" TJ smiled at her lover. "But I won't put you through such torture. Lay it on the table where I can reach it to look at once in a while." TJ's eyes filled. "I can't believe they did this." She began to cry in earnest.

"Hey, I think I might buy some stock in a tissue company." Mare gave a handful to TJ and barely got her little quip out before her tears came and she had to grab a handful for herself. She laid the plaque on the table, pulled her chair as close to the bed as she could, and sat down.

Pushing the button to lower TJ's bed as far as it would go, Mare leaned in until her golden head lay next to, and touched, TJ's raven hair. She put a hand up and caressed TJ's strong jaw. "I'm so glad they recognized your true worth."

TJ, tears still flowing, closed her hand around Mare's, moved it to her lips and kissed it, then laid it back along her jaw. TJ would have been embarrassed to cry so openly in front of anyone else, but Mare didn't seem like "anyone else." She was an extension of TJ, body and soul. Mare waited until TJ finished crying then pushed herself up enough to reach her and dried her face with kisses.

"Do you know what this means to me, Mare? I feel like I've been fighting a battle forever to divorce my father's life from mine. This is the first indication that I am succeeding. My first victory." Although hoarse from crying, TJ's voice radiated hope.

"There will be lots more to come, TJ. I know that as well as I know you." *Let's hope this boost to your battered self-worth soothes some of the pain of your recuperation.*

TJ took hold of Mare's hand once again, clasped it with her own, and raised their joined hands in the air. "To victory. And to us."

Keeping their hands together in the air, Mare joined her lips to TJ's waiting mouth and they wordlessly declared their love. When they parted, they smiled into each other's eyes as Mare echoed, "To victory. And to us."

Other titles to look for from
Yellow Rose Books

Destiny's Crossing, 2nd Ed. By Carrie Carr

Roman Holiday By Belle Reilly

Breaking Away By Tonya Muir

Seasons: Book One By Anne Azel

Mended Hearts By Alix Stokes

Tiopa Ki Lakota By D. Jordan Redhawk

Bar Girls By Jules Kurre

Tumbleweed Fever By LJ Maas

Seasons: Book Two By Anne Azel

None So Blind By LJ Maas

Safe Harbor By Radclyffe

These and other books from Renaissance Alliance Publishng, Inc., are available at a bookseller near you.

Printed in the United States
5437